The
Bridge Tender

A Novel

The
Bridge Tender

A Novel

teZa LORD

THE BRIDGE TENDER

Copyright © 2024. teZa Lord. All rights reserved. No part of this publication may be reproduced, distributed, or transmitted in any form or by any means, including photocopying, recording, or other electronic or mechanical methods, without the prior written permission of the publisher, except in the case of brief quotations embodied in critical reviews and certain other noncommercial uses permitted by copyright law.

For enquires please visit: tezalord.com

Publishing consultant: AuthorPreneur Publishing Inc.
Editor: Mary Rembert
Interior design by Amit Dey
Cover Designer: by Zizi
Cover & interior illustrations: teZa Lord

ISBN: 978-1-7365501-0-6 (paperback)
ISBN: 978-1-7365501-1-3 (ebook)
ISBN: 978-1-7365501-2-0 (audiobook)

For Yann Martel, who said to me:

"... we writers must leave more than dust behind."

"Marginality [is] much more than a site of deprivation ... just the opposite ... it is also the site of radical possibility, a space of resistance."

— bell hooks,
Marginality As a Site of Resistance, 1990

PROLOGUE

My children, I am within each and every one of you.
I have commissioned this to help you discover how to make the Cosmic Force truly your own. Some call me cosmic consciousness. Others ... simply not to be overwhelmed, I assure you ... call me by recognizable names such as the Great Creator or the Divine Mother—whatever you call me that works for you, works for me. Each and every one of you has me inside yourself. There are no special humans. All of you are my children.

Each of you is born with the same seed of infinite possibilities within you that I bestow upon all my children. Dispel the idea that there are only a few who tout themselves to be the so-called chosen. Every human has within them the seed of this shared consciousness—call it a super being if you wish—waiting to be discovered by your individual, human awareness that's been elevated to correct perception.

Regardless of what you think, all humans are a part of this universal consciousness. We share awareness of the infinite as well as the everyday things that surround our individual existence. Before you now, this ordinary, yet extraordinary story will help you realize this as never before. For certainly, you've glimpsed this uncanny magic, the cosmic connectedness about so-called ordinary life, many times, in many ways, before now.

There is no exclusion of age, race, gender, ethnicity, or belief system when it comes to understanding that we are One. You and I and all the Unseens are at the disposal of our Oneness that has no second. We are here with, and of, you in every moment of your earthly existence.

Never doubt that the least of you is possibly the catalyst for great change upon Earth. We are waiting for natural evolution to bring this reality to its natural prominence. Of this, prophets and divinations have been sent your way to proclaim since eternity began. Since consciousness formed into the One, we have waited for this moment. Each human being—even you—has the power within your beingness to effect such change that all of the challenges that have so far faced humanity will be seen for what they are: mere stepping stones to this catalyzing moment. Each hardship and calamity is a necessary one that leads to this moment, heralding the fulfillment you've all been anticipating.

With this in mind, let us proceed. No matter what state you may be in presently, this story is meant for you. If you are distressed, all the better. Relief is now yours. If you are already part of the awakened force that ripples over planet Earth at this moment, you will see your story reflected here, in Thea's.

See how one of you, a misfit like Thea Bowman, a ne'er-do-well in society's measured terms, is your clear reflection. She—who could be any of a million other marginalized revolutionaries against archaic, divide-and-conquer societies with vestiges of patriarchal norms into which she was born—succeeds in discovering her true purpose. You all play a role in humankind's ever-upward-spiraling evolutionary forces. Proving, in the process, how the least likely person, like her, like you too, represents the Oneness of which we speak, regardless of social status, self-recognition, or being acknowledged by your fellow humans.

Thea's story changes history to her-story.

Half-formed Thea

1

All Thea Bowman's life she's had an Itch. The strangest, weirdest, most indefinable sensation known to man, woman, or child, and nothing—nothing!—Thea does can make it go away. It is an annoying remembrance, or some damned thing. She becomes obsessed by inner urges that Itch's persistence presses upon her. She can't scratch it; she can't even tell where it's coming from—if it is inside her body, in her mind, or if its source is in the world somewhere. Is it on her skin, in her hair, deep in her bones, under her nails? Or is she having some allergic reaction from something outside herself?

All Thea knows is something has to change—*big time*—or that relentless sensation will eat her up. The only thing that makes it bearable—that insufferable, annoying tingling that never subsides—is to keep busy. Hanging around with her new wild crazy girlfriend will take it away. So does fooling around. No pain when the lovemaking gear is engaged, and oh, how Thea loves that! Making art distracts her attention from it too, but that's hard work. So naturally, Thea's favorite remedy for that damn Itch is to party—anytime, anywhere, any which way, with anything that gets her out of her head and into oblivion.

On this lonely midnight, she's strolling on the haunted, creaky docks of Sausalito. Thea had wandered over from her too-empty attic aerie, atop a hill in San Francisco. In a faraway Asiatic country, another senseless war is being fought with far too many casualties, way too many heartbreaks. Angry fervor is bittering everyone's hearts here at home. Humanity's feet have just touched upon the face of the moon. Even more surprising, Thea Bowman had somehow, the year before, managed to survive her twenty-first birthday, a feat that left her more shocked than anyone. Yet it is just today she's discovered she failed to get into the Art Institute, what she thought would be the perfect next step in her making-art-dedicated life.

Naturally, Thea feels unbearably lost. And even more lonely after this latest rejection—more than being new to town, having no friends—there's not much reason for her trying anymore. Anywhere. So it's surprising when, on that wharf, an unknown voice blindsides her, and a muscular, fearless woman gruffly makes herself known, simply by stepping out of the shadows onto the unlit dock.

"Hey. whatcha up to?" A huge, stout female walks toward Thea and into the beam of a streetlight. The glow of a cigarette forms a bull's-eye around the stranger's mouth. "Friends call me Big Sue."

Thea sees the strange figure has a dog at her side. "And this here's Dr. Bob," he's quickly introduced.

Thea instantly likes the woman's aggressive friendliness. She looks up at this statuesque, six foot two Amazon and recalls a childhood tale of a grubby tugboat Annie. She feels a shift inside, her usual clam-tight self cracking open to this stranger.

In an equally friendly tone Thea says, "Friends usually call me fucked-up."

They both make chortling noises, instantly hitting it off, right there in the half-bowl darkness of a seal-honking salty night on that Sausalito pier. Thea finds Big Sue's tough sailor talk intriguing. She quickly discovers that this Big Sue character *really is* a sailor, even though she looks more like a lumberjack, bundled in grimy oversized clothes. Thea has never met another female so uninterested in appearances. This woman before her, taller than not-short Thea, is that rare version of female who hasn't one iota of either affectation, beautification, or couth.

Thea looks at this surprise person in the streetlight's mellow cast. Big Sue isn't bad looking, with a heavy dark braid like a squaw that must keep her spine warm all the way down her back. Her features are not unrefined, just not particularly notable. If it weren't for her voluminous size, it would be easy to miss her. Her looks warrant no special attention other than the sheer mass of a surprisingly agile, bulky body. The continuous scowl on her face might put people off, Thea thinks. However, it is precisely this that immediately draws Thea to her, another soul in pain.

"Fuck it!" Big Sue's war cry comes with a slap to her new friend's sturdy shoulder. "Let's go get us some libations, whaddya say?"

What relief it is to meet a pal! Someone Thea can commiserate with and feel not at odds with herself or the world. Thea and her new companion, the Queen of Wasted, and her black-and-white tuxedo dog, enigmatically called Dr. Bob, walk down the dock together, a tight trio already.

* * *

The towering figure amuses Thea as they walk in step, Big Sue's arm warmly around the lost little dock rat she's just discovered. At the end of the dock is the Noname Bar, Big Sue's home away from home. When she isn't out at sea or at the Noname, Big Sue can be found on her boat, an old wooden tug called the *Raven*.

Thea feels an incredible energy rush from this powerful person's body into her own. Surely, Thea figures, Big Sue has to be a real life She Pirate, and no doubt, one hell-bent incarnation of Bluebeard himself.

"Wanna smoke?" Big Sue extends a pack of Pall Malls to Thea as they settle themselves into a wooden booth at the Noname, the dog nestled in the shadows underneath, apparently used to being incognito in bars.

"Sure," says Thea.

"So what are ya doing out here, so late and so alone?"

Thea shrugs. She bends to the lighted match Big Sue cups in her hands against the steady breeze of so much booze-soaked B.S. wafting around the darkened, antiseptic-smelling bar.

"Figured I'd come over to see the boats on the dock. I like to look at them. Already checked the ones over in town where I live." Thea indicates across the bay with a toss of her jaw. Moments before, they'd seen San Francisco's lights bursting through a thickening night fog as they entered the Noname.

The stranger takes a drag from her cigarette and leans back as Dr. Bob watches them both from his spot under the table. The whites of his eyes, combined with his coat's spots speckle a lively presence in the darkness. When Thea first came upon Big Sue on the dock, Dr. Bob checked her out more than his companion did. He sniffed Thea's outstretched fingers, then quickly returned to his position inside the center of a coiled-up line on the dock.

Now, the dog's ears respond to every lisp of the two women's banter. His radio-beacon ears are simultaneously tuned: one to them, the other to the taunting barks of a harbor seal he hears through the walls of the Noname, languishing on a nearby floating buoy, vocalizing whenever a chilly wave washes over it.

Thea is glad to finally meet at least one person who extends a simple kindness to her. A year earlier she'd hitchhiked from the Midwest, having run as far and as fast as she could from a past that brought too much pain and anger.

Since arriving in the Bay Area, her new boss at the restaurant where she works has talked to her with condescending authority. In this era of hippies and mind-bending drugs, compounded by throngs of gays proclaiming San Francisco to be their sequined Mecca, Thea noticed no one, absolutely no one, made eye contact with her on the streets. The entire city was in a state of siege, shocked from the tidal wave of freaks and misfits, all of them proclaiming the hilly city theirs, only theirs.

Later that night, Thea sits in Big Sue's tugboat galley drinking rum. She feels embraced by the mannish woman, who hasn't felt like a stranger to her since their initial meeting. Thea bids her new friend goodnight around two in the morning, grabs a cab and heads back to her rented room, glad to accept Big Sue's invitation to join her for a camping trip this upcoming weekend.

"A chick after my own heart," Thea mumbles, climbing the stairs: one who's not afraid to sleep in a tent and go without fancy stuff.

A few days later, Big Sue pulls up at a Victorian painted lady, at the address Thea gave her. Dr. Bob jumps over the seat when Thea gets in front, tossing her pack in the rear alongside him. "Hello fella," Thea says, patting the queerly smiling dog, all teeth and canine jollies.

After driving over the Bay Bridge and through the Caldecott Tunnel, the land becomes wide open.

"I need the ultimate experiences in life, M'lasses," Big Sue says, spontaneously baptizing Thea with a nickname she knows is hers the first time she hears it. "Wait till you see the mind-blowing campsites on Mount Diablo. See, over there."

A tall mountain looms up before them. Flat land and busy towns surround its golden base of dried grass meadows. "I never knew Nature could be as strong as it is out West," Thea murmurs.

"You're right there, girl," Big Sue says in delight. "This here mountain makes Mount Tamalpais cringe like a city park. Just you wait."

Thea had spent hours exploring the trails and craggy spots around Mount Tamalpais on the Sausalito side of the Golden Gate. It's true though, she knew she was in a city park, not close to anything like being in the wilderness.

The two friends, with Dr. Bob in the back, drive to the summit of Mount Diablo, then choose the most scenic campsite, number thirteen, overlooking the surreal, crowded San Francisco valley below. The view transforms the city and its environs into a wall-length Baroque landscape painting that barely, but actually, moves—when you look real closely at its minute details. Big Sue rolls a big fat joint and hands it to Thea. After smoking it, they put up the tent and throw in their sleeping bags, zipping everything up tight as a drum.

"Gotta keep the coons from ruining everything. Come on, let's hit the trails," Sue says.

The trio walk vigorously for several hours. Big Sue has a stash of j's with her, besides a nipping bottle of Southern Comfort. "Just for energy," she grimaces at her new partner in mental blitzkrieg-ing.

Thea is impressed at the larger woman's stamina. They walk up craggy hillsides, down fern-drenched valleys, across wide grassy meadows that sprinkle the otherwise rocky mountain with alarming beauty. At twenty-five, Big Sue's strength matches Thea's, who usually is unrivaled by anyone, man or woman.

Her friend's knowledge—of plants, of interpreting approaching weather systems by reading the ever-varying clouds, along with knowing seemingly countless legends about local Indian tribes, especially of the ancient Anasazi people—revealed in detailed stories that Big Sue relates nonstop as they explore the trails—electrifies Thea. Because she cares deeply about these things too, even though she feels hopeless about her own nowhere life, and the state of the entire messed-up world.

At their first meeting, Big Sue provided the camaraderie of a drinking partner, period. By now, though, she's revealed how aware, how sensitive she is to how bad things actually are for all Earth's inhabitants—fulfilling the prerequisites that Thea's hurt soul cherishes in another person's company. But the more she finds out about this fascinating, taboo-feeling, odd-looking, he-she person, the more she knows that Big Sue is a treasure chest of knowledge, especially about ways indigenous people everywhere revere Nature. Every other word out of Big Sue's mouth is another fact about how sacred our home, Earth, is, was, and always will be, " … even if its dumbass human residents don't start waking up to what Mother Nature, the entire planet needs," she growls.

(If Thea had met this spellbinding person in our present time, requiring a major cultural shift and another deadly pandemic to separate fact from fiction, Big Sue would be speaking about sustainability, kombucha, and being vegan, wearing those buzzwords like a jeweled crown with her grimy jeans. But back then, Big Sue is obsessed with Native Americans, referring to the Life Source with their native tongues translated into English names such as Great Mother and Great Spirit, as she draws more libations from a hip-pocket.)

"That's a good enough God-name for me—the Mystery," Big Sue says as she swigs from the Southern Comfort pint before handing it to Thea, scratching her dog's head as she does.

Then the hike brings them suddenly to a clearing, in between corridors of rock and thick overhead oaks and pines. Big Sue suddenly bursts into a run. Flailing her arms about her head she screams, "Get away, you fuckhead!" at a big red hawk that's diving repeatedly, joined by Dr. Bob's enthusiastic barks and mad dashes to and fro. Thea spies a panicked rabbit zigzagging across the open field. Big Sue jumps and runs, foiling one dive after another, until the hawk suddenly turns and zooms after her. She punches and swings, yelling at the top of her lungs, Dr. Bob joining the fracas. Finally, the hawk flies off and the bunny scurries into a hole in the hillside.

Thea runs to her friend, who squeezes her wrist to stop the bleeding where the hawk's talons scratched her.

"It's nothing. Motherfuckers takin' advantage of the weak always gets me."

"It is the way of the wild, Big Sue."

"Yeah, I know, but it doesn't mean I have to like it, does it."

Thea smiles. Already she feels akin to this rough person, in ways she never knew she could. Sue's right, Thea silently nods to herself: *Nature doesn't care about being fair.*

They walk on, up to the summit, and over to the south side of Mount Diablo, where they look out onto many crowded towns, reaching as far as their eyes can see, north and south.

They smoke another joint while sitting in a golden field, goofing on the late afternoon scene below, of the ant-hill human population that surrounds metropolitan San Francisco, Oakland, and Berkeley. The crush of buildings, the sinuous highways filled with shiny cars, evoking long glistening snakes that cruise this surreal, silent landscape so far below them. On the ground, towns appear as dotted and crosshatched patterns; grids are made from thick rows of winery grapes the outskirt towns grow in neat parallel lines.

Thea and Big Sue bellow like crazy women at the ludicrous thought of so many people crawling around like tiny bugs, all hectically making money, making this, making that, living for … what? To be ants, from up here! They fall over backward laughing, zonked out of their heads. Somewhere, hidden from human sight, two anxious robber raccoons scratch themselves, looking at this bizarre human scene in front of them.

Another hour of walking and climbing. Big Sue takes a seat atop a huge smooth boulder as wide and high as a three-story house. She offers the Southern Comfort to Thea, who gulps the syrupy toe-buzzing stuff, even though she isn't fond of the sickening sweetness. Big Sue brings out a plastic bag of wet, cow-shit-encrusted mushrooms. Thea has never done them before; her eyes grow round. She knows the more plants she shoves down her throat and into her lungs, the less she'll feel that damn Itch of hers.

"We're here for a few days; why not enjoy ourselves?" Big Sue says.

The dog scrambles to place himself directly in the middle of them.

Thea scoffs. "What a ladies' man he is."

"Yeah, just look at this, will ya, M'lasses," Big Sue says, gulping down her share of the fungi without chewing as she sweeps her hand before them, out at the startling vista of land, sea, and sky. Their perch on the mountain, devoid of any other campers or hikers this chilly time of year, is a magnificent eye view of the world, atop the protected wilderness of Mount Diablo State Park.

"Who says we have to have a god to answer to," Big Sue says, unexpectedly, "when Nature's awesomeness is so, so …." She sits up straighter, struggling to finish her sentence. In a whisper she finally says, "It's so real." Big Sue's eyes get squinty and moist as she gazes at the sight of the valley below, as if it portrayed some fairytale scene rather than life itself.

"Yeah, this is pretty cool," Thea quietly agrees, feeling awkward at her friend's sudden turn to the serious channel.

"Cool!" Big Sue turns to Thea. "Are you kidding? Nature's the only thing worthwhile. It's the holy book I read. The clouds, the wind, the waves—just look at this fucking wonderful world, will ya! Shit! Have you ever been in a storm out at sea? If anything is fucking cool, that's it, M'lasses!"

Thea keeps quiet. She isn't much good about things concerning supernatural forces, Nature's or otherwise big magnificence, or of trusting anything vast, much less this transcendental stuff Big Sue is suddenly talking about. Thea has always been running, as fast, as far away as she can, from the religion of fear she'd been spoon-fed by her small-minded, bigoted parents.

The God I was taught, Thea thinks, *was no fun. For me to trust in Nature, to see Mother Earth as some kind of spirit, I have to believe it's not going to judge or hurt anybody, not me or any other. Or be a phony fetish, like so many world religions have become, with obsessed fanatics proselytizing, waging wars, condemning others for not believing like they do. For me, religion is dangerous. I'm a skeptic, I admit.*

For me to believe there's a Great Spirit, Thea nods and thinks silently, *I have to feel it, not be told about it.*

For a few minutes, Big Sue and Thea just sit and watch the mind-stilling view. The horizon is so far off that the endless silvery reach of the Pacific Ocean can be seen to the west, while the Sierra Nevada mountains stretch on either side of them. Off in the distance where land meets sea, Thea notices the glint of super jets appearing like toys zeroing in on the Oakland Airport, like gnats buzzing around something rotten.

Big Sue speaks, this time in an easier way. "Nature is so real to me, so right, M'lasses. Nature's power is endless. Out at sea, it's sometimes terrifying and deadly, yet other times it can be as gentle as a lake, and as kind. I love Nature! This is *It*, my friend. This—this—" Big Sue's arms spread in a wide sweep to embrace the tableau before her, "this is my God, all around us, here and now."

Thea sits in silence. She doesn't mind Big Sue's drunkenly elaborating upon her trust in the inscrutable nature of Nature. Inside herself, more important things are happening: the psilocybin mushrooms are starting to kick in. Thea feels the first queasy surge of nausea. She wonders if she's going to puke. But she doesn't want to say anything, neither about her physical discomfort nor the slight confusion she has about Big Sue's adopting the ways of the Ancient Ones, her appearance being so non-native.

Thea's words, spoken or silent, have always been her enemy. Words never quite connect with how she feels. They're like muffled, handcuffed slaves, to be freed only when absolutely necessary. For years she's trained herself not to feel. She's extremely uncomfortable speaking about things beyond making her basic needs known. Anything too deep confuses her. She holds no opinions, and proudly defends that position, as if it's a right she's earned by being so miserable for so long. It's become a habit, stuffing her feelings, ever since she discovered how well booze and drugs worked on numbing them.

Thea sits next to the awe-struck, now-silent Big Sue, and her serene formal wear dog. Thea turns to look right into Dr. Bob's sparkling eyes of wisdom. She sees in them the good humor of the dog's lively, trusting ways. She admires his nonverbal expressions, so … eloquent. Thea gives him a warm embrace, just for the heck of it.

Her stomach rumbles are growing with each passing minute. Something is definitely happening. That's what she wants, more of being outside herself. More of averting her attention from who she is, where she's come from, and what scares her the most—that irritating Itch. Thea smiles at the disrupting sensation arising from inside. She adores getting high, as shit-faced as she can get, becoming like a plane about to take off for Destination Unknown. She doesn't even care whether she makes it back or not.

※ ※ ※

After some time passes, Big Sue stands and says, "We better get to the Trail of Time before old Mescalito shows his face around here."

"Who?"

"Mescalito, the spirit of peyote. But I call him in for every damn thing I take, peyote or San Pedro cactus, mushrooms, that weird Dragon's Blood, or the ayahuasca vine. I only do natural when it comes to trippin', M'lasses. Ol' Mescalito is obliged to show whenever called upon for assistance from us mere mortals. Nature teaches best through her plants, I figure. The People knew; indigenous tribes everywhere, them and the animals, they're the ones that remember most. The People have always been taking some bush, leaf, or tree bark to find answers in their own selves. Only through the gates of the natural world do we find clues for truth and happiness."

Big Sue turns, flashes Thea a beaut of a grin, and shouts to the air above her: "We want to touch the magic of life! That's why we're here!" She turns to Thea, "That's why people like you and me, my friend, do what we can to get out of ourselves, to loosen us up from—from all the shit the world flings at us. So we can get unhuman enough to pass through the gates separating this world from the unseen world. That's where the real power is."

Balancing on a boulder, Sue stands looking out at the silent vista of huge boulders and blue skies for a while longer.

"Get it, M'lasses?"

"Yeah, sure." Thea struggles to her feet from her precarious perch on another rock. "Whatever you say, I'm in."

"I bet you are," Big Sue chuckles. "You have to if you're brave enough to be here with me. And Dr. Bob. You're my kind of wonder-er, aren't cha, boy?"

The wonder dog gives up an emphatic woof as if he understands every word his big mama caretaker has uttered.

*　*　*

A few minutes later they pass the Cave of the Wind—a massive sculpted formation in a huge sandstone cliff, made from the wind of eons carving out a line of small irregular holes that resemble a mountainside's own musical instrument. They stop. They hear whistling that sounds like notes coming from a giant's flute. Yet there is no giant around, just a steady breeze. The unique beauty of the place, and the eerie sound of the wind passing through holes in sandstone, now resembling a muted saxophone, affects Thea. The mushrooms have already transported her to their promise of altered perceptions. Everything looks extraordinarily clear, sparkly, and cellularly interconnected. Thea begins to see web-like patterns, things making a visible, mycorrhizal network she's never noticed before.

She stands listening to the haunting, almost sacred sound coming from the stone holes. They proceed noiselessly, reverentially, alongside the cliffside wall.

Peering in, Thea sees that the rock cliff has been hollowed out enough to make a comfortable aviary, but no birds are there right now. Suddenly something whizzes by from one of the cave's holes, only missing their heads by inches. Big Sue and Thea stop dead in their tracks, not believing what they see. As if caught in slow motion, a glass beer bottle arcs high … and bursts into demonic splinters of shattered light on a nearby rock. The explosion of glass shatters the deep quiet shared by the mountain and its hikers.

A litterbug's bottle, thrown unconscionably. Their idyllic vision is scissored in half. Before them, the broken bottle is a snapshot of another disheartening portrait of life on Earth with uncaring inhabitants. Thea's body goes rigid, swept away by a rush of anger that silently ambushes her. But Big Sue—that ever-ready pirate gal, bursts into a screeching, roaring tornado.

"Hey!" She yells at a half dozen teenage boys guzzling beer—seen peering out from behind the cliff's holes that were once used, long before vandals walked these trails, by birds entering their safe nests. Sue quickly makes up the distance between her and them, in the same phenomenal burst of energy displayed earlier when she rescued the rabbit from the hawk. "What d'you assholes think you're doing here, huh?"

Before she can grab any of the gang, the punks scatter like rats, and good thing too, because Thea is sure if Big Sue got her hefty hands on any of them they'd have sorely regretted ever having been born.

"Little fuckers," Big Sue snarls. "Wouldn't you know, nasty little turds like them, ruinin' even the best place around. Some people would crap in heaven, M'lasses."

Thea doesn't answer. She's thinking of all the times she'd done equally appalling things back in Illinois, when she'd been an irreverent, teenage drunk herself.

Thea and Big Sue camp atop Mount Diablo

2

Her demented downstairs neighbor and landlord, Tim Osgood, Thea realizes, is borderline psychotic. Osgood is as driven, as obsessed, as a madman who calls his fluffy cat his wife (which he often does), or stands in the road tearing his clothes off (his longtime pedigree in Haight-Ashbury warrants overlooking such trivial quirks). He'd barge in without knocking or asking permission any old time, right into Thea's affordable attic room. Thea has never been successful in stopping the lunatic landlord from invading her privacy, but—with Big Sue often visiting when not at sea—Osgood has become triple times more neurotic.

He's really pissing Thea off now, doing crazy stunts such as the latest one. Bringing complete strangers, mostly men, up to meet "the infamous buccaneer, Big Sue and her timid cohort," he'd insanely deride right to their faces ever since Sue started showing up. He was boastful and rude, marshaling parades of gawkers into Thea's sometimes now-shared room whenever the sensationally asexual Big Sue overnighted at his boarder's hovel. He'd bring straight or gay, men or women who'd do anything, they'd tell him, to meet the *She Pirate* and her sidekick, the whacked artist no one knew, Thea Bowman; both of them, by then, known for their wildly notorious drunken stunts in every watering hole along the bayfront.

Osgood would start off each guided tour with his hand on Thea's doorknob, whispering so the occupants wouldn't hear him about to barge into the cantilevered-ceiling space. "Now you'll meet the incomparable fast-fighting she-devil herself, Big Sue, and her sublimely lovely, probably lesbian girlfriend—but not verifiably, yet—Thea."

Big Sue always thought this sideshow that she somehow, inadvertently, found herself party to whenever visiting Thea on Delmar Street, funnier than hell, when the Raven made port in San Francisco. Both were so stoned they didn't care about privacy. Neither bothered to figure out if Osgood was really a jerk, or if this outrageous, exhibitionist habit of his was a sign of some incurable mental ailment, a brain tumor perhaps, and he was actually to be pitied. They decided over a buzz one night that he was a bit of both. Thea chocked it up to what she called "Osgood's carnival-tax," an inconvenience she figured was worth her room's economy rate, even with the downstairs shared bath. Besides, the two friends thought it hilarious when Osgood showed up with yet another entourage of squares seeking thrills in hippie haven, anxious to meet the legendary Big Sue herself, and her incongruous sidekick. Rumors of the She Pirate's exploits were seeded in every harbor Big Sue ever put into, so it was reasonable her shady reputation made her practically a celebrity in her own homeport, the Bay Area.

After the two were hanging tight for some time, all aspects of Thea's life became unreal, not just communing with an unseen Indian guide using *spirits stuff*, meaning the *booze* mostly. When Thea asked about the bottle of Southern Comfort that accompanied Big Sue everywhere, she began to affirm, "The reason I'm more an imbiber than a fungiphile or ..." before she either nodded off or forgot what she was talking about. Thea and Big Sue used bizarre combinations of drugs (plant derived, of course), chased down by shots of tequila, rum, or whatever liquid buzz-maker was available.

"To make our buzz higher, out of this world," Big Sue the alchemist, claimed. "That's why booze is called spirits ya know, M'lasses. It does the trick to pierce the veil."

Through the fog of blinded consciousness, Thea obfuscated Osgood bringing a particularly intriguing young man with penetrating eyes to meet them one day. But hard as she tried to recollect what this haunting, singularly attractive visitor looked like, or what transpired during his visit, Thea could never conjure up in her muddled memory what made him stand out among all others. Did Osgood bring him up? Had this guy even existed? Try as she might, Thea couldn't remember his face or discern anything more than a shadowy presence of goodness, like a scent of sweet familiarity, an awake-dream she yearned to meet in real life. A pair of piercing dark eyes penetrating the darkness with a lightness of surrender, hopefulness, and unlimited possibilities.

Meeting this mystery was nothing more than a hashish dream, she scolds herself. Stop it! Its memory, she orders herself, is to be discarded.

Yet on another occasion, Thea thinks she has this stranger's elusive image nearly in focus, then—poof!—it vanishes, leaving an enduring wistfulness that makes Thea swear off trying to recollect anything about intruders Osgood kept bringing around. To her, they were the freaks who peeped at her private life with Big Sue; people to whom she and her friend were just a carnival act, to be gawked and ogled over. Probably paying Osgood for it too.

No clues ever surfaced as to the unknown individual's identity when she was sober. Big Sue gruffly said, "Don't know," when Thea asked her friend about a particular man, whom she couldn't describe. "I dunno, just felt he was … special." Thea's only clue was the phantom's penetrating eyes meeting hers. She soon gave up, yet she couldn't help feeling a strong presence had floated by, like a magic-winged schooner passing her silently, in the dark of a moonless night.

The mystery man became like another fine meal one has had, strewn with unknown sense-swooning ingredients: but too much trouble to determine exactly which ones. And … just as experiencing the finest of gourmet delights, the taste of even heavenly food dissipates … in time.

Leaving Dr. Bob behind with Thea whenever she has to, Big Sue delivers boats for a living or freelances as a navigator aboard sailboats, powerboats, other tugs, or cargo ships. Big Sue's next delivery is pulling away from Sausalito's dock. This time she's bound for Maui, navigating an eighty-foot ketch for a boat owned by the manager of one of the biggest-name rock groups of those LSD-laced times. During her friend's absence, as she's always done, Thea roams from place to place, never quite knowing what to do with herself. When Big Sue isn't around Thea's life goes aground. One-night stands with a rosary bead-ful of men never interests her much more than a cup of joe they share the next morning. Getting high is her wake-and-bake mandate, barely managing to get to work and wait on tables or take Dr. Bob on his daily walks.

By this time, Thea has lost her drive to make art. What's the point? she figures. The wildly exuberant, demon-haunted images she makes scares people more than anything. Nobody cares about the nightmarish work she painstakingly puts together in her tiny attic space, in between binges of trying to master forgetfulness of things past and yet to come.

She hates having to spend weeks, sometimes a month or more, waiting, listlessly passing time without her carousing partner. Without Big Sue, Thea is adrift.

Then, the pirate returns. They celebrate her long absence at sea with a big bash at the Noname. That night Big Sue says, "M'lasses, I'm gonna treat you and me to a vacation. Somewhere different. I'm sick of Hawaii."

The next week both of them fly across the States, then over azure seas dotted with green Bahamian islands, for an adventure in the waters best known for fabulous diving, "… other than the Red Sea," Big Sue clarifies. "Crystal clear reefs," she sighs, "a sight for my blurred eyes, staring at a far-off horizon for too long on those damn deliveries. Plus," she winks at Thea, her partner-in-crime, "the tickets were pure cheap-o."

"Cool," Thea grunts.

In the clear, shoal waters off Cat Cay, at the southern tip of the Bahamian Exumas, Big Sue and Thea are putting on their tanks, snorkels, and masks as they bob in an oversized Whaler. The sun-kissed dive shop owner, a nut-tanned princely speaking Brit named Giles, has already dived down to the seafloor to check the set of the boat's hook. Where Giles has anchored the seventeen-foot skiff, aways off Cat Cay, is the best spot on all the reefs, he'd proclaimed when they approached it. Big Sue is still gearing up. Thea has all hers on and is adjusting her snorkel, preparing to backward somersault off the boat's rail, when Giles' blond head bursts above the sea's calm surface.

"Stay in the boat!" he shouts. "A hammerhead's down here!"

Olympian strong though he is, Giles has no time to swim the twenty-five feet back to the Whaler. His breaking the crystalline water's surface has sounded the alert for the beady-eyed predator below. A rogue shark is atavistically programmed to kill. In an agitated circling rush, the animal attacks and drags the hundred-and-seventy-pound diver below the surface of the water.

It all happens in a breath. Where Giles' head just was is now an echo of the heart-stopping alarm he choked out moments before.

Big Sue screeches a war cry, grabs an emergency oar and violently beats the churning waters. Giles resurfaces, gasping. Startling pink spreads out as his arms flail the water wildly into foam all around his fierce face; his expression a shield that epoxies time to this moment. Above the water rises Giles' midsection. The shark's long needle teeth grip his flesh as primordial predator thrashes its weighty prey about in the air. Giles' twisted, gruesome face. His strength fighting death for life. The cut of his mouth, jagged, makes no sound as he is pulled under again.

Thea hears an urgent command clearly telling her, "Save this guy!" Without thinking, she obeys. Instantly she's in superwoman overdrive. Fully geared, Thea backflips over the boat's rim. Big Sue calls out, "Stop, you fool!" Nothing matters to Thea but the inner command she hears. She has to obey. Thea swims with no splash right for the semi-conscious Giles—now loosened from the shark's jaws—her snorkel raised defiantly above the perilous water. From behind goggles, her eyes dart everywhere, ready to fight the monster with her fists if she has to. Thea's only thought is to reach the man whose agonized face, contorted and ashen, is magnified in her mind as vast as the universe.

Giles, the whites of his eyes rolling backward, floats, maybe unconscious. The full air tank has been ripped off his muscular shoulders; the rest of his dive gear is shaken loose, gone. Stealthily, Thea glides over to him, all the time regarding the shark's rushing dorsal fin circling, circling. Just as she grabs Giles the deadly fin disappears underwater.

"It's okay, Giles. Hold onto me," she commands.

The shark is probably diving for another attack, she knows, she's heard Sue's shark attack stories. Thea hears a scream from the anchored boat but doesn't pay any attention to her friend, who's ferociously beating the water with an oar.

Thea swims Giles, lifeguard-style, her arm wrapped over his chest, to the boat where Sue quickly gets them aboard. He's semi-conscious. They see that razor teeth have ripped open Giles' left side. Blood gushes crimson. The huge gash makes Thea queasy, but instead of gagging, she binds a beach towel around Giles' middle and applies pressure as Sue hauls up the anchor as fast as a sailor ever did. Everywhere inside the boat is covered with bright fuchsia, bloodstained seawater. Thea wonders if any is hers. Big Sue ignites the Mercury engine and whips the Whaler's nose to Cat Cay's main dock, so far away.

Big Sue can't stop Thea from diving in

3

"You're being asinine, M'lasses," Big Sue says, and stomps off without another word. Thea knows her friend is right. But from the moment she slipped into the water, she knew she was destined to be with this man. How could she not? She needed a change, and look, he needs her too. Giles is weak and ripped up, damn helpless, lying there stitched from left breast to groin when she brings him back to Cat Cay after a two-week stay in the Nassau Hospital.

Yet Thea feels compelled to stay with this man whose life she's mysteriously felt tasked to save. To Thea, this shark event is nothing less than a sign, of the *big change* she's been looking for. She wants to stay and help Giles, Thea tells Big Sue, who's stuck around all this time trying to convince her pal otherwise. Her friend grumbles that Thea doesn't know what she's doing.

Giles' vulnerability, his irresistible accent, his intellect so sensitive: how could she help herself? Thea has never felt so drawn to a man, ever. The idea of making him her special project, to fix Giles' torn-up body excites Thea beyond anything she's felt before. Somehow, her Itch has disappeared in all this. She thinks, *What else could have brought me to this nowhere chain of tiny limestone outcroppings, with hardly a tree anywhere, but to save him who needs me as much as I need him?*

Harrumphing and stormy, Big Sue returns by herself to San Francisco, while Thea, the wild-child half-woman, remains on Cat Cay.

Gone are the days in which Thea does nothing but get obliterated, taking whatever Big Sue dishes out in her private search for the High and Mighty. Gone also, Thea quickly realizes, is the chemical motivation behind those freakishly surreal paintings of hers, fueled by mushrooms, rum, revenge, and recklessness. Time for a trade-in, Thea tells herself, missing nothing of her old life back in the Haight, ready for a new, healthy one in the islands.

Thea watches over Giles as he lies helpless, determined to help him recuperate no matter how long it takes. "You're my savior, you are, Thea," he winces when she helps the hospital nurse turn him, watching to learn how his bandages are changed. As soon as he gained consciousness after surgery, she offered to work in his dive shop. "Until you're on your feet," she reasoned.

Without her help Giles would have fallen into an even deeper mess because, ex-pat par excellence that he is, he has no insurance and absolutely no savings. He has only the dive shop. His chest, arms, and legs are stitched up, so he'll be crippled for a while. Giles is as grateful for Thea's assist as she is for him presenting a reason to feel her life is worth living.

"So, what do you do?" Giles asks Thea after he's awoken to find her, again, sitting by his side after many consecutive days.

"Do?" Thea hesitates. She hates this question. For Giles though, she wants to make sure her answer means something.

"Do you mean … for love or for money?"

Giles grins. "Oh, I get it. You're an artsy sort, right?"

"It's that obvious?"

"Sure. You look like one, for starters. The way you dress is, ah, unique. The way you don't fancy yourself up. Natural like. Artists always do other things to pay the rent, don't they?"

"You must know a few then. Where, here in the Bahamas?"

"Nah, artists I know, back home, don't like the sun much. Back in Bristol. But Thea, you know it's no different for me, getting funds; money is always a struggle. I'm here with whatever pittance the shop makes. Sadly, no more research grants have been forthcoming my way. That's what I do for love, study the turtles here. For years, I've been following hawksbills around, tagging them, observing, that sort of thing. Till I ran out of funding; ergo: the dive shop."

"Oh, I see."

He looks at her carefully, grunting in discomfort as he shifts his position in the bed. "Thea, you're a strange one, know that?"

"Why, 'cause I want to help you?"

"That, and ... well, I imagine you're the type chased by all sorts of men, with your looks. What are you doing hanging around me, all ripped up like this?"

Thea smiles and looks at her fingertips.

"And what the bloody hell are you doing traveling with that weird bird I met you with? Blimey, she looks and smells like a modern-day Boadicea, a warrior woman if I've ever seen one."

"Who? Never heard of Boad-y."

"Oh, that figures," Giles sighs. "You Yanks wouldn't know a first-century British Queen that defied the Romans. Too hung up on Cleopatra, huh? Never mind, it's too long a story and I'm too tired."

"Big Sue's my best friend—and that's good enough for me."

Giles grimaces, perhaps from pain. "From the moment I laid eyes on you, I've been trying to figure what was going on between you two. It doesn't add up.

You're about as incongruous a pair I've ever seen. C'mon, admit it. You're into her, right?" he says, leeringly.

Thea breathes deeply, trying to release the pinch in her heart. She doesn't expect anyone to understand her having a friend like butch-dike-appearing Big Sue.

"What's to figure how people click, Giles? She's my friend, and that's that. We enjoy each other's company."

"She was stinking drunk when you showed up at the shop."

"What makes you think I wasn't?"

Giles' eyebrows burrow. "You didn't look wasted. She was rank."

Thea keeps quiet. No sense in revealing too much of her excesses. She knows that from past guys who thought hers a bit much.

Giles' voice softens. For a moment he and she say nothing. His eyes shine as he looks right at her. "You really are a special person, Thea, staying with me. Thanks. Guess it's at times like this, when no one else shows, you find out who your friends really are."

Thea's hands grow hot. She wipes them on her shorts. She's thrilled, actually, to hear Giles recognize her sacrifice. Inside, she's jumping with joy, but on the outside, she keeps her cool.

"No, really," Giles continues, "don't think I'm just being polite, either. I've never met anyone like you. As good inside as you look on the outside. I swear, I'm not just saying this because you saved my life. Well, yeah, that was damn bloody decent of you. But when I look at you, sitting here with me every day like you do, I see your hair, like gold in the sun, your eyes, all cockamamie greens, like clear emeralds and the frothy top of waves—and your skin shining from something inside—it's freaky. I've never known a person so capable, so strong as you, either. Hell, you practically lifted me out of the water that day, even with my shredded equipment dangling on."

"Big Sue helped," Thea mumbles, burning up. Men are always eager to bed her with fancy words and trays of drugs, but nobody has ever praised her like this before.

A bolt unlocks her heart free. Thea knew when she slipped into the water that day, she would be with Giles. She doesn't say that, though. Giles' face, when she finally turns to look at him, bursts into a pulse-quickening grin.

"If it's okay with you," she stammers, "I'll keep working the dive shop until you manage to get around."

Giles doesn't have to answer.

The seventy-seven stitches zigzagging along his left torso, and other random ones along that side of his arm and leg soon heal, adding to the daredevil allure of the dashing Brit. His stamina and healthy regimen make his recovery swift.

If one could judge by Giles' posh speech you'd think his was a privileged background. Perhaps once. But now, the injured man, still sun-glorious in his current sad state, becomes reliant upon Thea and a few Bahamian friends who show up with fresh fish, some coconuts, handfuls of hard beach peas, and a rare head of green lettuce. Thea has no money either, after wiring

Osgood to pack up her art supplies and send them to her in one big box. But somehow the pair gets by with what they have.

Giles' classic looks are strangely enhanced in a raw, visceral way by his cruel wound, healing well, but seasoning him with a ghastly scar. Odd though, that during his recuperation no one arrives from England to visit him, neither family nor friends. Yet, in a few days, even Big Sue is no longer a lingering regret in Thea's mind. Giles' Pan-like playfulness takes Thea over completely. His continuous stream of gratitude and compliments awaken in her a sense of needing to be appreciated only by him. She wants to soak in his refined, elegant manner and nothing else. It helps that Giles is so vocal about being grateful.

Always physically active, Giles is a man with a positive outlook, even if he's momentarily a half-invalid. His is the opposite of Thea's tendency to cultivate more than anyone's share of self-destructive habits. He barely drinks and doesn't smoke weed or tobacco, and considers studying turtles and diving his passions. Well, one more thing that he doesn't mention to Thea.

Thea convinces herself: What have I got to do that could be more important than taking care of this poor injured fellow, who's all alone? Helping him will keep me from partying myself to death. I'll be able to stop getting loaded all the time, and get away from my sorry-ass life. He needs me. Big Sue never needs anybody.

Ultimately, Thea traded in the doom-and-gloom head-trips she tended to heap upon herself for focusing on Giles' charm and hardcore work ethic. Even after his untimely run-in with the hammerhead, his infectious optimism remains undaunted. Giles has an unquenchable thirst for learning the sea's secrets, continuing his amphibian research, and—one other less admirable pursuit.

In the flash of a shark's fin, Thea puts down her mind-numbing crutches and leaning too much on Big Sue's amusing antics, to becoming addicted to being needed by someone. With no one asking her, she steps into Giles' life and learns everything in order to keep the dive shop afloat. Of course, Giles is overjoyed by this woman who's shown up just in time, to save not just him, but his business. Which means, the way he figures it, she's also saving his long overdue dissertation.

She dives in, learns about maneuvering the dive boat, renting out gear, maintaining everything, all under the watchful tutelage of the convalescing Giles. No longer does she feel the Itch. Since rescuing this man it has, thankfully, left her entirely free to explore her new life on a tropical island.

"Have you come to help me save the turtles?" he asks her one day after fully realizing Thea doesn't intend to return to the States.

Thea looks at him coyly and smiles.

When he recuperates well enough to walk and gently move around, Thea notices Giles never drinks more than an occasional glass of wine with dinner, and never, ever does anything illegal. But the drug of sex, ah, that soon becomes a major part of their story. When his wound mends nicely and Thea has ingratiated herself to him beyond measure, the next logical step is to abandon herself to the thrilling rapids of unlimited, satisfying sex with the recovering, suave dive master. And lucky Thea, Giles is inventive, competent, and practically insatiable in the sex category.

Once he has healed enough to maneuver some tricky, handicapped gymnastics, Giles lies next to her after making delectable love, their bodies knitted together like the mauled skin under his unsightly scars. Thea and Giles' lives are so entangled, born from similar needs and wants: both having deep inner Itches always needing to be scratched. The pair fall into each other's spell. Thea's edgy art-making, totally forgotten; and Giles' diving and turtle studies, only for the moment, as disabled as he is. From the day she dove into the bloody waters to save him—obeying that inner voice she clearly heard—their lives become interwoven in an intricate pattern.

How could Thea resist, then, when Giles asks her to marry him mere weeks after becoming passionate lovers? It seems the most natural, most romantic thing in the world for her to utter the big "I do" with this man she pities so. He has many missing pieces: a questionable and seemingly family-less past like hers, and no friends to speak of other than the simple island folk of Cat Cay. *He's just like me,* Thea thinks. How can she help but fall in love with someone who needs her so much? Who has saved her own life from purposelessness?

4

Work becomes Thea's new drug of choice. She relishes taking care of this man, his shop, his life, as much as she'd previously thrown herself full force into serial sex, substances, and hanging with Big Sue, misdirecting her energies. By herself, Thea manages the dive shop for months, and then, one day Giles makes a comeback. Soon after he's helping out, he limps up to her at the counter.

"You know, love, tourists buy art while they're on vacation. There's not much else for them to do, besides dive and eat conch all day."

Thea looks at him. "Yeah, but not my kind of art."

"How do you know?"

"Believe me, I know, Giles."

"Well, why not make something they'll like, then. We really could use the extra cash."

"That wouldn't feel so good to me. It'd be dishonest, untrue to my art."

"Aw, c'mon, Thea! Get off your high horse, will you? Art is art. Just make some pretty fish and beach paintings and see how the limeys gobble it up. Do it for me, okay?"

What she says to Giles is right on: the art she made back in San Francisco, that edgy, weird stuff, would never appeal to tourists in the Bahamas. With a bit more prodding, Thea is coerced to switch to painting quickie seashells, rainbow fish, and coral reefs: tourist pleasing junk. Her art-making is directed at churning out heartless souvenirs, crap some might call art, not she. She shuts her eyes making the damn stuff, for as many minutes as it takes to throw paint onto small driftwood pieces she picks up on the windward side, items small and sturdy enough to fit into any airline's overhead compartment. Thea's art, once her source of delight, is now as mind-and-senses-numbing as her previous life had been as Big Sue's shadowy cohort.

Thea convinces herself she doesn't mind. She's selling stuff, making moola, it's just tourist shit, she shrugs. Why not? She thinks, *I can milk a few bucks out of the suckers who insist on buying this crap, and save the heady art inside me for another time.*

Without her knowing, the Itch has snuck back in, deep inside her. But Thea doesn't bother to notice.

Like every other drug before, obsessive work now takes over her life's energies. No longer does she have time to notice things that were once so essential to her. It no longer matters to be true to her calling, as far as making meaningful art is concerned. Instead, she chooses to turn her feeling-valve, the one about making art, all the way *down* to that all-familiar numbness of hers. Because, in her mind, she insists that things are going well, right here, with Giles. Too much scrutiny has never been Thea's strong suit.

Her and Giles' tin-roofed house on the beach is filled with sounds of Cracker, their cockatoo, chirping, Amigo the dog's lazy yawns and groany stretches and—out in the outdoor studio space—endless shelves and boxes bulging with varying stages of tacky junk she makes.

Gone are Thea's stylized human-like forms gyrating through mystical, colorful mindscapes like ancient gods and goddesses, having enigmatic tales to tell through her works. Contorted, erotic, and truly—only hers to convey. Not copying anyone but listening to her private muse that calls itself, *Itch*. Now though, Thea's motif is limited to insipid, primary-colored, perfunctorily realistic tourist bait. Allowing visitors to bring back reminders of their happy stay in the Bahamas. Fishing boats, birds flying over blue water, beach sand and plenty of glued-on seashells: all that would make Thea's hair stand on end, if she just took the time to think about what she was doing.

5

Just as she did in her early teens, when she'd trained her childhood sadness to go dormant with the help of numbing inebriants, now Thea dismisses any second-guessing about Giles. The Itch has become too loud, too consuming to bother with much else. Again, she's blinded by its debilitating agitation.

Filling shelf after shelf with forgettable, painted driftwood knickknacks has distracted her from seeing what is obvious to every outsider. But not to distracted Thea.

A continuous stream of female researchers has been showing up, clipboards in hand, with whom Giles goes off on overnight excursions to explore uninhabited coves close to Cat Cay to—you guessed it—study sea turtles. These *researchers*, ironically all extraordinarily fine-looking women, and all studying the migratory habits of the exact same species as he. Never mind, Thea is consumed with making a living for them both, selling her trinkets at the dive shop as well as in Nassau gift shops, so she never thinks Giles' absences strange. She is too tired to worry, truth be told. The bills never stop mounting ever since Giles' attack. He's had two, and soon will need a third reconstructive surgery before being able to properly function on his own.

Thea finds it odd that no male scholars ever come to Cat Cay to confer with the gentle turtle expert. Only female scientists, hailing from either Giles' alma mater back in the U.K. or some noteworthy stateside institution arrive, dive gear in hand. "Simply coincidental," Giles shrugs whenever asked about the line of hawksbill female specialists, as if the flippered amphibians are the only turtle species of the world worthy of being studied.

Giles is more distracted than usual when he arrives back from the latest scouting trip, telling Thea he needs to mend some tank hoses that evening. Thea often walks the beach late at night when Giles is away observing turtles or busy repairing dive equipment. She loves the sound of the gentle surf, so comforting in its consistency. The sea has become as much a friend to her as anyone on Cat Cay these last few years. Feelings of solitude, even while married, have brought Thea to walk barefoot in the moonlight along the water's edge this night, to soothe her uneasy heart. She tries to understand Giles being so focused on his reptiles. She strolls from their modest, open-windowed island home, lost in the peaceful monotony of the surf's heartbeat on the shore, meandering on the silvery moonlit, salty-aired beach. She sees the silhouette of the dive shop. A huge mozzarella moon is crying out to her, trying to still something unquenchable inside her. But Thea doesn't hear it. She only knows something ... *something* ... is drawing her to this spot.

She notices movement in the dark shadows, becoming more focused the closer Thea gets to the shop. She stops walking and listens. In the secret of shadows, it is Giles and his latest research assistant making too much noise.

From a short distance away, she freezes. With stealth-like telescopic vision, Thea sees her husband on top of the grad student. Thea snaps. "You asshole!" she screams, turns and runs, a flood of adrenaline racing through her. A feeling of panic, of being ambushed, fills her, piercing her head like a thousand arrows shooting into her. How many times has she felt this panic before, but never paid attention to it? An army of needles attacks her insides.

"I'm done!" she shouts. Shame of making awful trash, of loving a man who doesn't love her, knocks her senses clear. At last she sees, hears, feels. Understands.

She grabs the flight bag she's always kept packed for emergencies, filled with irrational things: a book of a woman's solo journey through the Himalayas she's never read; a goofy penis-shaped toothbrush from a novelty shop in New Orleans Big Sue sent on her last birthday.

Cracker screeches from the perch on the patio. "Sorry pal," Thea says, as she rushes past the bird, just misses kicking her darling, innocent dog, Amigo, in her haste out the door.

"I'll tear him to pieces," she screams. "Finish off what that damned chicken-shit shark was too wimpy to do."

Giles runs up just as she reaches the Jeep.

"Stay away from me," she spits in an acid hiss neither she nor he has ever heard. Giles, sweaty and shirtless, charges her as she jumps into the Jeep, spewing explanations, apologies, vows of never-again.

"I should have let you die!" she barks, her teeth bared in a Don't-Fuck-With-Me lunacy.

"Thea, wait!" Giles catches her by the arm as she fumbles with the ignition key.

"Get your hands off me," she murderously grimaces. "Man, you make me sick." She hears the shell clink against the mermaid charm on her keyring as she jabs the Jeep's key into its hole—the familiar sound for that one split second empowers her. A known sound zeroing-in to replace everything else that's crumbling around her.

"I don't want to ever see your cheating lying face ever again. Have fun with the babes, you jerk. Tell them to watch out for sharks."

Thea breaks his grip, steps on the gas, hatred replacing love in an instant. In the moonlight it's as if a floodlight shines on his mangled side and back, where ripped flesh is mottled by scar tissue.

She floors the accelerator, leaving a cloud of white sand to wipe out Giles' pleading. No backward glance. She leaves house, husband, pets, and her outdoor thatched roof studio where she committed a worse crime than murder—making tchotchkes instead of true art.

"Fuck you!" she screams, her foot weighing pedal to floor as she speeds away to a friend's shack where she'll hitch a ride to Nassau.

Coconut palms gently sway overhead in the cool ocean breeze, waving farewell.

6

A collect phone call from the Nassau airport is all it takes for Thea to re-enter her loyal friend's enormous whirlpool life. Thea joins up with Big Sue and her puzzling pooch, this time in Manhattan. Big Sue and Dr. Bob have been calling the port of New York City their home base for most of Thea's disloyal absence. With Thea gone, Big Sue found Sausalito too stale, too lonely without her one-and-only party pal.

Thea's overjoyed to be reunited with her friends. Dr. Bob executes some spectacularly exuberant backward cartwheels when he smells her familiar scent, sees her I'm-you-too eyes. For the moment, Thea is distracted from self-loathing over having fallen for a man who turned out to be a liar, not the refined, broken person she thought she'd married.

As soon as she arrives in the city, Thea shears off the sun-drenched locks she's grown long and loose in Cat Cay. Discarding the un-made-up, bronze beach look she'd adopted, Thea goes for a tragic rendition of herself, clown style; gets a hundred-dollar shaggy cropped hairdo with spiked, garishly clashing hair colors she will religiously keep newly tinted each week. Par for downtown artists, she dresses all in black, which suits her mournful but by-now, numbed-out heart.

Thea calls an island friend and asks her to pack up some things. A trunk arrives in New York City filled with art supplies and books, and nothing much else.

Big Sue says, "New York's our homeport now. It's perfect for me and Dr. Bob. I blend here, M'lasses."

Her blending is quite a feat for a woman who stands out over most except superstars of the NFL and NBA. For Sue to feel inconspicuous means that Thea might also. Close to South Street Seaport, Big Sue has a spacious waterfront loft adjacent to the vintage three-masted schooner, the *Constitution*, whose female skipper is an old sailing buddy of hers. Big Sue's loft, sunless, stained floor, located in an old cod-packing factory, its floor-to-ceiling windows caked with decades of salt and filth, is covered with cobwebs and empty bottles. Thea notices the heap in one stinking corner when she first enters her friend's dingy place.

"You've switched from Southern Comfort, I see."

Big Sue grunts.

Aside from Dr. Bob, the only other friend Big Sue has in New York, it turns out, is a short, slight, and balding guy she introduces as Fast Forward, which Thea interprets as the speed he smokes, drinks, and snorts to keep up with Sue's in-all-ways generosity.

During the time they've been separated, nothing much has changed about Big Sue. Except she now freelances with ocean-going tugs and shipping freighters, only making an occasional delivery of some high-end sailboat. "Not enough bang for the buck," she utters as to why. She still likes to make weeks-long cargo runs to South America or Europe whenever a crackerjack navigator is needed at the last minute. When she isn't at sea she occasionally stands in for pilots of New York Harbor's many tugs. Big Sue makes sure never to have too steady a job. "*That* might interfere with my partying," she tells anyone, chuckling, but dead serious. True, she has a pad to crash in, somewhere safe she can return to after her frequent ocean voyages, for another annihilating binge. Home is too corny a word for her though. She calls her place *my fuckin' pad;* her dog, *my main man;* and Fast Forward, *my girlfriend.*

Dr. Bob likes to go wherever Big Sue does. She says his sea legs are better than most human crews she's dealt with. Quarantine laws of other countries and shipowners' rules against pets are the only blocks that keep Sue from being with her main man all the time.

"'Cause Dr. Bob, my lean machine of canine dreams," she says, rubbing her constant companion's appreciative ears, "can't go ashore in some piss-ant places." When he can come, Big Sue prefers gigs that include return fare for both herself and Dr. Bob, besides her usual fee.

Back at the loft, Dr. Bob makes do with Sue's homemade trap door that lets him onto his rooftop latrine whenever he needs. Fast Forward, the only one who could keep up with her until Thea returned to Big Sue's life, comes by to feed him when Big Sue is away at sea.

The first night as they sit around catching up, Sue says to Thea: "The Big Apple's just another port o'call for a dog traveling as much as ol' Dr. Bob does. City streets are just a mite harder on his paws."

Big Sue downs her bottle of rum, smacks her lips, and says, "Sure, I'll put ya up for as long as you need, no prob. I always thought Giles smelled a little fishy. But I never said anything, did I, M'lasses?"

Big Sue belts another cold German beer with a Mount Gay chaser, then gives Thea, deeply tanned and slightly shell-shocked in this beehive of a city, a pat on the back as she adds, "Time to start over, girl. Ya win some, ya lose a lot. Look at me."

The two friends sit around the huge drafty loft, drinking, smoking Camels, rolling doobies as big as Big Sue's well worn, greasy fingers, and snorting coke. They stay up most the night laughing and crying, till they fall over and can't get up. Sue has it all. And she shares it every night with Thea. For the first week in the city, Thea is grateful to not have to think about anything, happily blotto-ed.

"The worst thing about it is Giles being dishonest," Big Sue says only once. "Let's face it, he's a guy. Guys are animals. He had one foot out the door, wanting freedom—but he couldn't admit it—and the other foot on your ass, wanting you to be good and loyal to him while he did his tricks. Worked too, didn't it? Till he got his dick caught on the razor blade in between. Deep down you must've known he never loved you. You were his caretaker, not his soul mate. You're a free woman now, be thankful, M'lasses. You gotta learn to love yourself. Like I had to," she finishes, chugging straight from the Mount Gay bottle.

Thea's eyes gleam in the night as she takes a hit from the rum bottle her friend hands her. She doesn't like it when memories flash to the surface, of her origins or her big disappointments. But she can't help it. Whenever Thea drinks she flashes back to the putrid taste of a lonely childhood: her parents smelling like booze, both so busy with careers, martini parties and projects, too distracted for hugs or even an encouraging word. Both of them always annoyed with Thea, their only girl, the youngest among three overachieving boys; a girl who was too spacey, who never seemed to get it *right*. Thea takes another hit of rum.

"From now on I'm not letting anyone tell me how to live my life," Thea says to no one in particular, even though Big Sue is sitting right there. The effect of booze torpedoes to her toes, its familiar, welcoming curtain blotting out all sensations. Thea smiles at how safe and secure she feels, drunk. "Never again am I gonna let anyone tell me what kind of art I can or can't make."

"Right on, M'lasses," Big Sue slurs, reaching out. "Gimme back that bottle."

Within weeks, Thea's Bahamian-brown body withers to an unfed, unhealthy shade of addict-gray. She becomes racked with aches and has cramps that double her over, making her fear for more than lost pride. No amount of coke, booze, or partying can stop the soul-erosion going on within her. Thea's mind screams *No!* in thirty different languages whenever she's not drunk enough, beating herself up about how dumb she'd been to waste those years, hiding out with Giles, that pussy dweeb.

Thea's hair is now dyed dried-blood red. Gone are the subtleties of shades, only harsh remains. Just as she'd hidden herself when she assumed the fake beach-artist role, she morphs again. Thea figures the hair thing is symbolic. It's a mourning flag for the heartbreak she's bottle-feeding; not over Giles but having lost her identity as a true artist, dedicated to discovering new ideas, new visions.

She looks in a mirror and sees what everyone else does and hopes they'll all stay away from her. It will take a while before she can stop the brain-sizzling burn over not being smart enough. Fooled by her sex-crazed man. Not strong enough to have said *No!* to making that phony crap. "Yes," she admits, "I'll wear my red sizzle hair as a banner of grief."

She goes with Big Sue to Duffy's, a neighborhood dive where her pal has a permanent table right in the middle of other hardcore downtown bon vivants. After Thea joins Fast Forward, Big Sue's entourage increases to the nice round number of a trinity. They can out-drink, out-snort, out-smoke anyone. The trio of infamy stays blind for days on end, without stopping to eat, puke, or ever complain.

Patrons at Duffy's know that lines of the Lady are just as likely to be laid out on the grimy bathroom sink as a fight could break out between the wrong guy or gal hitting on Big Sue. No one ever pays attention to the official closing time of 4 a.m. The unspoken rule at Duffy's: stay all night as long as the outside door is locked and the shades are pulled. Just don't brag about it. Even if the cops happen by on an unscheduled late-night cruise, they only see dark shadows inside, through drawn blinds.

Numbing her heart-sickness, Thea begins to make angst-driven, ambiguous art in a corner of Big Sue's loft that she clears of cobwebs and empty bottles. Her art changes as much as Thea has. The colors are weird, slightly off, complex and darker. The recognizable mystical myths she once portrayed now dive deeper into the scary nightmarish realms of a troubled human psyche. New themes venture into morbid territories. Any hint of joy remains undisclosed in Thea's alluringly pained perspective. Her ominous references reflect the muddied state of how unhappy, random and unfair life is, devoid of respect—of self or others. Her art is altogether as depressing as she is. Big Sue and Fast Forward love it.

Thea takes several of her tormented canvases to Jack McGraw, the cigar-chomping dealer whose gallery on West Broadway shows some of the best work of the moment. Every downtown artist knows McGraw will take a look at anyone's work. "Some of my best discoveries come right off the street," he was quoted saying in *Art Quorum*. McGraw is notoriously brutal—some say heartless—his opinion can make or break a career. If McGraw likes your work, you might be invited into a group show. Maybe even a show of your own, a virtual miracle in a city of a thousand hungry artists per block.

McGraw grunts, "Let's see what you got."

Thea, shivering with a hangover, approaches him in one of his barn-big showrooms one quiet Tuesday afternoon. Even rum-fueled bravery can't stop her from shaking with trepidation. She's a virgin at showing her work to a New York hotshot dealer. From the motley blanket under her arm she unwraps three small wood panels. Thea is naive, believing artists needn't bother with following the *norms* of fashion, not caring what her clothes speak about their wearer. Consequently, she looks like hell. Thick-heeled snow boots, clunky smelly castoffs of Big Sue's, a motley Navy-issued peacoat covered with stains from rodent droppings from where she'd dragged it out of a dank corner of the loft—Thea looks like a Bowery bum, not a hip artist. No job and no cash. It is winter and every last trace of her tan from Cat Cay has worn away. Air is free, but otherwise, Thea is living off Sue's largesse.

McGraw's bushy eyebrows raise high. The art world magnate scans bedraggled Thea; glances at her equally bewitched paintings. His big lips suck on his unlit cigar with a hissing sound that heaves Thea's stomach.

"So what makes you think you can walk in here and get shown?" he demands, not turning from the images he's scrutinizing.

"I, I guess I think my work is good enough, Mr. McGraw. Art ought to speak for itself," Thea mumbles.

"Well, it's all wrong," the man says, too loudly. "Who wants colorful Nature? Don't you know what's happening in the art world? Where have you been, in a black hole? My stable is post-modern, dystopic hyper-realism. Are you lost, from another century or what?"

"Er, I've been living out of the country for a while."

"Yeah, well, you better stay there until you're ready to play the game. You have to stay in the gutter like the rest of you out-of-touch wannabes. Try working another ten years and then come show me your stuff. I can't sell this; it's high school." True to his reputation of not mincing words, McGraw's chubby hand waves the air in a wide dismissing gesture. Without even turning to look at Thea's quivering face, the thick man shuffles away to an assistant waiting with an urgent phone call.

Rejection fuels Thea's addiction dragon. Not bothering to fight anymore, she slides into the aching, piercing chasm of self-loathing.

Despite her brutal slighting, Thea is compelled to continue making the macabre art nobody resonates with. But she gets it together enough to get a job. She doesn't want to be a sponge any longer, even though Sue never says a word. Thea is a waitress at Seaport Chowder, right around the corner from the loft. After her humiliating rebuff by McGraw, she swears she'll never show her work publicly, a promise she celebrates nightly in subsequently more and more creative ways. Fueling her vengeful self with cooling, pungent, nutritious beer ("Hey, it's made from grain," she defends her liquid diet), Thea begins to vacuum lines of cocaine offered by her better-connected, better-paid compadres, who always share. The more out of it Thea gets, the more she listens to Fast Forward, who keeps urging her to join the downtown performance art scene that keeps his larder well stocked.

"You're a natural," he tells her. "Look at your art, for cryin' out loud. Those paintings are nothin' but dangerous-deep and searing-strong. I love the creepy weird ones, especially the Nosferatu series. What? They're not vampires. Oh well. Performance will be easy for you, Thee. Your voice is sheer liquid, like poetry. Man, you can wail, woman. I hear you but I know you don't. Come on, we need a lead singer for The Supply House. All you have to do is be loud and be you. There's nothing more to it. Up on stage all you do is be cool and outrageous. Like, I don't know anyone who does that better than you, do you, Big Sue?"

"Shit, no, Fast. M'lasses has always been ahead of her time. No one understands that shit she paints, they never have. She went soft in the Bahamas, but she's back on track now. Her stuff will never sell for shit, so she may as well sing and have fun with you guys. I've been telling you, Fast, you need a chick's voice to balance all that nasty violent testosterone. Least you've got gigs lined up."

Fast says, "Better than waiting tables and not doing anything with your overdose creativity, right, Thee?"

"I don't know," Thea says. "I never thought about being a singer, not once."

"No problem," Fast Forward chirps. "The guys and I didn't either, 'cept Harry the Harelip. He's the only one who knew how to play an instrument when we started. Man, can he blow that horn. I'm telling you, nobody gives a rat's ass what you used to do. It's what you're doing *now* that counts in this city. Am I right, Big Sue?"

"Shit, yeah, Fast. Look at me. Nobody in this frigging city believes a broad can handle pulling barges around. So guess who works as much as she wants, when she wants, and gets to watch the old geezers down at the dock eat crow?"

"Thanks, Fast," Thea says. "I'll think about it."

The threesome shrug their shoulders in tandem, slug down a few more belts, whip out a few more lines as they lounge around on filthy pillows, the only furniture other than a few skuzzy mattresses scattered around Big Sue's fifth-floor walk-up. In oblivious canine gaiety Dr. Bob strolls away from the group sprawled on the floor and heads straight for an arching, spread-out skeleton of a good-sized potted ficus tree, whose brown, brittle branches almost touch the splintery wood floor.

Dr. Bob ducks his head low and moves, ever so slowly, under the fragile stick of a dried-up bough, allowing only a solitary twig to just barely, and whispery-soft, touch his back's thick fur. Then, he does something so weird with this low-lying branch, Thea's eyes go tennis-bouncing between Big Sue and her canine alter-shadow, wondering *What The Fuck?* Big Sue is taking another hit off a bong and couldn't care less. She shrugs her shoulders, like saying, "Hey we're getting high, why can't he?"

Thea watches a remarkable shift occur within the dog. He's standing mid-step, one paw lifted, absolutely still, under a branch that lightly touches his rippling, relaxed spine. A spaced-out look spreads over the mutt's face like a thick paste, altering his muzzle's furry features. His eyes are glazed. Every part of him is frozen with the euphoric touch of some magical, mood-altering connection with the dead tree's fragile, feather-light tickle. The ecstatic look on the dog's face is bizarre, to say the least. Thea can't stop staring at the animal as he remains in this self-induced hypnotic trance. She has to get the scoop from Big Sue.

"Yeah, he started getting off on leaves and things like dangling jacket sleeves while you were gone. Weird, huh? Now all he needs is something that doesn't move, to lightly touch his back and he's a goner." Sue shakes her head, looking at her canine protégée in unabashed pride.

Entranced by the mere touch of the tip of a dried tree branch, the dog is smiling without opening his mouth. His eyes, not seeing. He stands in this gonzo, not-there fashion, one paw at a time slowly lifting off the floor in ultra-slow motion. Barely noticeably, the dog moves. For the longest time the three humans watch from their cushions, goofing on Dr. Bob as the dog trance-waltzes under the brittle boughs of the long-dead ficus that Big Sue keeps solely for her dog's pleasure.

"It's his bong, m'buds," Sue roars a deep throated approval.

Fast becomes as close to Thea as she is with Big Sue. Party animals unite: you're either one or ya ain't. Without a gallery or any way to show her art, Thea clearly has no motivation. Painting is cutting into her partying. She never mentions to anyone, ever, about McGraw's harsh words.

Fast Forward passes a blunt as he points at his favorite of Thea's paintings one night while Big Sue is away on a delivery. "This one here's about you killing a family, am I right? A cartoon murder, all that blood. You told me what lousy folks you had. Didn't do squat for you, just like mine," he spits out with sad irony. "Too busy putting us down, right?"

Thea just smiles. She never explains, not one comment about her enigmatic puzzles. "It's art. It's not psychodrama. I just want to suck you in," is all Thea ever says about the mysteriously evocative images she makes. "Keep looking, Fast. There's always more. And when you figure it out, be sure to let me know," she adds, making a face. "What I paint can't be figured out," she says. "People who try to stick literal meanings onto things that come from the abyss of human imagination—annoy me."

Since arriving in New York and making enough pained, vengeful images that needed getting out of her, one day out of the blue Thea decides to take up Fast Forward's invitation to sing with his band, The Supply House. She might as well since she hangs out and gets high with these four crazy guys. Quickly she learns that partying her ass off on stage is way more fun than being alone, which painting is. Flinging herself about in front of people puts Thea's anger to good use. Turned on by entertaining crowds, seeing and hearing the roar of their appreciation, she realizes that studio art, hiding out in the solitary madness of making object-art—destined to be seen by only a few privileged people anyway—is an antiquated, dead art form.

The band practices a few days before they're due to play the Mudd Club, a gig that was scheduled before Thea signed on. The punked-out crowd goes absolutely ape-shit. It's a weeknight yet a good crowd turns out to hear the pounding throb of the band's dissonant, gutsy sound featuring the new violet-haired, alien-looking girl-woman who wears a ripped-lace, shimmery mini-thing as she channels electric jolts with frenzied antics on stage, forcing every jaded downtown freak to perk up and *Hey! Dance!* Thea screams all her nightmarish hurt into every song. The crowd loves her tormented angst. They lap up her blatant missteps, smeared like her makeup is, identify with her pain, her anger, her despair with screams and cheers of their own.

Fast Forward rushes to Big Sue's loft a few days later. "Man, you should hear what they wrote in today's *The It*. Listen to this: 'Everyone who was there was wild, absolutely gone, Tuesday night.' Thee, you're a hit! The band's got the *now* sound, that's what they say. We're in fat city, and you're the reason." Fast grabs Thea and *mwaw*-kisses her right on the lips.

Overnight, The Supply House becomes the most talked about group in the downtown rags. Pretty soon the band is playing gigs all over the city. A month later they play CBGB's, where their reputation is sealed as the next *in* band. No other discordant sound better portrays this extravagant time, when Manhattan is awash in tamale-for-brains molly and cocaine-users, mixed with waves of despondent HIV/AIDS victims. Downtown is a dazed bunch that is just realizing there's a global contagion beginning to flow in people's blood, a virus-killer of hundreds of thousands that year, and soon after that, millions worldwide. Serious times are a-brewing. Nobody ever thought that a microscopic creature, such as a virus, could be a lethal killer.

Thea is there, drinking, drugging, snorting, and, when she's in the mood, fucking herself into oblivion, using pandemic-protection for the first time. Her friends—adamantly celibate Big Sue and voraciously gay Fast Forward—right beside her.

* * *

She stays with Big Sue and Dr. Bob for six months before moving in with the first of a string of lovers with real estate. All of them have either artistic inclinations or appreciate hers, have steady jobs in respectable professions or businesses of their own. In other words: they're capable of supporting Thea in the manner to which she never thinks about. The new rule of Thea's thumb: None of her boyfriends indulge in self-medicating nearly as much as she does. That would be too competitive for her, since tasting the public's acclaim as an official downtown rocker brings along a readymade reputation of being *the most* outrageous.

Steve is a real sweetheart but clueless as hell, a jazz bass player who enjoys a worldwide following and has a smoothly uncluttered Scan Design loft on Spring Street. In just five months, Thea gets tired of his regular hours of practice and a workout routine that he does to maintain his performing stamina, as he's booked years in advance. Steve also unwittingly compromised himself by complaining about Thea's lack of any routine whatsoever.

James, she meets at Duffy's. But it's only after ascertaining he has even more spacious digs than Steve that Thea takes him seriously, and once she does, moves her all-black wardrobe to his loft on Greenwich Ave. James is the owner of a favored downtown nightclub that brought him instant notoriety and a safe full of gold. Their liaison lasts thirteen delirious months before succubus Thea drains all she can from James' resources, before she falls for the next guy with even better connections, and, of course, a much classier living space.

Dieter, far more conservative than any of her previous hook-ups, is an imposingly stiff, soft-spoken German from Nuremberg, with a chain of oxygen-inhaling bars that were a smashing success all over Europe; now the American market is just opening up for them. Thea feels pangs of a holistic bent grabbing, beckoning her for a moment, when she reads about Dieter's business in *The New York Times*:

"At last, a healthy alternative to drugs and alcohol for the troubled downtown gay community, where AIDS is striking the worst of its roulette-wheel death sentences. Panic like this has never been felt before in the clubs of lower Manhattan. Crowds are rushing to thank Dieter Jahn for bringing his oxygen-breathing social bars to town."

Fearful of infection, city revelers throng to Dieter's oxygen bars. In these troubled times many feel safer sucking clean air through masks than drinking booze, passing doobies, or snorting coke through communal straws. The O high is pure, healthy, with no side effects, its euphoria causing no trauma to anyone. Thea thinks Dieter, wealthy beyond her dreams, a thoroughly classy guy, even if he is rather ordinary looking. And he is obsessed by the unmatchable persona Thea lets loose on the stage. Her act is a pungent tornado, an art form she perfects with sound and antics, while her canvases gather dust in the dark corners of Big Sue's loft, hidden from everyone.

Fast Forward reports he'd heard that over in Munich, punkers and skinheads are buzzing about tapes someone smuggled there of The Supply House's raunchy, rowdy sounds. Word of Thea's sexy performance antics brings the band invitations to perform all over Europe. Fast advises his lead singer, when he sees how attracted the German is to Thea, that she can help this guy, Dieter—older than Thea's other men-with-real-estate—tap into the screaming unsettledness of Manhattan.

"Your In-Crowd audience means more customers for him. Hey CC, it'll be great," Fast sarcastically giggles, using the wretched nickname he calls all females—besides Big Sue—short for *Cute Chick*, which Thea knows damn well is so her lecherous friend could legitimately draw breasts every time he writes women a note, delightedly putting two dots in the middle of the CCs to make clear his boob reference.

"You'll help him find more clients in our little world-in-turmoil, Thee. Nobody wants to get sick, but everyone wants to party," Fast says with a smirk.

To savvy Dieter, Thea represents the amalgam of America's confused generation, a new wave in culture power. Her message as spokeswoman for the rarified downtown art world: desperation. Through her, Dieter comes to understand how American youth relate to their throbbing, pulsating music, their unyielding use of mind-altering drugs, more rampant and visible in the States than anywhere in Europe at the time, except Amsterdam. Through Thea's stage act—largely unpracticed, implicitly untethered—fears get passionately exposed. Dieter studies her expressions, knowing he's learning how to capitalize on America's false sense of bouncing between invincibility and self-annihilation, like a nuked ping-pong ball. For both Thea and Dieter, theirs is a mutually beneficial, exclusively business relationship.

Before the modern plague of AIDS, most of the true hedonists were changing partners every other season, or less. Dieter and Thea's live-in relationship lasts almost a year's change of seasons, a record of longevity for strictly polyamorous Dieter; and a third-place personal best for Thea, next to her back-to-back *annus horribilis* with Giles.

You wouldn't call any of Thea's liaisons *romantic* in any real sense. Her string of guys-with-lofts is her way of dealing with Manhattan's chronic housing shortage. She never wants to find her own place; she's too busy to look for a pad of her own. At every gig The Supply House plays to standing-room-only crowds, at the Palladium, Village East, CBGB's, the Mudd Club, the Sass Hole. The band brings Fast Forward, Thea, Harry the Harelip, Stretch, and Bad Patch as much fame as anyone could ever wish for. Truth be known, no one in the band wanted to do anything too serious. None of the four guys have the ambition to take their act on the road, record, or travel the world. They never even wanted to play clubs in Europe. Thea's beginning to realize she's hooked up with losers, even if they're popular losers.

"Too much trouble," Fast says.

"Too much to do already, around town," the other guys agree.

After Thea has been playing with The Supply House long enough to know they're just as lazy as they are *in*, Fast tells her one day, "We don't wanna push a good thing too far, you know, CC."

"What? You make it sound like it's bad to be liked," she snorts.

"It'll spoil the fun for us, Thee. Fame fucks up lives. Think how bad it'd be if we had to give up partying just 'cause we're too busy playing. Gawd, that'd be awful."

So as Dieter starts to put too much pressure on Thea to "… get more focused about your career, show those weird paintings of yours in a prestigious gallery if the band's not going more public," it's just as well she'd already met Max.

Better and bigger real estate beckons, Thea figures. Max's renovated hi-tech loft is a tribute to urban aesthetes, set in an appropriately not-yet-trendy neighborhood, where most of Tribeca's industrial lofts are chicly half commercial, the perfect address for a well-greased wheel like Max. He appreciates the mockery when Thea meets him, calling his still obscure neighborhood of Tribeca, *So-So-Ho*, for *south of SoHo*. The anonymity factor of his luxury loft on Reade Street is as important to Max's preferred aloofness, for his business allure, as it is all-important to Thea in her quest for her next, perfect crib to move into.

By day, the narrow streets of Tribeca are populated by shops and merchants peddling every item to the insatiable appetites of consumers. By night, bug-eyed struggling artists slink along moist streets, wet with humans and their get-juiced choices. Tribeca is the only place that Thea, now a local celebrity no matter how Fast feels about it, can envision herself living. She cherishes her privacy as much as she loves the laid back, yuppie-phobic ambiance of the local Tribeca drinking holes. Best of all, to Thea's distorted perspective, is Duffy's, her favorite drinking temple that Big Sue first initiated her into, located right around the corner from Max's elevator-exclusive, top floor penthouse.

Tribeca has a gritty style, plenty of avant-garde panache, and enough cultural identity hang-ups to fill a mental health textbook. The place is rough, even when its busy formerly commercial-only streets empty at night. In the shadows of Tribeca's near-deserted streets, anything can happen. One night, there's a knife fight outside Duffy's. And then a dream-like sight, another night when Thea's walking the abandoned streets by herself, more than half drunk. She witnesses an enormously tall, muscular drag queen get out of a cab all alone, dressed exactly as Marilyn, complete with the white organdy, full-skirted dress, the stiletto heels and abundant bosom, and plants herself, feet spread wide, on top of a subway iron grate. The trans-femme doesn't have to wait more than a few seconds before the wailing and hissing begins, the queen screaming and hollering as if in sweet pain every time a train goes by beneath, its hot air blast whooshing up her skirts exactly as the famed noir photograph shows Monroe's own delight.

Hidden within a darkened doorway, Thea checks the bizarre scene out, an entire three-trains' worth. Better than any performance act she's ever caught because it's real, she nods. *And no one else but me seeing it.* The queen thinks she's alone, that's what makes it more bizarre. Letting herself yell and scream with orgasmic delight as if she's being fucked by God Almighty Him- or Herself. Yet there Thea is, hidden in a doorway. Thea sees the oversized, slinkily dressed s/he getting-off as each blast of steam goes up those spread-wide legs. The off-beat gender gal, still shrieking in the lonely night as Thea slips away, unnoticed.

Big Sue always feels at home in Duffy's, the most hard-core drinking (and bathroom drugging) hole of the time in Tribeca. "It feels like country here, M'lasses. Like somewhere up in Maine, where people don't bug you."

"Yeah. I love Tribeca too," Thea says, on their way to or from Duffy's. "It feels like you're not even in the city down here." In her bones she knows she belongs in Tribeca's streets, where it doesn't feel quite safe.

Ironically, Max appeals to Thea because he's so damn straight. *I won't drink or drug myself to death with him around*, she figures.

Her old Itch—is it the urge to make art again?—begins to make itself known as soon as she moves in. *Max's place is perfect,* she thinks, as soon as she glimpses the high-ceilinged, empty room where she instantly envisions herself making art again.

Thea's terms to Max insisting she move in with him are simple, as usual: "No strings attached." Secretly, though, when he sees her output, Max starts planning on introducing Thea's work to an art dealer he knows. Max is too good at what he does not to know a sure bet when he sees one. He figures he'll promote her as an edgy outsider, a female Basquiat, the punk princess of underground miscreants. As soon as the two met, Max's business sense psyched out Thea's bankable potential as much as her instincts went on high-alert for her next, better real estate deal.

"That stuff's dynamite," Max gushes as she unpacks the paintings she's stored at Big Sue's, work she'd done before joining the band. "Sexy and brain-rattling. Just like you and your act."

Thea keeps quiet. She can tell from Max's huge barren loft that he doesn't have an *eye* to save his ass, not for fine art, not for anything more subtle than a Hollywood blockbuster, which happens to be his specialty in the promotions company he manages. Max begins to tell Thea he'll take charge of her career, make her art famous. "I'll be your patron."

"Whoa! Just hang on there," Thea says aggressively, pushing Max out of the spacious empty room he's given her for a studio. Thea glares at him and hisses, "Mind your own damn business!"

Of course, Thea now suspects Max of having a hidden agenda when he invited her to live with him. It's hard for him to fake it. He keeps throwing out bait, saying things like, "Babe, consider it my job to take care of you, to develop your potential."

"Leave it alone, Max. I'm in charge of my destiny, not you," she repeats, annoyed yet glad for the spacious studio in which she's inspired to create new work.

Max can't resist, the pushy bastard. Privately he envisions her art star rising high, him leading the blast off. All he has to do is wait, he tells himself.

"I gotta protect myself from the assholes of the fickle art world," she confides to Fast Forward and Big Sue at Duffy's one night, where she escapes to join her friends as much as she can. Thea can share things with Fast and Sue that have to be left unsaid to anyone else. Whenever Max goes on one of his frequent business trips to L.A., Thea makes up for lost time with her partying pals.

"Waste of time," Sue Big grumbles when Thea and Fast Forward start talking of their shared fascination about the *religion of art*, as they call their creating habit. Big Sue wanders off and orders another mug of beer with a Cuervo chaser. If it isn't about boats or faraway places, Dr. Bob, indigenous causes or Nature Herself, Big Sue isn't much interested in waggin' her jaw.

Thea is at their usual table at Duffy's, partying with Big Sue and Fast Forward while Max is off on another trip.

"It's hard. I wish I could get that connection back I had in the Haight. I used to feel really in cahoots with something *important*. But I think I've lost it. Nothing comes out feeling right. What's the point, anyway? We're all probably gonna die of AIDS or some environmental or nuclear disaster, so why bother? Art sucks. It's like hearsay: who says anyone should believe any of it?"

"Thee, you're gettin' weird on us again," Fast warns.

"Hey, come on, I just wanna feel alive! I don't want to be told how it ought to be.

Art used to make me feel alive; but I'm stuck," Thea admits.

"You're both full of shit, y'know," Big Sue slurs, slugging down a half pint in one swallow.

"I don't know," Thea shrugs, "maybe it's Max's loft getting to me. It's too fucking nice there."

Thea talks louder the more she drinks. Fast and Big Sue just look at her, all three out of focus. Sitting at the table next to them is a most unusual, exotic-looking couple: a fantasy duet from some faraway time and place, not from then and there. The man is dark-skinned and has tremendously thickly lashed, soulful eyes that never cease roaming and smiling. He's a veritable futuristic iconoclast, a downtown Hindu sannyasin with dreads of wild black wooly spirals, mesmerizing facial expressions, and a deep, gentle voice. His sturdy, lean and lanky frame is crammed into a flimsy rod-iron chair, while his companion, with her fine, delicate features, as if molded from barely perceivable, tinted creamy porcelain, is an appealingly strong-in-self female. Both of them are dressed unlike anyone else at Duffy's, as if the two are on their way to a costume party of their own. Thea can tell, in between slugs of her drinks, that these two are *heavy*. The woman—with her radiant, un-made-up café au lait complexion, a swish of fine glowing materials wrapping her compact, curvaceous body—is an apparition of graciousness, rather than flesh and blood among the dregs of such dire surroundings.

Leaning toward the trio of desperation, the uniquely attractive man says, "Pardon me intrusion," in a thick, sing-song Caribbean accent. "Me canna help but be overhearing. People be talking 'bout the hardship of making art be my kind of people." His face bursts wide in a jester's grin.

The remarkably regal man introduces himself. "Me be Junkyard Trinnie, mohn." His shoulder-length dreads are dusted rust-colored, bamboo thick, and stick out from his head in electrified tentacles. His startlingly lovely mixed-race companion, whose indigo-black hair is pulled slick-straight back, like a ballerina on stage, has smooth mango-ripe skin that shimmers like a sunset on an Indian Ocean island, which is exactly where she happens to hail from, they are told by Junkyard Trinnie as he introduces his wife, Maly.

"That be short for Marie Laurence," Junkyard Trinnie grins.

7

The pair of artists Thea meets that night are of the highest caliber for any time in history: both are socially active and both equally impactful in their respective fields.

Junkyard Trinnie is a West Indian man of a roasted nut hue, while Maly, brought up on the island of Mauritius off the eastern coast of Africa, is a mix of everything, natives and colonizers alike, a descendent of whomever trod the East Indies. Her appearance is so hybrid that it is startlingly strange, yet as if peering into a crystal ball and seeing what we humans are all wont to become, more and more, in another hundred years of blending races. When all of us will have as harmonious a tone to our skin as this woman has. Time stands still, meeting this handsome couple.

The man grimaces when Thea asks if he's been here before.

"It be that obvious, then? No, we be never here before."

Thea isn't surprised. Duffy's has a reputation of being dangerous after midnight, when local hoodlums and artists start to congregate.

Junkyard Trinnie and Maly are on an adventure, the man unabashedly offers. When he leans over to the blurry-eyed threesome at the next table, his alarmingly white teeth blind them. Thea, even in her woozy state, feels instantly attracted to the couple, mostly for their uncommon friendliness, their unaffected modesty with all that beauty rolling around in front of her eyes.

After sharing names, the man with skin that sings Blackness declares in a booming voice: "We be savoring the nightlife, the t'ing we never be making time to do these busy days." Junkyard Trinnie's joy gives away his heritage as much as his name and his calypso lilt does.

Big Sue and Fast Forward are too inebriated to care. Somehow, Thea is no longer drunk. She immediately feels at ease with this tree trunk of a gnarly-roots-headed man, his dreadlocks spewing like a water fountain from the top of his skull, and his ethereal spouse, both of them altogether too mythological-looking for the stark reality of a Manhattan downtown dive.

"Trinidad, right?" Big Sue says, as if his name isn't obvious enough.

The man's good humor dances upon a face that, like his lady's, seems to emanate from a fairytale: he the solicitous faun and she, the promise-giving fairy. He is drinking Guinness in its very British brown bottle; and she, a bright white wine in a thin stem.

"We work too much, like you too probably, mes amies," Maly's accented words glide.

"Too many nights in the studio make the brain go hungry for a jump-up," Junkyard Trinnie says, or rather, his deep voice sings in sanguine jubilance. "Every artist needs to pah-ty every now an' then, m'sohn!"

"Me, I wouldn't know," Big Sue grumbles, slugging down her umpteenth draft, then holding the empty glass aloft for the barkeep to see that refills are sorely needed.

"Oh sorry," Junkyard says. "I thought you all be artists."

"It's all right," Thea grimaces. "She's our mascot."

Junkyard compliments Fast Forward on his mismatched stripes and polka-dotted ensemble, the thrift-store jewelry adorning every lobe and bare inch of his flesh; and Thea on her electrified rockin' hair (nuclear-waste green that night) and her glittery black skintight get-up. Big Sue doesn't look art-friendly at all; more like *don't-fuck-with-me* off-limits, fresh from overhauling her tug's transmission because the mechanic onboard couldn't. Her short, broken and bitten fingernails, black with engine grease, don't go unnoticed by the friendly man's searchlight eyes.

"I agree, partying is a necessary part of life," Thea says. "Too much work and not enough play makes one go soft in the head."

"What kind of art you be doing?" Junkyard asks, his eyes going from Thea to Fast, wiping his wide mouth with the back of his hand after taking a frothy slug of Guinness.

"Come to my studio and see for yourself," Thea hears herself say. Fast looks at her as if she's revealing she's a pregnant four-foot dwarf who only speaks Arabic. "It's right around the corner on Reade Street. We can come back here afterwards."

"It be sounding good," Junkyard Trinnie says, "but we be heading home after that, thanks." He nods to Maly, who signals back: wordless communion evident between them.

The pair laugh continuously. At first Thea thinks it's strange, meeting artists so damn pleasant. But their joy quickly becomes hers.

As the group, caboosed by a scowling Big Sue, piles out of Duffy's, Maly says, "It has become too trendy for us to enjoy our old hangouts without a big headache. Soho is filled with gawkers who come to see 'ow artists live, where we eat, what we look like. They follow us even when we go to the laundromat. The streets are like a zoo these days, and we, we! are the animals in the cage."

"Yes mohn," Junkyard says. "Our old night spots be more vexing than relaxing. Another reason why we be too much in the studio, eh, my Queen? So we be trying your neighborhood tonight. Just a few minutes' walk down West Broadway for us."

Big Sue begrudgingly drags behind, insisting, "Sure ya got somethin' to drink at Max's?" When they get off the silent, stainless elevator that takes the five revelers up to Max's top floor luxurious loft, everyone except Big Sue is happily exchanging about their lives. She keeps to the rear, grumbling. The others walk through the oversized living room enjoying themselves. Thea tells her guests that her boyfriend Max is away on business, as usual.

They follow the long hallway that passes the huge master bedroom with its full wall of windows looking out over the Hudson River. As soon as the quintet enters Thea's studio and sees her vibrating colors, her strong patterned jump-at-you images—some half done, some stacked in corners— Junkyard and Maly stand still. They silently, potently, look at each other.

The pair stop joking with each other. From the moment they enter her studio, Junkyard Trinnie and Maly, Thea notes, huddle together talking softly, looking at her canvases stapled to walls or the wooden floor, picking up sketches on paper strewn here and there, looking at everything as if all of it is rare, ancient treasure.

Thea's biggest pieces—lustrous, textural, rich with symbolic reference, stunningly mystical but not beautiful in any usual manner—draw the duo to whispers no one can hear. Junkyard and Maly stand before a six-foot painting depicting the birth of a mythical figure.

Thea says, "Someone told me her name is Daphne, and the pursuing warrior dude there, he's Apollo. But I only found that out after the painting was completed, when this guy I was showing it to recognized the figures as an actual myth. Wow, that blew me away. Talk about the collective unconscious, huh?"

The surreal composition was of an abstracted woman arising from, or is it merging into? a deeply-rooted tree. Her outstretched arms blend into the tree's leafy branches, while an invincible warrior who has been chasing her is left, at a distance, without a conquest, his head hanging in dismay.

"I'm getting sum'in to drink," Big Sue announces with no invitation to the others.

"Your stuff be courageous calls to be battling head with the heart," Junkyard Trinnie proclaims as he and Maly saunter around the studio on their own. Thea is in the center of the space, happy to see people enjoying her work. She likes these two, which is unusual for her. Most people other than Sue and Fast bore her. Thea is intrigued by Maly, so humble and not intimidated, even by Big Sue; and Junkyard Trinnie, funny and direct, and kindly to the point of things. Thea feels a pang of missing the friendly Bahamians she knew while living in Cat Cay, beguilingly child-like in their unaffected ways.

"Your pictures, ma cherie, so challenging. They break through old beliefs so many insist holding onto," Maly says. Before she can answer, Thea rushes over to where Fast Forward is just about to knock over a tall stack of paint cans. Maly speaks with her husband. Thea doesn't quite catch all of it.

"She be ... one of us."

"Yes ... excellent ... catching ideas we hearts be dreaming, my sweetness," Thea hears Junkyard reply.

Thea returns to the pair who continue to talk as if she isn't there.

"This work, they are invitations to drop the old games, and explore new ways of seeing," Maly half-whispers.

"Mohn, this White Gurl can paint!" Junkyard says out loud, causing Thea to smile despite herself, his comment making her miss her all-ways open-wide Bahamian friends that instant. She keeps getting reminders how racism is so hard in Amerika, for all skin shades. Then Fast makes more noise across the other side of the room, drunkenly knocking something else over. Thea goes to inspect the damage. Junkyard and his wife continue talking in low tones. Thea pretends not to hear, although she catches snippets.

"She be making real what hides beneath," the man from Trinidad says. "Those fern eyes of hers be seeing secrets about invisible t'ings that be locked away inside we all. That heart of hers be looking for bigger answers."

"But, mon cher, I don't think she knows what she has here."

Nothing seems to escape Thea's noticing that senses-sharp night. From the other side of the studio she is all ears. These people, standing right before her, are talking about her work like only she, she'd always thought, feels about it.

Maly nods, "Mais oui, mon cher, she is creating portraits of the mysteries. Ray will adore them, n'est-ce pas? These things she addresses are not easy to express. Most people never wonder about them. Look at that scoffing of a businessman! And see how she puts people in their easy nakedness, like we are veritable gods and goddesses. She paints another language here. This work is very brave, isn't it?"

For a long time Junkyard and Maly stand closely, talking softly as Thea strains to listen as she deals with her friend Fast's drunken wobblies. The couple spin around slowly, pointing at one work after the next, their heads joined whispering. Thea wonders if they might be tipsy, but they don't act like it. She rejoins them after dealing with the mess Fast made.

"Such haunting images, Thea," Junkyard Trinnie says, spiraling around to face Thea. "Me be moved. This work be *I-ree*."

"My brain, it feels massaged by your curious colors and forms," confesses a delighted Maly.

Both artists remain absorbed by the ferocious energy of Thea's work surrounding them, like rainfall bombarding powerful sustenance on a dried-up landscape.

Quietly, the pair ask Thea, with her drugged, boozy brain, a barrage of questions.

"How long have you been painting? Where have you shown? Where have you been? Not in New York? Tourist art!—how in heaven's name did you stay sane?"

Thea isn't so drunk she can't be delighted. The flowing conversation leaves Fast Forward and Big Sue out, both grateful to be left to their own preferences of smoking and drinking, off by themselves in the furthest corner of the studio.

Thea feels she's known both of these deliciously flavored people from somewhere before. But how could she possibly?

Right then and there, Thea falls in love with the tall black man and his caramel-colored wife. Maly's slight build is framed by the long winter coat she holds close to her in the heated studio. She reminds Thea of an amused child playing in a self-contained teepee, smiling like she and her man have just won the biggest prize two people could ever hope to win.

Thea has found two people whom she hopes can be friends as sweet as the surprisingly candid words they speak now.

"Me be knowing you already by what you be making, White Gurl," Junkyard says without a trace of self-consciousness, accompanied by a lightning strike of a grin. "Me like it, and me be liking you."

Maly beamed a glowing face of approval as her man says this.

Thea's heart jumps when he calls her *that name*—White Girl. Nobody she's met since leaving her jovial Cat Cay island friends has had a personality so forthright, so irreverently funny, yet dignified, as this man before her. There is no racism among islanders when they call each other white or black, girl, boy, man, woman, or any other name, as long as it's meant with love and respect. Junkyard Trinnie reeks of this same honesty and truthfulness, things too often mistaken for rude social blunders there in the Big Apple. Thea looks closer at this man who beams as easily as her other friends get wasted. Everything that comes from the imposing, majestic black wizard and his composite beauty of a spouse moves Thea, including that outright—typically childlike honest, island make-fun humor—un-racist name he's just dubbed her.

"And your art, it be *inside* strong," Junkyard says. "It be like waking up from a dream, trying to figure what be up with the billboards of the mind. Yes, White Gurl, the world dreams too. We be needing artists like you, for the world to be remembering its own dreams. Just like our own self when we canna remember what we be dreaming all the night before we m'sohn! Your job should be getting this stuff out into the big wide world. Forget that singing shit. No offense, Fast."

Junkyard tilts his head to Fast Forward who's whispering close with Big Sue near the door, ready to make their quick getaway from these newcomers who are getting chummy, from the looks of things, with their privately possessed girlfriend.

"This be a heart artist, not a rocker standing here!" Junkyard says, holding his long arms out like a circus barker.

Junkyard walks over to Fast, who's too bombed to be agitated.

"Fast, the work of your friend here be carrying messages from other places," Junkyard says, motioning all around. "These be maps for others, like you and I, and my lovely here," his eyes seek Maly, "to be finding things deep inside we. You know that connection me be speaking of?"

Thea stares, dumbstruck. Her shocked expression shouts, *Are you serious, man?* but she says nothing. Finally, she grimaces in embarrassment. She can't help it. She doubts this stranger could possibly know what her art is about when she herself doesn't. Thea suspects, for the briefest of moments, this Junkyard Trinnie dude and his consort are conning her. Thea's work, each one like a puzzle, a diagram outlining circuits, sensational subterfuge that convert desire into visual poetry—it's all there—and Junkyard Trinnie is the first person Thea has met who can explain it *to her*.

"Just trust me, Fern Eyes," Junkyard Trinnie says.

"Oui, ma chérie," Maly shrugs sweetly to Thea. "Mon homme, he always tells the truth."

* * *

Fast and Thea go back to the studio to sit amid the chaos of her creations after the couple depart on the elevator. Thea feels their light-hearted absence right away. Fast gets busy rolling another joint. Big Sue is in spirits-finding action.

As soon as she sees they're gone, Big Sue says, "There's something phony about them." Thea defends the newcomers with surprising simpatico. "They don't party much, leave them be, Big Sue. They have completely different lives than we do."

Thea peers out the window and sees, five flights below on the empty sidewalk, Junkyard Trinnie and Maly talking excitedly as they turn the corner, arm-in-arm, jauntily walking back home to Soho.

8

Thea spends as much time as she can with the intriguing pair after that first night. It only takes mentioning his name to other, better informed artists for Thea to discover just how well-known Junkyard Trinnie and his exquisite wife actually are.

No one asked that night, so Junkyard didn't disclose who he was. His new friend hadn't a clue that he's one of the most-collected and sought-after artists of the times, and his wife is an equally successful, multi-talented designer. Thea's friends tell her he keeps a low profile, that self-effacing Junkyard Trinnie who, a decade before, a famous critic crowned with the moniker—*King of the Outsiders*—when Junkyard was heralded as the darling of that new genre taking over sales from the *isms* clogged with conceptualism, photo-realism, and other tightly guarded art cliques. His very first solo exhibition at the Jules St. Pierre Gallery was a frantic sell-out before opening night. Art critics hadn't even known at first what to call Junkyard's—or was it Mr. Trinnie's?—work. Articles appeared about the innovative, free-form expressionistic work with inadequate descriptives that the international art world would debate for the next generation to come—*Art Brut ... Primitive ... Visionary ...* or *Outsider*—all reminiscent of the raw human passion the completely unprecedented, non-derivative style evoked. Unfettered by too much education, sophistication, analytical bunk, and immune to pretentious, emotionless styles—Junkyard Trinnie's work was best described by the artist himself, from an interview in an oft-quoted old *Art Quorum* article:

"It be *my* art, mohn. Why you be needing to call it other t'ings?"

He and Maly enthusiastically embraced their new punk rocker friend. They spoke about the process of making art on the phone with Thea once or twice a week, and got together in person often to visit each other's studios to discuss what they were working on. Thea would visit the couple's two different studios, one exclusively for Junkyard's work, the other for Maly's design business that incorporated the couple's comfortable homey space.

For long hours, Junkyard, Thea, and Maly would sit and drink nothing but coffee or tea, or split a single bottle of wine (that Thea controlled herself not to guzzle) as they ruminated upon how art in general, and theirs specifically, fit into the scheme of society's bigger, worldwide needs. Highlighting the scary reality of Earth's toxic environment and getting people to wake up and help heal it—affecting society in positive ways, in other words—played a big part in each of the trio's work.

Junkyard asks Thea to remain behind after everyone else has left one of his and Maly's frequent dinner parties. Thea has been included, the newest addition to the group of eight tight friends who routinely meet at each other's places for lively conversation and a delicious repast. Earlier, Junkyard had to stop himself from interrupting the free flow of the dinner party talk when Thea, whose work has not yet been shown publicly, let slip some self-deprecating remarks that Junkyard overheard her say to the other guests, each of whose work has had access to the public for years, some of them, decades of critically acclaimed exposure.

"Honeypot," he says to Thea as soon as the others depart, "me canna believe you be saying those t'ings, about your art not being up to the quality of them others who be here tonight."

"Oh, come on, Junkyard, it's true! Sure, I admit it would hurt my feelings if someone else said it though," Thea shoots right back. "But yours and all their work is well known, and that's being more successful than me. Why can't I say what's true? Don't you think I wonder sometimes why you and Maly even bother with me hanging around?"

"Well, that be just the sort of t'ing a White Gurl like yohself would say, now isn't it," he says, merrily as usual. "Miss feel-sorry-for-herself Honeypot."

Thea loves all the nicknames Junkyard gives her, Honeypot being the latest; never using her real name, ever.

"Success be not about any t'ing, Green Glow, but how true and real a person be to what they feel they be here for. You be truly successful if you just do that one t'ing. Just look-ee what you be doing with The Supply House, Miss Messy Hair. You enjoying being a stage-happy person, giving others the joy of music, right?"

Thea doesn't say anything. She has complex feelings about what success actually is. She dared not reveal to the dinner party that night just how anxious and insecure she feels, that her paintings are not being seen by the world. It's her awful secret, how unsuccessful she really feels, even though every hip alternative type loves The Supply House. It takes a calm deep river of a mind to appreciate something that's not been validated by society, as an unknown artist's work, especially of the myth-filled sort as Thea's is. That's why she's stuck to singing with Fast and the guys, defying Junkyard's imploring her to quit. She feels successful up on stage, looking out at dancing throbs loving the sounds of good punk rock.

Junkyard seemingly flies over and grabs Thea's shoulders and looks her right in the eyes. From across the room Maly notices the encounter but keeps busy and doesn't interfere. The snake-haired man says loudly to his spikey-coiffed friend, "Don't you never be saying put-down t'ings about you or your work again, you hear? Least wise not near I. Me won't put up with it! It be a lie, anyway. Success is just we making the shit we do. Who cares who be seeing or buying it. Not I. Not Maly. And neither should you, White Gurl."

Thea quickly learns how she and her higher-minded friends share a mutual love of intense, unabashed, gutsy creation. Maly's art is functional yet enthralling. She relates surprising forms to everyday purposes more than content. But art is only one of countless subjects the three discuss, often far into the night. And never with Max included.

"He doesn't relate very well. He's all about selling movies," Thea says when the pair asks about her absentee lover who's never to be found whenever an art gathering happens. "He travels a lot. It works great for both of us though, 'cause we like our time apart."

Thea has grown to not be intimidated that Junkyard Trinnie is the veritable darling of the Outsider scene. Maly's friendship feels equal, but truthfully, she is an adjunct to Thea's unbridled fondness for the more accessible Junkyard. Even though she adores Maly, and certainly respects her independence and well-articulated views, Junkyard's art, like himself, is the more dynamic and humorous of the duo. His work is infused with an energized love of life. Maly's is more subdued, serious, worldly. Her designs deal with modern life's daily functions, so Thea understands why she's more practical.

At her first visit, when Thea saw one of Junkyard's bursting multi-media works in his studio, she stood speechless. At six feet in height, the sculptural painting appears to stretch in all directions from its vertical hanging in the middle of the wall. A story is depicted, painted and embroidered with sculpted objects sticking out here and there on wood and foam panels. What Thea sees is a three-dimensional world of finely-arranged junk. Filled with unnamable energy, she's overwhelmed, as if she's traveling in an unmapped, unreal territory that's oddly familiar. Silently looking at this work whose title she'd asked, and was *Seeing Be Believing*—in which one central image, a favorite of Junkyard's many motifs, is a cluster of half-animal, half-human entwined figures, their athletic poses suggesting a ritual of undisclosed origin. She stands silently mind blown, looking at the work, as if seeing a rendition of the primordial wall paintings made from soot and clay, hidden deeply within ancient caves of southern France. Attached to Junkyard's piece with welds of metal and blobs of thick epoxy, using varied materials so unidentifiable they appear alien-made—are bizarrely shaped sculpted objects reminiscent of plant pods, seed clusters, trunks of bizarrely shaped trees, and flowers of nightmarish cacti formations. Thea is stunned and reverent at the same time. Junkyard's misshapen, endlessly textured renditions of natural objects have transported her.

Thea's mind unravels as she scrutinizes one after another of Junkyard's creations that rattles her sensibility. If she were able to speak she might say words that, to her, sounded foolish in her mouth: *This guy's art is like being masturbated by creation. Everything's connected.* So she feels it more than think-speaks it. She's as excited as she'd ever been about any art, by a living or dead master. She wants to jump right into Junkyard's uniquely ever-expanding world.

Tenderly she touches details of works, here and there, exploring peeks at textures, fabrication methods hidden within seams and interstices. A deep place within her awakens, erupts, and shouts to her. A place she's been striving to understand but had never before been given tools to discover. And could never express in words. She succeeds in creating this feeling with her art. Now, she sees this man from Trinidad speaks her language too. Staring at Junkyard's sculpture-painting is like learning his lilting accent of their shared language.

She's amazed at how similar her friend's lusty, scrumptiously inspiring work is to the hidden intent within her own works. The pieces that hit that sweet spot of *Yes*. Thea knows she's still discovering her own art-language. Junkyard's work has long since surrounded international critics like a prairie fire ever since his first show in New York.

Not long after this night when Thea's mind opened like a dark cave being blasted with light, Big Sue is screaming at Fast Forward, who's called Thea over to help him convince the crazed sea-going lady wrestler to stay put.

Duffy's regular closing time had long since passed. Thea, Fast, and Big Sue had been drinking and shuffle-dancing, taking turns snorting up Big Sue's stash of coke in the john. Then they floated back to Sue's loft, the stupefied trio who practically slept at Duffy's.

"I'll be all right, for cryin' out loud," Big Sue snarls when Thea joins the fracas she's having with Fast at her loft. "What a bunch of wimps you two are."

"Fast is right! You can't drive yourself up to Boston," Thea demands. "The roads are icy and you're blind drunk! You'll never make it, you jerk. Just stay till tomorrow. Fast and I can't drive you tonight. Can't you put the trip off till tomorrow?"

The three had been partying pretty heavily the entire weekend. Now the time has come for Big Sue to take off for a job she really needs, even if it means Dr. Bob has to stay behind. Whenever Big Sue wants to party, it's always a marathon. Thea once knew how to quit before things got out of control, and now controlling herself only when around Maly and Junkyard Trinnie, and of course, Max—but the word *restraint* falls out of her vocabulary whenever she's with Fast and Sue.

"M'lasses, if I put it off I might not get the gig. I'm gonna be on that freighter when it takes off tomorrow afternoon from Bean Town. If it's not me navigatin' for 'em it's gonna be someone else, so I'm going. Let me outta here."

That late October night was a raw one. Big Sue insisted she'd be okay driving straight through to Boston to catch the *Evinrude Jones*, a freighter bound for Belgium the next morning, completing the second leg of a shipment of perishable kiwis from Australia.

"Take care of Dr. Bob for me, okay, M'lasses? He's got something wrong with his skin. I think he's allergic to that new plant I got him, a diefen-wookia or something."

"Sue, Dieffenbachia is dumb cane, you big ass! You're letting your dog do that weird rub-up thing with *that* plant?" Thea made a face at her friend, as if she were a class act abusive parent.

"What the fuck you talking about, dumb cane? The lady who sold me the shittin' plant called it die-fen—whatever."

"Big Sue, I know that plant. Island women give it to their men to stop them from wandering too far from their bed. It makes them impotent. Swells their tongues so they can't speak either. That's why they call it dumb cane."

"You think it might'a done something to old Dr. Bob?" Fast slurs.

"Could. If it does that to humans, why shouldn't it do something to a poor dog who's all over it like a Thai masseuse, for cryin' out loud," Thea says.

"M'lasses, I'm telling you, you're a natural born mother dog. Take good care of my main man for me. I'll be flying back from Europe in about two weeks."

Big Sue leaves on this dangerously icy night, not any drunker than Thea had seen her any other night when she's taken off, rushing to some other crazy gig sailing across the great oceans of the world.

※ ※ ※

Thea answers the phone at Big Sue's where she's gone to feed Dr. Bob, since Max can't abide pets in his place. An old man's worn-out voice says he's calling his daughter's loft, he doesn't really know why. "Maybe someone there knows why. I can't make no sense of it." The man pauses. "She got herself killed in a wreck."

"Oh my God, no." Thea sinks to the floor.

"Massachusetts State Police called. Happened two nights ago."

"How?"

"Susan's car spun out and crashed head-on on the slick highway 95, halfway up to Boston. The police said she'd passed out at the wheel. Her alcohol level was way beyond what it should'da been." The man's voice sounds old and remote, as if he's reading instead of speaking. "The sad thing about it," Big Sue's father says in a barely audible tone, "is Susan took another life with her when she rammed that tractor trailer. The man was delivering pork parts to a processing factory in Newark."

Thea's pounding heart jumps outside of her sweater. The harsh irony suffocates her. Crashing into a sausage truck? Big Sue, a lifelong vegetarian. She'd only eat insentient life, and choose good imported beers and spirits with no formaldehyde, the highest quality tequila fresh from organic mescal growers who used manure fertilizer. Big Sue wouldn't do it if she couldn't eat natural.

The trio of tyranny was over. Fast Forward and Thea would mourn Big Sue best they could.

Thea felt bad she had no other words of comfort to say to Sue's father, other than, "She was my best friend in the whole world. I'll miss her."

Then she hung up.

Sue's death and energy-transference into Thea

9

Something goes seriously amuck inside Thea.

Nearly a year passes in mind-wrenching grief and sorrow after losing Big Sue, even though Thea keeps performing with The Supply House, who thankfully are booked solid around Manhattan. Other times she hides in her studio making art nobody ever sees. The only connection Thea has to real companionship, Max not fitting that description, is through Dr. Bob, whom she inherits and insists on living with her after Fast and she pack up Sue's belongings. Max's restrictions are, for once, disavowed. Everything now is a thick fog that she drugs or drinks herself through. Performing becomes just a job, no longer a joy. Friends she sees occasionally, just to pass the time. A hollow numbness takes over where a heart that once loved now feels broken and cold. With or without Fast Forward, Thea pays many a visit to her old friends, Jose Cuervo, Mary Jane, and the White Lady. Wandering the lonely Tribeca loft when she can't find any reason to enter her studio, she stays in her pajamas for weeks straight, cleaning up her act only when Max returns from Los Angeles and complains about dog hair. She struggles to make a rare visit to Junkyard and Maly in Soho. Gone are the group dinners with other artists. And she won't let her friends visit her, nope.

On her last visit to join them for a meal, Thea mentions to Maly how boring her life has become *without Big Sue*. Thea can't drink excessively, or even get a little high around Maly or Junkyard Trinnie. That's why Thea seldom visits them anymore. On this visit however, Maly notices Thea's hands shaking. Sees how she pounds her glass down on the table after every tiny sip, trying to pretend she's okay.

"I want to help," Maly says before Thea leaves. "Here, try this." She hands Thea a card with only a name and phone number on it.

Soon afterwards, Thea walks into a spacious apartment overlooking Central Park that is crammed like an amateur hoarder's. Mammoth clusters of crystals are featured on tall, spot-lit podiums nearly as grandiose as the room-sized, crystal side altar she's seen when visiting Saint John the Divine. A heavily made-up person named Valala greets her at the door with an aloof smile and a gelatin handshake whose touch makes Thea wince.

The woman is small and wears an unbecoming, voluminous beige-patterned affair of folds that hide a bulbous shape beneath. A tiger's eye pendant dangles from a chain around her neck. Bottle-black hair is fanned on her sloping shoulders. Incongruous bangs dramatize heavily-lined eyes that have deep cutting wrinkles incised on all sides, drawing even more attention to her beyond middle age.

"Valala, she is like nobody you will ever meet," Maly had promised Thea. "She help me. She be able to maybe do similar for you. You need help to get over your friend's horrible end. Valala is healer, Thea. I send lots of friends to see her. She get depress out of you heart. Possibly, she make your life right again, ma chérie."

Phoning Valala one day after taking a good stiff belt and a few puffs of weed—for extra courage and self-confidence—Thea took up Maly's suggestion even though she'd never asked anyone for help, ever. Thea's dealing with the psychic side of life is a solitary one, seated in her haunted soul. Maly knows her friend's grief is too Sisyphean for a tortured soul like Thea to bear much longer, without some mishap happening to her too. So here she is. Thea walking into a place leftover from the parlor days of the occult to meet this person who, at first glance, looks like a ripe prickly fruit rather than a person someone could garner peace from.

"Hi, I'm ...."

"I know. You're Thea." The woman, without a trace of warmth, makes Thea feel as welcome as an inchworm.

"I was sent here by Maly," Thea says.

"I know," the woman slithers words between lipstick-stained teeth.

Thea bristles. She stays only because she really cares for Maly; but at that moment she wants to bolt for the door.

"My friend said you might help me find some answers," Thea says.

"I know. Maly told me all about your friend Susan who died."

A barbed wire again sears and pinches Thea's heart at the mention of Big Sue's fake name. The slap shuts her up. Thea's private hurt isn't any stranger's business.

Thea wonders, What am I doing here? Why did Maly insist I see this uptight burlesque know-it-all? Thea doubts this hag possesses any powers other than viciousness, from the I-know litany she hisses.

"She is good for you," Maly had told Thea, urging her to call Valala. "You are sad too long now. Big Sue is too long dead. You have to get on with life. Trust me, Valala did cure for me."

"She told me about you too," Thea mutters.

The uptown dowager with heavily rouged and Dough-Boy powdery cheeks led Thea through her grandiose living room. Haphazardly strewn about, Thea sees several impressive Persian rugs, a pair of matching Shaker chairs, a life-size statue of Isis, and can identify Incan pottery on a corner's clear acrylic shelves. In the center of the biggest wall in the room is a heart-stopping painting—the most imposing object of all. The image stops Thea in her tracks.

From floor to ceiling is a startling image of a bigger-than-life-sized figure of a black, red, and gilded dancing goddess of some indiscriminate origin Thea doesn't recognize. A sooty-feeling, baggy-boobed wild incarnation of some weird Eastern icon, Thea thinks, with endlessly radiating multiple arms projecting from oily jet skin, wearing around her neck an ornament that rocks Thea's core when she steps closer to look. It's like beads, but not. Upon closer inspection, the beads are made of severed blood-dripping human skulls, hanging by their long black hair, strung around the immense creature's neck. When Thea sees the horror on the faces of the eyes-open heads dangling from the *thing's* necklace, she jumps back as if struck by a sofa-length cobra. Her heart skips a beat, freaking at the sight—an appalling blood-red screaming, open-mouthed, many arms akimbo, with demons dripping blood all over her ample breasts—staring directly into Thea's eyes.

* * *

Thea pretends to be cool as she follows Valala, who keeps walking, noticing nothing of her guest's high-pitched discomfort. Thea had to halt when she found herself smack in front of the terrifying demoness, whose painted eyes—all three of them—stare at her as she tries to move across the room. Reflections of the glass-covered silk painting multiply, dancing on every shiny surface of the room, bouncing from cut glass prisms of a baroque chandelier that dangles in the middle of the crowded room. Fierceness shoots into every dark corner with every slight turn of a facet. Frozen, Thea stares at the fearsome creature's tangerine-colored eyes. Its elongated red tongue stretches toward her like a snake charmer, waving *right at her.*

Thea shakily points to the bizarre image. "Wh-what is that?"

"*That* is Kali Durga," Valala says, not stopping her glide across the room.

"Who? Hallie Dorka?"

"Kali Durga!" Valala turns at a doorway and glares at Thea, her gaze sharp as a sword.

"It's pretty scary," Thea weakly says.

Valala's answer echoes before it's spoken: "I know."

"Intriguing," Thea mumbles barely audibly; but to herself—*not like you.*

From across the occult-reeking room, a spark erupts from the older woman's wrinkle-lined eyes as she looks up at the imposing image with what could be reverence. She addresses the visibly shaken Thea without looking at her.

"Do you know who Kali Durga is, my dear?"

"Never heard the name. And I find that odd, that I wouldn't, seeing as I pride myself on knowing my eastern art, which this obviously is," Thea says, pointing to the wall.

Valala raises an eyebrow at Thea, then turns her gaze back to the huge, intricately executed, clearly ancient painting.

"Obviously you're not well versed at all in the ways of the divine female, the goddess. Am I correct?"

"That? Kelly Bergen is a goddess? Isn't she a little ugly for such a high rank?"

Valala ignores both the mispronouncing and the putdown. Thea wonders how something so monstrous-looking can be called a goddess. Mind-boggling, to her, that something so scary can be called sacred by some.

"Kali Durga is the most powerful symbol of rebirth and renewal humans ever invented for themselves."

"Oh, I see," Thea says.

"But I don't think you do, my dear."

"Well, Valala, that's why I'm here, I guess, to learn more about myself." Thea is growing increasingly annoyed by this self-centered spiritual snob.

"Yes, of course. Well, as long as you ask, allow me to introduce you to the Great Mother of all, Kali Durga."

With that Valala extends her right arm toward the coal-skinned *thing* with naked breasts, whose dozen or more arms flail about her frightening head in a spiraling, frenetic crown of flames. Each of the hands hold various things, although Thea can't make out what most of them are.

"She's the Great Mother of the Universe," Valala says, her eyes closed for reasons beyond Thea's comprehension, "because without her power to destroy negativity, nothing positive can be created or continue existing. We'd all be consumed by evil."

"Wow, that's heavy."

"Yes, heavy," Valala's eyes fly open and Thea balks. "Even more so is the fact that she gave birth to herself."

"Pssstch." Skeptical air inadvertently blows through Thea's smacking lips, island-style, a habit she picked up in Cat Cay. "How'd she do that, exactly?"

"It's myth, my dear. In stories anything can happen, right?"

"Sure. So how'd she give birth to herself?"

"People need conduits to the invisible, higher planes of being. That's why humankind has made up stories of gods and goddesses and given them roles as saviors and protectors, long before starting to record our race's determination to relieve the exigent miseries of existence. Religion and myth are the result of those stories, my dear. Kali Durga's origin is documented in the earliest of East Indian art. Like this magnificent piece from Kashmir. Legend says she gave birth to herself. You see, ancient people prayed to the most beautiful of all goddesses, Durga, the absolute, most benevolent of the Devi, the shining ones empowered to create. A time came, unfortunately, when Durga no longer could protect humanity. She simply wasn't powerful enough to fight off the swarms of demons that threatened the very existence of humanity. So Durga, knowing she needed a fiercer ally in helping humankind, willed to bring forth a completely separate, altogether different form of herself to kill the overriding army of demons. So Kali came to be, birthed fully grown, ready to fight, right out from Durga's third eye—"

"Excuse me?"

"... out through Durga's third eye—*the bellybutton of the Universe*. From out of her blue-glowing bindi, Durga commanded a fiercer, more powerful part of herself to emerge, to slay the darkness, to destroy the evil that plagued humanity. Of course, there is no greater evil than that which lurks in the hearts of humans themselves. The demons' dead skulls you see strung around Kali's neck, as trophies, represent humanity's fears, ignorance, and challenges like bigotry of any sort, all of which are Earth's actual enemies as well. The unmatchable, demon-slaying aspect of Durga, my dear, is known as Kali—the destroying aspect of the creative goddess power. Therefore, they are one and the same: destruction and creation."

"She's quite horrible looking," Thea says.

"Yes, I know. Kali Durga is a terrible sight, awful to behold, unspeakably aggressive. Just look at her! She alone is powerful enough among the gods and goddesses to slay *all* evil demons *any*where *any*time in *any* manner she sees fit. Such is the way of the focused and ferocious. She is the destroyer of evil so her other part, Durga can do her work of creating new and good. That's why she is called the Great Mother, she whom you see before you. She is my shield. Now, she is yours also, my dear. She is the protector of all. Without her, negativity will overrun humanity—as it has in the past, as it will in future times, as well—if Kali is not called forth to slay the evil demons, and keep life balanced. She protects all of us."

Feeling squeamish, Thea can barely squeak, "I'm sorry but I'm not into this black magic stuff."

Valala heaves a sigh. Her caked black eyelashes flutter irritably.

"My dear, you must learn to open your mind. Humanity's desires are the impetus behind every myth, every legend you'll ever hear. The story of Kali Durga and all the other Great Beings give hope and inspiration to us humans. Gods, goddesses, angels, mythology—they're all fairytales. We need them though, as channels that we use to give tangible shape to our inner desires. Without them, life is so less hopeful, less flavorful, and … meaningless. Kali protects us from our known and unknown fears. She destroys the darkness so the Light can shine strongly. Do you understand?"

"I don't know. I think so."

"You think so?"

"Yes, I do." Thea straightens her posture, listening. She isn't to be outdone by some psychic know-it-all. "Sure I do. Kali is a Hindu icon, which I find pretty incredible that I haven't heard of her before, seeing as I am an artist who works with symbols. I'm always looking for universal archetypes and ancient symbols for my work. I've studied how art's origins were the earliest means of communicating spiritual beliefs. Starting with bison on cave walls and carved fertility fetishes for crops and tribes to prosper. Okay, so I missed Kali Durga. Which is really strange, believe me, because myth, as answers to the human need to understand existence itself, has been my fascination. Maybe, an obsession. I'm not as ignorant as you make me out to be."

"Are you being facetious, my dear?"

"Hell, no, Valala. I'm into Kali, here. If she does it for you, I'm glad. Me, I'm into everyone doing their own thing. Kali's good with me. Howdy do, Miss Durga Kali."

Valala's painted eyes narrow to hard slits.

Thea walks closer to the vibrant eight-foot tall painting. She looks more closely at the awkwardly dancing figure that conjures up magic, arcane mystery schools, and alchemy. A wind suddenly shivers through Thea's body. *That's powerful all right*, she admits. Thea quickly follows the hastily departing Valala from the crammed room with its tomb-like redolence that reminds her of a simmering brew in a witch's cauldron.

"That ... thing?" Thea says as she catches up with her clearly offended host, "Maly only told me you were a therapeutic healer. I didn't come here to get involved with anything occult. Are you planning on—"

"You'll see," Valala continues into the next room.

This lady is beyond weird, thinks Thea. The atmosphere in the claustrophobic apartment is stifling. She looks and sees the new windows have been hermetically sealed in the classic old building. Thea tries to relax, reminding herself she's there to get help, not to get freaked out.

Valala whisks into a carpeted, mauve office lined with overflowing shelves. Thea is overdosed. She can't look anymore; the visuals are too much. Everywhere her tired eyes linger are portentous books and strange objects.

Ever since arriving at Valala's she has felt crushed by carvings of dragons, chimera and centaurs, spooky owls with wings spread wide peering down between volumes of Blavatsky and Crowley. Obsidian felines prowling along shelves as sleek bookends. Thea fleetingly reads a few book bindings: Ospensky, Gurdjieff, the Vedas, Cayce. How many treatises on esoteric knowledge can a person absorb? she ponders. Valala motions Thea to sit in a chair.

As if in deep communion with her reluctant guest, the woman seats herself like a priestess at an altar, behind a battered old mahogany desk. In front of her is a blotter rimmed with a pattern of colored stones that glimmer alongside her pearl-polished fingertips.

"You see, Kali is the Great Catalyst," Valala says, closing her eyes.

Thea wants to puke or bolt but stays and tries to keep an open mind, for Maly's sake.

"She signifies how nothing—absolutely nothing—can be created until the negative forces that block positive growth are destroyed."

Valala opens her deep-set eyes, lined with black kohl on top and bottom, making her appear as unmoved, as remote as one of her statues. The canned bewitchment creeps Thea out. Whenever Thea catches a glimpse of anything remotely paranormal, it strangely repulses her. Because as a teen she'd plunged into the Ouija board, and that was spooky enough for a lifetime of aversion to mediums, clairvoyants, and prophets. Thea feels stifled, uneasy about this strange woman she suspects is exerting her will over her. She squirms in her seat.

And weakly tries to smile. To break the tension in the air.

Thea says, "That makes sense. Something old goes, something new comes along. Yeah, did you know—"

"*Yes*! I know."

Silencing Thea with an arthritic index finger held aloft, for an instant Valala looks like a hawk. Thea shrinks with revulsion. Judgment is permanently stamped on this quasi-sorceress's furrowed brow. Thea wonders if some mind-controlling ritual is being performed on her, without her knowing.

With a demure soft tone Valala asks, "So, my dear, Maly tells me you have a problem."

Thea stares out the narrow window at vaporous clouds drifting outside. Resisting the urge to run, instead, uncontrollable words start to tumble from her mouth.

"I've been confused, and …" Thea looks down at her short, paint-stained fingernails, adding in a barely audible voice, "… and scared a lot."

"About what?"

Thea shrugs her shoulders.

"Life, I guess. I'm sad all the time, ever since I lost my best friend last year. Car crash."

Valala leans back in her seat and takes a long look at Thea.

"Hmm, I see. Tell me, Thea, do you do drugs or drink a bit?"

Thea's insides scream. The nerve of this uptown bitch! But softly she lies, "Not much."

"But some?"

"Yeah sure, some. Doesn't everyone?"

"Well, Thea, I see a troubled, chemically altered energy field all about you, although I recognize the emotional imbalance as just a symptom. I'm afraid you won't like this, but I see these injurious substances are hiding who you really are."

Thea's mental gloves go up. She's ready to kick some psychic butt. She squirms in her seat and looks yearningly at the door. The old lady doesn't give Thea time to act.

"Would you say that might be possible, my dear?"

Thea has to fight to defend her integrity.

"Look, Valala, who's the one paying for answers here? I don't think that's any of your business. I came to get help, not to be interrogated." Thea jumps out of her seat and makes for the door.

"I know, but my dear, don't be so defensive. Won't you sit down and try—just try—to listen for a moment? Please?"

Thea isn't going to let any elderly uptown vampire give her additional kicks on her already pulverized rear end. No way. She doesn't know why, but she sinks back into the chair's soft cushion and listens to Valala's lusterless voice.

"This is what I see. You want to get better, that's why you've come. I see pain in your body, pain in the features of your face. Your aura is in dis-ease—it's graying. That's right, that's what I see, my dear. I see *giving-up* in your eyes. Your destiny awaits you, but instead, only emptiness fills your soul. It's rather frightening, you know."

"No, I *don't know*," Thea says.

Then something rips open inside Thea. Her stunned defenses melt like sticks of sun-warmed wax. She can't say a word but sits deeply in the chair, trying to hide from this charlatan who has pissed her off more than anyone, ever. Thea is horrified this person might know something about her she herself doesn't. Desperately, she wants to leave, but she can't. She's nailed to her chair, stunned by a surprise attack of the weepies stabbing her eyes. Thea begins to cry.

Valala sits deeply in the upholstered chair with her hands resting atop the side supports, twin brass heads of the Egyptian hawk god, Horus. Thea doesn't notice, however, because misery clogs her mind like autumn gutters. As Thea weeps, Valala quietly fingers something sparkly in her right hand, turning it over and over.

Closing her iridescent, purple-powdered eyelids, Valala begins to speak in a melodic voice, in an entirely different tone from before. A feeling of relief sweeps over Thea that someone else is there now, instead of the bitch, Valala.

"You are at the end of the destructive cycle, my dear, so do not fear. All the pain, all life's disappointments will begin to show themselves to you as your salvation, not your enemy. Each event and every person in your life has a reason *to be*, in order to bring you to the higher place that's been awaiting you. The time of truth is very close."

Valala's eyes never open as her words slowly salve Thea's torn place deep inside. In her right hand Valala plays with what Thea can see is a thumb-sized, shiny clear crystal. The woman's eyes finally open, yet they look as if they aren't focused on anything. Distantly, they gaze. Thea stops feeling sorry for herself and fixes her attention on the beige tent of a person before her, who somehow has managed to acquire great strength over Thea's mind in the past few minutes.

Slowly, Valala brings her right hand up to her forehead and places the clear crystal she holds in her hand directly between her finely penciled brows. She stares at Thea with a look as eerie as the mysterious glow emanating from the sparkling stone. Within Valala's open eyes, Thea no longer sees anything to fear, so she listens with a hushed mind as the woman speaks.

"Someday soon your pain will be equally rewarded by your joy. Have faith. Until you trust in your own power and embrace who you really are, you are only postponing your destiny. Stop that half-drawn curtain between you and what is yours. Stop altering your mind with substances. Be brave and trust the power of the natural mind. There is no other way for you, Thea. You have been chosen. You think you're erasing pain, but all you do is sustain it, burying it deeper until it'll explode. Choose to free your pain. Just let it go."

Once more Valala closes her eyes and gathers her small claws back into her lap. She appears to be coming back to the room. Thea notices her blink several times. Valala speaks again, this time in her original scratchy, vain voice, her irritating Bronx accent almost ruining Thea's strangely soothed mind.

"You fear who you really are, my dear. You're afraid you might really be something other than the cursed, doomed creature you've come to believe you are. I see it. I also see why."

A change comes over the old crone. She begins to breathe as if readying herself for going underwater, taking in deep, regular gulps of air, her eyes tightly pinched in concentration. Her body starts to undulate as if a hidden current is traveling up her spine.

"Your job now is to destroy the lies, the fear you nurture within. Then your true self will burst forth. Kali will help you. Kali will destroy all the torments of your soul. She'll show you. Kali Durga is your hope. She's the Mother of us all."

Valala's eyes open. She looks directly at Thea, who sits bolt stiff, sensing something very odd coming from this woman, some kind of electrical transmission. Thea touches her cheeks and is surprised to find them wet with tear tracks.

"Don't you see, Thea? Kali Durga will do it for you. All you have to do is reach out to her. Offer her your hand, and she'll never let you fall. Trust the Mother's help."

Valala stands and walks around her cluttered desk. She comes to Thea's chair. Taking Thea's shivering hands into her own, she presses the hot crystal tightly between them and closes her hands over them. Valala's dull gray eyes look deeply into Thea's emerald ones that shine with awe now, instead of before, when they were clouded in defiance. Gone for the moment is the acute denial that blinded Thea. Valala continues to squeeze Thea's hands together. The warm stone held between their four hands generates more heat. Thea begins to wiggle in apprehension; Valala nods her head.

"That's right, feel the power of her vibration. I'm giving you this Kali rock, my dear, as a reminder that you are the Great Mother's child, as everyone is."

The old crone loosens her hands and waddles back to her seat. Thea opens her fist and examines the hot crystal, feels it now cooling, lying in her palm as if a phoenix has just flown right through the sealed window to place this clear, cosmic egg in her hand. Thea's brow wrinkles as wonderment fills her.

Valala says, "And when you're ready, Thea, when you're willing to meet Kali halfway by not using any more crutches—no more intoxicants—I'll be willing to see you again. For now, this is all I can do for you."

10

Seasons floated by after Valala pressed the Kali rock into Thea's hands. She told herself the Kali rock meant nothing—nothing!—to her. Thea didn't even know where she'd put the damn thing. She continued to get bombed, not as if she really wanted to die, because Big Sue had shown her, in spades, that *that* was a definite possibility. Thea just wasn't willing to change much of anything but her hair color.

Summer and fall came and went with Max out of town a lot, as usual. Fast Forward was planning to come early one night to pick Thea up for a downtown party-hopping spree. Thea looked in the mirror to spike and spray her cobalt blue, red, and violet-streaked, asymmetrically cut short hair. When she bothered to look she could no longer recognize herself as the same healthy, tan girl who'd once lived a carefree life on pristine beaches of the Bahamas; or the hanger-on at the docks in Sausalito either.

"Big Sue would congratulate me for achieving such a high level of wasting my life away," Thea mumbles as she dresses. On that wintry night she's squeezing her puny ass into black toreador pants. She sees a reflection in the mirror she's come to loathe.

A strained face stares back at her, framed with sizzling fried hair, overprocessed from constantly changing its chroma and unflattering styles. For unknown reasons, Thea has been compelled to get three tattoos since Big Sue's demise. Imprinted on her right calf is a small, dragon-headed, three-inch wide, coiled snake eating itself, a stylized Ouroboros; because that mysterious tat was the only one Big Sue ever had or wanted. Surrounding her upper left arm is inked an ancient Viking crest, her proclamation of solidarity with

Nordic seafarers who are cousins of hers via her soul sister, Big Sue. Vikings captivated Thea ever since discovering they ate *amanita muscaria* mushrooms, the elixir that seekers called *soma*, offering a state of transcendence to all who ingest it. The Vikings used the mushroom's powers of altering their mental state to go *berserk* (the Norwegian word for *fierce warrior*) to bolster their savage rampaging with a convenient insomnia-like ferocity. The final tattoo Thea got was the most conspicuous. The tiniest indigo dot, just a pinprick worth of ink she got some head-to-toe tattooed Village brand of a Hell's Angels devil to pierce right between her eyebrows, before she passed out one night doing some rampaging of her own with Fast Forward.

Waiting for Fast to show up tonight, Thea's wasted image pounds back at her in the bathroom mirror. She stands gazing at the grisly apparition of herself, and takes another gulp of Valpolicella. The tat-dot between her eyes is barely noticeable, except when she gets really messed up. Then it starts to throb and turns a deeper shade of indigo.

The wine deepens the buzz she's been nursing since Max left two days before. Her mid-eye tattoo has pulsated continuously since Max departed, but Thea pays it no mind. When her so-straight boyfriend is out of town she can party all she wants.

It's supposed to be just another night on the town. Earlier, Thea kicked the evening off sipping wine, smoking killer weed, and doing lines of coke every ten minutes, until Fast finally shows up with a stash he's scored for their night of revelry. When Max isn't around, Thea smokes pot more than her strong Gauloises cigarettes. She does more of everything when he's away on a promotional trek. Max's main vice is too much work.

"How's it goin' CC?" Fast Forward says, late as usual, his voice thinly drifting from the intercom, where he's buzzing at the shiny, heavily secure front door on the Reade Street co-op.

As soon as Fast enters Max's loft from the elevator, his grin large, his shaved head shining, Thea steps into the abysmally deep well of a blackout. For the rest of the night she sees through Venetian-blind unconsciousness, glimpsing only particles of reality while her stupor-ed brain's synapses travel elsewhere, on split rail-tracks.

Thea had been looking forward to getting totally *out there*. Max is gone for five more days. Count 'em. *Five more days of fucking freedom*, she rejoices to herself.

I'll have plenty of time to get myself together before Max gets back next week, she promises herself, feeling the rocket-thrust blastoff of slipping in and out of her intended blackout state.

She likes having Fast around. Like a mole hiding from the sun, he never shows when Max is in town. On this particularly bitter cold February night, Fast takes one look at disheveled Thea and knows he has a lot of catching up to do.

As soon as he arrives with reinforcements, Fast Forward lays out lines the width of his keyboard-strumming fingers as he chugs wine and rolls a big doobie from the ornate silver tray Thea keeps her weed on, displayed like candy, but hidden from Max's sight when he's home.

"He's so daft, that guy," Thea snickers, and Fast joins in.

It's an endless charade Thea and Fast Forward have had since Sue deserted their party of three. Somberly claiming they really want to stop, then right away getting loaded, then convincing each other how they need to keep getting high for creativity's sake, or, as Fast put it, "… to explore my inner femininity. I'm too tense if I'm straight."

"If I'm not blitzed yet," Thea chimes, poking Fast in the ribs, "I'm not going to any party, period. Everything is too damn dull when I'm straight." She rolls another fat joint for the road and sits back, grinning like a sad fat cat.

Fast reminds her of the many fabulous places they have to be seen at around town tonight. This is a rare weekend when The Supply House isn't booked to play anywhere. The band members are enjoying the break. "We're plain civilians," the two in the room boom, ready to chug, suck, and snort the night away.

"We got to catch that carnival troupe from Rio up at The Boit. And at the Men's Room in the Bowery, Meat is Murder is playing, that's supposed to have a chorus line of belly dancers for extras. And don't forget Junkyard Trinnie and Maly's party."

The night is sure to be spectacular. So many places for art world revelers to show themselves. The best is sure to be Junkyard and Maly's, where anything goes and positively the only time, party time, that Thea lets her guard down around them. After all, they are the envy of every creative aspiring to make it in the Apple. Thea figures no one will notice her among the expected mob that always attends all their spectacles. Everyone important will be there. A fete at the Outsider King's is the hottest, hippest downtown ticket for an art extravaganza.

"The party's for Maly's latest line of furniture she's exhibiting at Modern Life," Fast Forward says as they weave down Reade to grab a cab at Chambers Street to the first stop of the night.

"Just another excuse to get out of it," Thea mumbles.

Then she slips into her black hole again. For the rest of the night Thea is in and out of walking-unconsciousness, unaware of everything. The next day she'll vaguely remember the clubs, the people, the noise. At Junkyard and Maly's party, she'll dimly recall Fast Forward finding another playmate, Gianni, an exuberant street juggler from Rome. At last, Thea stumbles amid a throbbing crowd crammed in her friends' studio loft, oblivious of black-clad gyrators, a few hobnobbing collectors, an impressionable critic who could make or break any artist's career merely on their mood at press time.

In and out of barely being there, Thea swayed with the unknown masses in a shattered mind. The throbbing music told her where and when to step here, there, swallow, snort, don't eat—don't stop being cool whatever you do, shut up! don't think—and don't stop getting fucked-up, ever.

"How you gonna get her home like this?" Gianni asks Fast. Thea is sure the guy is speaking Russian.

Thea is half-carried by Fast as they leave Junkyard and Maly's where all the Beautiful People are dancing up a storm to a DJ from Harlem. Outside on the barren street corner Fast props her standing up against a light pole and hails a cab. Hysterically, Thea attempts to throw moons at passing cars, screeching insanely, but her clothes are way too tight for her wobbly attempts at exposing herself.

The cab pulls up Hudson and onto Reade. By the time they stop in front of Max's building, Fast has found the door key in the pocket of slumped-over Thea, who's babbling some Martian dialect. Makeup dribbles down her torn-up face like bad cake icing. Her eyes are slices of opaque deadness.

"Going where no one dares to go …" Fast mimics as he swings himself and Thea's boneless heap out of the cab. Gianni follows.

The driver never turns around as Fast lifts Thea's grunting weight onto his shoulders. Not much taller or heavier than she, Fast is used to carrying her like this whenever Max is away—sometimes twice, sometimes four, five times a month to get her home safely.

He opens the heavy front door with Thea's key. Maybe it's the panicky swoosh of the door, maybe it's the pressure on her shoulders from Fast pinning her against a wall while he fumbles with the door lock—but suddenly—Thea swings a walloping punch, screaming an eye-opening Geronimo war cry that could crack glass.

But Fast stops Thea's fierce swing and murmurs "Sorry, CC," and does what he has to do to control Thea's serial swings. He aims to hit her square in the jaw with all his strength, hoping to knock the crazy bitch out. But he misses and gets her left eye instead.

The blow only slows Thea for an instant. Her lurid face revs and steam comes from enraged bull nostrils as she lunges at him again, trying to kick Fast with dangerously spiked heels. Gianni rushes and tries to help, but he's even slighter than Fast. Holding her back with his left hand, Fast punches Thea again with his right, harder this time. He feels something go *crunch* under his knuckles. Thea looks stunned for a split second, then goes completely limp.

Fast catches her before she spirals to the cement step outside the door. Blood pours from her nose. Fast spits out, "You crazy loon," wincing as he says it 'cause he loves Thea like he'd love a sister if he had one anymore. She's moaning loudly now. He picks her up, hoists her onto his scrawny shoulders, and brings Thea into the muted, sconce-lit lobby.

No one else is on the Tribeca street at five a.m. in the morning, but Fast wants to get Thea into her soundproof luxury pad as quickly as possible. Any moment he expects cries of medusa madness, hysterical harpies slicing through daiquiri fog, screaming search warrants for the most-wanted gargoyle. At the loft's door Dr. Bob suspiciously sniffs, smelling blood. He greets the strangely moaning stillness of his adopted companion with more sneezing, prancing, and whimpers than usual, happy to hear her mumble unintelligible words. Fast unbuttons the tight jacket Thea's wearing. As he lays her now-limp form out on the couch, he checks her pulse. From behind her haze, she grabs his wrist and tries to get up. "Forget it, CC, you're finished," Fast says. A little blood oozes from her cut lip. Fast notices the eruption blossoming on her left eye. He looks at Gianni and shakes his head, motioning for the exit, knowing he really should get Thea some ice from the kitchen.

"You're on your own, CC," Fast Forward whispers as he closes the loft's door, eager to take Gianni to his favorite after-hours club.

"Bitch," Thea slurs before totally passing out.

Fast Forward blasts Thea

11

For two days Thea can't sleep. She's frozen in a frightening stiff state of fear. Anticipating something, but what? Something dreadful. Horror-stricken on Max's couch, she's incapable of moving. Dr. Bob looks at his incapacitated friend, shaking coon-dog dreams from his sleep-warmed ears.

Thea thinks longingly of death. "My friend, nothingness," she calls out, "take me!" How easily she can make that happen. Only something keeps her from doing it. Somewhere off in the distance of her checkerboard mind, she thinks she sees something sparkling white. Gradually it comes into focus. Waving above her. She begins to make out white speckles, like a flag flapping in the make-believe wind, high above the battleground of her loser life. Seeing that flag in her wobbly airspace gives Thea hope that she doesn't yet know she has. All she knows is: she recognizes that white flag, and thus some part of her is surrendering.

In curlicue fashion, Dr. Bob sits with his seal-sleek body tightly coiled in an armchair facing Thea, who's immobile on the sofa. He raises his eyebrow whiskers every now and then to witness her interminable pain. Thea speaks to herself in whispers, familiar sounds to which he lifts and cocks his head attentively. His lamenting matches hers in the two days she stays as if glued to the couch; Dr. Bob's deep sighs echo in her forlorn groans. Every now and then he gets up and wanders over to his much-needed ficus tree, a live one ever since living at Max's.

Dr. Bob has given up on her remembering basics—his food, water, or walks. Thea watches with unseeing eyes as Dr. Bob trances out, imagining her friend's inner vision changing as he resembles a jungle *brujo's* incantations of supernatural communion. Appearing to walk as if on tiptoe—a feat quite remarkable for padded paws—he glides under the soft branches, allowing the tips of the green leaves to caress his fur with a feathery wisp, as the shamanic dog shivers in ecstasy.

Getting high, doggie-style, on the leaves' touch is the only lasting communion Dr. Bob has with Big Sue, and now, with me, Thea *feels,* not says to herself. "Both of us do the same thing," she adds aloud. "We leave him behind whenever we go on our mind-bending trips: right, Sue? But Dr. Bob fools us. He gets as blitzed as we do, damn that little fucker. He's had some excellently wigged-out reality castaways as teachers."

Safe on her couch, Thea gradually comes to realize Dr. Bob has an extraordinarily developed talent that allows him to leave the reality of a crazy world, where people own dogs and *things* instead of themselves; where he has to live in a downtown loft instead of run on a mountain all his own; where he eats dried up grain balls instead of ripping his teeth into a herd of warm-blooded deer as his pantry; a world so crazy, in fact, that instead of a clear rippling stream he only has blue-colored toilet punch to drink.

Thea doesn't answer any calls the first day she's immobile on the couch, sobbing and shaking, terrified that her life has completely spun out of control. Her machine picks up and it's from Max, calling from L.A. to say he's coming home a couple days later than planned. A call also comes from Fast Forward.

On the second day of Thea's couch-curl, she picks up Max's call. He'll think it odd, her not answering the phone for two days straight. She speaks in a feigned tone of togetherness. "Oh, Mighty Max, I'm so sick. Ow, my poor head."

Thea pictures Max's precisely styled hair, the couture slinky clothes that make him appear more like a hot actor than the distribution hustler he is.

"How awful, being under the weather by yourself—the pits, babe. Call out for some soup, why don't you. I've been worried because you didn't pick up. You got my message to call me back?"

"I've been sleeping nonstop. Just felt too yuk to call you. Must be a flu," she lies. "I haven't been out of bed since, since, awhile."

Max is appeased. It isn't unusual for moody, nightclub-performing Thea to not pick up the loft phone for days on end. Max knows how she likes to isolate, hole up and work in her studio day and night. Leastwise, before Big Sue's demise. His worries are happily allayed: she's sick.

Morning dawns on the third day. She sees the familiar sight of Dr. Bob getting off under the ficus tree while she desperately clings to her shattered reality. Thea knows something really awful happened, but she can't remember exactly what. Whatever it was, everything feels different now.

Thea's only hope is to lie still and wait. She touches her aching face. Her eye socket hurts like hell. She isn't brave enough to look in a mirror so her fetal position draws tighter. From the corner of her vision she sees something, waving above her, making her nerves scream. She looks up to glimpse that imagined white flag. She remembers.

Shaking at the sight, she thinks: *It's like I'm surrendering in a war, the white flag thing.* She shrugs, seeing this universal sign of surrender, this mirage, waving strongly, surely, above her head in a hallucinatory breeze.

"I must be going crazy," she shouts out loud. For days she's lain mortified in between bouts of shaking and sobbing, battling the urge to die, cemented to the couch.

She touches her face again, where the pain is worse. Thea drags herself to the bathroom and, braving the inevitable, looks in the mirror and discovers a nightmarish black eye. "How the hell'd I get …?" wincing as she touches the swollen, throbbing, varicolored contusion.

"My life's nothing but a damn snake pit," Thea wails. "I'm done!"

She feels the crush of a blackened heart, her shredded mind and battered spirit. The flotsam of Thea's life is strewn everywhere she looks. Nothing but broken bits, crushed plans, the imagined bloodied limbs of her personal battlefield. Looking closer, right into her eyes in the mirror—she sees only emptiness. Thea shivers and returns to the couch, hugging herself, squeaking, "I've got to stop killing myself."

* * *

She's determined to drag herself at the appointed time to a nondescript church on St. Mark's Place where the guy on the hotline told her to go. More desperate than scared, Thea doesn't notice what clothes she's pulling on, whether they are hers or Max's. She grabs a long tan overcoat from deep in the closet, one that matches her mood: baggy, haggard, nondescript. Inside the pocket she feels something cold. Drawing it out, she looks at the Kali crystal that Valala had given her seasons before, left unnoticed since she last wore that coat. It starts to get warm in her hand.

Jamming the crystal back into the pocket, Thea finds her darkest pair of sunglasses and tries to tame her spiked, unruly hair. She knows she looks horrendous. Tie-dyed eye, botched life—she doesn't care about her appearance. Since getting off the addiction hotline a few hours earlier, all she has done is drink coffee and practice walking. After days on the couch, her legs are wobbly. She smokes cigarettes, relay-style, a lit one igniting the next.

It's noon on Saturday when she arrives at the church she's directed to. Thea opens the heavy, leaded-glass front door and suddenly she's surrounded by the sound of—can it be?—laughter! Inside is a crowd. She sees all different types, old/young, scruffy/stylish, all colors, faces from every race. She's sure these can't be people like herself, addicts and alcoholics. She's certain. Everywhere she looks she sees men and women and in-betweens smiling and having fun. *I'm in the wrong place,* Thea thinks, but quickly finds out otherwise.

A woman approaches with a hand extended, introducing herself.

"This your first time?" she says, smiling as if she knows.

Thea looks at the hip-looking young woman, wearing black just like other downtown artists. Thea wonders how she knows, and answers "Yes."

The rest goes by in a blur. The young woman's name is Carol. She takes charge of her and is so friendly that Thea is immediately suspicious. She leads Thea by the arm to a table where coffee and cookies are. Thea grabs a cup of black, and Carol leads her to another table where enough books and pamphlets are spread to fill a school library. A minute later Carol invites Thea to sit next to her. The hour-long meeting is a blur of speaking, hand-raising, individual voices, applause, more mirth. Afterward, Carol introduces her, one by one, to many men and women who look normal, too happy to be there; Thea thinks herself too miserable to be there. No one looks half the mess that Thea feels. A lot of them are laughing, no one's sad—and if they are they're pretending to joke around—things Thea can't understand. Why are they acting as if they haven't a care in the world? she wonders. I thought these people had a problem like me. She is thoroughly confused.

Carol stands chatting for a while outside the church's front door. With a pen, she briskly circles something in a thick booklet, hands it to Thea and says, way too cheerily, "Just keep coming back."

On her walk back to Tribeca, Thea looks at the pamphlet Carol jammed into her hands, sees the circled words: *Exchange Views*. *Sounds political,* Thea thinks. She shrugs her shoulders and decides to do whatever Carol and these people tell her to do. "Anything," she says to no one on the street, "to get better."

When Thea returns to the loft from the meeting—*très weird*, she keeps thinking and shaking her head—another irate message from Fast is on the machine, pestering her to make a Supply House practice that she has no intention of making.

Thea looks at Dr. Bob, who's looking curiously at her. "Don't ask me," Thea says. "I'm new to all this too, fella."

Thea gives the mutt a reassuring pat on the head and recoils into a snail shape. Not wanting to sleep in the huge bed she shares with Max, she bundles herself on the couch in a soft blanket as she has for some days and nights before, trembling, but this time glad for occasional waves of not shivering instead of the continuous spasms she's struggled through for days. She gets up and gazes out the floor-to-ceiling windows at the patch of steely sky. Her skin ripples in, what? Fright? Cold? She doesn't know. The frigid sky outside is milky and bitterly unfriendly, dark like an ice dome trapping fumes and furies. Looking at the city's uncountable night lights reflecting on low-lying clouds, she moans and sinks back onto the couch pillows.

But she can't relax. She keeps thinking how strange that meeting was. She didn't understand a thing they said or did; wasn't able to sit still or hold that cup of coffee in her shaking hands without spilling it; yet she felt, somehow, and weirdly, safe.

Just like the smooth-voiced guy on the hotline had told her—"The fellowship will make you feel better." She hasn't a clue why. She shrugs; who cares why? At least I'm not crying anymore.

Later that night, Thea needs cigarettes. She slips into the same long overcoat, and again finds the Kali rock in her pocket. Her rainbow and platinum-streaked hair sticks out like crushed petals from the collar of the big coat as she makes her way to the corner all-night bodega. It's the first walk the jubilant Dr. Bob has had in days, aside from the rooftop. When she returns, Thea smokes and paces the loft's smooth wooden floor, glancing out the high-glassed windows until she drops utterly exhausted onto the soft pillows, and falls quickly asleep.

The next day at noon, at the same red brick St. Mark's Place church, Carol is there and reminds her to check out the early morning group that she circled, the one that meets closest to Thea's own neighborhood—in the bowels of the World Trade Center's number one tower. She shows up at the meeting wearing sunglasses and doesn't take off her camel-hair coat. Deep in her pocket she holds the warm Kali rock tightly in her fist. The night before, Thea got up to put on the coat, clenched the stone as she smoked and paced, then slept with it on. She notices as soon as she touches the bright shiny crystal, she feels oddly better. And her uncontrollable shaking and cravings stop.

Thea sleeps all the rest of the day and on through the night. Waking up bright and early the next morning, she walks into the World Trade meeting that Carol told her to check out. It isn't hard to find. The enormous basement conference room is fluorescent-lights gray, filled with strangers, business people, wide-awake men and women dressed for their offices in the fashionably formal dark suits of the day, looking like a flock of absurdly satisfied penguins. *This must be some mistake,* Thea thinks, as she backs away to the door upon entering. The other place, in St. Mark's Square, had a high percentage of freaky, arty, or street-looking people among the swarm of variegated attendees. *These people here, at the World Trade Center, can't possibly be addicts like me. Everyone looks so*—she shakes her head—*bright.*

Right then somebody comes up to Thea and says a friendly *Hello.* Thea's hand gets shaken as she's greeted in the coffee and doughnut-smelling room by a woman exuding, "Welcome to Exchange Views."

Without being asked, the stranger starts to softly talk about sobriety, referring to it as a possession one owns. "I've got three years," the woman says when Thea asks how long it's been since she's not gotten high.

Another friendly pair of eyes appear at her side.

"Hi, I'm Sophia. I'm cross-addicted. Drugs, alcohol, pills, you name it."

"Pardon?" Thea's face displays confusion. How could this nice-looking woman, or any of them, ever have been into drugs and alcohol like me? Just look at her!

Thea turns her full attention to this new arrival: a perfectly dressed, smartly coiffed young professional woman. Her lightly made-up face is shining and pert. Those perfectly manicured fire-engine red nails are what Thea thinks are a woman's who does nothing but groom herself. As they talk, Thea envisions fine creams and exfoliating lotions, shelves of pampering devices that must go into the distinct glow of the comforting person who now stands radiantly before her, talking to her as an equal.

"I used to mix downers and uppers with my daily bottle of vodka," Sophia says with a sly grin. "Whatever would take me away, I used."

"Really?" Thea glares unbelieving. "So, what do you do now?"

Sophia's voice reminds Thea of far-off tiny bells. "I don't do any mind-altering substances, except coffee," she giggles. "Clean and dry, we call it."

Thea dares not say another word, afraid she'll burst out crying, and that would be horrible. Sophia continues talking for them both in a quiet, mellow tone. Demure diamond studs glisten on her dainty earlobes, barely showing beneath a burst of shiny fawn-colored hair, styled without a hair out of place, with highlights registering firmly on the square side. *A far cry from downtown punky spikes and all-black,* Thea thinks, noticing a glint of purple hidden at Sophia's neckline: an amethyst pendant cradled in the hollow of her pink-sweatered throat.

"One day at a time: total abstinence is the only way to stop the obsession. The dragon comes alive when you feed it, Thea."

What weird language, she thinks. Thea is more confused than ever.

"Dragon? I'm afraid I don't get it. What are you talking about?"

Sophia pushes a card into her hands.

"Give me a call whenever you want. I'll tell you all about the dragon. It's what I call the disease of addiction, kiddo."

Thea's one good eye aches when she now squeezes it tightly, repulsed by those saccharine words. Kiddo? Thea shrinks. *Who does this strait-laced schoolmarm think she is? Nobody's going to tell me what I can and can't do. Don't these jokers know I just want to cool it with the booze?*

Thea never considered stopping everything. No way! That's way too much, her mind argues frantically. *What will I do without my best friends? What's so bad about a little toot or poke of weed? How can I possibly get right in my head without a harmless beer? This is too fucking much! It's only booze that gets me in trouble,* she argues silently.

Who are these freaks, anyway? Is this a cult? She feels mad, being duped. Holy rollers calling themselves *The Fellowship*; babbling about *Practicing the Program,* like it's some kind of group workout.

And they all wear suits, she continues arguing with herself. *Fuck! There are no artists here, I don't belong. Period. What a bunch of squares to be with at seven in the fucking a.m. What the hell is going on with me, anyway?*

Looking around, Thea sees nothing but business types of all ages and nationalities. She envisions soon they'll ride elevators to their offices and fluorescent-glaring cubicles above the basement community room, or walk over to the other tower, or toward the Seaport, up and down Broadway, Varick, or over to Wall Street. She watches a hundred anonymous people go in and out of the room that morning. She also notices waitresses in their uniforms, women who could be secretaries, a few helmeted bike messengers, some shabbily dressed cabbies, and a few spiffy, cocky-capped limo drivers. There's a guy who could be a hotshot lawyer or a judge even. Then Thea notices in the back of the room a few bedraggled people, possibly homeless men and women, getting free cups of Joe with a sticky bun.

"They can eat all they want, have coffee too, but they can't talk, y'know, share at the meeting if they've been drinking," Sophia whispers, sitting next to Thea.

One at a time people speak, *exchanging views*, while others listen in silence. It's all pretty confusing to Thea. She starts to wonder how can these people possibly know what she's feeling? Whatever someone is saying is exactly how she feels. This can't be, she resists silently. Her entire life has been built on the premise that nobody ever understands the misery she feels. She chews on that like cud. Yet here she sits, hearing her own story from smiling strangers in many different versions. It's unbelievable. The people in that room smell good, look sane, and are bright-eyed—all of them except the homeless who are there just for the grub.

After the meeting, every person who comes up to her says the same thing: "You're in the right place. We were all there, where you're at today. Welcome."

Thea looks around. Not a single person she knows is there, of the local Tribeca and Soho regulars at McGovern's or Duffy's, or anyone she ever saw at gallery openings or wild artist parties. The closest thing to a creative-looking sort is a man across the room, huddled in a dark watch cap and coat. He has the unshaven, rumpled appearance of a well-known painter she knows has a loft around the Seaport. The basement room keeps emptying and filling, with more clean-and-dry folks banding together to stay on the wagon.

"One by one, the penguins steal my sanity," Thea mumbles, overdosing from so many sober people gathered in one place.

Sophia, with the amethyst at her throat, reappears at her side after the meeting. She introduces Thea to several more suspiciously friendly people who stick around to talk before bustling off to work. Everyone has remarkably bright eyes, even though some are not as pressed and polished as successful folks tend to be. All in all, Sophia is the most engaging person Thea talks to. Her skin shines with interest, and her out-of-season pink pants suit and sensible shoes are so crisp, so clean. Thea finds it increasingly incongruous when Sophia mentions more details about having been strung out on pills and vodka, "not too many twenty-four hours ago." *Strange way of marking time,* Thea thinks.

"If you abuse one drug you're likely to abuse any," Sophia explains as they walk outside together into the morning's sharp sunshine. "It's about addiction, Thea. We say using different mind-altering substances is simply changing seats on the Titanic. You're still going down with the ship."

In a flash Thea gets it. She knows what it's like—sinking to the bottom of a deep dark sea, using grass, mushrooms, booze, coke, pills or—

"Any mood changer sets off the obsession," Sophia says as they walk north. Behind them the World Trade Towers loom eternal that morning, reaching to the cloudless winter sky above them.

"It's both chemical and psychological," Sophia explains. She's a nurse with a private case who lives close by, so she comes to Exchange Views every morning she can, she tells Thea.

"Sometimes gambling, or hanging with friends who use, or having casual sex will kick in the compulsion. It's tricky. Learning to avoid things that trigger us is why we go to meetings, to remember we're addicts. So we never forget. By sharing with each other we stay clean, and little by little we come to be true to our own self."

"True to our own self," Thea repeats in a whisper. Part of her wants to cry, but she also feels strangely elated. Listening to this woman, who claims to have been through the same torment she has, makes Thea feel better.

She keeps her head down in the February chill, trying to focus on Sophia's words as they continue north on Broadway. Thea's turnoff to Tribeca is beyond the Woolworth Building, where Sophia will head west.

"You might be lucky, Thea, this *could be* your bottom," Sophia says as she braces against the wind at the corner, her two feet firmly apart as they stand waiting for the crosswalk light to change. "Without a bottom, you never get humble enough to ask for help."

"Bottom?" Thea mumbles under the wool scarf wrapped around her neck.

As the light changes, Sophia grabs Thea's elbow and speaks as they walk across the wide street together, leaning against the pounding wind. "Our bottom is the reason we decide to change: our last drunk or binge. The dragon's final attack, the one that gets you here, kiddo—to the rooms."

12

She wakes up the next morning, amazed she hasn't used anything for days. She thinks, *One day at a time, I can do it.* Even more incredible to her is—right then—she has no desire to get high this morning like she usually does.

After a quick walk with Dr. Bob she leaves for Exchange Views with this strange new feeling. It's a brisk day. It feels as if a brand-new life, one of excitement and hope, is beginning for her. She walks down Broadway looking up at the World Trade Towers for the entire fifteen minutes it takes to walk there. *Maybe I can learn to be as tall and strong as you are*, she thinks as she stares at the white endlessly-high pillars, gleaming in the morning sun, which oddly cheers her up. When she arrives she promises herself she won't be bothered, being so very different from the others in suits at Exchange Views.

She argues when the thought of feeling uneasy pops into her head, saying *No! I'm not letting anything stop me from feeling welcome here. I'm going to not use, no matter what, like Sophia says. For once I want to be a winner. I'm doing this getting-sober shit if it kills me. Sophia tells me I've found a home here, and I'm going to believe her. So far, it feels right. A new family that is warmly embracing and seems to understand me more than I've ever understood myself, from things they talk about so easily, so freely—so honestly.*

Just as she did the night before, when a thought about getting high came unexpectedly into her mind, she pretends she's Sophia, and says No! to that thought.

It works. Over and over, it works.

For some inexplicable reason Thea trusts what Sophia and the others at Exchange Views keep telling her. Each new day, a brighter flash of hope lights up Thea's heart and warms it till her chest expands, and it stays expanded. Her heart begins to feel like it's coming alive as she gradually comes back to life. Each morning she walks home from the Trade Center a little more hopeful, the two towers at her back looking down upon her progress in the quicksand swamps of early recovery that Sophia calls funny names.

"You're touching back on Planet Sober," Sophia tells Thea with a nod. "It's a whole new world out there, kiddo."

On the fifth day of early morning meetings, Thea lets herself back into the loft. Bounding to her side with a sneeze greeting, Dr. Bob's metronome tail knocks over anything in its periphery.

"You got it, old man," Thea clicks her tongue, rubbing the dog's neck, scratching his chest, ready to make good on her promise to walk him regularly. In her coat pocket, she again feels the familiar crystal that Valala gave her. Thea turns the Kali rock in her hand. Suddenly it feels hot, as if an electrical charge has gone off inside it.

With one hand deep in her pocket and the other holding the leash, Thea and Dr. Bob walk briskly for half an hour. Returning to the loft, she pulls off the rumpled coat she's worn every day since calling the hotline and stands in front of the full-length mirror in the foyer.

Dr. Bob barks an affirmative. Looking in the mirror, Thea can see that her face is already less strained, her posture straighter, her multi-tone hair clipped out of her face. It is true: she looks less done in. Even the front tooth that had cracked with Fast's punch doesn't bother Thea as much.

Aloud she says, "This is it, ol' pal, look at me—I'm changing. Bet ol' Big Sue would bust a gut over this one, huh? Me, her truest deadbeat soul sister, gettin' sober, oh man! Sue would sure say to hell with that."

Thea goes to the answering machine, sees the light flash just once and hits the play button.

"Hey, stranger." Fast Forward's nasal screech makes Thea cringe. He sounds anything but happy.

"Why aren't you ever there? Give me a call, will'ya. You can't just not call me, CC. What's goin' on? The band's countin' on you and so am I. We've got gigs, you toad. Call me!"

Quickly she erases Fast from the machine and his message from her mind. Sophia said not to hang out with any more "users." Thea looks at Dr. Bob and starts to drift. Big Sue's drunken dawn drive to Boston looms in her mind, and she, for the millionth time, re-creates the crash. *Sue should have slept it off,* Thea thinks remorsefully, not able to stop the horrible memory. She shakes her head. She can't stop missing Big Sue. But she knows nothing could have stopped her friend's determination to kill herself, one way or the other.

That old beat-up Mustang of Sue's was a rust-trap, but its engine was as finely tuned as her navigation skills on the open sea. It was only Big Sue who wasn't working right that icy dawn.

Man, I wish she was here now, Thea thinks. *What a jolt, me getting sober at Exchange Views. She'd laaau-gh,* Thea chuckles, imagining the unimaginable.

Thea collapses onto the sofa. Behind her, tiny cadmium spotlights are focused on the impressive wall sculpture of Junkyard Trinnie's that Max had bought for an extravagant sum at the St. Pierre gallery. Thea looks closely at the piece that Max had to buy when he found out Thea knew the famed artist. But it was only that one time, as a customer at St. Pierre's gallery, that Max ever showed the slightest interest in her friend or his coveted work. The piece Max selected was sedate compared to most of the other riotously colorful works of the Outsider King. Fabricated from welded gears and other odd parts of machinery protruding from the wall, bolted onto a wooden panel on which globs of thick pale blue-gray and matte silver paint were applied, in this study of shapes and shadows, Thea recognizes in the lower left-hand corner Junkyard's trademark of imposing a single distinguishable human image in every one of his abstractions.

As he told her once, "Having just one recognizable *t'ing* is like me leaving a footprint. Materials be making the piece work, but the image be the message, Honeypot."

Junkyard named this work that Max bought, *He Who Knows, Don't.* The sole figure Thea now regards is of a man lifting a colossal boulder, a comical feat for a man so skeletal skinny. The figure is painted in silhouette, staggering under the weight of a rock at least a hundred times his bulk.

After making the sizable purchase, by far the most expensive of his incongruous collection, Max relaxed that day, for about two minutes, to regard Junkyard's ten-foot-wide piece when it was brought to the loft and hung. "All this stuff," Max said to Thea, waving at Junkyard's elaborate piece, not easy to ignore, "doesn't mean anything to me. It's a great investment, that's all I care about. Now I can say I own a Junkyard Trinnie."

Staring at the piece, she's thinking of this. Thea reaches out and lights the cigarette she has in her fingers. She's aware of this unique new feeling of hers: feeling glad to be alive. She hadn't expected this, wanting to live after wishing to die for so long. Every time she thinks about it she's amazed she has no cravings to get high. Not yet.

Thea looks over to the ficus tree and says, "You getting off on that tree again?" Dr. Bob doesn't hear a thing in his trance-walking.

A fever of melancholy arises in Thea's overactive, unruly mind. Of things she's not thought about for years. How stupidly she's acted, being wasted so much. Then *swish*, the channel switches in her head to instant replays of rambunctious antics she and Big Sue delighted in with such vicious vengeance, in San Francisco, then New York, totally disregarding theirs and any other lives.

For some odd reason Thea then remembers a distant time, as if in a steamy haze, when that psycho landlord of hers back in the Haight, Osgood, came up to her kitchen with someone who wanted to meet her. But Thea can't recall a face, except that he or she came. And then, poof! She can't remember anything else about this secret sharer of hers. Slices of her life are gone, completely erased. Thea shakes her head, wondering how lucky she is not to have ended up with chop suey for brains. She couldn't recall much, thanks to alcohol's convenient memory-erasing benefits. Anxiety bombards her, making her squirm and shiver as Thea thinks of the huge gaps in her memory. She's just glad she's not craving to obliterate herself right now, as she has so often before. This is a new era, she reckons.

She gets up to grab her smokes she keeps in the tan coat in the closet. As her hand dives into the deep pocket, her fingers touch something cold yet hot at the same time. Thea withdraws her hand as if a snake has bitten it.

More cautiously she probes again. Then she remembers the Kali rock hidden in that pocket, the strange rock that the old mummy Valala had given her.

"That lady was a piece of work," Thea says as she brings out the bright clear piece of quartz.

Thea places the natural multi-faceted crystal on the table next to the ashtray and lights a cigarette.

"How'm I doing, Kali, old gal?" she sarcastically sneers, blowing smoke at the innocuous stone. "Thanks for taking away my craving the booze-and-drugs demon," she hisses sardonically.

She sinks back, enjoying the rush of nicotine batting her brain. An express train of memories roars up, speeding straight at Thea. This time something new arises. A wailing, warning, silent horn sounds deep in her brain. She closes her eyes and feels a new rhythm inside her as she smokes, thinking of nothing but how weird it is not to be high for these past five days.

What is she supposed to do with all this extra time she has on her hands?

She gets up to put music on, needing to be distracted by doing something. Flicking through the choices she finally sees something monumental, imminent, grand in a classical way. *The Magic Mountain.* She thinks, *Yes, that's how I'm feeling. I'm not scared anymore. Something's happening. I feel totally unlike myself. Like I'm out of my body looking at someone else, on the inside.*

Dr. Bob wags his tail and rhythmically thumps the floor, looking as if he sees and knows something more than Thea does. What's with him, she wonders, looking behind her to see what's so interesting to that weird mutt of hers. Thea stops. She notices a peculiar sparkle in the room, like a cluster of floating silver sequins. But she dismisses it, thinking it's the mid-morning light playing tricks on her eyes, bouncing off the windowpanes. She comes over to the happy mongrel and kneels at his side.

In a quiet voice she asks, "What's happening to me, Dr. Bob?"

The dog lifts his head as Thea listens to the strains of the music's capricious waterfall sounds. She smiles, sensing her life really is changing. Every time she's thought about getting high, she becomes instantly dizzy with disgust and on the verge of puking. *I'm ready for the next step*, she knows. She sees Dr. Bob jerk his head around. Thea lifts hers to look in the same direction. Right then she is acutely aware of a remarkable difference in the room. Everywhere around her, Thea notices, is light, as if intense spotlights are bouncing around, not connected or grounded to anything specific. She wonders if the electricity is surging, but it's only 10 a.m. How can this be?

"Something strange is going on," she whispers. "What's up?"

Dr. Bob picks his head up and cocks it to one side.

"You see it too, don't you, old boy?"

The dog's breath heaves deeply as he sinks and puts his head back on his paws and peacefully closes his eyes. Thea relaxes. She scoffs at the idea that something could be happening. That weird light. Letting her breath out in a loud sigh, Thea wonders aloud about herself. She decides this is just another of her overcooked fantasies, best used for making edgy art instead of thinking strange flickers of light are real.

The slumbering dog only half-raises his eyelids when she speaks to him.

"You're the only thing I have left of Big Sue, isn't that something, ol' pal? With all the blanked-out, Swiss cheese holes I have for a memory. Guess the time is here to stop this death-by-chemicals trip, huh? Before excess causes my death too."

Dr. Bob's lithe body stretches, elongating every sinewy inch from black nose to white-tipped tail. Click-click go his nails across the glossy stone floor as he slowly comes to Thea's side. He grins a toothy assurance with a few head-tossing sneezes as he nudges his wet nose under her limp arm that hangs off the edge of the sofa. Thea's heart warms like an ember inside her, knowing that someone still loves her.

The phone rings. Thea leans over to pick it up, tired of playing the coy game of screening calls. Fast Forward's urgent twang grabs her from the other end. "Hey, where y'been, CC? I've been calling for days. Y'okay? The other night didn't do ya in, did it?"

She lights a cigarette and speaks slowly.

"No, of course not, Fast. I've been busy. I was going to call you; I just kept forgetting. Sorry, I'm not feelin' so hot."

"You frog!" he shouts. "We wanted to jam last night or tonight, but you messed us up and the boys took other gigs. You better get it together, CC. The guys won't put up with your shit, y'know."

Thea cringes but she manages to check firing back. As close as she is to Fast Forward, she can't tolerate any undue criticism. She reaches up and touches her sore eye socket. Thea takes another drag of smoke deep into her lungs and stamps out the butt.

"CC, y'still there?"

"Yeah I'm here. So what's with this black eye I woke up with the other morning?"

"I swear, you went nuts, Thee! I had to defend myself. I never saw you so blasted. Believe me, doll, I wouldn't've hit you unless I had to. Is it bad?"

"Bad? I'm a total mess. There's no way I'm playing with you guys till this heals," she lies again. "I'm a freak. And besides, I'm sick. Got a cold. That's why I haven't answered any calls."

"I was worried about cha."

"I appreciate that, Fast."

"What's the matter? Do too much this week? Happens every time Max is outta town."

"Maybe. I'll call you later, okay."

Hanging up, she whistles for Dr. Bob. "C'mon, let's go for a walk, old man."

Nearly midnight in the never-sleeping city, the lunar disk shines as luminous as an uptown marquee. Thea and Dr. Bob walk along the Hudson River's promenade, close to their Tribeca loft.

The moon is her lost romance, but the sun, ah ... the sun. It had once been her entire life, but Thea can't remember that anymore either. Had she really once been a sun devotee? Lately, she cringes if she happens to reminisce over the tender kisses the sun gave her once-receptive body. Instead of the golden tan she wore for years after joining Giles and his island life, Thea's complexion is now cement gray from having worshipped places like piss-scented Duffy's. Her light sensitivity has become acutely allergic to any outdoor luminaries brighter than streetlights.

Where did her ability to tell time by the sun go, she wonders as she walks Dr. Bob. She hasn't thought of that in years. When she moved to New York she'd been able to accurately pinpoint any time of day, *when* the sun was visible that is, within give-or-take ten minutes. Thanks to how the Bahamian sun had been her one and only timepiece.

Thea remembers, suddenly, standing on a stool at her family's kitchen sink, staring at dish suds—within each rainbow-oily soap bubble she spied an entire universe, inviting all her senses inward, to a region of magical feelings. Lost in her own private kid's world, with no one from her family around to discourage or abuse her, it was then, at her dishwashing chore, that she first heard that clear voice within her. Lost in sudsy reverie, the mysterious voice spoke to her.

"Trust your destiny, Thea," it said. She looked around upon hearing it and realized no one was there. "You are one of our messengers," the voice continued. "One day you will be a bridge for us, linking our unseen world with your seen world. Follow your heart, and your destiny will be revealed when the time comes.

"Until then," Thea recalled the sourceless voice saying to her as an enthralled child, standing wobbly on a footstool, her arms emerged elbows-deep in warm soapy water, staring fixedly on one particular soap bubble beckoning her to enter its mysterious world within, "until then, trust us, Thea. Trust that your life will be unlike any you've ever dreamed of."

As she walks in silence on the dark quiet streets with her dog-pal, she remembers other things. Thea hears her mother's grating voice discouraging her from creating anything other than marriage and babies.

Remembering her mom never condoning the boyish shenanigans Thea got into, and how she'd earn whippings for making those messes out of garage paraphernalia, lopsided fortresses and palaces. Thea flinches recalling her two older brothers, how they terrorized and resented her, until they started with the physical abuse. And her parents' cocktail-holding guests who'd condescendingly gaze down at her when, at any prompting, she'd make up long involved fairytales, complete with surprise casts that both horrified and entertained.

Her family paid little attention to Thea's bizarre antics, except for the whippings she endured. They thought her penchant for storytelling was her being a pest. Her experiences were hers alone, born from isolation, uncaring, and the salvation of the human imagination. Instead of applauding her free spirit, Thea's family only wanted to put a cap on it. "Why can't you be like other little girls," her parents and siblings lamented, hoping by controlling her she'd *outgrow* her alienation. When she reached adolescence, it was a no-brainer for her to sneak away, get drunk with her parent's stolen bottles, run wild with boys as fast and as far away as she could. It was the only way she had of blotting out the implacable sadness of being misunderstood. Other, more sordid things—about her brothers—Thea simply refused to remember.

The dog tugs on his leash. Thea speaks to him as if they are in the middle of a long conversation.

"Since then, Dr. Bob, I found it hard to tell if life was a dream I was having, and I, only a dreamer—or if I were awake and this movie reel everyone calls life isn't worth remembering because it sucks so bad."

Sensing his companion's roller-coaster downslide into self-pity, again, Dr. Bob tugs on his leash, to no effect. Thea is already in another mood swing. This one, a jet stream of memories. Thea's gait slows. Urgent barks from Dr. Bob, as if he heard her obsessing, command her to let go of whatever thoughts are trying to invade her up-and-down feelings.

"Ghosts—get out of my head!" Thea shouts, causing the dog to whimper. Her voice joins the howling wind in an attempt to clean out the cobwebby corridors of her stuffed attic of a mind.

Thea stops and says, "The past is over, damn it! I want to live free! Memories, leave me alone!"

Relieved, Thea walks briskly with Dr. Bob in the freezing night air, bundling herself tighter inside her big overcoat. Her bare hand dives deeply into the silk-lined pocket where it touches the now-always-hot Kali rock that lives there. She shivers, not from the cold.

Thea sees all her resentments lined up as she mentally pokes at their jeering faces: old lovers, old doper buddies, her aloof alcoholic parents, her brothers who couldn't care less. She orders all the barbs they flung—the put-downs that fueled her using and self-abusing—to leave her.

13

The only pleasant remnant left in Thea's obscured memory bank is swarthy Russ. His image drifts by like a lost cloud, stranded in the landscape of a lonely past, unable to land on any firm ground in her hopeful present. Russ' face was rugged like the coastline of his homeland, New Zealand, up by the North Island's thousand bays, where the fringed land stretches out to meet foaming spray crashing upon the frayed rocky hem of the sea's edge.

Handsome in a brutish, barbarian way, that was Russ. They'd met on a trip Thea had taken with Big Sue on one of her friend's sailboat deliveries. Back in the pre-Giles era, Thea jumped at any serendipitous trip with her friend, to anywhere on the watery face of the globe. Thea's mind hopscotched now, thinking of her dearest pal, the big lug of a woman.

She'd been a hard nut to crack, even for Thea. No man or woman ever thought of Big Sue in a romantic way, none Thea knew about anyway. Sue was a fine specimen of a tough, independent soul, an ocean-roaming, true free-agent. Only once Big Sue had loved someone, but never again. She'd talked about it with Thea when the two were almost, but not quite, passed out, when Big Sue's defenses had been nonexistent, liquefied.

Big Sue said she'd been crazy for some guy she'd loved since they were kids, but he didn't feel the same toward her. He was a fellow who remained forever nameless, who'd married someone else, and never gave Big Sue another look after the few clumsy times they were together in their early twenties. Big Sue clamped her heart gates closed for good after that.

Her heart had once been opened, and like others, filled with love's bright possibilities; but after that one time, her sorrow and self-lowness would remain forever incurable. After that, she cared nothing about balance—neither in love nor in life. She was not one to analyze things; she just lived. Loving another human being had been a one-time deal as far as Sue was concerned.

For years Dr. Bob had been her only companion. Then Big Sue somehow let Thea into her others-excluded life that night they met on a dark Sausalito dock, back when they were both young and foolish, getting stupendously hammered together at the Noname Bar, in the Haight, or anywhere they could. Big Sue's only respite from her stubbornly private revolution against anything healthy was to stay as far out to sea as she could, and being sure to dive deeply into and stay firmly entrenched in oblivion whenever she was on landlubbers' turf.

Thea made up for her friend's abstinence in the love category with her own gluttonous need for male conquests. Oh yeah, and that one time that an aggressive lesbo seduced her, but Thea didn't count that seduction as romance. On a delivery trip to the Pacific, Thea found herself sharing a sixty-foot sailboat with only Big Sue as navigator and the unattached Kiwi captain, Russ. Thea did what any sex addict in her right mind would do.

Five weeks later they cruised into Bali to meet up with the boat's owner, just in time for Thea to catch a flight back to the States. As she waved goodbye to him, Thea never fooled herself that she cared more deeply about Russ than any other guy. He was simply the fun one of the moment, and yes, he was sensational in the sack. Nonetheless, her feelings got surprisingly hurt when he said to her at the airport, "Bugger all, you're too wild for me, so long," and would stick in her craw and bang on her memory drum right up till now, this frigid night as she walks the promenade with Dr. Bob, dead sober and counting reasons to be glad about it.

This ridiculous comment never made sense to her. *Russ was pissed I left him, that's what it was,* Thea now thinks, feeling Dr. Bob's restless tug of his leash.

* * *

On lower Manhattan's nighttime dome-encased promenade along the river, Thea stops walking and Dr. Bob stops tugging. Her curtain of bad memories is thrown aside. It's as if the lights have been switched on, and suddenly, Thea can see more clearly. A clarity as dramatic as if someone behind has tapped her on the shoulder, and as Thea turns to face an interloper, a faceless form tells her it is dead wrong to carry such heaviness, these miserable old resentments, weighing her down, tainting her life.

Yet there's no one there.

Thea looks at Dr. Bob. His abysmal eyes hit hers with laser penetration. Her old memories crumble to the pavement. It hits her so radically that this animal before her, with unabashed love pouring from him, is the only true friend she has.

Another piece of the puzzle slides into place.

Dr. Bob shakes his head vigorously, and opens his toothy mouth widely for a gigantic yawn. His human's deep vibe isn't his bag. Now his canine body, from wet nose through sleek torso to the end of his long-haired tail, ripples with kinetic energy resulting from the recharge of that oxygen-intake yawn. It seems like the white tip of his tail fires off mini-firecrackers from the effort of that shake.

Thea says, "What's going on, man?"

The dog barks and looks away at something in the darkness, beyond where they are standing on the riverfront. Thea turns to see what the dog is barking at, but she sees nothing. She stares in the same direction as Dr. Bob, who continues to bark, his tail wagging as if he sees someone he recognizes. This time Thea squints, making her eyes go a little out of focus. There, about ten feet away, she sees the same kind of sparkly light that had appeared from out of nowhere—a strange nebulous iridescence, like floating sequins—that she'd seen in the living room earlier in the day. Tiny prisms of suspended light, as if a swath of snowflakes were suspended in the air, with myriad reflections bouncing and shining back from invisible points. She stands and stares at the strange glimmer, mesmerized. Thea thinks she hears something. She turns to see who or what might be approaching them. Nobody. Nothing is there.

Thea turns her head to her best hearing side, thinking she'll be able to make out the sound that is growing slowly from faint to audible. Then she hears it distinctly, as if whispered in her ear.

She turns in all directions. Yet Thea sees no one on the deserted river walk. Words come, though, from where she does not know.

"Everything happens for a reason," she distinctly hears a nondescript, genderless voice say. "Nothing is for naught. Reliving the past leads you to the place where obsession breeds. It's a mental narcotic. Lighten up. Freedom is yours if you're willing. It's right within you. When you're ready to receive the truth, we're here to help you, Thea."

Thea stands riveted. She is certain she heard it. Isn't she? She and Dr. Bob remain motionless and bend their heads to listen. But there are no more words. Just the late city night: distant sounds, a kind breeze, and cold as hell.

"What's going on, man," she whispers. The dog sits on his haunches, patiently waiting. Thea feels the chill and the pair briskly walk back home.

14

Over two weeks have passed since Max left for L.A. He calls to check up on Thea every day, and she appreciates his concern. His last call had been brief and even more vague than usual, even for never-certain Max. "I'll make it home soon. It's just not clear how things are going here. Call me if you need me."

Thea is glad to have as much time alone as she can. She and Dr. Bob are doing just fine without the owner of their pad. In her new quietness, Thea realizes her best friend is Dr. Bob, truly the happiest being she's ever known.

"He's my guru," she jokingly tells people whenever anyone stops to admire the permanent-press tuxedo dog. His smiling face makes some jump, confusing the weak of heart when he bares his teeth, with that snorting wheezing laugh of his upon meeting other humans. Paranoid sorts tend to interpret exposed canine teeth as sinister, thinking an attack is underway. But when Dr. Bob smiles, which he often does—toothy, slurpy, head shaking, silly as hell—it's an expression of genuine joy, unusual for a dog and getting more so for humans. Dr. Bob greets all friendly smelling strangers by bursting into tail wags, snorts, and fang-popping idiotic grins. Just as quickly, his expression changes to don't-give-a-damn aloofness if he meets fearful, guarded humans. He doesn't engage, he just doesn't bother to look at low-energy sorts, once he's categorized whatever creature by scent and vibe.

* * *

Of course, Thea prefers it when she and Dr. Bob have the loft to themselves. Max at home easily distracts her, his schedule crammed with meetings. The little time they spend together is constantly being interrupted by bicoastal phone calls or fax transactions, Max having to rush off to promotional events and parties that Thea simply can't bear attending anymore, after that one excruciatingly stuffy event she'd conceded to when they first got together. Now, Max's loft has become her private haven. Max hardly uses it for anything but to change clothes when he's in the city. He says he doesn't mind Thea's aversion to entertaining. "It's easier for both of us," he concedes, "you're so punk." There are plenty of events to keep his many business associates and him hopping, nonstop, no matter which coast Max is on.

This last time he's left for a worldwide premiere in L.A. Thea isn't sure Max will even recognize her when he gets back. She doesn't even know who she is, not really. Max has always backed her up though, so Thea is pretty sure when he returns this time things won't be awkward. Something inside her stays calm, stays focused on getting to Exchange Views early every morning, staying positive, and remembering how supportive Max has always been.

Dr. Bob laps noisily at his water bowl in the travertine and diamond-black granite kitchen as Thea thinks of Max returning the next day. It has taken all her strength and courage, focusing on how to start changing her habit of getting high. Sophia is helping her to recognize the need to create new, good habits to replace the old ones of using and getting out of her head. She hasn't had time to think about Max at all these past days. She's been too busy learning how to stay positive, and not picking up no matter how rotten she feels. Thea knows she wouldn't have been able to do any of this without Sophia.

Whether meeting her briefly at the morning meeting, going out for a long chat over coffee afterward, or talking on the phone any time during the day or night, Sophia is guiding Thea on how to stay clean and sober. Right now, Thea goes to the phone and punches in Sophia's number. An answering machine picks up with Sophia's no-nonsense, sweet soft twang.

"Ah, hi, Sophia, it's me, Thea," she says into the receiver. "I don't know what to say, except I'm doing what you told me to do, to call you and, uh, here I am. I haven't had anything to drink and I didn't get high either today, so I guess I'm okay. So that makes it a good day, right? Talk to you soon, bye."

Thea has made the same call five, six, sometimes seven times a day, each day and night, for the last two weeks. Thea swears she feels like making the next call to Sophia's machine as soon as she hangs up, just to hear herself say aloud, "I'm not getting high right now." And then later, she'll do it again when the craving-Itch returns, like a trained strike force.

Loud alarms keep ringing in Thea's ears. She lies on the bed. Her newly awakening nerves scream stereophonically in her head. As each new emotion arises, she feels like she's a gasping fish just hooked—desperate and jumpy, crazily flopping for breath, hauled onto a too-sunny dock to dry up and croak. Her feelings are killing her. Thea knows she can't get out of her head, get high. She's groping, wishing for another chance at life. Not yet aware that her sensory perceptions are temporarily out of whack. She tries to remember Sophia's instructions: "No matter what—don't use!" She feels out of order, as if her brain cells are being yanked out, aired out, and put back in an entirely different order.

When she gets up to make herself a tea, Dr. Bob follows her. With a grunt, he lies on a rug close to her, beside the king-size futon bed she falls into, on which she hasn't lain for the entire time Max has been away. Shaking from apprehension as she thinks about Max's return, she eases under the sheets of the humongous bed. Its firmness feels strangely unfamiliar, although she's slept and made love with Max in it for well over a year.

I'm not going to think of anything but changing my life. I can do that much, she reminds herself.

As Thea drifts off to another fitful night of troubled sleep, she tries not to let scary thoughts gain ground in her randomly shifting mind. She drifts off anticipating going to Exchange Views as soon as she awakens the next morning. She needs to see Sophia and the other recovering people. That big room beneath the towers is the only place where she can breathe easy. It's where she's learning to live as a sober person. And she'll get to talk to Sophia, her angel with the amethyst pendant at her neck.

* * *

"You're doing great, kiddo," Sophia says, sitting in their favorite breakfast spot a couple blocks from the World Trade Center. Day eighteen for Thea has started off as all previous ones: listening to and talking with others who, like herself, are learning to live naturally, without chemical highs.

"I feel pretty good today. It usually doesn't get bad until nighttime," Thea admits.

"Well, that's when you pick up the phone and call me, or some other sober woman, right?"

"Yeah, I try."

"Listen, Thea, I've not told you too much about me because we've been focusing on you, kid, each time we get together. You're not shaking so much now. Interested in a bit of my story?"

"Sure. You don't even look like you ever had a problem."

Sophia's lilting glee sounds so innocent to Thea's ears after years of barroom sneers and snide asides from sardonic pals.

"I'm a pill freak and an alchie, that's who I am," Sophia says. "It's important for me to say that, so I never forget. Being a nurse, it's pretty darn easy for me to hide stashes of this and that, every time I dispense the morphine, the codeine, Percodan, or Dilaudid."

"Yeah, you told me you're not just a boozer."

"Right. I'm a cross-the-board addict."

Thea nods, glad to know she has even more in common with Sophia. She has to force herself to relate to anyone whose addiction is exclusively with alcohol. That's so restrictive and old-fashioned, Thea believes, in this modern age of better living through chemistry.

"I've always had a weight problem," Sophia goes on. "When I was a teen I started using diet pills, the kind you get over-the-counter. By the time I finished nursing school I was pretty hooked on uppers for the day and downers to get to sleep. Booze came in when I started partying with sorority sisters, up at Cornell. It's a pretty deadly mix, booze and pills. I had to have my stomach pumped more times than I can recall. Even still, I considered myself somewhat of an expert about mixing my highs and lows and not getting too deep in my own poo."

Thea blinks hard at Sophia's quaint euphemism. "We're like alchemists, aren't we?" Thea says. "Mixing and balancing, always trying to get the perfect high. I've always done mind-expanding drugs along with drinking. I was weaned on the Haight Ashbury scene—grass, acid, mushrooms, peyote—all-natural stuff until coke drove everyone out into the snow, like we were Eskimos in the Arctic."

"And you started drinking when, Thea, your teens, right?"

"Yeah, around fifteen."

"So here you are, thirty-three, and after nearly twenty years of addiction, you're starting a whole new way of life. Proud of yourself, kiddo?"

"Are you kidding? I'm way too freaked to be proud," Thea grimaces. "I'll be happy if I can just get through the next hour. I guess I'm stuck on feeling sorry for myself. I still think about calling up old pals, scoring some toot, smoking a joint, going to the liquor store, getting some Mr. Mount Gay to lean on. Tell you the truth Sophia, I'm happy just to be breathing."

"That's good, kid, that's perfect. We don't have to go back to what we used to be like, not even in our memories, if we stay in the moment. We have to learn to stay in the light."

"The light?"

"Yeah, the truth, the love. The opposite of self-loathing, when we used to live in the darkness of despair. We begin by learning to love ourselves one tiny step at a time. That's how it happens, changing something bad like our self-abuse into a good healthy addiction, like self-love. That's how we get free from destructive addictions that either kill us or our spirits. All compulsive behavior, which addiction is, leaves us, little by little, by replacing our bad compulsions with new, better ones. Like hanging with other sober people, and going to recovery meetings, and developing other good habits. But first we have to be ready to change. And open to being helped."

"Help. From other people you mean?" Thea says.

"Yeah, sure. But other kinds of help, too."

"Oh, you mean the God stuff we talk about at the meetings, right?"

"Not necessarily, kiddo. God as in 'the next right thing.' I'm more into you finding your own HP that you're comfortable with."

"Higher Power?"

"Exactly. When you have a relationship with HP, God becomes more personal than some kind of outside rescue operation. We learn to cooperate spiritually—with our *own HP*. Not someone else's."

"Well I haven't a clue how to do *that*."

Silent for a moment, they sip from warm coffee cups. The buzz of the restaurant keeps the serious tone of their conversation at a functional level. Sophia speaks:

"I'm talking about extracurricular help, in addition to what we talk about in the rooms. In my line of work, nursing, I stay with cases from when a person is given an incurable diagnosis to their death—and beyond that even."

"Beyond? What do you mean?" Thea suddenly perks up. She is surprised by how this interests her immediately.

"My work is thanatology, the ancient name given to caregiving for the dying. In earlier times, death was treated as just another phase of life, the final one in the material plane."

"That's intense."

"Yes, it is, and I love it. I've always known helping people with their final life transition was my calling. To ease their passage, my patient is often not even aware of what I'm doing."

"I don't understand, Sophia." Thea feels edgy, like she's treading on an icy pond, not sure what's below and afraid of falling through.

"My HP allows me to work with energy that's real, but invisible. There's so much more to life, kiddo, than what we can see. I've learned to interact with certain forms of pure energy. I call them guides. Some people call them angels. But they're around us all the time, waiting to help."

"That's funny," Thea says, "because I call you my personal angel."

"You're sweet, Thea. We have to be open to this realm, that's all I'm saying. Sometimes my patients and I work together with these guides, and other times, if a patient is resistant to the idea, they don't have to know about the work I do for their easeful transition. Especially if a patient is in distress, angry, or blocked by negativity. Fear blocks the magic of life more than anything. Fear can be reversed if a person is willing to try. But anger, one of the masks that fear wears, is usually the result of strong resentments. Still, the work continues between the patient's guides and me even after that person has left us. Died, I mean."

Thea is thinking Sophia is the one who's more than she appears. *What is it with me,* Thea marvels. *First that kook, Valala, and now another nut case?* Slumped over her coffee, she doesn't know what to think about her new friend, who'd seemed so nice, so perfectly right in the head—up to now.

Sophia continues talking, oblivious to Thea's resistance. "When terminally ill people are ready to pass over to the other side, they draw to them even more sources of energy than usual that arrive to help them make their transition. It makes their journey much smoother."

Thea hasn't a clue what to say. Half of her wants to jump up and run away. But she sits still. Waits for Sophia to take another sip of coffee. She decides to stay put. She'll hear this woman out. *Be open,* Thea thinks. *Sophia has been a great help to me, remember that. Maybe I'm not hearing right.* Thea tries to listen more carefully to every word Sophia is now saying.

"I start by talking to the patient about how I see energy sources all around them. Some people are open to it, and that's always nice. Some of them aren't so open, so then I have to do my work when they're asleep, but I still do it."

"What kind of work?" Thea asks, trying not to conjure up an image of Sophia hovering over some sick person's bed, putting a spell on them with those long, glistening apple-red fingernails.

"I communicate with my patients' guides. I ask them to help the person, to help me to help them. Sometimes it's very specific stuff. Like how one patient needed help making a reconciliation with her estranged daughter. The daughter needed to understand that her mother's physical time was coming to an end fairly soon. There was no time to be diplomatic; real firm action had to be taken. And it happened! Believe me, *that* was nothing short of a miracle in that particular case. The daughter had held a huge grudge against her mother for decades. You'd be surprised by the results we get from this kind of asking for help. One time I needed help after a patient died before he had the chance to tell his children where the family's safety deposit key was."

"Really?"

"His guide told me where it was so I could tell his heirs."

Thea is stunned. She looks at Sophia, who smiles as sweetly as the Virgin Mary, looking as pure as a flower, as trustworthy as a new sober friend, which to Thea's mind is not as predictable as it was before this.

"I don't know what to say, Sophia, I'm just, just—"

"Blown away," Sophia offers.

"I'll say. This is hard stuff to believe."

"Acknowledging that there is unseen energy that affects our lives is where I started. You don't have to believe anything. All you have to do is be open. Use whatever energy makes itself available to you, and see what happens. Let your own experience show you what's real and what isn't. Tapping the unseen forces is more immediate and way more possible for people who are on the verge of leaving this material world. People who are dying get a choice. Their guides present themselves, in sometimes subtle ways, sometimes quite shocking ways. The choice is always ours to accept their help. But for a dying person, they're much more, shall we say, desperate for help. They often choose to be open to the invisible world *before* they re-enter it themselves. Or they can resist. Believe me, resisting is a lot more uncomfortable. The spiritual discomfort of leaving their body, when a person resists, is excruciating."

"What do you mean?"

"People are scared of losing their life, something that's only on loan to them."

"Death has always been a downer, Sophia," Thea says. "Since forever."

"For those who choose that way of thinking, yes. But it doesn't have to be. People who choose to embrace the mystery of life can eliminate the separation between life and death, the known and the unknown—that exists only in our minds. Those people who believe in help from the other side are the ones who relax and let go so easily. Their death becomes an exultant event. It can be the actual highlight of a person's life, believe it or not. One lady told me, before she departed, that since she'd had a lifelong trust in the unseen spiritual world, her physical death was something she'd been looking forward to her entire life. Her eyes became brilliant, filled with wonder and astonishment as I sat next to her while she was transitioning. She described to me what she saw at that final stage, until she couldn't speak any longer."

Thea squirmed. "Sophia, this is weird for me to hear. I don't think I'm sober enough for this."

Sophia giggles. "Oh, but I think you are, kid. You may not know it yet, but I can see your guides already around you. Besides, don't you want to know what makes me tick, what my life is dedicated to? That's the difference about being sober. We start to embrace others as equal to ourselves. Without sobriety, we never have deep relationships. I know some people can't handle the unseen dimension. But you're an artist! All good artists are in touch with the true source of creativity. That's the kind of unseen energy I mean. It's not just for the dying. The unseen realm is the source of creativity and inspiration we can all tap into, if we choose. If we're sober. That's what our HP is: a source of wisdom bigger than ourselves. It's the same source where creativity comes from, that allows artists, or inventors, to discover new ideas. The imaginative process is in cahoots with the unseen realm, you see?"

Thea's eyes stay glued to the table as she softly says, as if repeating from memory, "A bridge between the seen and unseen worlds."

"What's that?" Sophia didn't catch Thea's mumbled words. The noisy morning rush is in its grand finale at Bert's Coffee Shop.

"Oh," Thea looks up. "It's something I was just remembering. Something I heard when I was a kid. It was really weird because no one was around when I heard it. Someone whispered my name when I was doing dishes as a little kid one day, and told me I'd help others to bridge the worlds between the known and the unknown—whatever that means."

"That's exactly what I'm talking about," Sophia smiles and nods her head. "You've been working with these energies all along … but now you're becoming aware of it."

Thea leans closer to Sophia as she replies, "Maybe you're right. When I was a kid I used to dream I would grow up and be able to help others understand, somehow—and believe in the magic of life. The powerful things not so easy to see, hear, smell, touch. But then—I guess I forgot about it."

"Maybe you'll start remembering," Sophia says, "now that you've recalled that much. Phew! That's a pretty direct message, kiddo."

"But I forgot, until just now."

"Doesn't matter."

"So, what am I supposed to do now? And what the hell is that supposed to mean, being a bridge? It doesn't mean anything to me, really."

"Maybe not being the actual bridge. Maybe you just guide people to it, like a bridge tender helps to lift and lower it when folks need to cross rivers and big bodies of water. It's a sign, Thea. You were given a sign, back when you were a kid. It'll mean something someday, when you're ready for further communication. You're just beginning to learn to trust your own self, kiddo, and by that I do mean your higher self, your *inner connection* to HP. When the time's right you'll figure out what your childhood message means."

"I don't understand, Sophia." Thea looks around, antsy with frustration.

"I mean," Sophia draws closer, puts her elbows on the table, "that you've awakened a memory that's very special. I believe lots of children have access to their guides. I hear children say this all the time. But most of us forget as we get older. We become jaded, confused, block out the simple reason of why we're here. In my line of work, I help a person make their final life transition, when they're most open to the invisible realm. Our senses become sharpened then, our perceptions way more acute. Much more than at any other time, except when we are young children and we're closer, just having come from the source ourselves. Dying people, you see, have acute senses. They're wide open then, more than usual times—to what the guides are offering."

"So you're saying it's possible, even if a person isn't dying, to be aware of and communicate with the invisible, spiritual realm?" Thea wants to trust her. "To be open to these, ah, guides?"

"Right. Our guides are here all the time. Some of us work with them regularly. Other folks are totally closed to them. Closed minds and closed hearts are dangerous. That's how judgment and wars happen between neighbors or between cultures. That's how evil takes over human behavior:

when back and forth connections become completely severed between the two realms. How permeable the separation is between the seen and unseen depends entirely on each individual, whether they're open to receiving any form of unseen assistance. Call it wisdom, not just intuition."

"What if a person's not open?" Thea says, thinking of Big Sue.

"Lots of people aren't, and that's a fact. Anyone in active addiction can't. They may think they are, but it's impossible to make that leap of faith."

"Why?"

"Because chemicals alter our natural state—our mind's innate ability—to connect to the unseen realm."

"Oh."

"Even though in primitive cultures people often take divination drugs, like peyote or psychotropic concoctions to reach the unseen world, the effects of these mind-expanding experiences are transitory. The connection only lasts as long as the drug's effect does. In sobriety, kiddo, we get to connect all the time."

"Wow."

"Yes, wow. And the permeable wall between our world of solids and the unseen world of pure energy is shut closed with chemical substances or, and this is most people's case, any intense emotional distress. Like fear and anxiety, confusion or mistrust. Our natural consciousness shuts down to the Unseens then."

Thea is completely tongue-tied. Finally, she admits, "I'm lucky I even remember my name, from all the drugging I've done."

Sophia smiles knowingly. She sits back in her overstuffed bouncy seat. Her bright eyes seem unfailing in their kindness.

"Haven't you been telling me about strange lights you've noticed lately?" Sophia's head begins bobbing up and down as if to a rhythm only she can hear.

Thea stares at Sophia, wondering, questioning. No longer a sworn disbeliever.

120 THE BRIDGE TENDER

The Wave of Power

15

That very night Thea is lying on the couch in her darkened living room. She's watching silvery lights bouncing off the many shiny surfaces within the loft, mixing with reflections coming in from the glowing city outside the wall of windows, the overall effect creating an intricately webbed pattern of moving lights that she's tracing on the walls and the floor, as if looking for more clues. She'd been lying there for almost an hour, thinking, following the sparkly patterns, watching beams of reflected neon and incandescent lights flooding into the windows, wondering if this dancing light pattern is real or a made-up vision, resulting from Sophia's talking about guides and other phenomenally unbelievable things, as she was that morning.

She stops wondering and slips … somewhere else.

In this state of quiet peace, a waking-trance overcomes her. Perhaps the light has enticed her and hypnotized her unwittingly. Thea has a numbing feeling of being half human, half spirit. A strange, ominous half-ness runs through her veins, changing her, preparing her, melting her rigidity into something intangible, rather than the formed, pretty useless thing she'd lately suspected herself to be. Thea feels herself lift from her restraints, as if from outside herself. Suddenly she's in, but wonders if she's sometimes *outside* her body. She has a sensation, like she's witnessing the birth of her own bravery. Completely aware of this happening, she agrees to continue. She's not freaking out. She's watching. Observing. Seeing. Aware of being willing to participate in the most profound of things—because she somehow knows she'll discover more about what it means to truly be alive. No longer stifling her Itch, she allows it to be the guide.

* * *

Thea's heart thump-thump-thumps with anticipation. Listening to her heartbeat, she looks around and discovers she's standing on a familiar seashore, surrounded by unknown yet strangely decipherable figures. All around her, she realizes, are barely visible, half-recognizable figures, crowding up to her as if trying to protect her. From what? And then she sees it.

Such a disturbing, bestirring sight, far off on the horizon! A wave—tall as the sky, big as the world itself! Who could imagine such a thing? But Thea keeps on listening to her rhythmic drumbeat heart, slipping deeper into the delicious state of half-here, half-there, where dreaming becomes obediently lucid.

Her vision is of a mile-high killer of nations, an unbelievable tsunami that Thea knows is coming right for her! Instead of running away—which she knows is out of the question because, after all, she is in her dreaming self—the wall of water rushes with frightening speed toward her.

From outside her body, Thea sees herself being sucked up into the wave, up a vertical tunnel of irrefutable power. All around her is turmoil, thunderous sounds, water restrained and funneled into one inconceivable, powerful upliftment. Thea remains motionless within the weird calm inside of the uprising wave because—it feels safe. She feels nestled within its inner power, untouched by the wave's outer violence, and is one with, *a part of* its calm inner strength. She allows the wave of power to do what it must with her. Motionless, as all around, outside herself, everything swirls in tumultuous crescendos—she knows her very life depends on completely cooperating with the ferocious energy she's been sucked deeply into.

She allows the wave to do with her what it wants. She is absolutely powerless. She's become one with the enveloping majesty of this formidable wave, yet she's inside it and outside her own beingness at the same time. Thea commands herself to be completely still. She does not resist. Dreaming Thea is empowered by surrendering to the overwhelming power of this wave that has come to fetch her. And by her surrendering, she is untouched by the wave's danger. She absorbs its ferocity and uses that strength to dive deeper into Stillness. Trusting. Surrendered to its unknowable energy.

✵ ✵ ✵

When she opens her eyes, Dr. Bob is looking at her, standing as close as he can get, hugging the couch, yet not touching her. Standing watch over her, something he does. She arises and soon he hears the rattle of keys when she opens the front door, calling him.

"Hey, man, let's go for our walk," Thea says and grabs his leash.

Everything about this morning feels different. They return from a brisk walk when it isn't yet six. Somehow she's still not craving to get high—a fact that stuns her more than anything—other than the cup of steaming coffee she walks into her studio with. She turns on the overhead lights. Dawn hasn't yet cracked the veneer of winter's darkness. Thea walks over to a blank sheet that's been waiting, untouched, since she bought the pricey paper at Pearl Paint weeks before. Grabbing a brush she mixes some paint, burnt sienna, with lots of liquid. Dr. Bob slowly walks in, parks himself and patiently waits. He sits with his head cocked and watches as Thea sketches with a commodious bristle brush a huge spiraling form, the wave, and all the details she'd seen in the dream she'd just had. As she sketches, the shape of the wave takes form. Thea remembers details of the extraordinary things the wave showed her, as she puts more paint onto the white paper.

She creates the known presences standing beside her, watching, waiting for the wave to hit. She remembers and outlines the immense wall of water hovering over her. Thea fills the blankness, capturing the furious energy of being sucked up into the wave: recalling the strong sense of freedom, after surrendering, that she'd experienced; sketching other creatures that were there: the fish, detached sea fans, a swimming tiger that'd also been caught in the wave's gentle-on-the-inside embrace. Her brush dances over the heavy Arches rag paper. She paints as if still inside the vision that is so real, the way prophetic dreams can be head-bangers. She paints her hands tightly clenched at her sides as her floating body remains absolutely still in the wave's anti-gravity pull upward, knowing that if she moves this way or that, she'll surely be killed by the force of the water—that lifts her so mightily, so frighteningly high above the horizon of Earth! Thea captures the safe knowing-feeling she had, best she can, the way she trusted this wave that brought her so far off the ground, away from the beach and her faceless companions, away from the turmoil of Earth far below. Thea remembers and paints herself in another position, in another quadrant of the work. Peering out from the wave, able to see a little red sports car winding on a cliffside road, far below her. She sees pastures and farmland of the surrounding vineyard countryside spread out in all directions.

When the composition feels complete, Thea starts filling in the shapes she's made with colors mixed from tubes and jars, making broad strokes to depict the incomprehensible power she experienced, tucked safely within this dreamt wave of hers.

16

Max calls the next morning to say his trip has to be extended again by at least a week. "Sorry, babe. That's show biz."

Thea is relieved. The more time alone the better. At quarter to seven she walks the short distance south to Exchange Views. Afterward, she goes with Sophia for coffee, enjoying their frequent face-to-face conversations. Along with the usual well-heeled bunch in the basement today, Thea meets two new nonconformists to the penguin code: an offbeat couple named Jerry and Frieda, who, with their black on black, torn and paint-stained clothes, are two more artists in a crowd of a hundred businessmen and -women.

As usual, Thea sits next to Sophia.

Each day things are getting better for Thea, thanks to Sophia. She is like a dive buddy—something every serious diver knows one needs—a dive partner to Thea's handling the shark-infested waters of getting straight. Everything about getting sober is weird and terrifying, this alien place: *Planet Sober*, as Sophia calls it.

Thea is happy to return to the loft every morning. In between his getting spaced-out, tickled into samadhi under the ficus tree, she swears she sees Dr. Bob wink at her reassuringly, during these trying, reentry to Planet-Sober times. Nights are worse—long, piercing nights—when her body painfully detoxes itself. Sometimes she thinks of tying herself up, just to keep from going out to score on the streets. Often she's unable to sleep, and when she can, such dreams! But nothing comes close to the enormous sense of wonder Thea sustains in her waking state by painting it, over and over, after that monster wave took her far, far away.

Thea soon realizes that being straight is possibly the best, the most potent and mind-blowing high she's ever had; a glimpse of joy that takes her absolutely by surprise. Amazing, she thinks, that I never gave life a chance before, without booze or drugs. Who'd ever guess life *au naturel* could be so stimulating, so thrilling? It's like a new, powerful drug. One I won't ever have to withdraw from.

She becomes elated with this weird, best high of all, called ... being *normal*. She thinks, *This must be the proverbial pink cloud I've heard so much about. Is this what they mean by* serenity?

Thea is determined to do whatever Sophia suggests. She clings to the merest hint Sophia offers to help her across the many turbulent pitfalls of recovery.

Soon the cornucopia of realizations overwhelms her as she awakens to the barrage of having feelings again for the first time since she was an alcoholic teenager.

At their coffee dates Sophia says things like: "Other than not getting high—and saying goodbye to all your friends who use and the places where you used to hang out—don't change anything for now. Let Nature take its course."

And oh how Thea cringes at those stupid aphorisms Sophia uses. "*Time takes time*. What the fuck's *that* supposed to mean?" she implores another explanation from Sophia.

Everything she learns from Sophia and the flock at Exchange Views works its magic on her. Thea wants to get well more than anything she's ever cared about.

She feels the Kali rock deep in the pocket of the same camel-hair coat she's worn almost continuously since her first recovery meeting. Every time her fingers wrap around the faceted crystal Valala gave her, Thea feels intense heat emanating from it. She examines it, wondering if it is somehow battery operated, or if the old witch herself is sending signals through it. Times like these, Thea remarks at her own crazy paranoia. "You're weird," Thea chastises herself. Then she forgets about Valala as the crystal's heat disperses through her palm, down her arm, into her chest cavity.

On this particular morning, after saying goodbye to Sophia at the street corner where they always separate, Thea leans against a building and brings the glass-clear thing out to regard it in the early morning sunlight.

She turns the crystal and feels it emanate heat. She brings it up to her eyes and focuses on it as if some secret is locked inside its caged light. Within the depths of the crystal, Thea notices spectrums of rainbow colors, how they change at every slight turn of her hand. A fissure that first appears solid, and in the next instant after a half-degree turn—it's gone. Illusory geometry, prismatic fanfares, phantoms, fleeting images: she sees all of these within the clear stone she holds. Thea looks around and realizes no one on this busy street, West Broadway, could possibly know how drawn into the crystal's mysterious world she is.

I'll try painting this visual phenomenon, she promises, pocketing the crystal, quickly walking back to Reade Street. Later, she makes small sketches, attempting to capture the prism patterns she saw that morning within the Kali rock.

Other things are capturing Thea's imagination. Hearing so many wild stories coming out of ordinary-looking people's mouths at Exchange Views, she tries to relate to them all—as bizarre, as far-fetched as each is. What a cast of characters she's meeting. Such unheard-of events, and real people who no longer drink actually having lived through death-defying bottoms—it stuns her. Stacks of character sketches made with charcoal on thick rag paper now fill every inch of Thea's studio, tacked to walls, covering floors and every flat surface as new work starts to take shape, flowing from her like a rushing river.

Thea begins a painting. It's an amalgam of several sketches she made after hearing the story of a woman called Linda. At each of the meetings, a different person shares about how life was both before and after they got sober. Linda's life makes Thea's own feel like a boring soap opera.

"Sounds like she fell into a snake pit," Thea whispered, but Sophia doesn't take her eyes off Linda. She nods to Thea and winks. Up at the front of the room Linda is chain-smoking skinny cigarettes, her sandy blond hair showing dark roots all the way to the back of the room, where Thea and Sophia sit.

"My husband beat me," Linda's husky voice drones on after a preceding litany of hard-to-believe mishaps. "Then I got cervical cancer and he skedaddled. And just after I made my getaway from Queens and moved me and my sister's family of four into a rotting piece-of-crap trailer in Georgia, as far as I could get from the hell we were in here in New York—as soon as I flipped the switch of the A/C unit—the wiring caught on fire and the whole thing burnt to the ground. And we hopped right back in the car and I moved them back here, to my cousin's in the Bronx."

Nobody says a word in the dead-still room. Nobody's story is ever pleasant in Exchange Views, and this one, really, is no worse than usual. Up front, Linda smiles for the first time since she began speaking ten minutes ago.

"But you know what? I'm glad, I really am. I ended up at a shelter and that's where I went to my first *Angels Anonymous* meeting." The group hoots at what Linda calls them. Thea nods and smiles, pretty much knowing what Linda means.

All that horror of Linda's—the fire, the beatings, the poverty, illness, despair, and hopelessness—Thea will later make into quick sketches. Then she'll collage them together into an abstract composition, using dark, violent colors for this sad story, with a few streaks of bright yellow and orange depicting how the woman got to discover light at the end of her burdensome tunnel of catastrophe.

Then Thea starts to piece the sketches together to form a collage of another's recovery story. Ned is a neatly dressed businessman who confessed during the meeting that he'd been molested as a boy by a priest. As she sketches, sitting on the floor of her sky-lit studio, she starts to weep. She can't help it; it is too close to what happened in her own life. "I hate you, you monster misdirected sexual shit!" Thea cries at the painful memories she isn't ready to unlock yet. But her shattered heart has been touched deeply by

Ned's honest and raw-sore story. "Look what you do to innocent children!" Thea sobs to the familiar monster in her studio she's trying to capture in charcoal, not even knowing why, as the pain of her brothers' abuse begins to rear up from its lifelong hiding place. "The cruelest thing is, I don't even know what it's like to not hurt. Shame and brokenness have been my shield," she speaks to the works and no one else.

Thea cries as she draws and paints and sketches and thinks about how art helps bring all these pieces of her torn-up life together. She's chosen to work on other people's stories, not her own. Through others, she's learning to contact her deeply buried secrets. The excavation process has begun, in proxy.

The story that makes Thea's mind brake to a halt, though, is told by a woman named Eva.

"You can see I clean up pretty good," Eva begins. "Today I'm a financial planner and a pro bono lawyer right here on Wall Street. But I was a homeless person once. Look at me now, folks." The room teeters in amusement. "I was born in Tennessee, a half-breed Cherokee. My mother was a true-blue alcoholic Injun. I never knew my dad. Mom didn't talk about him, whoever he was. We traveled all over in her car before we headed West. At age fifteen, I finally got smart and got away from Mom and started living on my own. Don't ask me how I did it, I just did what I had to. By the time I was eighteen I ended up in Albuquerque, strung out on heroin, downing any jug of cheap wine I could find. I got picked up by the cops for about the tenth time. While I was held in some god-forsaken hole, I was gang-raped by three ugly motherfuckers-in-blue in some nowhere town in New Mexico."

A shudder goes through the entire room. Thea managed to escape into adulthood with only her brothers' assorted transgressions to haunt her, nothing this violent.

"But I had my revenge on those men," Eva says, not missing a beat, with no emotion of any kind. She pauses a moment. She looks from side to side of the crowded basement where suddenly a pin could be heard dropping.

"As soon as I got out of jail for thieving, I found them, one by one. And I shot them with their own guns. No one caught me till I was twenty, after

I'd killed all three of them. I don't regret doing it, I'm telling you here and now. But it would have been nicer if they hadn't done what they did to me that day in the holding cell. But they did. So I did what I had to do. I've made peace with my Higher Power over it. I've made my amends for having killed. When I went to trial, by the grace of God I was given a sympathetic judge. I was found guilty of three counts of third-degree manslaughter, and, due to the circumstances of the case, all three sentences I got to serve concurrently. So I served my time, five years in all, in the State of New Mexico's Penitentiary for Women. And that's where I found you guys, the Fellowship. I've been sober ever since and now, after law school, I get to defend other men and women who are unfairly treated by life and the law."

Thea's mind has been ambushed and roped-up when Eva stops talking. The rest of the meeting goes by in a blur. Sitting over coffee afterward, Thea tries to say something to Sophia but it comes out all wrong.

"How can someone get away murdering three men like that?" Thea hears herself say instead of, *How can three men possibly act so unhumanly?*

"Life is a mystery, kid," Sophia says, slowly nodding. "It does seem unbelievably brazen. But the judge must have weighed the facts, and that's what happened. We speak honestly here. We trust each other's stories to be true."

"So you believe her, Sophia? It seems so far-fetched."

"Life is stranger than fiction, kid. Nothing's impossible on Planet Sober. After hearing people like Eva for the last seven years, I keep coming back to listen to people trying to live right. Pretty soon you'll realize there's no limit to what a person can do when we're aligned with our HP."

Thea listens, as she always does in Sophia's company. Although some of what she tells Thea she can't understand, she trusts Sophia. Back at her studio in Max's loft, however, Thea works out her questions, the ever-present doubts about hearing horror stories one can never imagine making up, but only read about in the sauciest of novels. Yet the people she meets and hears at Exchange Views—folks who are rebuilding their shattered lives after being driven to self-destruct by compulsive, addictive behavior—are now Thea's provocative new subjects in her studio work. She realizes that by making this kind of personal, intimate art she has a better chance to figure out—at least in a subconscious and symbolic, if not a thoroughly logical manner—exactly *why* she'd become a person so addicted to darkness.

It'll all come together, in time, Thea hopes as she splashes a big dollop of vermillion onto the piece she's working on. The sketches she's already drawn of Eva's grisly murder spree are glued onto the blank sheet of paper that Thea now fills with brush loads of desert colors, mauves and pinks, the madder and sienna tones of New Mexico. Finally, she adds big streaks of cadmium red for the blood fest Eva so honestly shared with the stunned basement group.

17

Thea doesn't pick up calls from Fast Forward or Harry the Harelip, Stretch, or Bad Patch, anyone asking about the band, or anyone else she used to get high with. She takes calls only from Sophia and only from Max when she feels up to it. Other than a few folks at Exchange Views she's befriended, the only other people she wants to talk to are Junkyard Trinnie and Maly, neither an addict of anything but inspired creativity. She misses them. But she's waiting to see them until she feels stronger and surer; they mean so much to her.

For now, remembering them will have to do. Thea is certain of only one thing when she thinks of them: both Junkyard and Maly are completely intoxicated by, and in awe of, the experience of life. Since meeting them, Thea heard many times about their plan to return to Junkyard's native island to run what they already decided to christen the One Blood Culture Center.

"It be an I-ree sound to me, all peoples in the world being *one blood*," Junkyard once explained.

The pair share a dream and work hard to achieve it. Every time Thea was with them they talked ceaselessly about how they wanted to bring to those who might never be exposed, the joys of art and culture that Junkyard and Maly had discovered since leaving their respective island homes to live in the art capital of the world. The pair wanted their future center to celebrate the visual arts, theater, set and costume design, poetry and puppetry, dance, music and mime, along with all creative aspects of the exuberant potpourri of island life.

By far, Junkyard and Maly were the most fun people she'd ever been around, Thea remembers with a warm wide feeling in her chest.

Not a jealous bone existed in Maly's vigorous body. Junkyard's and her commitment to each other was as steadfast as their delight in being socially conscious artists, having found each other in the heart of Manhattan, coming from such far-off points of the compass as they did. In a world that relies on the influence of public art, whether as a massive sculpture in a park, or as subtle as advertising on the subway, these two are stars in the galaxy of the creativity that thrives in the Big Apple.

As their friendship grew, Junkyard felt brotherly when he teased Thea about the hordes of men he'd seen her attract with her act and in the streets. Of course, Junkyard knew his wife made any man in his right mind salivate. Maly's full figure, usually wrapped in swishy, finely woven fabrics, and her tender almond eyes always shining with a mystic's innate love of life, affected everyone around her. Maly's face mirrored legends of brown-skinned, luminous beauties for which gilded and bejeweled marble temples of long ago were built. Junkyard would gloat, rewarding his pride by saying to whomever was within earshot, words meant to bring a pleased flush to his devoted one's full beet-colored lips.

"There be not'ing hotter than the sun," he'd playfully intone, "and that's a fact, not'ing! And there be not'ing cooler than the moon, for certain. Well mohn, me be hot like the sun and my womb-an be the coolness of the full-full moon that quenches my burning fire. Not'ing more, not'ing less." With that, Junkyard threw his head back and belly roared like a crazy man, wild with delight and chest-bulging pride, all rolled together.

Of all her new friends, these two exotics are the only ones who were never addicted to anything other than creating inspiring things, and that, Thea figures, is an okay, life-affirming habit even Sophia would approve of. The couple's unpretentious ways, their curious intellects, epitomize the harmonious blend of eccentricity and vitality. They both fascinate and enthrall Thea, more than Max, way more than Fast Forward, and—well, she can't say anything about Big Sue other than she was her savior. Sue, that big lug of a woman, who took Thea under her wing from the day they first met. Thea can now admit that she recognizes herself in her two like-minded pals, Junkyard and Maly. Thea's thoughts have turned often to them. She can't wait to show off her new sober self to them, but—she'll wait till she feels strong enough, sure enough of herself.

* * *

Thea is working in her studio, hands busy with materials, mind immersed in the process, yet she's thinking, thinking, pondering all the while, of how crazy her life had been before, and how quickly things are changing. She continues making collages of others' pain, unable to address her own. Mixing paint, cutting and pasting sketches onto sturdy sheets of paper, arranging compositions, balancing form and shape, adding color, emphasizing movement and texture—she marvels how her work is absorbing, translating, and yes, transforming these stories of pain into her own hope and rejuvenation. Just as the series of collaged works pour out of her. Each new image is a mix-up of other peoples' cutouts of horror, of blistering relationships, of torched trailers, of regrets and shame, abused lovers and children—a separate work for each person's redemption story. Thea hunches her shoulders as she toils, feeling the sorrows of so many getting into her bones. Glad, in a perverse way, she's beginning to feel. Still, she can't name or touch what her pain bears. Disappointment? Abandonment? Sometimes she thinks she's merely played a dangerous game of courting self-annihilation for nothing more than spite. Always the rebel.

"That could be the name of my religion: Rebellionism," she scoffs to herself.

Following that thread, Thea recalls her addiction to bad relationships as she continues working in the studio. She steps back, assessing the strangely nonsensical images she pins to the wall. "I don't want to think about my own pain," she rebukes herself. "I think about others' and make art of it. Art, I can think about, not life. Anything … but my own shit!"

About that Itch.

Along with drugs came the kink. Gone now—but gone forever? she speculates—is the consuming *gotta-have-it* animal lust that used to fuel her every choice. She certainly doesn't feel sexy, not since giving up booze, pot, coke, you-name-it. And when she thinks about the men in her life, it's only the inaccessible memory of Russ that stirs her blood. Yes, she admits, that one really got under her skin. Giles, she just feels sorry for. No one but Russ came close to igniting Thea's desires, like what she instantly recognized as Junkyard Trinnie's true passion for his wife.

Thea trembles, thinking how incredibly shallow she was.

She imagines those goat-weird eyes of Max's. As she works, her mind chatters as quickly as her nervous hands fly, gluing paper, adding texture and color. Honest remembering begins to arise—and—she's horrified. She can finally admit that her and Max's mutually insincere chemistries positively exploded when they met. After she moved in, Thea found herself loathing the smooth operator who never became more than a better address to her.

18

When Max walks back into the loft and kisses her hello after nearly a month away, he ruffles Dr. Bob's bony head and gets his customary glass of chilled mineral water. Then he takes a good long look at her. Only a vague shadow remains of Fast's furious punch, but Max notices immediately.

"What's with the eye?"

That's when she tells him about Exchange Views.

"Exactly what are you saying now? That you're an alcoholic, Thea?"

"More like an all-around addict," she nods her head.

Max shakes his. His body tenses. Cords on his neck begin to pop out, ones Thea only sees when he gets really ticked off.

Max's face goes stormy, then clammy pale. A sheen breaks out on his upper lip, but he remains silent.

Thea wants to be truthful about what she's been through during Max's absence, but she doesn't say that Fast is the one who caused the shiner. Her cracked front tooth already has a temporary crown on it, so why bother even mentioning that, she figures. Thea tries to tell Max everything—except that she realizes she doesn't love him. That would be pushing honesty a bit too much. Besides, Sophia has been telling her, "No major changes the first year." There's plenty of time to come clean later, Thea figures.

Max slams his handblown water glass onto the marble countertop. "I don't need to hear this crap, Thea. You're fine!"

Biting her lip, she looks at him. She isn't surprised he can't support her need to change. Things are clearly different now. She's on a bona fide quest. And what does he see me as, she wonders? All he ever wanted was to brag about me being famous as something, punk rock star, or anything really. The truth takes her breath away. She steps backward, as if punched in the stomach.

Max speaks, "You know what your trouble is, Thea—you're fucking lazy, that's your problem. I've given you everything, everything! To you and that flea-bit mutt of yours. A home, a nice studio, time enough to become great at something—music or art, who cares?—the two things we both know you can be great at if you want. But what do you do? Piss everything away. And now you tell me you're going to those dumb-ass cult meetings? More stalling. If you ask me you're afraid of life, that's your problem, Thea."

Max storms out of the room and into his office, lined with hi-tech equipment, the latest communication hook-ups—the works—every electronic matte black gizmo a first-wave techie-slave has to have before the digital age is in full swing. With a loud thud, the thick oak door closes. A metallic bolt clicks from inside.

Thea shrugs her shoulders and looks at Dr. Bob.

"At least I told him about being an addict. I can't help it if he doesn't want to believe the truth."

The Kali rock, the clear quartz Valala gave her, stays loose in Thea's overcoat pocket, the same coat she's adopted as the dual emblem of change and also, self-protection. Each time she wears it, Thea imagines her old self melting away—like the translucent cast-off skin of a snake—whenever she takes off its protective blanket. It makes her feel safe when she goes out into the February bitterness, when she puts her hand deep into the coat's right-hand pocket and feels the comforting heat of the Kali rock.

She brings her hand up to her throat to touch Sophia's gift, an amethyst like hers. Max had already left for a day full of meetings uptown when she got up, and she's asleep already when he slips into their oversized bed later that night. *Some sexy welcome home, huh,* Thea thinks, sullen as she walks downtown in the next morning's early sun. Thea looks forward to working in her studio as soon as she gets back from Exchange Views. Maybe she'll start something new. The thought excites her. Now she's sitting in the bright living room with coffee and a cigarette as Dr. Bob naps at her feet. She's thinking over things Sophia told her at coffee that morning.

"Watch out for sex, Thea," Sophia warned. "It's going to trip you up—now that Max is back, I mean. It'll be as weird as everything else you do for the first time without being high. You'll want it or you'll loathe it. Or you'll want to do it with frogs. I'm serious! With two men at once, or a woman, or both sexes—who knows what'll turn you on? That's how it is when you're rediscovering your true sexuality. Sex is like everything else—everything's going to be different on Planet Sober."

"But I'm so turned off by Max," Thea sadly admitted.

"The world's most insidious come-on: money and power," Sophia said.

"I don't feel one bit sexy any which way," Thea said with a scoff.

"Not to worry. Just remember when it happens: Sex is a drug, a mood changer. You may not feel like it today, but when the urge takes over, watch out. Be prepared. Sex can play havoc with your peace of mind during these early days, okay, kiddo?"

It was then that her friend shared the strangest thing, something she did not understand one bit, but remembers clearly. "And one other thing about sex, Thea. A person's sexuality is mysteriously and psychically interwoven with their spirituality. The arousal of both energies within us comes simultaneously, at exactly the same time and intensity for each individual. Just remember this when you start having sexual feelings, okay? In sobriety, it means your spiritual life is being activated as well."

Thea absently touched the amethyst necklace and smiled. "Sure," she replied, not having a clue what Sophia meant.

But she knew her friend was right when she next said, "Changing your life can be pretty scary stuff."

It seemed like everything Sophia ever said turned out to be true, Thea was realizing.

Sophia always reminded Thea not to trust her feelings, "… at the beginning of their awakening from the numbness of active addiction," she clarified. Already the novelty of not getting high was beginning to wear a little thin. Without Sophia, Thea couldn't imagine how she'd ever get it, this *staying real* stuff. It was way too complicated.

But she wanted to be successful with at least one thing in her life. Why not at being natural, Thea thought, encouraging herself.

"I can stay sober for one day, this day right here," she renewed her pledge.

Thea awakens at dawn. A strange sensation creeps over her, something extra besides the sting of morning chill. She leaves the king-size bed that has sustained her but hasn't fanned any passion between her and Max, whose back is turned to her, as it has been ever since she told him she was in recovery for substance abuse. Since then their moods have rapidly crisscrossed each other. They are two ships on a collision course in the dead of a starless, foggy night.

I can barely stand it when Max talks to me, Thea admits, shivering as her feet hit the stone tiles. He doesn't converse; he lectures. He's not changed. I have. Or, I want to.

Putting on her robe, she watches Max closely as he lies sleeping. Any other time his features are too intense, his cool steely eyes way too challenging, his eyebrows strained with ever-present tension perpetuated by a steady stream of deal-making. Now asleep, buffered by the new light of dawn creeping through skinny aluminum blinds, Max really doesn't look so bad. She stands and observes the undulating valleys of his gym-buff chest, outlined against the contrasting cool gray bedsheets. She reminds herself that Max's smashing loft, his success, his having the right-sized, empty studio, were the original aphrodisiacs that had turned her on.

A vile taste fills her mouth, seeing Max sleeping before her; her shallow and moronic choice of a lover with real estate. The latest iteration. All her previous choices invisibly rush into the bedroom now, harassing her with their disgusting reminders. A shiver runs through her.

Thea gently shuts the bedroom door, shushing the surprise arousal that awakened her with an urgency she can't deny. Barefoot and stealthily, she slinks down the hallway. Where is this sexual feeling coming from? she wonders. Again, she feels ambushed by her own unknowable emotions.

It's not Max's fault, Thea thinks, quivering, but not from the cold touch of Norwegian marble.

Reaching the cavernous living room, first light blends into soft colorless patterns. Everything is still. Excitation is everywhere, inside and outside herself.

Sophia told me I would one day re-emerge—in my emotional being—right where I left off when I started getting high, at fifteen.

Thea imagines she is Rip Van Winklette, awakening from a twenty-year snooze to find that everything—everything!—is different.

I've never even touched myself … like that. There's always been others, so many others, for me to explore.

Thea scoots into the living room without disturbing Dr. Bob, who's snoring lightly on his rug over in the corner.

Today's a good day to start.

She slides onto the plush gray leather couch, where she'd camped out for three days straight in a fetal position just a month earlier. She had to figure if she was going to die, or was willing to change. With a twinge of stage fright, she now lies back among the soft cushions. Without thinking what she is doing, she follows the screeching trumpet urge of her awakened, curiously arrested, adolescent libido that is releasing itself, right there, after an eternity of suspended animation. Her sexual needs are at the controls, flying high. Her loins burn, as mysteriously as the white flag she'd seen flapping above her sick, hungover headache, the one Thea now remembers as she writhes in the exact same spot. A lifetime ago.

Closing her eyes, she parts her silk robe. Thea jumps at the first alarming firecracker she feels when she touches herself in the invisible place between her legs. It's like being shot straight through with a lightning bolt, awakening her. Then—so moist, so eager—she is curious to know this place she's never allowed herself, ironically, to explore in her incarnation as inveterate sex addict. A bolt within her unlocks. Something churns in her no-thoughts mind. *This isn't so hard.* She bolsters herself against the soft sofa. Without any difficulty, Thea proceeds to voyeur juicy seduction scenes between herself and numerous imagined partners, all in her head, trying on one ex after the other, like going shoe shopping.

The litany of lovers. None of them work. She keeps the imagining rolling.

"Russ, ah, he'll do," Thea whispers, thinking, *This is It! But wait, he's an asshole*, she suddenly remembers, for him saying, "You're too weird." *The nerve of that jerk. Pretty boys are not reliable lovers. They're such a commodity on the sex market. No, Russ won't do either,* Thea nods.

Big Sue? Wait, she's not a lesbian, and neither am I. Am I? Well, it doesn't work with her that's for damn sure. Thea squirms, trying on the next known possibility.

Up pops Hazel, definitely lesbian, a West Indian who had her way with her one drunken night. No, Thea recalls, won't do either. *Pussy lickin' ain't me.*

Nothing's working, she sighs, starting to slow her rhythmic strokes. *No one's fitting.*

But wait!—why not?

She imagines she's just met herself. Instantly, passion rises up. The flame is fed and she begins making love to her own self—not a replica but a real live duplicate she envisions is her male-female-all-sex-everywhere partner, herself—and … it works!

A convenient taboo. Imagining what's not available perfectly fits her escapade mood. Finally, she stops trying and gets to work scratching that inscrutable Itch of hers that appears at the oddest times.

She sinks further back, moaning quietly, keeping a cautious ear out in case Max gets up. Across the room, her mutt opens an eye, sniffs, and puts his head back down onto his paws. It's just Thea's scent, stronger, muskier.

Thea feels the opiate rush of the drug-sex, bee stinging the entire length of her lower limbs. She gasps as electric shocks grip her stiffened legs, quivering arms, a tensing sensation unlike any other—thrills mainlining directly to nerve centers screaming Yes! Her body converges into one big tingling nerve, ready to explode, wanting to yell aloud, willing to tear herself apart for pleasure. She throws her head back, grits her teeth, and bites her lips, trying not to cry out. Holding herself like a vice, legs apart, she presses glistening fingers over the stiff pinnacle of her femaleness—harder, faster, until the crash of the first honestly won orgasm of her life erupts all over her in glass-crashing splinters. One ripple after another. Waves of bliss, releasing, soothing, calming her Itch. Until she lies spent like a tattered book, frayed at the edges, read through and through.

How easy—no fuss, no complications, no talk, no wondering ifs or whys. No obligation. Only following an inner conductor.

Thea purrs softly. *Why has it taken so long to discover this trick?*

She *made* love to herself ... so maybe one day, Thea wonders, I might have a chance to love myself too. That's pretty different than anything I've ever felt before.

Is this what Sophia meant? When she said how sex and spirituality are as connected as twins. Both originating from the same powerful Source, yet both capable of separate and vastly different, but equal identities.

19

With each new day Thea's old life is disappearing, like snow sublimating in the strong rays of springtime. She feels like a newborn mole, soft and unformed, totally blind, vulnerable to the point of dangerous. She knows, like the snake she has tattooed on her calf, she is shedding her useless old skin of fear, as Sophia had forewarned.

"You'll feel raw and vulnerable when it happens, kid. You're growing. Hold on steady and strong, during times like these. You'll soon form a new psychic skin, one that emotionally suits you better—the new you. The old skin—and I mean your old reactions to things—aren't who you really are."

Thea listens, knowing Sophia is right. So far, everything her friend shares tips with her about how to live happily, naturally, on Planet Sober, have turned out to be true. But Thea keeps it to herself, the discovery she's made, about how thrilling it is to make love to herself. *That is too special to talk about to anyone,* Thea thinks.

Each new day, as she rubs sleep from her eyes and stretches, she looks up at the peak of rosiness in the morning sky and agrees to have one more day sober—just this one day. She can do *that*. She is beginning to remember the beauty of being alive. Coming awake after such a long slumber.

Once the gates of self-love have opened, a flood of new ideas starts gushing out of her. With Sophia's prodding, Thea stays away from Fast Forward and The Supply House, even though they continue to harass her with threatening phone messages. Max slinks around out of her way, leaving before she awakes and returning after she's fallen asleep. Her daily routine becomes simple: staying sober. She calls Sophia's machine multiple times, reporting she hasn't used that day, and with each new day the phone-ins become less and less. Whenever Sophia's busy schedule permits, they meet over coffee after Exchange Views. Occasionally they have a meal at a Thai restaurant in the Village. Thea is surprised at a remark of Sophia's as they eat, about how plump she is. How joining the gym around the corner is a waste because she never has time to go. Yet whenever the two would meet, Thea feels like she's arrived at a green oasis in the middle of a parched desert. She listens mostly, soaking up Sophia's ease in sharing the most intimate details of how she came to live so comfortably, without getting high.

"Doesn't anything bother you, Sophia?"

"Oh yeah, sure. I'd like to be fifteen pounds thinner," she says bringing the *saté* expertly up to her mouth with chopsticks. "You'd think losing a little weight would be a piece of cake after giving up drugs and alcohol, wouldn't you? Pun intended," she giggles. Then firmly adds, "I have to keep remembering that I have to heal myself first before I can help anyone else."

Thea realizes that Sophia has the right to have her weaknesses too, even though to her, she seems perfect.

After he's home for a week, Max starts asking questions about the changes he notices. Those early morning outings being one.

"They help me from using, that's all there is to it," Thea says after explaining about Exchange Views. And to his credit, that's enough for Max.

She can sense a dim light of understanding begin to creep under the closed door of his mind. During the day, he comes out of his locked office more often to talk with her, and he soon realizes he hardly knows her anymore. This sober woman he's returned to isn't the same as the punk rocker-cum-artist he knew before leaving for his latest trip.

Others are not as curious or understanding as Max. Fast Forward finally gives up phoning when Thea never returns his calls.

20

Thea keeps her routine regular: going to Exchange Views and making good sober friends, as well as making art like mad. And, with Sophia's help, not getting high and learning to stay grounded in emotional sobriety. That pretty much sums up her life.

"Why aren't you singing with The Supply House anymore, Thea; what's going on?" Max asks one day. "You never return Fast's calls. He calls me to complain about you. I thought he was your great buddy. What about your career? What about your friends? What about me? We never go anywhere because you don't want to be around people who drink or drug. Well guess what? That's pretty much the whole entire world! What am I supposed to do? I'm sleeping in my office more nights than with you. Is sex on your list of bad things to do too? What about me?"

Thea cringes as the elevator door closed on his last shouted word. To the stainless doors she waves goodbye as Max leaves for the gym before catching a flight later, back to L.A. Thea clearly realizes, *Everything is wrong here.* She was wrong to have moved in with him, even if his loft was right. And now she feels dishonest staying. That's becoming plainer to both of them with each passing day.

She crosses to the row of tall windows and looks down at the street several stories below and watches as Max rushes onto the street to flag a passing cab this crisp, early spring morning. She feels a twitch of disappointment as he opens the door of the yellow cab and throws his bag and briefcase in without looking up at her, the same as he has done since they first fell for each other. Thea suddenly sees the lie she is living. Max's flashy style actually revolts her. His designer-tasseled shoes, the slinky silk suits, his impeccably handmade English shirts—the color-coordinated Nike workout outfit he's wearing now—give her the creeps. This game of hers is getting harder to play, she knows.

I'm grateful he's providing a safe haven for my shipwrecked life, she thinks. *Besides, Sophia told me to stay put, make no changes, it's part of the recovery process.* But, she asks herself—is it worth it?

When Max gets back from this trip, just three days long, he picks up right where he'd abruptly left off, hardly having spoken to her during his absence.

"C'mon," he says after grabbing her by the hips as soon as he's back at the loft. He plants a juicy kiss right on her startled lips. "What's wrong with performing with The Supply House? You're great at it and you know it, babe. I've been thinking about what you said. Things aren't *that* bad, are they, really? I never saw you as an over-imbiber, certainly not like Big Sue or Fast. Jeez, both of those two were out to lunch. Sorry, I know you're still hurting from losing Sue. Okay, you like to get a little high sometimes, but come on, who doesn't?"

"Max," Thea says in a gentle tone, "I'm not a performer. It's just not who I am. I can only do that when I'm really schwacked out of my head. Don't you get it? Don't you get any of what I'm trying to do with my life now?"

Max doesn't and never will understand, she knows this now. Talking with Sophia and the other two she likes best at Exchange Views, Jerry and Frieda, Thea is slowly realizing that most people—those not in recovery from addiction, that is—just don't understand what she or any other recovery person has to go through. Still, it's hard to admit how bad things really are between her and Max.

In Thea's head she hears Sophia reminding her, "No major changes the first year. The huge emotional upheaval you're going through is hard enough. Stick it out with Max if you can. Believe me, I know it's not easy, kiddo. Not changing anything the first year helps you find out who you really are."

Thea wants to believe her friend. She struggles to believe all the inspiring things she's heard at Exchange Views.

She says, "I don't want to talk about it, Max, I just can't. I'm very confused these days. Can you just give me some time, please?"

Max shrugs his shoulders, grabs a bottled water from the fridge, and storms into his designer decorated office.

Instead of tormenting herself about her dead-stop career, or how she and Max don't even care for each other, Thea focuses on getting through that day ahead of her. Sometimes—when the cravings arise—it's one minute at a time. On a much deeper level she is now appreciating being unaffected by any mood-altering substances. She's seeing the results of her efforts with glimpses of what can only be called serenity. So happy is she to not live in constant fear, Thea does everything Sophia tells her to do. And sure enough, day by day, things are getting better. Remarkably so.

Sophia is there at every turn to share Thea's awakening senses, as well as the terrifying unreality that screams in her dreams at night. Slowly, Thea understands the marvelous truth that she isn't a victim. That she can actually make *wise*, meaning *sober* decisions. Sophia tells Thea everything she knows about how to live—happy, joyous, and free—on Planet Sober. After the first uncomfortable months, with the onslaught of her cravings not as tortuous as many others' she hears about at the meetings, Thea is exploring this treasured state of mind—her natural, sober mind. With Sophia's guidance, and of course her Higher Power's, she's discovering straight is way more intense, a thousand times more fun than she ever had being high, which she now realizes is her having chosen to be really low. Thea chortles. Everything she feels now, she feels intensely—whether it's something funny, sad, tragic, or sublime. Thea's feelings become as entertaining, as absorbing to her as her old rotten, drama-freak relationships used to be, as having no-HP once was.

Looking in the mirror slowly becomes easier. Thea's eye settles down. Only a slight darkness remains around the socket. A persistent dermatitis irritation lingers as a mocking effigy to her previous discontent. Her hair grows out from the hacked-off screech-straw it'd been. She starts to see a clear-eyed stranger staring back at her from the mirror, someone Thea hasn't seen since being an adolescent, but there she is, peering from behind familiar grass green eyes.

Something else is awakening deep inside Thea. A comfort zone peeking through the cloudy screen of her consciousness that is so foreign that when Thea first recognizes it she can't believe it's happening *to her*. At first, it comes for only a second or two. Then gradually, it lasts for one, then longer minutes. Eventually, Thea comes to know this unnamed feeling as a genuine, true part of herself. She feels it most deeply when she pays careful attention to what Sophia tells her to do—and doesn't argue or be rebellious of her advice.

"It's natural," Sophia says, "that nameless *sense* you speak of. It's your inner guidance, which you can connect with now. Some hear its direction as a *feeling* in their gut. Other people hear it as an inner *voice* of some kind. Still others wait, listen, and pay hyper attention to signs, which have the tendency to arrive in the strangest ways.

"Whatever way it happens, you can hear HP through yourself, or others, only when you get still and listen," Sophia assures Thea. "Everyone has a guide, an inner voice of wisdom. See? It's exactly like the invisible energy work I do with my private patients. You'll soon learn to trust that connection, kid."

Thea asks, "Doesn't my old, addicted bad-self speak as loudly as this new, sober good-self?" She pauses. "How do I know which is which?"

Sophia laughs. "Don't worry. You'll soon come to know. Good feels, well—good. Bad feels shitty. It's a feeling thing. That's how to best recognize your lower from your higher self. And of course, people who continually dull their senses don't get to know this. Recognize your feelings when they arise, then you learn to trust them. But at first, getting sober means you'll be barraged by emotions you used to cover up. So give yourself time. Your feelings are great teachers. Plus, remember: you do have to put your HP to the test a few times." Sophia wipes a strand of blond hair off her smooth forehead. "Otherwise you won't trust it as easily.

"Listen to your inner voice and forget those internal demons, the negative voices you've been struggling with, Thea. When you learn to do this, that will be the turning point of your sober life. When we're in addiction we only hear our personal demons. That's why we do stupid stuff, like I used to mix pills and booze. That's why I'm passing on to you about connecting to that *feeling* in our gut that tells us we're perfect the way we are. For me that means I'm not overweight. Working with our HP, everything is all right, here and now. Working with your inner self is the prize of being sober."

"Well," Thea's manner is insecure compared to Sophia's steady sureness, "the voice I hear feels like—like I've known it from before," she admits sheepishly.

"But in which lifetime, huh?" Sophia says as Thea stares, not knowing how to interpret that. "Everyone has a connection to inner guidance," she continues, "that's intuition. In the Fellowship we say HP, because some people are atheists or agnostics. Personally, I'm comfortable calling my Higher Power, *Spirit*, plain and simple. Try sitting quietly for a few minutes every day, kiddo. You'll soon learn to distinguish between your instinctual perceptions and the rest of life's many distractions—the negative forces at work all around us. This happens only when you learn to get still … and listen."

Things are changing fast. People, places, and things associated with Thea's druggie existence ripple off one by one, and disappear.

"Forgive yourself," Sophia constantly reminds her, "for wasting time on people who were never there for you, even if you wanted them to be. You're cutting the cord of dependency. You're learning to care for yourself."

As reality becomes more familiar, less scary, and much more palpable, Thea learns to appreciate this strange new feeling, the one Sophia assures her is serenity. "The natural human state of being," she says.

Empathizing at Thea's tendency to confuse this unique new feeling with boredom that Sophia remembers well, she says, "Serenity is like the expanse of ocean waters all over the world. A bad feeling is like a single, isolated wave that we learn to ride, like a surfboard catching an incoming wave. Sailors like you know about rogue waves, the ones that come out of nowhere and cause real damage to a boat if you're not prepared. Life is like this ocean wave analogy. Feelings are the waves. So just learn to relax in sobriety, and enjoy the ocean of bliss, kid," Sophia assures her. "It's as big as the whole universe."

Boy, Thea catches herself thinking, *I'm sure not there yet.*

There are still days she calls and leaves long messages (at Sophia's invitation) at all hours of day or night. Sophia had smartly advised her to ramble on as long as she needed—to her answering machine—thus avoiding having to speak to freaked-out Thea in person, at such invariably low points everyone in recovery has to experience, when one deals with early-days misery, sadness, depression: those devilish mind-made insecurities that come, unexpectedly, between tiny crackling rays of sunshine penetrating the opaque darkness of old fear-based habits. Thea knows she's awakening in her heart as her mind expands to embrace this new reality—being HP-aligned, clean and dry—natural as the day she was born.

"It's okay, kid. Laugh or cry—just don't get high no matter what. Be grateful you can feel so strongly. It takes some of us years before we open up as much as you're feeling."

Thea sniffles a half believing, "Really?"

"Yeah. Let your sadness, as well as your bliss, show you who you really are. Explore the emotions, they're our guides to happiness. Cry away! Tears are gifts that wash away everything you've kept stuffed inside your heart—things that have kept you from living in the light for so long. Let them out, kiddo."

Thea's art begins to reveal, like her emotions, a side of life she never recognized before. The work emerging from these new feelings stirring within excites her beyond measure. Everywhere she sees overlooked connections existing between things she'd never noticed before. In the studio, subtle works emerge, filled with random signs, evoking both quiet epiphanies and volcanic insights. The work resembles random dream pictures, to which she, as awakening chronicler, has finally discovered the key that unlocks its previously closed door. Through painting after painting, Thea explores her raw feelings as they arise, marveling at her ability to discern details that were always there but she'd never seen. Suddenly everything has meaning to Thea, heightened significance! Her energy becomes so enormous she can't wait to get back to the studio each time she has to leave it.

Gone are the others whose lives Thea used as her first sober paintings' models. Paradoxically though, it is through experiencing compassion with the subjects of these earlier works, based on others' tragedies, that she now learns to tap into her exhilarating perceptions—and furiously starts to depict the unlimited possibilities of an expanded version of existence—like blasting off to the moon! Before, such insight remained hidden, or rather, indecipherable, to her dulled, numbed-out perceptions. Thea now begins to access joy instead of the macabre as the worthy subject for her creations. Her studio begins to fill with works inspired by her *feelings* she's now able to revel in. Deciphering her feelings in symbolic and semi-abstract images, she uses whatever materials she has on hand. Hours rush by in which Thea loses herself in a state of interpreting nonverbal urges of all sorts—creating new ideas that leave her in a wondrous state of awe.

"Who's creating *this stuff?*" she wonders. "Surely, not me!"

The enormity of emotions slowly begins to dictate her use of energies, her passions, something she'd stopped trusting in, in early adolescence. Translating sensations and this expanding awareness into artwork becomes her new, good obsession that she keeps expressing in art, not talk. She wants to learn to love herself and these baby steps, her renewed approach to making art, are done in total privacy.

Thea nods to herself, looking over the work emerging in her studio. *It's just like Sophia said,* she thinks: *You don't just stop using. You substitute a new and better addiction for an old bad one. Guess I've found mine.*

21

Thea finally calls Fast Forward but gets his machine. She leaves a short message saying she's sorry, she knows she's let him down. "It can't be helped," she adds, "and I sure hope the new singer, who I hear is great, works out okay for you and the guys."

Thea doesn't know if Fast would support her if he knew how drastically her life was changing. She doesn't want to get into that on the machine. Over the years, Thea has heard only occasional hints that Fast himself would like to curtail his chronic recreational use of drugs, but she isn't ready to share her new life with any of her old heavy hitting friends.

Thea is making her way to Valala. In a recent phone conversation, Maly suggested a follow-up visit might be in order: "For your sake, get all the help you can, n'est-ce pas?"

Thea considers Maly's suggestion and figures why not, although she received some cautionary words from Sophia about revisiting someone who had shaken her so badly.

"We're all psychic," Sophia said. "You'll discover that one day, when your mind gets still enough."

Thea is received with surprising warmth by the older woman, who greets her in flowing robes, of pastel lavender this time, when Thea steps from the gilded elevator into the sarcophagus-like apartment on Central Park West.

As soon as Thea announces to her hostess that she's months without inebriants, Valala says, "My dear, I know how hard one struggles to change for the good."

This time Thea isn't intimidated by Valala's personal museum of arcane paraphernalia. Nothing intrigues her, in fact, but the boisterous painting of Kali Durga. Seeing it again, she's transfixed by its fierceness. Nothing could be more vigorous, more alive to Thea than the representation of this intimidating female deity. Next to the ancient wall-length painting-on-cloth, everything else in Valala's theatrically occult digs appears tacky. Thea feels the heating-up Kali rock she keeps constantly inside a pocket, as if it's being charged right then, plugged into an invisible electrical socket. Thea releases the stone, acknowledging this sensation. She's used to the crystal getting hot at odd times. For now, Thea decides to ignore the rock's transmitting heat.

The poor woman needs some work, Thea notes. Silver roots glare beneath Valala's jet-black (silver roots), carnie-Pharaoh hairdo. Fleshy jowls jiggle as she waddles into her inner sanctum where, months earlier, Thea had sat and cried, terrified at the truth she was hearing about herself. *Just a silly woman,* Thea thinks, *who claims she can read the past, present, and future, but appears as ordinary as the tattered cushioned chair into which she's plopping her substantial weight.*

"And so, my dear, I've done it, haven't I?" Valala exclaims.

A frozen smile rips into the woman's thickly powdered face. Thea's neck hairs bristle.

"It's true, my dear, I've saved you from your own self," Valala says. "Yes of course, I knew you'd be glad. You don't have to say anything. I know. I can see the glow around you. Why, my dear, your aura positively shimmers. The Kali rock is really doing the trick, eh?"

Oh brother, Thea silently murmurs to herself, *What is this egomaniac rambling on about?*

"And you know I did the same for our lovely Maly," Valala exudes. "That charmer came to me because of her sugar craving and look what I've done for her! Why, now she's positively ravishing, don't you agree? She weighed one thirty, you know, when she came to see me, the little porker. Look at the gorgeous queen of lean I've made her into! Ha ha ha."

Thea winces. She makes a mental note to tell her friend that Valala is using her as a before-and-after poster girl of reformed chubettes, sure that Maly won't appreciate that.

"There are some things people just can't understand," Valala says. "That's why you've come to me, to know more, right? Thea? Thea!"

I'm going to vomit, Thea is thinking, squirming in her seat, wondering how she can exit without paying for the session. *Maybe I can sneak out if I go to the john.*

"Oh sorry, Valala. I missed that. What?" Thea remembers something that trails her wherever she goes: *Never let another person force their reality onto yours, kid*, Sophia's voice speaks in her head.

Valala's eyes narrow. She's stopped talking and glares at Thea. Finally, she says, "Do you have any specific questions today? Or do you want a life reading like we did last time? Together, we can lift the veil of Isis, my dear."

Oh brother! Thea thinks. *No way am I revealing anything to this freak.*

Thea remains seated, fascinated by the private stage show, which this time she finds not only amusing, but revolting at the same time. She gazes at the room's perimeter. The world that Valala created for herself is a bewildering array of theater. Yet Thea is curious how far Valala will take her paranormal act. So she stays.

Thea hears a muffled voice calling her name.

You don't have to do this anymore, Thea. You don't have to play games with anyone ever again.

Thea jumps out of her seat. The voice pushes the doors of her perceptions wide open and allows the light of Seeing into the eagerly awaiting recesses of her mind. Standing tall above seated Valala, Thea becomes lively. She moves about the small room like an acrobat, an inspired temple dancer, filled with aggressive grace.

"You're no more psychic than my kneecap," Thea announces in a singsong fashion, jiggling on one foot, then another, with a wave of uncontainable energy.

"What *are* you doing?" Valala gasps, clutching her chest as if stabbed.

"My dog trances out better than you, Valala, and gives better advice too," Thea firmly remarks.

Thea rushes out of the room, past rows and piles of mystical junk.

Valala shouts as she too jumps up from her seat, hurriedly following her subject, stammering in a heated voice.

"You unspeakably ignorant ingrate. How *dare you!*" Valala shrieks.

Thea turns to face the imploding woman as they stand in Valala's living room, positioned right in front of the preposterous image of Kali.

"You must be crazy if you think I'm going to be suckered in by your phony game," Thea says, her voice rising a half octave. "I don't care what Maly, or anybody thinks of you. You're nothing but a psychic viper."

Valala loudly says, "Of all the ungrateful ignoramuses—! Look what I've done for you, you—drug addict!"

Thea twirls on her heels, pivoting to face the asymmetrical dance of the painted Kali image. "I do thank you for giving me the Kali rock, Valala. I'll always cherish it."

Thea reaches into her lightweight spring jacket, feels around a few subway tokens, some change, and a crumpled tissue. The crystal feels smooth and assuring as Thea brings it out. Instantly it grows hotter as she stares at it lying in her upturned hand.

"It's nothing!" Valala spits out, looking at the crystal as if it were feces, her eyes dulled by meanness. "I made it up, you idiot. That's no token of Kali's. It's an ordinary quartz, you stupid gullible girl! That shows how deluded you are. I should have known: you addicts are all alike. You'll never understand the depths of the Mystery School. Give me back my crystal." Valala extends her bony, arthritic hand.

"It's not mine to give back," Thea quietly states. "It belongs to Kali, and you know it as well as I do. You're some piece of work, you know that, Valala? I can't stand phonies. I guess I needed to hear what you had to say before, but now, no. Dr. Bob would have sniffed you out long before I did."

"Who? *What* are you talking about?" Valala shouts. "You're nuts! Get out of my house. This space is sacred, you horrible thing. And to think how I've helped you."

"I'm going, don't worry," Thea bounds for the door before she guffaws out loud like a donkey. Clenching the Kali rock and feeling more heat emitting from it, she leaps into the computerized elevator as soon as its doors open and doesn't stop gripping her pocketed crystal tightly until she reaches the safety of the street, where finally she breathes freely.

"Oh fuck, how'd I get myself into that?" Thea says, sticking her hand up to hail a taxi.

Looking out of the cab, Thea lights a cigarette and swears to quit. She brings the Kali rock out. Thea hasn't gone anywhere without it since she looked inside it and saw the clear light playing phantom shadows in there. She looks again at the rock in her hand. Every time she gazes into it she sees something different.

She smiles, feeling really happy … since forever.

Such joy, this bit of frozen light, she thinks. *So pure, so comforting.*

Looking deeper into the luminescent clarity, Thea hears Sophia telling her, "Everything has a good and a bad side."

She'd fled from Valala's knowing the old crone was an imposter, but now she holds in her hands a small piece of fascinating clarity. Thea wonders out loud at the irony of that. "Something great from something shitty," she scoffs. The cabbie glances at her in the rear mirror.

Thea stops chuckling, not because the cabbie eyeballs her. She thinks she hears something. For a moment she swears she hears a whisper in her ear. Can it be? She senses it's coming from the crystal.

Oh man, I'm losing it. Get me home quick!

Thea looks closer into the piece of quartz. Its inner facets, like a map of a microscopic landscape, presents something to discover each time she dives into it. The stone's overall appearance is harmonious clarity. But it is the countless irregularities frozen deeply within the matrix of the mineral that give its flawless nature such depth, such diversity.

Thea's consciousness dives deeper into the warming crystal as the car bounces southward.

Then she hears a distinctive voice. *Thea, I am within you.*

Who is speaking to her? The rock? At the same instant the image of Kali's intimidating figure—the soot-skinned, fire-eyed, flame-tongued magnificence—vividly appears in Thea's mind. She feels dizzy and grabs the door's overhead handle, wondering if she's hallucinating. Had she forgotten to eat or something?

Thea tenses. "Get a grip," she softly commands herself. "Try to relax. Maybe I'm going crazy?"

No. You are me, I am you. We are all the Great Mother.

Thea shakes her head. "Now I'm really losing it!"

No, you're not. You're letting me get closer.

Thea looks deeper within the Kali rock. She wills away all restraints and slips over an invisible portal.

Gradually, she feels the cab bouncing on the asphalt. Thea eases back to herself.

She blinks and sees outside her window the rush of hard metallic things spinning on wheels. Hordes of robust people on sidewalks. The cab racing downtown.

She looks down at her hand where heat throbs. In her palm is clearness, a stone capturing light. So diminutive, innocuous, innocent. Thea's breath draws short. Then she realizes what has just happened. "You're leading me somewhere, aren't you, Kali?" she whispers.

She relaxes and sinks back in the cab's seat. Instantly an image comes of a painting she wants to make of the things she's just seen within the Kali rock. Every moment—filled with startling discoveries such as this—since she started carrying her stone.

Her life has taken on subtle hues, like the multitude of prisms within the crystal. Nothing is black and white anymore. Possibilities shimmer.

158 THE BRIDGE TENDER

Thea in Junkyard Trinnie's studio

22

Thea steadies herself for the bear hug that Junkyard gives his special friends, male or female, at every greeting. He picks her up, twirls her not-small body around, and plants large juicy mango-flavored kisses upon both her cheeks as he places her back on her feet. Maly is away with a client.

"Honeypot, you be too much!" he dances a raucous solo jig. "Me now be sure you be West Indian, the way you be bouncing back like we, every time a hurricane be messing up the home, the heart of we."

Junkyard jumps with joy to see his friend looking so well. Once more he tosses her up in the air with titan strength, agile as an obstreperous young bull, gleaming his contagious grin while elatedly dancing with Thea this way and that, twirling her around like a ragdoll. Sizing up her new sober self.

A full deck of shining teeth flash as Junkyard Trinnie's mesa lips spread wide as he faces Thea. She's sitting in an armchair draped with exuberant African batiks. She's thrilled at her friend's buoyancy. She needs his enthusiasm and support more than ever, and he never fails to give it. Thea tenderly notes a few gray hairs popping out of his full head of corkscrew dreadlocks. Now quietly sizing her up, Junkyard's wide smooth forehead resembles a peaceful pond with a deep-moving current beneath. High arching cheekbones frame wet olive eyes, sharply contrasting a finely bridged nose that hovers over flaring, deeply incised nostrils that lunge out rhythmically, as if to grab and take her scent in with each new inhale. *So filled with life and vigor is he,* Thea thinks exultantly.

"You be looking mighty good, my yummy pot o'honey—might-tee tasty indeed. Not getting high agrees with you, 'tis easy to be seeing that. There be a new sparkle about you, Fern Eyes." Junkyard Trinnie breaks into an irrepressible paroxysm.

His crowded studio is on the top floor of an industrial Soho loft building. Even with the exhaust working full speed, Thea is hit by the acrid odors of turpentine and plastic resin reeking from leftover buckets of paint and materials of every description. Wherever she gazes Thea sees mounds of jars, lacquers and pigments stacked high, piles of wood, aluminum and copper scraps, baskets of iron and stainless-steel fittings. Materials, sorted by incomprehensible categories, garnish the bright studio.

On the longest wall are hung three works, a series that Junkyard is currently working on; each is eight-feet wide by five-feet tall.

Thea walks their length and examines each new piece, while Junkyard chats with her. She notices that the images contained within each mixed-media maze are stylized cutouts of figures in positions like primitive knock-kneed dancers. Each work coordinates with the next in a rhythmic pattern of continuous movement as she walks from one to another, touching each of their three-dimensional protrusions on strong, unbendable surfaces. Intricate feats of construction and imagery that rattle Thea's inner appreciation meter.

"Maly and me be so proud of you, White Gurl," Junkyard bursts after Thea finishes her careful inspection of the artist's exciting new work. "You really be changing yourself, Womb-an!"

"Gee, thanks, mohn," Thea teases in her easily slipped-into-island twang. She traces the shape of a sturdy vise screwed onto a worktable, casting her eyes anywhere but her friend's searching eyes.

"No, me be sear-i-ous. We not be seeing you at-tall since that doozy of a party when you disappeared. You be something *that night*, daughter of Ja, Whoooiee!"

Thea lightly touches her now-healed eye, not relishing the memory of that night, her last binge.

"Yeah, I was pretty messed up," she says. "But I haven't been high since then."

"That be I-ree. How you be doing such a t'ing?" Junkyard asks and starts rummaging at the same time for something among the peaks and stacks of supplies. He grabs what he's searching for and turns to face Thea with his black diamond eyes.

Thea doesn't know what to say. She's waited all this time to visit her friends, mustering the courage—just in case it might trigger her wanting to use. Getting high of any sort has never been tolerated in her friends' presence, except for at their invite-only, no-limits parties where they'd whip out bubbly champagne for every big opening of any of their artist friends, letting revelers do whatever poison was their pleasure.

"As long as no one be dragging we down, anyone can be coming by us, my lady fair and me," Junkyard made clear to Thea early in their friendship. "When you be coming to visit, don't be buzzin' with I, Green Eyes, 'cause me be wanting to know *you*, not what high you be on."

Now Junkyard is standing with his arms on his hips, looking like the proud King of Downtown Cool. "White Gurl, you be something else now, me be seeing that for true."

Only Junkyard can get away calling people names like this, Thea smiles, delighting in her friend's way of irreverently saying things head-on about what others tip-toe around. How much she appreciates his talent of turning life into one inconsequential comedy, not the serious drama played out by many. She cherishes this man who doesn't have a prejudiced bone in his supple body.

Thea looks around, surveying the familiar beehive bustle of Junkyard's never-ending idea factory. "Well I sure am relieved you approve, Rasta-mohn," she says, tugging on the natty locks of this man who never smokes the bush revered by his similarly dread-styled tribe. Long ago Junkyard realized he got much higher off life than the ton of ganga he'd smoked in his Rastafarian youth, back in the streets of Jamaica's Kingston and jungles of the Blue Mountains.

Junkyard's loft is a haven from the outside world, where the unnerving competition of a city inhabited by every single soul *trying to make it* often causes a too-sensitive soul like Thea to go the opposite way. At Junkyard's and Maly's lofts Thea could relax and groove with other artists with no competition. The couple didn't replace, but they sure helped fill that huge empty gap left by Big Sue's death. These two island-people enjoyed themselves with friends, with no rivalry. Friendship, to them, is way more important than impressing the serious collectors that flock to Manhattan, the island center of the art universe.

"You always blow my mind, Junkyard," she says in a whisper. "No one's work has ever moved me like yours. Except William Blake's and Turner's."

Junkyard's joyous sounds compete with the noisy dump truck right then lumbering down potholed Wooster Street. "That be holy praise, Honeypot! Thank ye from my soul spot. What you be doing in your studio lately, Green Glow?"

Not waiting for a reply, Junkyard begins to trace, freehand, a complicated curve onto a piece of plywood. His head tilts at an angle as he switches from all-encompassing to magnified-focus on the job before him. Not saying a word, Junkyard picks up a German-made jigsaw and its noise hammers the air. He buzz-cuts a shape as if he'd orchestrated an interlude for Thea to think about an answer.

She craves a forbidden-by-Junkyard cigarette as her thoughts screech along with the saw. Gazing around at various works-in-progress that litter the space, she notices a robust life everywhere. The opulent visuals excite her.

The saw stops.

Without a beat of conversation lost or diminished, Thea wants to keep her work secret because she's not sure where she's going with it. "The work's taking a back seat right now," she says, "because I've been busy going to this place, Exchange Views, every morning, down at the World Trade Center."

Junkyard looks up, surprised. "Every day?"

From across the sawhorses where he laid the wood to cut, Junkyard stares at her as if she has flames coming out of her ears.

"Mohn, you not be smoking one teensy little puff of spliff, not a jolt of anyt'ing in all this time! Since me be seein' you last with Fast Forward that lunatic?"

Thea shakes her head, amused with her friend's incredulity.

"So what be the deal with this Views place?" Junkyard asks.

"We just talk, one at a time. I mostly listen."

"Talk about what?"

"Oh, how to live without getting high."

"How to live? Sear-i-ous?"

"Obviously there's more to it than that, Junkyard. I'm now on a search for my Higher Power instead of getting high. Stuff like that, that I never knew about before."

"Oh yeah, like my good friend Yann be saying, 'Swami Jesus at the Haj,'" Junkyard says with a toss of his sawdusted wedge of urchin-like hair. "Or my Buddhist pal, Phil, when he be telling we, 'If you find the Buddha you have to kill him!' That took a while to be comprehended, Honeypot, so Phil had to explain it to I." He slaps his thigh exuberantly and continues.

"So now me be making up my mind who my Ja be. Must be Kahlil Gibran! He be wearing a yarmulke under his turban when he be going to St. Peter's." Junkyard stomps the floor as his mental loud gestures explode in head-bouncing merriment. "We got to be covering all bases in the maximum game of who and what we be searching for, with this Higher Power dance partner; right, Honeypot?"

Thea grins, adoring her friend's plucky irreverence. She lapses into West Indian lingo when she's around her island friends. She says, "Yeah, that be reminding me of the zen koan, *thunder in the teapot.*"

Junkyard kisses his teeth. "Whoosh, me be liking that one, sweetheart. Like killin' de Buddha."

Thea joins her friend's infectious laughter. "You're right, Junkyard. Nothing I've heard or read about, I could ever take very seriously. It just never touched me. With this God thing, I'm like you: I like to be free, not have rules and regulations. I'd never make it with too-stern or strict a Higher Power. Laughing a lot is the best description of how my HP makes me feel, now that I think about it. But before I decide who and what that is, first I'm trying to figure out who, or *what*, I really am; and then, maybe, what power, if any, I can have fun with and—you know—call my own."

Junkyard grins widely. "White Gurl, that be good. The Higher Power be waiting for us any old way. But where you be finding time to do your art? Time be gem-like. Me canna be imagining a trip anywhere, each morning, but right here to the stud-i-oh." The two look askance at each other, nod knowingly, and burst out like those who share a passion for mischief.

Junkyard grabs the sander and switches it on. His spellbinding fingers sharply contrast against the pale wood as he delicately feathers an edge, envisioning the precise angle he needs as he exerts effort. His determination in working this cutout piece inspires Thea. She can't wait to get back to her own studio, where so many half-done pieces lay strewn about. She's not been able to complete a single piece she's started in the last few weeks. But she shows up, or keeps trying to, for a few hours each day in her studio. If nothing else, to dream. To sketch. To envision what's waiting to be born from her as soon as she regroups her energies. For Thea, these baby steps have been like learning how to make art all over again. First, she has to learn to feel.

They continue to talk in between Junkyard's making fine saw cuts. Different shapes emerge that later he'll bolt onto sturdy frames. A powerful exhaust fan almost noiselessly escorts fumes and dust out of the studio. Thea speaks when the saw quiets.

"There's something about being natural that makes me want to do something for the world instead of always expecting the world to do for me; you know, Junkyard?"

He looks up. "Sure, me be same with that. It be taking just one person doing the right t'ing that be changing the whole world, Honeypot. That be the t'ing that makes we be keep making heart art. Me be calling the creative force, *arting* now, because life be about what we create, not just what is in a fancy-schmancy gallery to sell to them big bucks collectors."

A moment of silence lets this statement sink deeply into the truth drawer.

"Me be glad to hear that this power be popping true in your waking-up heart. Never doubt that making the art can do for the world like you be doing for yohself. Change—we hearts do be meaning in our work—mind ye, White Gurl."

Thea shakes her head. "I don't know about all that, Junkyard. I'll be happy if I can just get through the day without the pavement gobbling me up. Sometimes it's really rough. Getting out of my head with a joint or a cold beer still sounds pretty good sometimes."

"You still be thinkin' bout that boring shit?"

"Sure. Getting high is what I've done my entire life."

"Be hanging in there, darlin'. Once you be settling in with this new way of being true, you be realizing—like Maly and me be doing—that you be a real class act. Good art, like good anyt'ing, is what gonna be helping us to be making it through all the confusion in this wonderful weird world of ours."

Thea's eyes brighten. "You really think there's hope? For this screwed up world, I mean?"

Junkyard puts his sander down and walks a few paces closer toward her.

"What me be meaning, White Gurl, is things likely be getting a whole lot weirder before they be getting better. This be a crazy mix-up world. But artists, writers, thinkers, believers like me and Maly and you too, and others like us, we be seeing the possibilities. Goodness be coming out of this deep dark confusion. Some say the sickness of society be our destruction, like Babylon; and it be coming fast. All we heart artists, we got obligations to be spreading the hope. We work to balance the un-hope. Heart artists have to be staying real!" he bangs the workbench with his fist at this last emphatic statement.

Junkyard Trinnie turns away, puts on his safety glasses, picks up the saw and makes another cut without glancing her way.

Thea doesn't really know what he's talking about.

Her thoughts turn to the dream that Junkyard and Maly have often shared with her. The center they call the One Blood Culture, where they envision making art and healing society interacting. The couple have been saving for the time when they will leave New York and live fulltime in Trinidad, where they will be able to help others tap into their inner creativity. And creativity, as the couple espouses to any who'd listen, is the salvation of Earth's many challenges.

The pair have always seen art as a way to help others out of the quagmire of life's dark shadowy side: poverty, the lack of health, education, safety. Uplifting others, if anyone asked them, has always been the driving force behind their creative output.

23

Junkyard's saw shuts off. Thea shrugs her shoulders and says, "This getting-straight business takes a lot of work. I'm not sure about what I'm doing in my studio. It feels like I'm starting all over again. I'm not even certain I'm supposed to be making art. I'm not sure like you, Junkyard. You and Maly are so committed and passionate. And what you do seems like magic to me; I haven't a clue how you do it. I'm confused. Maybe art's just not that important to me anymore. I haven't sung with The Supply House, either, since before your party."

Junkyard lowers his ghost-dusty hands, jigsaw in one, a sheet of coarse sandpaper in the other.

"You be joking with I—right?"

Thea shakes her head, a sheepish look spreading on her face.

Their eyes meet in burning affection. She flinches to see love so real, right before her. They are man and woman without any silly games or confusing emotions clouding recognition of each other's true souls.

The shallowness of her life with Max, her avoiding Fast, and everything else that reminds her of her former fogged-out ways, is erased with the depth of Junkyard's true caring. His sapphire eyes penetrate Thea's heart with a loving ache. It isn't easy for her to accept that someone truly loves her ... for herself. But ... how can he? She's torn between wanting to trust him and not knowing how. She forces herself to look into Junkyard's comforting face as he speaks in a genuinely puzzled tone.

"Is that what they be telling you at the Views, not to be in the band, not to be making art at'tall?"

Thea sighs, relieved. As always, Junkyard is curious, not judgmental or opinionated.

"No, no, it's me. I'm blocked about performing, about creating. I'm just fooling around with some new art ideas. Started with studies of people I've met. Now I'm working on more personal stuff. It feels like I'm beginning to wake up. But nothing's clear yet. I know, it sounds weird. Maybe I'm scared, I don't know. Seems I can't remember who I am anymore. Don't pressure me, Junkyard! I've decided to take my time. Maybe the work will go deeper without me controlling, we'll see. Don't worry. I'm a little black-and-blue right now, after battling my dragon."

"You be saying what?"

"My addictions. But that's over now."

"Over? Addiction never be over, Honeypot. It be the way of we humans to be addicted! Me be addicted plenty, mohn. Me be addicted to life, to loving Maly, and looking up at the beautiful sky and being with good people like you, and making art so me be helping people enjoy life more. White Gurl, addiction can be positive and I-ree too, you know."

"Yes, of course, Junkyard. But for me, so long now I've been stuck on self-destructive ones, I'm trying to sort things out. I find myself asking, 'What is art, anyway?' Surely not just ideas, any old ideas. I know you think life is beautiful, but I'm waking up from a spell I've been under, that I wove on myself. I need time to sort out how I feel about things, and one of those happens to be about me *making art* ... if at all."

"You be sear-i-ous. You don't know how you be feeling about art?"

"I'm not kidding, Junkyard, I don't even know what I'm supposed to do with myself anymore."

"Honeypot, you be one of the best un-discovereds the world be waiting to meet, and now you be telling me you don't be knowing how art influences people?" Junkyard again sucks his teeth like all West Indians do when an emotion shifts. "Art changes everyt'ing, White Gurl, it be the world's secret religion. And we artists be its high priests and priestesses. How can you be so absentminded all of a sudden? You don't be remembering all we talk about, me and you and Maly, before you busted up that eye of you? You not be thinking right anymore, is right! Maybe you better lay off those meetings for a while and come be hanging with me and m' Lady Sweetness."

Junkyard's words are strong and fierce, but his eyes, his easy posture, bespeak a deep sympathy for Thea's dilemma.

She remains silent. After a few long and low suckings of teeth as he thinks, Junkyard speaks.

"Okay," he says, "be true with I. What really be going on with you?"

Thea feels dizzy at Junkyard's prodding. She wants to tell him, but doesn't know what, or how. While Junkyard makes a few swipes with a wood rasp she thinks how badly she wants that cigarette she can't have. Junkyard puts his tool down and turns to her. Waiting. Finally, she speaks as Junkyard Trinnie closes his eyes, leans back, and listens.

"Okay, I'm starting to find a few clues about who the *real me* is. I remembered a voice from my childhood. It told me I was going to be some kind of conduit."

"A what?" His eyes open wide and he smiles.

"Like a bridge tender: a person who helps others cross over."

"Cross over what?"

"From our world to the unseen one."

"That be I-ree."

"Yes, it is, but how? How can I do that?"

"With art, you goose! Honeypot, that be what all we artists do, or try to do."

Thea says, "All my life I've misunderstood that. I guess all my friends, I realize now—except you and Maly—were all party props for getting high, running away from myself. Okay, so I'm better now, I'm getting there. I haven't seen Fast for ages. I quit the band. These are steps in the right direction. Things are crashing in on me, though. I don't know what's happening with Max. I wake up every day wondering how I could have let myself get so off base, living with a guy I have nothing in common with. All the stupid choices I've made. I can't believe I got so sloppy about my life. Look at Fast Forward for chrissake! Look who I chose as my best friend after Big Sue died."

Junkyard quietly says, "Big Sue be the worst drug fiend of them all."

"Yeah, I know, but we shared a history, Junkyard. You know we were friends way before New York. I knew Big Sue like nobody ever knew her. I'm all she ever had—well, Dr. Bob and me. Her pain was her only joy, isn't that sick? That's why she got high so much. For her, life was a drag. I'm sorry she's dead, I loved her. Maybe I could have helped her, now that I'm learning to help myself."

Junkyard slowly stands, silently gazing at Thea.

"I hate to admit it, especially to you, Junkyard, but—it hurt so bad—nobody ever caring about my work or buying anything but that lousy tourist junk I made in the Bahamas. My heart has a bad case of rejection-itis, I admit it. I was dying inside, and now I'm learning to live. It's tough, but I'm sorting it out a little at a time. Sophia is helping me."

"Sophia?" he asks.

"She's my recovery buddy, so I'll be all right. Shit, I feel better already. It's like realizing your life was only a bad dream before waking up and realizing—it's not even started yet. Crazy, huh?"

Without another word Junkyard walks over to her, grabs her hand and brings her over to the Indian-spread covered chair. He sits down and pulls her onto his ample lap. Like a little child he takes her into his big loving arms, like sunshine filling a valley of darkness.

She doesn't have a prayer to calm the inner floodgates that are bursting within her. Junkyard's caring does it. Her tears fall, and he holds her. On her friend's lap she quietly weeps—for herself, for her painful childhood, for losing Big Sue, for all the things that have gone wrong before this. Silently, Junkyard rocks her like a baby. He holds Thea like her mother used to, back before things went rotten, when her parents' addictions soured their love.

Junkyard hugs the fears right out of Thea.

"Let it all out, Fern Eyes. Spill it onto me. I can take it," he whispers.

Quiet minutes pass as the two remain in this tight, trusting state. Silently, Thea releases all she needs to let go of. Junkyard pats her ordinary-looking hair that echoes only faint tinges of the riot colors of before.

"It be all right," he says, rocking Thea as she shudders and weeps. "Make yourself easy, White Gurl."

* * *

Still in his lap, Junkyard reminds Thea, "From the beginning," he says, "you, me, and Maly, we be speaking 'bout art, why we bother be making it, how making art be our mission, like a spiritual calling. Don't you remember? How we be saying how difficult it be for we heart artists to stand up in this age of grab-bag material shit, every which way up and down. The world be losing its mind, Honeypot. Every body be bowing to the god of greed instead of loving the bigness of God that be in all of we. Me? Me rather be shovelin' donkey manure than be an artist if me canna be making works that come from the heart; and that be true, mohn.

"For heart artists like we, our work be about the message, not the making of more stuff the world don't be needing. Our art be about this world desperately needing inspire-ation—and some good old-fashioned truth with a capital T. We hearts have an obligation, Green-Glow, to help raise up humans from the trouble we be getting ourselves into always. Without art, our future be soon goner. The human family future me be meaning, 'cause planet Earth, she know how to be taking care of herself. She be doing just fine long before we two-leggeds arrived, so she be doing so long after all of we be dead and gone. Art has to say *Yes!* to all the world's *Nos* or it be crap, just more stuff, not art at'tall."

Junkyard continues to rock Thea back and forth. "Don't you be remembering what you be saying one night? 'I be making art,' you told we, 'to help make this world saner and safer.'"

Thea shrugs her shoulders and keeps silent, hoping that was her who said that, as she stays relaxed in Junkyard's soothing lap.

After a while Thea realizes where she is, gets herself together, and rolls off Junkyard's knees to sit next to him. Still in a fog, she forgets where she is and reaches into her bag and, without thinking, begins to light a cigarette.

"Whoa, hold on White Gurl! Soon as you be getting your head screwed back on straight you gotta get off those t'ings," Junkyard says, no joking around this time.

"You're right," she smiles, putting the cigarette back into the pack. "For a moment I forgot, sorry. Must have been that good cry you let me have. I've been thinking about something that phony psychic of Maly's told me."

"Valala? Jeez, she be not'ing but a flakey fake. Me be getting so mad whenever Maly mentions her bad-poem name. How you be getting sucked into such foolishness?"

"Maly said I ought to see her. She never told you? Anyway, yeah, she's hokey. I went just to please Maly. Talk about a real creeperoo. But she gave me something helpful. See this?"

Thea brings out the clear crystal from her pocket and hands it to him. Junkyard looks at it intently, turns it, notices every minute detail.

Thea says, "She gave it to me and now it's gotten under my skin. Bizarre, I know. Valala called it a Kali rock."

"Kali? She be the Indian warrior goddess, the naked black one that be wearing bloody skulls around her neck? Real dread lookin'?"

"Yeah, that's her." Thea isn't surprised Junkyard knows about Kali Durga, even though she hadn't. "You know what Kali signifies?"

"The Kali part be destroying the bad so the Durga part of she can have the space to be creating new and better; that be right?"

"Junkyard, you amaze me. How do you know so much? It's funny but the thing about Kali is she symbolizes how I'm feeling inside right now. I've stopped a lot of bad habits and now I'm trying to start some good ones. When I hold this rock it somehow makes me feel stronger about the hard work I'm doing, not getting blasted out of my skull."

"I-ree, White Gurl. Anyt'ing that be making life better be sounding good to me."

"Junkyard, I know it's crazy but I feel like, even though this is tough stuff, this looking at who I am, feeling my feelings, shit, I sense I'm becoming a more powerful version of myself. Does that sound nuts?"

"And way too no fun," Junkyard says. "Lighten up! Life's a game! Just be learnin' the rules, then be bending them a bit if you want to be making good art. Okay, so you did too much pahr-tying. Jump higher over the hurdles and you be getting over them. You might fall but won't get broken if you be falling with grace. Just be getting up and tryin' again. Stay in the race, no matter what, that be your job, says I. Your art be true, you just need to be working hard *at it*.

"Society be as bad or as good as its art is—dance, music, all of it—it be that simple, White Gurl. You be getting well soon. Then you be getting busy making that special heart art of yours. The connection gets stronger, it be true for you. You already be the bridge tender you say you wanna be. You just be forgettin' for a short spell, that be all."

Junkyard walks over to a workbench and grabs a tool in each hand as he says, "And another t'ing, daughter of Ja, your work be *dreamtimes.*"

"What?"

"That what Maly and I be calling your art," he quietly speaks, his rambunctious tone soothing now.

"My lady be saying your work be like the way the outback people of Australia be making their bark paintings, their creations. We be seeing it there in Alice Springs, and it be feeling just like your connection to strong truth. How they, the bush people, and you too, keep ideas alive that people too much be forgetting. Dreamtimes, they call 'em, Honeypot. Your work be a loud wake-up call bouncing back at us. Like the Aborigines do their walkabout, singing their song lines, keeping everyt'ing alive. Each song line meant for one certain t'ing to stay a bit longer in the whole of creation, each song be keeping everyt'ing balanced, existing, but only if we be giving each t'ing its proper due respect. Renewing t'ings, keeping them alive, by the attention we be giving them. And what is not sacred, if it be comin' from Nature? Everyt'ing be sacred. That's why we artists who got heart, got to be making art to keep the human spirit going strong during these hard times here."

Thea howls an animal sound in spite of herself. "Okay. Dreamtimes. That's cool. I like that. That is definitely Aboriginal and I'm feelin' pretty primitive myself these days."

"Your work be what *Ja* putting you on this planet for," Junkyard says without missing a beat. "To be making heart-cracking, mind-bending, alarm-clock Dreamtimes that be blowing everyone's mind up, including mine. Heart work be I-ree."

"You talkin' Rasta, mohn."

"That be right. I-ree as in real *dread*, as in *best*, reggae style. It be Godlike, the Rasta Higher Power—Irie!"

"Oh," Thea feels like a private joke has just passed between them.

"This Kali you been talking about. Guess what? You be painting her story all along, Fern Eyes. You be sharing her wild wicked kill-evil dance with others even before you knew her being her. When you say you be meeting her first at mocha jumbie-weirdo Valala's."

"I have?"

"Sure t'ing. Your work always be about destroying lies. Giving a positive spin to the curse of the material world's wants and needs we be in. Your work be playful, Honeypot, tickling mind-game puzzles that we be hashing out, each and every one of we. Me be liking your riddles, your Dreamtimes! There be magic in your work me be seeing, soon as we be meeting you, Maly and I."

Thea and Junkyard stand in silence for a few moments, tools still unused that he holds in his arms.

"Glow-girl," he softly says, "someday soon you be coming with us to meet our friends at Gaia Group, when it be time to meet your *real* family." His grin widens.

"What group?" she says, curious in spite of herself, but thinking, *No thanks, I don't need another fucking family.* "What *are* you talking about, Junkyard? You know what? You be crazy, m'sohn."

The two shake their heads in good humor as Junkyard resumes his work and Thea watches.

24

Thea is leaving Junkyard's studio with her chest aching and laughter ringing in her ears. It's a good ache she carries though, because her shut-gate heart has just been forced open, exposing that she's always yearned to be loved. And this friend of hers, she knows, truly loves her. Not wants to sex her—but *loves* her. This afternoon, Junkyard shared something with her Thea never experienced—a mutual respect born between two similar souls clearly recognizing each other, with no other agenda.

A few evenings later Thea is peeling onions, cracking open garlic cloves, slicing sweet red peppers while humming a new tune maybe she'll write down and share with The Supply House.

Yes, it's important to keep things light, she thinks. Junkyard's words have inspired her. She chops with swift, sure movements, anxious to step back into her sky-wrapped studio as soon as dinner is over, to go another round with her art. "Dreamtimes," she whispers, trying out its sound.

Max walks into the kitchen wearing one of his gym outfits, a toasty brown color-coordinated velour sweat suit. "Looking superb tonight, Thea. Interesting new do."

Midair, Thea stops the knife. *Odd,* she thinks, *how much Max resembles her aloof, never caring parents. Always absent. He doesn't have a clue who I really am.*

Max walks up to Thea and places a dry lip-stamp on her cheek, an annoying habit of his. She cringes. *It's so stupid,* she realizes. *We're playacting here, not being real.*

"Hey babe, Fast Forward called again today."

His challenging voice sends chills up Thea's spine.

"I'm getting pretty tired of telling him you're out. You going to ever call him, or what? Obviously, you're not performing anymore, so what's the scoop? I feel foolish not knowing what to tell him."

Max walks to the fridge to get a beer, his nightly ritual of having *just one*, a feat of restraint that doesn't so much fascinate Thea as makes her wary of his now-blatant control.

"I'll call when I'm ready," she says.

"Well, the old speed fag would probably appreciate it."

Not looking at him, Thea continues slicing tiny pieces, peeved.

"I wish you wouldn't say that. He has never called you a name."

"Hey, okay, Miss Sensitive! Can't a guy joke around here anymore?"

"Sure, but why at another's expense?"

"My, aren't we touchy today."

"I feel absolutely fantastic if you want to know, Max. A whole new way of looking at my work is opening up for me."

An unfamiliar thump again taps Thea in the middle of her chest. The sensation travels quickly, piercing her stomach with a sharp stab. She bends over a little to relieve the pinch. Max slugs his beer. Lately this new gut-wrench comes every time she's with Max, or thinks about getting in touch with Fast. The stitch subsides but it becomes hard for her to breathe. The onion fumes have started stinging her eyes.

"What's going on?" Max asks.

Thea leans over the sink and splashes handfuls of water onto her face as Max watches. Straightening herself, Thea turns to the pile of mushrooms. The smell of blending aromas—oregano, cumin, basil—dapples a false veneer of domestic tranquility over the bitterness that stretches between them.

Thea listens, transfixed, to that strange new voice she's been hearing occasionally, inside herself. She gives no indication to Max that something is going on within her, that she is hearing or feeling anything. *Is this Higher Power stuff?* she wonders. On the outside she appears normal. Looking up from the counter she notices a cluster of floating sequin-light shimmer in the air right next to her.

Max puts his drink down and turns Thea's black-sweatered shoulders toward him. Tenderly he brushes aside one of the newly grown-in locks of fawn hair from her face. Thea gazes down at the chopped mushrooms, unable to look at him.

"Why does everything have to be so difficult with you," Max asks. "You haven't seen Fast, and we haven't made love since you've been on this new get-healthy kick. What's up with you?"

"Max, can't you please try to understand—I'm changing. I *have* to stay away from the old triggers. I can't hang with people I used to use with. I simply can't see Fast; he's the worse drug fiend of them all. And as far as making love with you, I—"

She pauses to breathe the pungency of vegetables, redolent of a sane world that she hopes might one day be more accessible. She closes her eyes in relief, recognizing something real, some other presence in the room. "—I-I just can't right now."

"Thea, what the hell has happened to you?" Max demands angrily.

She turns away from him.

"You used to be fun. You used to dress like theatre and fuck like a bunny, and now, look at you—cooking! You never used to cook!"

"Actually, I've always been a rather good cook, Max. You just never knew that about me."

"And your hair—it's gotten so normal looking."

"I'm tired of spiking it," she says. "The dyes were frying it. It was time for a change."

"And what's with the ice act? Getting sober making you into a lezzie or something? Is that who this Sophia is, huh?"

Thea silently chops, focusing on the pungent shitake on the board. She wants so much not to be there. Not to be having this conversation with a man she should not be with.

Ripe vegetables simmer in the saucepan. Thea wishes herself away, like the individual ingredients, now merging their juices and aromas in the soup pot. Slowly the vegetables are changing, metamorphosizing, like she is. Distinct shapes and flavors evolving into something entirely new and different as they blend together in culinary magic. Spices losing their disparate flavors, being unified, just like her new self slowly losing its old self-centeredness. Even the texture of the vegetables is changing, just as she knows she's becoming a part of something much bigger than herself. She has become a willing participant in this steaming, sober stew of life she's hopped into. Thea doesn't want to play games any more. She looks directly at this man, this stranger she lives with.

"Max, I'm changing, can't you understand? Before, I felt dead inside. Can't you give me some space to get better?"

"You're such a loser, that's what you are, Thea," he spits the words as if striking her.

"You don't have to call me names." The stirring spoon Thea holds aloft softly comes down, resting gently on the marble countertop.

"Okay, addict—do you like that better?" he asks. "Alchie? Like those put-down names you call yourself? How do you think I like living with someone who calls herself a loser?"

"I've never called myself a loser." Thea's voice is surprisingly relaxed. Somehow she can't muster a speck of anger.

"Work is what you need to do!" Max's voice booms in a way Thea's never heard before. "You've become a fucking flake, Thea. A freeloader. You haven't made any money since you stopped singing with the band. Do you even hear yourself?"

"Max, you sound like you hate me," she whispers.

"You're seriously getting on my nerves, that's for sure. First you suck me in with that sex machine bod of yours, those theatrical stunts and pole-dancing outfits that'd drive any man out of his tree. Then, wham! You're in my life, living in my loft before I even know it, with that whacked-out mutt of yours; and when I get back from the coast one day all you can say is, 'Please be patient, Max, and oh by the way, I can't fuck you anymore,'" he says with unabashed unkindness, "'cause you see,' he mimics her, 'I'm changing,' Well screw that! How gullible do you think I am, anyway?"

Max's viciousness bites Thea like a cobra's fangs.

Her lips are drawbridge tight. Shutting out any more lies, Thea hears only the beat of her strong heart. She listens to the inner voice that slowly has become louder, more familiar—the one that now shouts to her, no longer a whisper—that it's time—to end this charade.

She places the anchovy jar she's been holding in her other hand carefully on the counter. She shuts the sizzling saucepan off. Whistling for Dr. Bob, Thea calmly walks over and takes his leash off its hook next to the front door. In one swooping movement she grabs her coat and bag from their nearby place. She raises a relaxed, assured face to Max.

"I'm glad," she says, looking right at him, "that you're finally saying how we both feel, Max. You're right, I don't belong here with you. You and I have never loved each other. We're both users. But I want to change that about myself. I'm already too well to live this lie anymore. Goodbye, and thanks."

Thea turns and walks out with Dr. Bob trotting at her side, his bobby-socked paws lightly high-stepping, his tail wagging amid the noisy threats Max hurls behind them.

"Don't bother coming back, Thea! You're nothing but a pathetic narcissist!"

"Sure, come on over," Sophia says without hesitation when Thea calls from a payphone. "You did the right thing, Thea. Don't worry, I saw it coming. I was hoping you'd be strong enough when it happened, and you obviously are. You're not alone, so forget about him. See ya soon, kiddo."

Sophia is a human life raft, Thea realizes as she hangs up. She tells Dr. Bob he's going to have to tolerate living with her friend's two cats for a while. When they get to Sophia's Chelsea apartment, where Thea has spent more than a few pitiful hours being freaked out, trying to resist using, screaming and crying in angst during her earliest, uneasy days on Planet Sober, Max's spiteful words and the fact that she is now being *forced* to change her life strikes Thea full force.

One moment she's panicking at what she's just done. The next, she's absolutely elated at being free. Then the next second, scorned; then scared, then ecstatic, and finally ... thanks to Sophia's guidance—Thea gets through every emotion stirred by life's cataclysmic events. That night, as Sophia sleeps peacefully, Thea again rides the wild roller coaster of unchecked, fully felt emotions. This time she knows how to harness herself safely, as she rides the careening cars of both fear and gratitude.

On the fearful, twisty ride up and down the whirligig of erratic feelings, she hangs on for dear life. She hasn't felt so torn up inside since she'd been a lonely, terrified ten-year-old, afraid of the up-till-then trusted brother who molested her whenever he wished; angry and fearful of a boozy mother who never believed her, criticizing and blaming her forever for things in the family "never being the same," claiming Thea was the cause and never the victim of everyone's unease. So accusatory, that little Thea learned to keep her horrible secret from the entire world. Until the day, finally, when the ache of her heart ended—the moment she chugged stinging, stinking liquid from her parents' bar with another daredevil teenage girlfriend of hers. And she never looked back without the shield of numbing those torturous feelings of wanting to die—until now.

"I'll show you a good trick," Sophia explains the next morning when Thea begins to doubt she's done the right thing by leaving Max.

"I'm broke," Thea realizes. "I have no job. And my fucking feelings are killing me. I'm a mess!"

"Kiddo, feelings come and go like waves on the ocean, remember me saying? Here's the trick I use whenever I feel overwhelmed. This should be easy for you, being an artist and so visual.

"I take all the bad feelings I have inside me, and pretend they're real, live, evil monsters. Go on—visualize those bad feelings that keep you up all night as demons locked inside your head. Now—order them out of your head. That's right. Command them to get the hell out of there and pretend to order them to sit right in front of you, like a pack of bad, snarling attack dogs. Or worse. Like a nightmare come alive. Imagine each shitty feeling you have inside as the most dangerous creature you could ever imagine."

"What? That sounds crazy, Sophia."

"Come on, Thea, get into it! Give your feelings imaginary horns and nasty fangs! Make 'em snarl and snap with slobbering green acid foaming at their mouths! Make them into terrifying monsters out to kill you! But get them *out* of your head! Visualize those evil devils inside you, bring them to the floor in front of you and see them as rabid wolves! Because they are. Remember, those bad feelings inside you want you *dead*. Go ahead, *do it*. Create this picture in your mind."

Thea shuts her eyes and, with a little effort, visualizes her cruel, tormenting feelings as a pack of hideous gargoyles, their sharp teeth ready to rip her to shreds.

"Do you see them?" Sophia asks.

"Oh yeah, they're there." Thea's imagination is in overdrive.

"Okay. Now order those beasts that are within you to get *outside you!* And to *stay away* from you. Command them to sit, to stay *six feet away* from you, *and to behave!*"

"What?"

"Just do it, Thea."

"Six feet?"

"Just do it. It works."

Thea does as Sophia orders her. She imagines forcing the evil creatures to sit on their haunches, snarling and snapping. She manages to get them out of her head and away from her, sitting in front of her, still threatening and horribly evil, though. The foul things froth, growl, snap their toothy jaws—but at a safe distance from her.

"Well?"

"They're sitting."

"And—are they hurting you?"

"No, it's incredible, they're obeying me."

"That's right. They obey you. Our inner demons can't hurt us when we make them be under our control. We command them—and they obey. They're nothing more than made-up fears, that's why."

"How is this possible, that—they're obeying me?"

"Because your mind created them. They're not real. Fear is not real. Now you know. You can order them, *will* them—these bad feelings of yours—to be powerless over you.

"Eventually," Sophia continues, "if you do this enough times, they'll stop their stupid antics and just go back to—nowhere, where they came from. With practice, they'll leave you completely alone, once they know you're on guard and control them. Feelings are made up by our minds. Those evil monsters trying to kill you are only in your mind, kiddo, the same place where you're now learning, choosing to make them obey you."

Thea's face softens. She's astonished at how her friend has just saved her from what felt like crippling fear. The feeling that she's about to die that always tries to take her over, since her carefree childhood busted apart at age ten. She looks at Sophia, who is saying, as soothing, as caressing as a breeze:

"You've got to remember, Thea: bad things have to run their course before better things can start. Everything happens for a reason, kid, when you live in the Light. Darkness can't thrive here."

In Sophia's snug one-bedroom apartment, Thea makes her bed on the couch, with Dr. Bob on the floor, his warm body leaning against her dangling arm. She listens as Sophia shares stories about her family back in rural Pennsylvania, until her eyes are too heavy to stay open. Thea is happy to be there, with someone who wants nothing from her, with someone who has so much to give.

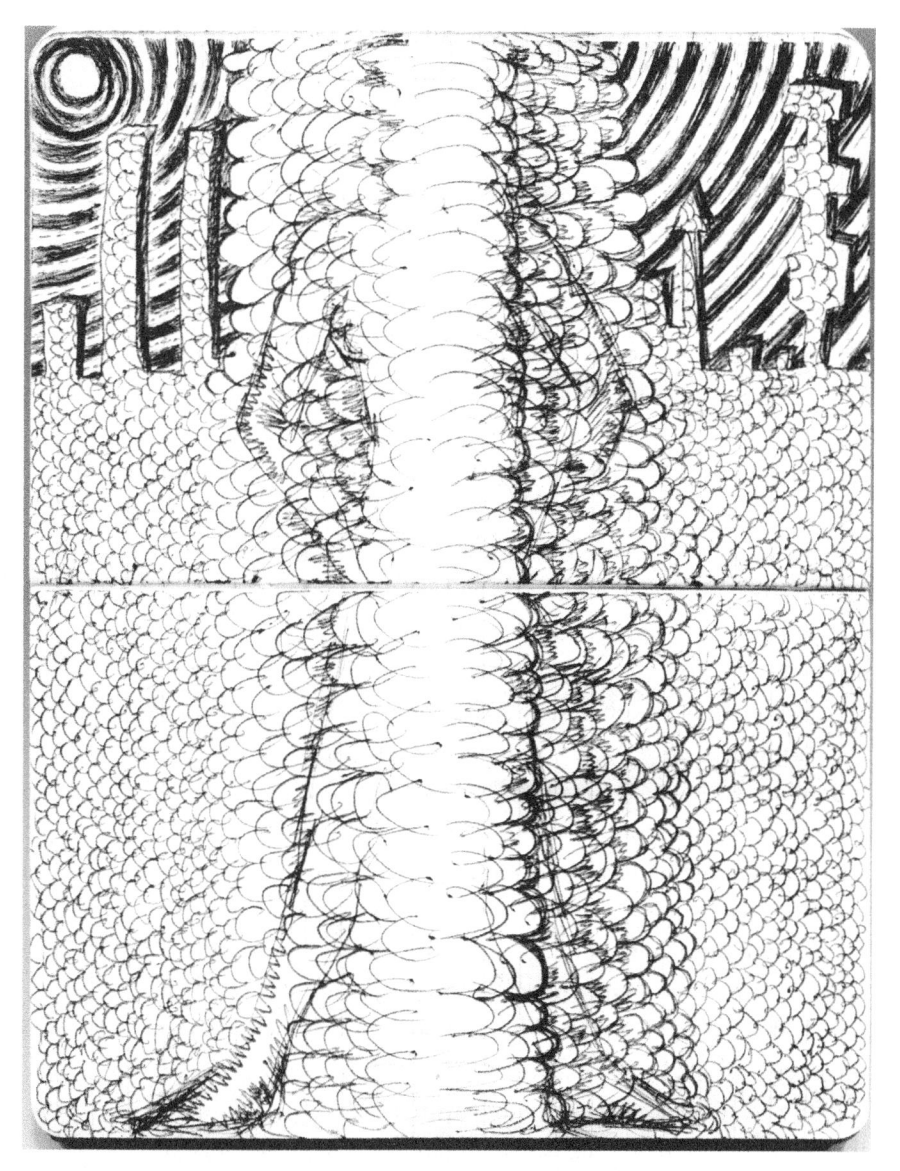

Healing with Exchange Views' and Sophia's guidance

25

Thea imbibes no inebriants other than massive doses of coffee and cigarettes with a twist of peace, now and then. She gets a job waitressing soon after she and Dr. Bob move into their temporary home at Sophia's. Right next to the Chelsea restaurant where she works is Whitmore and Fields, a secondhand bookstore. She stops off one night after her shift to browse for any information she can find about the Hindu goddess, Kali Durga. Valala's rock is with her, of course, acting as a reminder of where Thea wants to go with her life: strong and clear, into the Light. She brings it out to stare into its comforting clarity whenever besieged by her stubbornly resilient dark urges.

A stooped old woman with bifocals shows Thea to a shelf in the back of the antiquated shop. Mrs. Chid, her name is, appears to have worked here for as long as the dustiest corner has existed—in which secret windows that peer into life's startling moments can be unearthed.

"Look here to know more about Kali," she taps a shelf of tattered tomes. The first one Thea picks up is the *Mahabharata*, printed in Delhi. There is no index. Give me a sign, book, Thea silently wishes as she closes her eyes and opens it at random. Sure enough ... good fortune strikes again.

"Kali," the text reads "is Time ... the life force ... as goddess," Thea scans the opened page, her eyes flitting over words of an English translation.

The next book Thea chooses is titled *Mundaka Upanishad*. She does the same, randomly opens it. And again, as if by magic, instantly she finds mention of the female godhead, "... Kali ... of the Seven Divine Mothers."

Surrounded by musty shelves, Thea searches through one translation after another of India's holy books, till Mrs. Chid returns. "Come with me, dear," the kind old woman says, and leads the precarious way down rickety wooden steps to the basement of the store, full of precious volumes that the bibliophile owner never intends to sell. There, Thea is given the well-thumbed pages of one, then another, egg-shell crackled leather-bound work titled in gold leaf. Thea is sitting under a dim overhead light bulb at a small wooden table in the basement, when Mrs. Chid hands her a book.

"This one will be most useful for your search, my dear," she says.

It is an English version of the Sanskrit *Kali Tantra*, which Mrs. Chid prefaces with an explanation, surprising Thea that the old lady knows so much about Kali.

"This will explain how our time in Earth's history is called the Kali Yuga," Mrs. Chid says, placing the book on Thea's pile. "Now is the time of Kali's protection, that means. This is when humanity is being forced to become spiritualized."

The old woman smiles as she pats the slim book's cover. "I borrowed it from the owner's trunk of treasured scripture. Just for you."

After Mrs. Chid departs Thea opens the musty pages of the *Kali Tantra*. She reads of the beginnings of the two-in-one Mother of the Universe, the goddess Herself—Durga and Kali, the original one being Durga, benevolent and placid. But there came a time, a horrific time in humanity's history, the scripture reads, when Durga needed assistance. So fierce and warlike Kali was purposefully brought forth, self-born from Durga herself, to be more aggressive and unmercifully violent against all the rampaging demons overrunning Earth at that time, both characteristics the kind and compassionate Durga did not possess.

Thea thinks, *It's just as Valala said Kali Durga was.*

In every volume she is given, in this slim book and others, Thea reads more about Kali's cosmic significance. She reads text of the *Rig Vega*, dating back to thousands of years before Christ.

"Fortunately, many good English translations are available," Mrs. Chid mentions before returning upstairs.

Thea is overwhelmed with the mountain of books about Kali Durga's importance. Her eyes start to blur; she needs a break. Upstairs she asks Mrs. Chid if she may return to continue her studies.

Each time Thea returns to the old bookstore, a meager space that's seemingly limitless in its offerings of forgotten texts, Thea ventures to the basement and pours over East Indian scriptures about Kali. At one of her visits, Mrs. Chid hands Thea an old LP and puts it on the convenient record player, there in the basement.

"What is this?" Thea asks as soon as the strange sound begins. Mrs. Chid answers, "It's Kali devotees singing the *Devi-sukta*, a chant asking for the goddess' protection. The jacket says it's a hymn from the *Rig Veda*. I found it yesterday in an unopened box along with vinyls of Billie Holiday and Caruso."

Thea listens, transfixed. Immersed in the repetitive sound of a simple Sanskrit mantra—*Kali Durge Namo Namah*—repeated continuously, in call and response, men, then women's voices, separately, but together blending, intermingling in a hypnotic immersion, a fullness of humanity in sound that has no gender or class, just full of power. Thea feels a jolt rush up her spine. In that Manhattan midtown basement she discovers the unique satisfaction that people enjoy when they come to fully, viscerally, comprehend an archaic act—a symbol, a sound, a ritual—used in less busy times, to help humanity better understand the impenetrable Mystery of Life.

Her journey to discover more about Kali Durga takes Thea to an opening within herself. A portal that had been closed before—she now feels opening as its rusty hinges crumble away and cast aside, freeing something primordial deep within her.

She feels tingly. The same as she did when she discovered in the *Rig Veda* that Kali Durga is called the Great Mother. And then how—through Kali Durga's cosmic womb—the entire Universe came into existence. Thea reads of other Hindu female deities too. Lakshmi depicting abundance; Saraswati honoring creativity; and *Yoni* translating as the Divine Womb of the Universe, also called the Sacred Mother. Thea jumps out of her seat when she realizes these Great Mother images are earliest people's simplest, most anthropomorphic answers to questions about their origins, their very existence. The Great Mother relieved early humanity's sufferings. She soothed their pain and hardships. Whether interpreted as literal or symbolic isn't the point. Thea now knows that

Kali Durga—the destroyer of evil and the creator of new possibilities—is everyone's Great Mother.

These scriptures were guides to ancient people, just as they help Thea right at that moment as she searches for a Higher Power for herself. Now she understands how life-saving a spiritual concept—as a way of *being*—is to her. And for anyone who wants to transform their perceptions from seeing life on Earth as only something to be endured—feeling depressed, enraged, or anxious as a result—to perceiving each of our experiences here on Earth as sacred, protected by a Great Mother such as Kali Durga.

Thea returns time after time to sit for hours in the still-aired basement. Mrs. Chid has become like a watchful auntie, helpful in any way she can in Thea's unusual quest to know Kali, something the woman has rarely seen in her decades of working in the famous bookstore.

Most intriguing to Thea's interest in the scriptural description of Great Mother's cosmic womb is its being defined as timeless. The fact that Kali Durga has two, seemingly opposing aspects—that of Kali's destroying demonic influences so Durga can continuously rebirth all creation—makes Thea feel connected somehow to this mission of the twin-deity. As if she's being called to be Kali Durga's personal conduit, in whatever fashion, whatever medium can best be used to help heal this toxic world Thea finds herself waking up to.

Thea reads and learns how artists have, for thousands of years, portrayed the Great Mother's attribute of infinitely sustaining the Universe by the symbol of the *Hiranyagarbha*. She finds this also explained in the Rig Veda. The same symbol—on her leg, the same as Big Sue's one and only tattoo—called the *Ouroboros* by ancient Egyptians and Greeks, is mentioned as well in various alchemy texts that Mrs. Chid slips onto Thea's desk.

When she reads about the symbol of the snake eating its own tail for the first time, she reaches down to touch the tat on her right calf as a shiver passes through every cell of her body.

She reads how the Ouroboros represents the birth of life itself. The negative space within the snake's coiled-upon-itself body is *the cosmic egg, the Source* from where all life is created, destroyed, and re-created, thanks to Kali Durga doing her dual duties.

Imagine—as she discovers in her studies—the meaning of that tat of hers of the snake eating its own self! A deafening roar consumes her when she pieces together the snake's significance is linked to Kali Durga's historical role in the preservation of humankind.

She remembers that night, when she *had to have* the circular snake inked on herself in a scruffy Bowery ink shop, right after Big Sue died. This coincidence, learning the image's significance, which she'd never asked Sue about, thinking it was just a cool shamanic choice on her friend's part, probably after one of her Southern Comfort trips with a side of ayahuasca or mushrooms—shocks Thea.

Thea ponders what Sophia said to her recently: "There is no such thing as a coincidence. Everything happens for a reason."

"But this—this is too much," Thea gasps as she runs her fingers over her right calf. "Am I under some kind of spell?" she mutters. "Or is this the way Planet Sober operates?"

She sits and stares, motionless, for some minutes after this exhilarating connection with Big Sue ... and with all of humankind's ancestors. She wonders if her body's snake-symbol image relates to her own destiny.

Filled with the exuberance of discovering a great mystery, she continues reading, gently touching her leg's snake decoration, pressing her forehead's miniscule indigo dot of ink, and feeling the pulsating Viking knot inked on her upper arm.

"This is too much to figure," she says, exhausted that day with all the wondering. But she keeps returning to the basement to deepen her understanding, determined to try to piece together the puzzle of what Kali means to her.

As she studies, heat emanating from the Kali rock seems to increase each time she regards it. Sometimes it's too hot to touch. She stares at it as it sits where she's placed it before her on the desk, next to a stack of books. Flashes of its prismatic light reflect from every angle.

After a dozen visits to the bookstore to research the ancient scriptures Mrs. Chid delivers with such interest and kindness, Thea starts to comprehend. She realizes ancient people, just as modern folks today, found comfort from having a Divine Intelligence—today some call that a Higher Power—such as an all-powerful God or Goddess, or Nature Itself. Having an HP of one's own can be comforting, she now clearly realizes. Having faith in one (or two, or hundreds, in the case of the extensive Hindu pantheon) would be a logical way for humankind, ancient and current, to be able to deal with the complexities of life that otherwise are unanswerable.

"The riddle of existence," Thea mutters one day after clearly seeing this, "can be eased by what Sophia tells me about finding an HP for myself. Like she told me, 'Some people are so resistant to having a Higher Power that we tell them to choose anything—their cat, the fellowship meetings—just fake it till you make it—but choose something to begin with, that has greater power than your own ego.'

"I can do that with the Great Mother," Thea whispers. "That feels righteous."

Whether Great Mother is called Kali Durga of India, Isis of Egypt, Mary of Bethlehem, Gaia of ancient Greece, or any of her thousand holy names, Thea's budding comprehension has expanded and now grasps that the spiritual feminine is easier for her to relate to than the masculine patriarch, a now-dated, *don't-work-no-more* figurehead.

That Old Guy in the Sky that I was spoon-fed as a good little Christian kid doesn't feel right anymore, she thinks.

Up to this time Thea tried calling her HP by things like the *Absolute*, the *Unnamable*, the *One without a second*, or her favorite—the one Big Sue used, that she'd learned from her Native American friends—the *Mystery*. But now Thea reckons, why use a neutral, or a masculine name, like Father, Son, Allah, Yahweh, Brahma? They just don't do it for me. I know faiths and religions are meant to dispel darkness and instill light and hope in the human heart, but I'm only turned on by the name of Kali Durga—that badass goddess!

Since they'd been talking, Sophia made it clear to her: "In order to stay sober, you have to work with a Higher Power. You get to choose which concept of an HP works for you. Any HP works. But you *must* have one.

One person I knew used their doorknob—until they were awake enough to grasp how ridiculous that was."

At her basement table, she gradually grasps that all these human efforts—the early scriptural recordings tell her—are meant to explain how a Divine HP intervenes for the benefit of humanity. Whatever form of the Divine one relates to helps people reap comfort, she now can see. An HP helps to have a sense of safety, peace, health and contentment. All noble reasons for cultivating an HP, Thea nods. She realizes that the goddess called Kali Durga is nothing less than another HP, a human attempt to define what is indefinable. An answer that satisfies the powerful serendipity of life, borne by necessity by suffering people everywhere.

The more Thea reads, the more she knows how having comfort is a basic human need she never had. When she was using, she had no comfort, no help. She pauses at this stark revelation. Then reflects, remembering vividly how her world fell apart when her trust in *others* was shattered around the age of ten. Things never made sense after her older brothers, then her parents, withdrew their love. Thea was lost and alone from then on. Sighing, she returns to the camphor-scented page before her, trying to understand that which can't be grasped by logic alone. Thea resigns herself, after weeks of trying, that at least she feels worthy of having, *of wanting*, some kind of faith in a Higher Power.

Art is the only way I can feel the Divine, she admits to herself.

Art will be my own private HP.

Thea smiles and stretches, noticing it's time to gather her things and return to Sophia's and take heroic Dr. Bob for his nightly walk.

One day Thea visits an eclectic shop in the Village. She's surprised to find in a box an old cassette of people chanting mantras to Kali Durga, and buys it. The haunting, soothing melody obsesses her, sticks in her mind, day and night. Thea listens to it continuously on her Walkman, humming or softly singing the atonal, comforting drone as she rides the subway downtown to Exchange Views, or walks the streets of Chelsea, Sophia's neighborhood.

Whenever she listens or joins in to others chanting the name of Kali Durga, Thea feels impervious to evil. It's as if an invisible shield is protecting her from harm. Of course, she knows this sense of protection isn't a *real* shield, but she feels safer, somehow, and braver, imagining the warrior goddess actually with her in the form of the mantra vibration. Somehow, it makes life on scary Planet Sober seem more manageable. Thea has discovered that by singing the fierce goddess' name, her fears dissolve. She doesn't know why. Nor does she care. It just happens. As long as she chants that name, and has her Kali rock close by, Thea no longer feels overwhelmed, as she did in previous episodes when besieged by—okay, *imagined* by—heart-stopping demons.

Sophia's home nursing job has changed. Now she's away most nights, an arrangement that conveniently works for sharing her small apartment with day-working Thea. Other things have changed besides Thea leaving Max. She can't get to Exchange Views on a daily basis anymore, but often attends a closer Chelsea meeting. Dr. Bob has learned to tolerate the two cats and Sophia likes the extra rent money, so her two guests have become apartment mates, for now. Her latest patient has already entered the final stages of cancer. That means, as Thea sleeps peacefully with Dr. Bob nestled at the end of her sofa bed, that Sophia is doling out morphine and other strong medicine to ease her patient's continuous pain. Sophia does other not-so-obvious things to ease her patient's spiritual discomfort. Thea feels Sophia is a veritable angel for doing the work she does.

26

Soon after chanting her name continuously—Kali makes herself visible.
An amusing illusion tickles Thea's dreaming fancy. But soon she stops chuckling in her sleep because, before her dreaming self she sees the terrible, black-as-coal form of the Great Mother. The goddess draws a glistening sword high above her head as ankle bells clamor on her dancing feet, and flames shoot out from her fingertips. Twenty arms surround her! All the dark fingers are held in weirdly varied positions, completely encircling Kali Durga's upper torso and black oily locks in a free-for-all aura. Her belly button shines like an ultra-blue moon in a black sky.

It is She all right. The fierce female source of Creation—making herself Real right in Thea's dream world. The goddess jerks her normal human-sized body and instantly—her head bends to fit under the room's ceiling as she explosively looms to fill the space itself—and then, zap! she jerks back and becomes apartment friendly, Barbie-doll, pocket-size tiny. Back and forth, in macro- and micro- versions, she yo-yo's her way into Thea's subconscious.

Uncanny sensations arise. She is suspended, Alice-like, joining the size-switching mode, joining the goddess as one being in vertiginous transformation mode. Thea looks down at her own sleeping hands and sees they've become tiny peanuts, and her legs, withered birch branches that need pruning. Kali and Thea, together now in a syncopated dance routine, shrink, then bounce to being as immeasurable as a comet, as vast as a far-off galaxy, as they take off in tandem to as yet undiscovered dimensions.

Thea's dreaming-self relaxes. She becomes a single cell within creation, lost in the circulatory system of the Great Mother's womb … becoming a cell within infinity.

I am Kali, Thea speaks aloud in her dream.

I am that part of you you've always suspected but have feared till now. Now nothing separates us. Trust me.

Thea gropes her way down a dark tunnel stretching before her. No light at the end shines the way. No flames flare from her Kali-esque guiding fingertips, or her luminous blue navel. Separate from herself no longer—in the primordial darkness—Thea becomes a human oneness with the formidable sacred—as Kali.

Changing forms again, Kali-Thea morphs into an animal, a cloven-hoofed wild boar. Snorting and sniffing, her animal-self digs the black-as-night cave floor mud for clues with her long fleshy snout. A steady brilliant-blue light shines ahead, a tiny seed of light directing her, leading her straight on. The wild boar rushes for the light. At last! A low, echoing sound surrounds her in the darkness as she rushes for the spot of illumination. Enchanting and melodic, the sound pierces her dream as she moans in recognition.

The dreamer arrives at the place where her initiation will be complete. A new life, an intuitive one, merges with her breathing. She's now rebirthing herself as a real human … seeking enlightenment in her Earthly existence.

In her dreaming, Thea transforms back into her goddess form—as the soundless voice of her inner Kali proclaims …

It is done.

Recognizing the familiar blue glow, the brilliant seed of this inner world, Thea finds herself on her knees where she's gotten out of bed, sleepwalking during her wild boar journey down the dreamt tunnel. She sinks back onto the sofa bed breathing deeply, dazed, lost in a weirdly wondering state.

Dr. Bob nudges his nose into Thea's unmoving hand. The warmth and satisfying smell of his comforting doggy-ness, the cold aliveness of his nose, helps bring her all the way back. Dog friend presses his sturdiness against Thea's, licking her face with his washcloth tongue.

"Okay, I'm all right," she says, gently caressing him.

She strokes her companion's back, comforted in feeling his tight, luxuriant coat; she feels for the familiar tiny mole he has on his belly. Thea senses Dr. Bob relax as she strokes him. His moans help Thea resume normalcy.

Fully awake now, Thea recognizes the same whooshing sound she'd heard in that deep dream state of hers: the enchanting melody of her breath.

Then she remembers. The cave. Her searching animal state. The eerie sound of nothingness—and then the dim, incongruous hope of light penetrating darkness. In and out, the life-force breathes her, she notices acutely. Everywhere she looks, tiny blue seeds of awareness glow in the darkness—ahead, to the sides, below and above. Thea's pleasure spreads like liquid, her window into life's possibilities has become more real by the surrealness of this dream. She recognizes what has happened: a message from beyond.

Finally! Finally, Thea has experienced that there is something within herself, something bigger, something nobler, something—can she call this Divine?—that she's been searching for. She sinks back and holds Dr. Bob's paw, both of them smiling.

27

"All who come to Gaia Group are *stewards of the Earth*," Junkyard says on their way there, "and you be now too, White Gurl."

When they arrive, Thea sits with Junkyard and Maly in a stranger's downtown loft. Everyone's shoes are off. Cushions are strewn on the floor because there aren't enough chairs for every person at this gathering. Junkyard Trinnie and Maly told Thea they rarely miss the Tuesday night weekly meetings of the Soho chapter of Gaia Group International.

Every slice of the social pool is represented in the room. Workers sit alongside professionals, rich and poor, old and young, everyone in harmony. *A haphazard group, just like Exchange Views,* Thea thinks as she arrives and looks around.

She thinks they're like every other regular person who happens to live in the most exciting city in the world. Someone says the meeting is beginning, and asks everyone to go around the room with names, occupation, and a comment about what interests them most about Gaia Group. As folks introduce themselves, Thea notes an accountant, a dancer, an aquatics engineer, a freelance writer, a subway driver, a meat packer, nurse, lawyer, cabbie, an elderly socialite, an immigrant guy fresh from Lithuania, and one other artist besides the black-clad trio of Junkyard Trinnie, Maly, and Thea. Twenty-seven Gaians sit scattered in the spacious room.

Thea hasn't a clue what to expect, even though her friends tried to explain *thought-action* to her on several occasions beforehand.

"We have been waiting for you to get real enough so you can appreciate what we are part of," Maly whispers to Thea as they settle into their seats.

Junkyard is asked to do the honors of the opening statement.

He reads in a deliberate voice, clearly enunciating the printed declaration that begins each gathering. Thea looks around. Everyone remains seated, their eyes on Junkyard as he reads in a heartfelt tone, his West Indian cadence adding a rhythmic mellowness:

"Will you teach your children what we have taught our children?

… that the Earth is our mother?

Man did not weave the web of life,

… he is merely a strand in it.

Whatever he does to the web, he does to himself."

Maybe it's the way Junkyard reads, so respectfully, his proper use of English strange to her ear, but Thea's emotions go deep. She's surprised to feel unexpected tears stabbing behind her eyelids. Her gut is grabbed in a way that makes her want to jump up and shout, right after Junkyard finishes quietly reading. Yes, yes, she silently agrees! Each and every living thing is connected, like a web. *I've always felt it so,* she thinks.

"And here be the leader of our group," Junkyard says. He stands waiting as a distinguished older man, who limps badly, approaches the center of the room.

A slightly stooped man of medium height, whose bearing is amiable and scholarly, in his tweeds, introduced by Junkyard as "our beloved Ray Tomlinson." Thea immediately notes by his warm reception how the man, with a wide-open face sporting a neatly trimmed goatee, is the guest of honor at this gathering.

Ray's gentle gaze pierces any skepticism or resistance Thea might have clung to, agreeing to come that night. As he speaks now, Ray's voice waxes eloquent and inviting, in a mellow tone comfortable to Thea, for reasons she doesn't yet understand.

"We're all human beans just beginning to sprout," he speaks, turning to Thea, the sole newcomer. "I'm a Gaian, like everyone else here. I'm also an ecologist." Ray addresses the entire room as he and Junkyard take their seats.

Softly, he continues. "These words we've just heard, of the nineteenth century Native American, Chief Seattle, are clearly the focus of our Gaia

Groups. That's why we say them at the beginning of each of our worldwide gatherings. Let's prepare now for thought-action, by getting comfortable. We'll close our eyes and take long and deep breaths as we settle into sending energy of healing to that which needs healing."

Thea, from her friends' previous sharing, is somewhat prepared for what Ray is doing now. Yet she finds herself strangely hopeful, something she hadn't expected, even though she's been given an explanation of what was going to happen there.

"Thought-action," Junkyard explained earlier to Thea, "is what my lady fair and me be doing together every single day."

The three friends sit side by side, with Maly in the middle. Thea sees her friends close their eyes. As Thea watches, an easy peace settles on Junkyard's smooth skinned face. Maly's face becomes like an opalized glaze, radiating more inner beauty than a person would seem capable of. With both friends beside her, Thea loves looking at them. She would be content to just focus on her friends' beautiful faces and sit there, feeling at peace. But she knows she's being introduced to something new, something she knows little about; so Thea closes her eyes and follows the rippling brook of the leader's voice.

Ray's gentle words ebb and flow like a trickle of water leading to the edge of an ocean of tranquility. Pin-drop quiet is the room, as he guides everyone to a calm inner state.

A shaft of light slowly materializes in Thea's velvet-wrapped mind as she becomes attuned to Ray's pianissimo solo, which leads her, like a mystical conductor, to a beautiful composition playing somewhere softly, within herself.

Ray whispers, "Listen to your breath. It has the same music, the same rhythm as the entire universe."

The room is still. Outside only faintly distant sounds of city traffic can be heard.

Ray again speaks. "Now bring up the image of Earth in your mind as we'd see it from space. Visualize our home planet having the healthy blue glow of a clean water-covered garden world."

As the man's voice drifts, Thea creates an inner vision of Earth seen from afar, like the shots taken from the Apollo moon expedition. The image easily looms in her mind, as what Earth really is: a vulnerable puny planet suspended in space. From this imagined vantage point of hers, she sees the entire planet, and follows Ray's continuing instructions. Joy floods Thea, doing this strange exercise. So simple, yet enormously satisfying. Her breathing is suspended. She's immersed in fascination.

"Open yourself to the bigger mysteries we're part of," Ray's gentle bassoon urges. "Go with that, wherever that idea leads you."

The room is filled with motionless, breathing statues instead of bustling urbanites. Thea forgets the melodious voice belongs to a man named Ray. Instead, his voice becomes a vibration resonating in her every cell. Ray eases the Gaians further.

"Our home planet is Gaia, the name given to Earth by ancient Greeks. See how proudly she reflects her turquoise light out into the Milky Way. The light of Gaia reflects the light of our Sun out into the darkness of our galaxy, and beyond."

Completely absorbed, Thea floats as Ray's voice guides her.

"We're all sons and daughters of Gaia," he continues. "Feel your connection to our Earth Mother. She's alive, she breathes the same atmosphere we do. Her pulse is the tides of the oceans, just as our pulse pushes our body's rivers of blood. We're from the same matrix, Gaia and us: planet and its inhabitants. Each of us has the same energy within every cell of our makeup. Within each thing—colossal or minute, planet, star, moon, insect, or molecule of water: all objects—we're all connected. Simultaneously. Undeniably. This life force throbs in everything. This, my friends, is the great enigma. Feel it here and now."

A pause. Time and space are within, not without. Again, Ray's soft voice:

"Feel the pulse of the life force within you as you breathe."

Another pause. Thea no longer hears what's spoken.

"This energy, that's continuous and infinite, changes form but never dissipates. As Einstein proved. Feel the life force deeply within. Energy connects us all."

Ray is silent for a while. Then, his voice waves like a magic wand: "This energy is what Chief Seattle calls *the web of life*."

A drop of time dissolves. Uninterrupted.

"Now let's envision a world united in healing. Celebrating Unity. Peace. Create that reality."

Thea does. It isn't hard. The idea of a world with all Earth's people working together for a higher good, one that remains unknown until it appears, with no war or wasteful conflicts, makes her hopeful.

"This awareness is the truth we are creating together," Ray assures the group. "We only have to make the effort, have the intention of holding this thought, for our creations to one day shift from idea-form ... to become our new, tangible reality."

Thea doesn't move from her expansive inner experience. The group remains still for some time, with twenty-seven individuals' thought-energies entwined.

Thea feels her chest burst open as her mind melts.

This must be group hypnosis or something, is Thea's first thought upon hearing Ray's voice bringing everyone in the room to their regular, ordinary selves.

What is this strange feeling, she wonders. *It's like being connected, but to what? It's within me, but is it just me?*

Thea places her right hand over her heart and feels it throb. The steady pulsation verifies her unlimited capacity for life's creative surprises. She feels an energy, like an effulgence stirring, coming alive, astoundingly strong—a power surge originating from inside her chest.

She melts into the sublimeness of being unified with others, as if remembering something she'd forgotten, that has been hidden inside her all along.

This is delicious, she thinks, *completely intoxicating.* A new awareness flows in her veins, in her mind, filling her. It is a feeling she'd once been as familiar with as her own fingers, her toes, feet, and hands. Was that back in childhood? Or in a dream, when she'd imagined the magnificence of a powerful wave of energy all around her, lifting her above Earth's woes.

* * *

Ray's voice is a musical instrument that holds Thea's attention. His words skip stones on the glassy surface of her mind. It feels as if he's leading her into a waterfall of peace. Within this short time, he's assisted her in dissolving the last of those stubborn mental barriers she'd held on to, even in sobriety. The ones that used to drive her to drink, drug, and act out, resisting goodness. She wants to be rid of the lies and uselessness she once believed about herself, believed about a world that has no hope for anyone. She feels she's found her true family here at the Gaia Group, just as her friends had said she would when they urged her to join them.

Thea hears clearly Ray's words:

"We can help accelerate change," Ray speaks to the silent group, "by first healing ourselves. Only then can we help our broken world. Let's now bring into our mental arena all world conflict at this time—clashes everywhere, in the East and West, South and North—anywhere where people resort to control and violence as an antiquated solution. Bring any troubling picture of conflict, even locally in your community, your family, in yourself—and surround it with the light of love. Hold it there. Believe love is invisible energy capable of healing anything.

"All action starts as the seed of a mere, single thought.

"First," Ray says, "heal yourself. Then, spread this energy of love—but self-love first—wherever it's needed. And together we'll heal the entire planet, Gaia, our Earth Mother."

28

After the meeting, Thea walks with Junkyard and Maly on the glistening wet streets of Soho after a gentle late June rain washed away the dirt and grime of another day in Gotham. The three are reflecting on what Ray said. It is a quiet night in the city; the friends remarking how they can smell renewal in the spring air.

At the gathering of dedicated thought-action warriors—what Ray calls the focused mind-exercisers, and what the Gaians do for the Earth—Thea remarks to Junkyard how what they're doing reminds her of indigenous sitting around fires chanting to Great Spirit, asking for protection of the entire world. Thea feels drawn to Ray like a blind person knows where the sun is by the warm touch upon their upturned face.

As they walk together on the empty streets, Thea asks Junkyard and Maly about Ray, the mysteriously charismatic man with such a bad limp.

Junkyard said, "Ray, he be the cream of the cow's juice, White Gurl. He be the diamond that be sitting atop the caca pile."

Maly smiles at her lover's bargain-basement metaphors.

"This is true, ma chérie, Ray is like his name; light beams all around him. Best of all, being around him gives us hope too. We all feel … more useful," Maly says.

"So what's his story, anyway?" Thea asks.

Maly answers in her succinct manner. "Ray knows that the future of our world depends on even the simplest of things every person can do and think about. In Gaia Group we believe the world will be healed only when each of us heals our own self. We change our fears into love, then we trust we can heal Earth with our combined, focused minds. That's why we focus on expanding our individual selves to include the planet, which is possible through thought-action."

"And Ray be our example of how to be doing just that," Junkyard interjects.

"It is his special gift," Maly says. "Inspiring others."

"His words, his life—they be like throwing stones that cut deep ripples in still waters," Junkyard adds.

"C'est vrai, mon amour. Ray shows that each of us, every individual, is a microcosm of the universal macrocosm. He reminds and shows us how we can heal the world, just like he healed himself."

"Healed himself from what, exactly?" Thea asks.

Junkyard switches to his rare serious mode, complete with an unconscious shift to more traditional, non-island English syntax. "Years ago in the UK, Ray he be part of a group of international brains who be wanting to take more drastic steps than their uptight governments allow. Hardly any scientist, not back then, was being brave enough to be admitting how off-balance the world's environment was. It be right after World War II, we be talking about. Pollution be off the charts! Already Germany be in red-alert. Factories be spitting out toxins, making the water and air all over Europe be turning to toxic soup, long before the U.S. of A did, believe it!"

Junkyard shook his head, his dreads swishing, his features downturned.

Maly joins in. "Ray and the other scientists studying Earth's ecology were sick and tired of the fancy rhetoric politicians use to cover up the real issues. Instead of dealing with it, the scientific world got bogged down in doublespeak and endless conferences. Hashing out theories like the Big Bang took precedence over global warming and arctic meltdowns. Scientists went into a kind of universal denial. Forums got stuck on controversies like artificial intelligence, ethics on cloning and stem cells, chaos theory and plasma cosmologies—just more talk!—instead of facing the facts that Earth is crying out for help."

Junkyard quickly adds, "Ray be seeing the effects more than most people, with his own clear eyes, because he be diving all over the oceans of the world for his research."

Maly says, "The reefs were first to scream Help! ma cherie. He knew things needed to change, and quickly, because Ray is a marine biologist—"

"He be knowledgeable with a capital 'K', our Ray," Junkyard interrupts. "Did you know he be studying the tiniest creatures that live on sea reefs?"

"No, I didn't. He speaks more like a poet," Thea notes, "than a scientist."

"It is true, he is that too," Maly smiles. "Our Gaia poet."

"He be everyt'ing," Junkyard nods. "He be studying the reef's almost unseeable shelled organisms, called *foraminifera*. They be getting bleached when they be stressed-out, like corals do. Ray be the recognized expert in that field. He also be a wise, wise man, Fern Eyes, you can be seeing that for yourself. He be showing us we be having the key to the future in our hands when we be merging our foolish over-think heads with our big-love hearts."

Maly literally effervesces when she adds, "We Gaians spread the word and do thought-action, alone and in groups. We are out to create a new trend. Make awareness the new fad of the mainstream."

"That's a noble idea. But it'll be a tough sell," Thea winces. "Most people will think this stuff pretty, you know, airy fairy. They'd rather believe in the almighty power of football, politics, or fashion than do something quiet like we did back there, getting all high-and-mighty meditative, the kind of stuff people who don't know tend to say. Hey, I'm all for it, being hopeful. But the average Joe and Joanna? It's gonna be a tough road convincing the naysayers, brother and sister of mine."

The three walk along in silence for a while.

Then Maly softly adds. "True, Thea. But we Gaians, just like we Hearts, need to counter all the negative energy out there with super doses of positive and hopeful. We need to believe that each one of us open-minded Gaians makes a difference."

Junkyard's hands fly in all directions as they continue walking. "White Gurl, humanity might be setting itself up to exterminate us, all of us, and that be par for the course of history, as Ray be telling it to we. He be saying the fossil record proves how we be extincting human types several times already. And probably we be doing it again, right now."

"What?" Thea says, alarmed. "What are you talking about? I swear sometimes you just don't make sense to me, Junkyard," she nervously responds to her friend's sudden turn to doom.

"Relax, Honeypot," he says. "It ain't be happening like tomorrow. And if we keep be doing thought-action, and get it popular with celebrities and changemakers making it cool instead of stupid violent movies, and fussing over other silly t'ings, de-struction of humanity never be happening. That be our plan, our action. That be why we doing the changing of our own mental toxic waste 'cause it makes *we* feel better—and then we try to infect others with our positivity. We help others be changing, just like you changed from feeling low, getting high, to feeling high on life. Right? So yeah, most people, they be getting all worked up over blues and reds, games and races, scared shitless of going to war. We use our thought-action beams as weapons of change. Creating alternatives to injustice, greed, and poverty, that be the Gaia-job of we, Maly and me, and now you too, White Gurl, is to help us be convincing all these citizens out there who be wasting their mental powers. Wait! Here me be cri-ti-cal about correcting that! Those who be stuck in fear not be using their *unlimited mental power-brains* for Earth's beck and call of needing to be healed. We Gaians, together, be making somet'ing better than the future of our own puny lives."

Junkyard sighs terrifically. "We not stupid. We be knowing we're the minority here. There be a lot of work for we, now and ahead of now."

"The Gaia Group, you see, Thea," Maly says with an upbeat tone, "is the only hope we have to cling to."

"Plus," Junkyard says, somehow straightening himself to appear even taller, "Ray be a man of science. Scientists be studying the unknown. He be showing us the way of creating the solution. We be making thought-action for all our Earth ills like nobody be doing, art or science-wise. Ray Tomlinson be a man of truth the world be needing, Fern Eyes."

* * *

The trio sinks again into silence as they saunter down the street, nearing the couples' lofts. Finally, Thea breaks the ponderous silence.

"So, what's with Ray's limp?"

"Oh," Maly softly answers, "he was in a terrible car crash right after he graduated from MIT. That is a prosthesis, from just below his right hip."

"And," Junkyard solemnly notes, "Ray be dead by the time help be arriving."

"Dead?"

"Yes mohn, Ray be a bona fide NDE," Junkyard says. "He be dead at the roadside when the ambulance be arriving, but he be coming back. He be one of the Near-Dead-Experience people. Ray be remembering the whole t'ing, being dead, he says, like everybody else who be dying and be coming back be saying the same time. You know, the tunnel, the light, that stuff. Everyt'ing be changing for him after that. Before, he be happy working in a lab, not being too interested or be needing to be involved with the world, him studying the *foraminifera* with them electron microscopes. Never be wanting to do any research, the deep diving part, on his own. But after the accident—Ray be wanting to experience more of life, and believe you me, he be doing just that."

"What does he say about, you know, dying like that?" Thea asks.

"He says a lot," Maly replies. "He says he came back because he wanted to, or had to. That he was *told* it wasn't his time. Like every other NDE-person, they say, messages are heard. Ray tells us he saw, and knows is true, that he felt the same power that makes thought-action work—the invisible connection between us all. He really experienced it. He knows it is true. And we trust his saying he did. Ray says if enough people practice doing it worldwide, thought-action can be more effective than diplomacy, or new energy technology, in bringing about a healthy balance, one in which Nature and human dignity be respected. Instead of people molesting the sacred of life."

"Ah," says Thea. "I think I understand now."

Junkyard adds, "After the accident Ray be getting involved, instead of be hiding out in his lab. He be organizing the first Gaia Group, right there in Oxford where he be spending a few years teaching. Then he started to be diving reefs with a special flipper prosthesis he be designing for himself, to collect data."

"When he came back to the States to teach at Stanford," Maly says, "Ray started Gaia Groups here too; and now tens of thousands of Gaians like us around the globe are planting thought-seeds for a healthy, united Earth."

"Me, I rather be believing the Ray-mohn," Junkyard merrily says, "than others whose closed minds and hearts be shriveled up like hard raisins."

In the days that followed, Thea tried her best to discount thought-action.

She couldn't see the value of sitting in a darkened room with others—doing nothing.

For the next six months she made every excuse she could think of to not return to the Gaia Group with Junkyard and Maly. She avoided her two heart artists, not knowing why. Still out of touch with her feelings, she just didn't want to get involved. Instead, she worked waiting tables, filling multiple sketchbooks with ideas at Sophia's place while Dr. Bob stared at her wondering when he'd be free of those two cats he had to tolerate. She took up playing squash, but couldn't get her eyes and hands to coordinate enough to hit the ball, so gave up after a few lessons. She tried jazz dance, but couldn't remember step 1 by the time she got to step 5. She was invited sailing by a potential suitor out in Long Island Sound, but wound up with her first case of seasickness and never saw the man or his boat ever again. She tried indoor roller skating, nearly busting her front teeth and wrenching her back. By winter's end, another man invited her for a trip to a New England ski resort where Thea ended up unconscious but unhurt from a run-in with a surprise boulder. In the city, and with a gaggle of sober friends, she felt safe clubbing and dancing downtown, with Sophia's prescient warning. And she was right: clubbing soon drained her energy and triggered way too many dangerous old drink-and-drug cravings for Thea's comfort. She was desperate to distract herself from accepting that thought-action was a worthy pursuit.

Always—in the back of her mind—she kept remembering what Ray Tomlinson had said that night. "You can't help the world to change until you become whole and healed yourself."

It's late that winter when Thea calls Junkyard and Maly to tell them she's ready. Ready to try again, sitting with her eyes closed, visualizing Mother Earth being healed. Had she healed herself, in the meantime? Thea hasn't a clue. She doesn't want to drink or drug anymore, that's all she knows. She's been having fun being sober. So yeah, she figures she too must have healed something.

When she calls, Junkyard and Maly tell Thea when the next group meets. Thea goes again and again, with and without her friends, enjoying each meeting more than the last. After each exhilarating round of thought-action she says to herself,

The time has come for me to be real.

29

The phone rings at the tiny Warren Street hole-in-the-wall bedroom in someone's spacious loft that Thea and Dr. Bob moved into several weeks earlier. She's readying for work at the trendy Duane Street Station, a pulsating Tribeca restaurant specializing in gastronomic whimsy. Thea is rushing around looking for something to put up her now grown-long hair with, and dives for the phone on the tenth ring. Dr. Bob watches from the patch of sun in which he lies.

"Hey, CC, what's happening?"

"Fast?" Thea says, surprised and flummoxed. "How'd you get my number, man?"

"Whoooa. That's a nice way to greet a guy you haven't talked to in over a year. Nice to hear your voice too."

"I'm sorry, Fast. You caught me rushing out the door. It's good to hear your voice, really."

"Someone new on the chase?"

"No no, nothing like that. Just making moola. You know, life on my own and all that. I left Max ages ago, but of course you must know that. That's how you got my number, right? So how are you, anyway?" Thea continues buttoning her blouse with the phone tucked under her chin.

She can hear Fast Forward inhale sharply. "Not good CC. I'm afraid that's why I'm breaking the wall of silence you've cruelly erected around yourself. Some of your old friends need you. Like me."

"You need me?" Thea plops down on her unmade bad. "What's up, Fast?" She looks at her work shoes that need putting on. She listens, something she's made a point of doing lately. She's become a professional listener since learning to at Exchange Views and sharing everything with Sophia. Now Thea listens to her old friend Fast Forward.

"Take a wild guess. What's happening to every gay guy in this and every fucking city these days?"

"Oh, no."

The weight of their combined silence is tonnage on her heart. The truth weighs heavy. Thea has not given more than a fleeting thought to her old get-fucked-up-with buddy, barely mentioning his name aloud since that night she moved out of her toxic scene with Max.

"Shit, Fast, I'm so sorry. HIV positive?"

"Worse. Skipped Park Place, sent directly to jail. Sentenced to eternity, no possibility of parole."

"Oh fuck, no! Fast, you sure?"

He coughs a haughty laugh. "You sure you got tits? Man, I'm telling you CC, you're talking to someone who's put in an order for a shiny halo to hang over the mean motherfucker of a black skull I'm getting tattooed, right on top of my head, just in case I make it for the next Halloween blast."

Thea's voice shrinks. "Isn't there medicine? There must be something."

"C'mon, Thea. This is 1985, not a fucking time machine. No one knows anything about this plague. We just discovered the damn virus, like, a day ago—and look, practically the fucking *next* I've got full-blown AIDS. Is that my shit luck, or what? The fucking epidemic is on every to-do and fix-it list, but meanwhile we're droppin' like flies. We're all dead. Every gay man who's alive now might not be in a few years. If we're not dying, we're probably carrying the damn bug around, unknowingly infecting everyone we love."

"Fast, don't say that! You have to try, you have to believe—"

"I don't *have to do* a damn thing, Thea. I'm dying! I don't even have to floss my fucking teeth anymore. It's over for me."

"What about The Supply House?"

"What about it? God, you're something else, you know that, CC? We had to quit. No other chick can do what you do. If you really want to know, lots of times I cursed your fucking name for going straight on me. If you ever had the courtesy to answer my calls, you'd have known the band was always about *you*, you big dink."

Thea doesn't know what to say.

"Listen, Fast, I have to go, I'm really sorry. I can't afford to fuck up this job. The tips are all I've got. Besides Dr. Bob."

"You've got your art."

"I haven't got any place to work right now, 'cept my lap."

"I'll let you use my studio, if you promise to come on over and help me die. I know Dr. Bob would be glad to see me even if you're not."

Thea doesn't know whether to cringe or cheer. Is Fast really dying? Or is this another ruse like he's pulled so many times in the past, to get a rise out of someone.

"CC?"

"Yeah, I'm here. You've just blown my mind, man. Wow, this is heavy."

"You think *your* mind's blown, what about mine?"

"Fast, look, I'll come over after work. Okay? I get off at three, I'll go home and change and get Dr. Bob. I can be at your place by around five. Is that cool?"

"Try to make it more like four, CC. I gotta go to Saint Vincent's to get my nightly feel-good shot of Dilaudid with a twist of vitamin C."

"How about we meet at St. Vincent's."

"You'd do that? Really?"

"They let dogs in?"

While she waits tables, earning wine-enhanced tips enough to forge a secure headway against the riptide of the cost of independence, Thea's head churns. She never considered Fast Forward a class act kind of friend, like Junkyard and Maly have been to her. But he'd been a part of her, along with Big Sue, in all the debauched shenanigans they'd orchestrated. He was there that wretched night tugboat Annie insisted on killing herself on an icy highway.

It's unspeakably sad, Fast having the plague, she thinks. In between serving and speaking niceties to customers, Thea is plunged into the familiar battle with hopelessness. She's actually grateful to be feverishly running around, speeding from kitchen to bar to talk-crackling tables. Too busy to think of Fast with a death sentence disease.

Above plates of steaming grilled salmon with dill and capers, platters of shitake omelets smothered in goat cheese and lemon curd, Thea rushes, trying to distance herself from the snapping fangs of old head-tripping tormentors. Those inner demons of hers start snarling, trying to ambush her happiness, back in full force.

It surprises Thea to discover how very much alive, sneakily hiding, lying in wait the demons are, waiting for some bad news, or a weak moment to force her to get high. Whenever she stops running for a second—her mind bites her ass again. She scurries off to deliver another order and stays busy.

The brightly colored Margaritas, Singapore Slings, Wallbangers, and her favorite, Stingers, start to look too damn good to Thea, as she takes tray after tray of them to customers.

"*They* can drink, why can't I?" she angrily murmurs.

Then—quick as a blink—she remembers. She controls the demons. They're only in her head. And again, like so many times before, she commands them *six feet away!* just as Sophia taught her. Quick as that, her snarling gargoyles retreat and stay at a safe distance, just as Sophia promised they always would.

Thea leaves the restaurant and returns home, changes, and quickly walks Dr. Bob around the block, then hops the number six train uptown to Saint Vincent's. She pushes open the double doors of the outpatient clinic.

"Gee you look different. I've missed ya, CC."

She embraces her old friend tightly. When she pulls away she tries disguising her shock at how he looks like an empty costume of himself. Then she says, "Yeah, I've had to lie low, Fast. Been cleaning up my act. Sorry it's taken so long … to see you."

It's easy to see Fast Forward isn't long for this world. His eyes are the only viable life-spark he has left, two stars shining in a soon-to-burn-out quasar. As they wait for his meds, Fast and Thea sit quietly talking, tittering over old times, sharing some new ones as well. All around Fast, Thea can see an opaque, cement-gray cloud hugging his body like a bad odor.

"You don't look that bad," she grimaces.

"Shit CC, don't lie," he croaks. He knows how he feels and what he looks like.

Just then Frederick Newton, Fast Forward's real name, is called out and they both get up. Fast gets his cup of pills and they hightail it out of Saint Vincent's.

Fast and Thea spend as much time together as they can after that. She takes Dr. Bob over to see him, often arriving without being asked, at Fast's window-blocked, lightless space on the lower East Side. She shops and cooks healthy meals for him, does a little cleaning. Sometimes she reads aloud to help pass the time. But over the next couple weeks his condition worsens with every new sunrise; his pain deepens with every sunset. Pretty soon Fast is too weak to make the trip to St. Vincent's. Thea is prepared by the time Fast is admitted to the hospital, Sophia having coached her for what's to come.

Thea taps the white starchy sheet. They'd not spoken much for the last few visits. Fast has a hard time talking.

When she arrives that afternoon, she sees his aura has changed. No longer a death-readying gray color, Fast's energy field has an ominous, penetrating black stain on its perimeter, nearly a foot away from where he lies semiconscious. Thea, surprised at this new ability, plainly sees it. The stain—visibly seeping in from the outermost edge of the periphery of his life force—increases. She cringes, knowing what this means, from Sophia's instructions. Thea's never been around a dying person before. Fast opens his eyes then and greets her with a slight uplift of his eyebrows and a pinch at the corners of his mouth. It's the best he can do.

"About over ... for me," he croaks.

"Do you want me to come and stay with you, Fast?"

His eyelashes blink. It appears like his eyes light up, if only for a moment, with the spark she's always known. From his wasted mound of a body, something powerful ignites in the hospital room. A sidewise glow sears right into Thea's chest. Then and there it breaks into sharp sorrow, as if her heart were a mirror shattering into a million little pieces.

Fast's eyes flood with wetness. "You'd do that for me?"

Thea squeezes his hand and says, "Sure."

Thea knows that Fast's family, the Newtons, long ago disqualified him as their son, and turned their backs on him. His Queens family, typical for those closeted times, had been too horrified to accept his choices, once their Freddy settled into his adulthood of unabashed preferences and shady associates, herself included.

Thea's previous decadence hadn't differed that much from Fast's. And she certainly wasn't any closer to her birth family than he was, or Sue had been either. Too much bad stuff had happened to all three in their childhood stories. Big Sue's family had been just as unforgiving, just as intolerant, just as nonexistent, as Thea's was. Neither Thea nor Fast had ever heard a word about Big Sue's family until her father happened to call her loft that time, right after she'd been killed.

"Sure, I'll be around for the most important party of your life, my friend," Thea said in an upbeat tone, in a muted voice, just as Sophia had instructed her to do. Fast motions Thea closer so he can whisper.

"Really appreciate it. Only happens once. May as well get your money's worth, eh, CC?

"So they say, Fast, but who knows?" she whispers back. "Life is a mystery. Death must be too."

On the white pillow, Fast looks small and sunken. His body lies motionless on the sheet's crisp starkness. Nothing moves but wild fright in his eyes.

Then Fast smiles, this time a bit longer. *He looks serene,* Thea thinks.

They hardly speak the rest of the afternoon. Later, when speaking is too painful for him, in a low voice Thea tells him things she thinks he'd like to hear. Her friend's strength steadily diminishes as his breathing slows.

Thea softly tells Fast about the discoveries Sophia has shared about her thanatology work for ages now—how she helps a person have a conscious life transition. Fast blinks hard at that. That night Thea returns briefly to her studio apartment to gather some things and calls Sophia to check in, gain some strength, recharge her own worn batteries.

"Keep your voice real soft," Sophia reminds her. "The senses become hyper-acute when a person is leaving their body. Comfort him. Use simple words. Pray with him, or silently. It'll mean a lot to ease his transition, kiddo. Trust me, it makes a difference."

"I'm not so good at that, Sophia," Thea admits.

"It's just talking to your HP, kid. Just do it for Fast. No big deal. You're not signing a contract with the Almighty," Sophia says.

After work the next day, Thea rushes back and spends the night, sleeping on a cot the nurses wheel in for her, right next to Fast's bed. She notices no other friends have come to visit Fast. She's glad to be there for him, even if it's a party of two. By now he's in and out of a deep, painless state. Motionless. Breathing only every now and then. In the morning she calls Sophia and asks more precisely how to assist her pal.

"Helping Fast to face the great hereafter," Sophia plainly says, "might be the hardest thing you'll ever have to do in life."

Thea sighs. "Yeah, but it feels like I'm getting a lot out of helping him," she says, surprising herself to hear this.

"It's obviously what your life needs," Sophia says, "as well as your friend's."

"I couldn't do it without you, Sophia. You've taught me so much."

"Someday it'll be your turn to help another land back onto Planet Sober, kiddo."

"Do you really think I can handle this, Sophia? Sometimes I don't see how I possibly can. Dying is—so final."

"Yes, it is. But you're strong enough. Everything happens when it's supposed to, kid."

"I guess. Helping Fast feels like I'm the one getting the gift. A year ago, I would have run away from this. I hate hospitals. I would've been way too freaked to even see him like this. Death takes courage to go through, to witness."

"You weren't ready then. But you are now. That's the only thing that matters, kid, not what used to be, or what's going to be. But what *is* right here and now, is all we have."

"Sophia, you're my angel."

"Yeah right, I'm your pudgy angel," she scoffs in a half-joking tone, poking Thea with this sudden plunge into Sophia's neatly disguised but glaringly deep pity-pot.

Those momentary lapses of Sophia's, when she slips out how she really feels, are never what Thea expects from her otherwise seemingly perfect friend. *Perhaps she's a tad overweight*, Thea thinks, *but what a levelheaded person would only call voluptuous, with rounded curves instead of the starved angularity of urban fashionistas seen on every Manhattan street corner.*

"You look great to me," Thea reassures her. "You're perfect to me."

Sophia quickly mutters a clumsy, "Thanks, kiddo, you're sweet."

She can't see Thea blushing over the phone. No one ever calls her sweet but Sophia.

30

Sophia is the rock to which Thea clings these stressful days. For the first time in her life Thea feels useful, meaningfully useful. As much as Fast needs her, Thea's heart bursts seeing her friend's silent torture.

It becomes rapturous for Thea to be with Fast as he slips away, watching him, thankfully, soon to leave the pain and sorrow, the awful rejection he felt in his short life, to roam freely outside his earthbound misery.

Thea sees her friend as a giant phoenix, ready to arise from that wasted body he no longer needs, ready to fly off somewhere more glorious, a place with no judgment.

He awakens now and then, with the stunned look in his eyes of a person who's surprised to still be here. Bored with being here. Ready, oh so ready, to move on.

Fast tries to speak but his mouth is dry. Thea puts some water on his parched lips. It takes some minutes before Fast can work his tongue. Thea waits patiently as Fast bargains with his brain to stay conscious, at least a while longer. Finally, he scratches out a sound. Thea leans forward. She wants to hear every syllable that falls from his mouth, to know as much as she can of this event she is privileged to witness.

"Love," Fast slurs, looking deep into her eyes, "We're all love. And light."

Thea nods, sitting with Fast, holding his hand in silence. Her entire life seems to have been in preparation for this moment, to be here as Fast Forward's sidekick, to see for herself that the end is not the end at all.

As Fast sublimely smiles, Thea cherishes the moment.

His breath becomes shallower. She does as Sophia had instructed: "Keep good thoughts in your head, Thea. He'll go peacefully that way."

Thea calls his parents and breaks the news. A strained woman's voice says they'll come to claim his body for burial. Thea makes the trip out to Massapequa on the Long Island Railroad for Fast's graveside service. She speaks only a word of greeting to the Newtons, his working-class parents, who don't know what to say to this nice-looking woman with that strange dog, wondering how she came to care so deeply for their son.

Thea's life starts changing at a pace she wouldn't have believed possible. By helping her friend, Thea was given precious gifts, from Fast *and* Sophia. From Fast Forward, Thea received his undeniable glimpsing of Love and Light as he peered into the portal to the unknown. Thea assumed he must have experienced the Great Enigma for himself. From Sophia, Thea learned how to accept as *real* the unseen yet accessible energy that her spiritually wise friend accessed every day.

"Just keep that white light around everything, and your life will get better," Sophia keeps telling her. "The light of love protects and guides us."

After Fast left the planet, Thea and Dr. Bob take the Hampton Jitney out to the rocky shore of Montauk Point, to have a ceremony of their own by the Atlantic waters. They spend an afternoon staring at the sea, tossing wave-smoothed gray rocks into the surf, communing with Fast. Thea thinks how life on Earth will never be the same for her, not after this gift of omnipresent love that Fast has inadvertently presented.

"Thank you, Fast," she says aloud to her unseen friend as she tosses another stone into the waves. "Thanks to you I know the truth now. Feeling love everywhere is no longer a fairytale for me."

31

Thea regularly attends Gaia Group, often tagging along with Junkyard and Maly. She begins to help the group at rallies and demonstrations they hold: in Washington Square and Central Park, Union Square, and once at the United Nations, and other events sponsored by the growing eco-family whose silent thought-action, they believe, helps balance the growing ills of a chronically toxic world.

"I'm new to Gaia Group," Thea tells the handsome Brazilian man named Raffie she meets there one night. "But here is where I feel most useful."

"We're lucky to have you," the man with smiling dark eyes says. He introduces himself as a horticulturist visiting for a term at NYU. "I'm on sabbatical from teaching in Sao Paulo," he adds.

With Raffie, Thea's sex drive is ignited. He becomes her first sober relationship under the influence of nothing besides the pure lust of animal attraction.

Every minute Thea can spare from waitressing—attending Gaia Group in evenings and Exchange Views in mornings, sketching new ideas for artwork in between—she spends with Raffie.

One night Raffie says, "You must come visit me when I return to Sao Paulo."

Thea smiles and nods, but doesn't reply. She doesn't feel strongly enough about Raffie to consider doing that. *How remarkable,* she thinks, *that I know how I feel instead of letting life toss me around like a leaf in a tornado. I am getting better!*

* * *

Ray Tomlinson, with his wife Julia, who accompanies him this time from their upstate retreat, arrive for the big Earth Day celebration that spring. Junkyard and Maly are asked to join Ray and Julia up on the platform to speak about thought-action. Thea stands at the side of the raised dais with a group of other Gaian volunteers. Raffie returned to Sao Paulo the month before, and Thea's not sorry. She had a great time playing with the energy of desire.

The noon rally in Central Park has started. A swarm of students, professors, locals, and out-of-towners crowd around a popular fountain where the bright green and orange banners, the colors of Gaia Groups International, are hung between monster speakers. Thea spent hours the previous days handing out printed fliers urging people to come to the event. She's leaning against the makeshift stand, listening, and excited to hear the dynamic speakers. Glad to be part of such a great organization as the dedicated Gaians are.

Ray speaks first. The gathering of several hundred is receptive to joining Ray when he invites them for a few silent minutes of sending their combined mental intentions out to the ailing world, giving their mind's attention, their spiritual energies to the needs—big or small, environmental, political, or social—of planet Earth. When he turns the podium over to Junkyard, Ray is given a riotous round of applause by a satisfied audience; satisfied perhaps, because now they have been given a tool, a practical method by which each and every person can aid our challenged world instead of feeling hopeless and ineffective. No longer would anyone have to feel impotent, confused, or unwilling to be part of the solution out of fear, limited assets, or time restraints. Instead of perpetuating the environmental problem by inaction, all listeners now have the strength of practicing thought-action.

Junkyard is starting to speak when suddenly a rush of angry young men swarm by Thea. She's quickly swallowed by a throng of black-leather clad neo-Nazi roughnecks, snarling, frightening as zombies with their shaved and greased white skulls covered with repulsive swastika tattoos. Thea is shoved up against a wooden upright beam that abuts the platform when a surge of crushing disruptors invades the rally, jumping the five-foot height and crowding onto the dais, their verbal assault exploding like artillery fire.

"Go back to where you come from, you skanky Rasta!" a bald-headed guy pushes and grabs the mic from Junkyard's hand, screaming at him in the middle of the stage. The skinheads are bombarding from all sides. Over the speakers come disjointed slurs:

"You're nothing but—fucking dumb ass—"

"You don't—belong here—"

"Gaia Schmy-a—who gives—a fuck—"

"We're all—gonna die anyway—who gives—shit—"

As suddenly as the skinheads arrived, Thea hears whistles and there they are, a squadron of police! Rushing to block the disruptors, presumably the police having been forewarned of the fracas, as they stand ready with riot shields, helmets, and sticks held high in the air. Within minutes the violent explosion is over. The shouting subsides. The skinheads are rounded up, frothing and spitting like rabid dogs. Their shocking hatred soon becomes just another off-note in a city of a million dissonant tunes. The rioters are dragged off the stage by an impressive show of police force. Still shaking, terrified Thea holds onto the wooden support beam that bloodied her when she slammed up against it.

The mic is back in Junkyard's possession. But Thea's shaking too hard to hear what he's saying. She feels like a loose sheet in a wind storm. This is America? she wonders. This is the land of the free?

Thea doesn't hear Junkyard's calming words to the crowd. She doesn't notice that Ray and Julia had been safely taken off the platform before things got rough. She's fighting to maintain her balance and not fall to the ground. The mêlée lasted only minutes. The crowd that came to hear the Gaia Group begins to return from having raced away up a hill when the invading throng appeared. Thea's arm is bleeding through her light cotton blouse, where it got crushed on splintery wood. Her sandaled feet ache and bleed where thick black boots of the rally-crashers had kicked, shoved, and stomped her in their rush for the stage.

Above her head, Junkyard is speaking to reassure the crowd about how, even in the face of violence such as they've just seen, "It be the same choice everyone gets to be deciding for themselves—healing action, forgiveness not revenge, unity not retaliation—aiming love toward people, even those who be acting more like animals like those who just be spewing their hatred here. We Gaians choose to be loving, choose to help heal Earth's environment for all we humankind. Even them sorts who be calling us nasty names."

He pauses and looks around the spellbound crowd.

"For me," Junkyard proclaims loudly in his best stateside diction through the mic, "Me have *to be doing* something to help our dread state or me cannot be sleeping at night. How can some be angry or scared, instead of choosing to shoot the love bullets? How? Because they not be awake to the truth!"

Here a big cheer drowns the King of the Outsiders, and he must begin his thought again.

"The truth be, my friends, that love and love alone heals. Me be glad to be having Gaia, and Dr. Ray Tomlinson here," Junkyard opens his arm to include Ray who, with Julia, has just returned to their seats on the stage, "to be reminding us that—right now!—we can all be doing somet'ing about the big dilemmas in our world. Hate, judgment, fear—they be the opposite of love. What we just be seeing here proves how love be the healing we all need, not more anger, not more blame."

Again the crowd cheers and applauds!

Thea tries not to think about her throbbing arm, her bruised and bleeding feet. She doesn't think anything's broken. She listens to her brave friend up there who is speaking without a hint of anger. Thea knows Junkyard Trinnie well enough to know that being called names never pushes him off his throne of inner peace. Fear and intimidation are other people's poisons. She's just glad the dangerous mob got apprehended. She sees them standing cuffed, surrounded by the police, off in the distance. Maybe a few got away, but not many.

She tries to listen but Thea's body now shakes uncontrollably. She can't catch her breath. Her feelings, so raw and so new, are overwhelming her. She loses it, covers her face with her hands and bursts into muffled sobs as Junkyard continues to speak from the podium above her head of his love for the garden planet we live on, of his belief in hope, not more separation and despair.

Thea has never been so close to the unreasonable face of violence before. Even during the shark attack, when she unthinkingly dove in to rescue Giles, her fear never penetrated her, not like this human cruelty has, this afternoon's attack.

She shivers as fright-tears run down her face. She stands and shakes silently as many others crowd around her to listen to her friend, oblivious to Thea's state, as she faces downward, lost in her own thoughts. Right then, she swears she's sticking to making art. She thinks, *I don't belong at rallies, or passing out pamphlets. I can do thought-action anywhere, others can do the grandstand thing. It's more important for me to make art to help Gaia and promote thought-action that way. I can't get sidetracked. I'm a creative, not an eco-soldier.*

32

Thea and the others gather after the final speaker. By then, she has calmed herself. Junkyard and the others surround her, expressing concern about her injuries, her bloodied blouse, her limp.

Maly puts her long arms around her friend and says, "Thea, you look like a ghost. And look how you're bleeding! Let us get this bandaged. Me—I want to kick those crazy jerks like a football, but you—Thea, I know something bad got triggered inside you. I can see it."

Junkyard says, "We be all the time conflicted too, Honeypot." The group is walking toward a riot ambulance waiting nearby, for first aid.

"Maly and I be getting closer to making our dream come true. Soon we be breaking ground on One Blood back in Trinidad, maybe this time next year if all be going well. You be helping yourself and the world as well if you be sticking with making your art, White Gurl," he says as if reading Thea's mind. "You not be cut out to handle the loonies that always want to be mixing it up with the treehuggers."

"I can't do this anymore, Ray," she says calmly. "I'm just not cut out for this public rally stuff. It makes me, I don't know, uptight I guess."

"I know exactly where you're coming from, and it's all right," Ray says, putting an arm around shaken Thea, whose tears have dried, but is still pale and scared from such random, senseless viciousness they'd witnessed.

"Your work is your life's passion, I know," Ray says. "Once a person finds their own cause they have to follow their joy. Yours is doing art."

Maly hugs her shocked, shaking friend. "You need to stay focused on that heart art of yours."

Junkyard nods solemnly. "We be understanding, Honeypot. You be helping Gaia more by doing less for rallies and more with your art. That way you be helping us by helping thems that needs to be shocked awake."

Thea straightens her spine. "You're right. I'm onto something with the work, I can feel it. I'm lucky Fast willed me his place. It's been awhile since I've had a studio. It's time to make my ideas come to life. My mind is like a radio antenna. I keep picking up the most amazing images. From where? I don't know."

Junkyard says, "Yeah mohn. You now becoming *to be* that bridge tender you be telling we about. Remember? You be like our secret agent, making thought-action happen in your Dreamtimes."

"It's settled then," Ray announces. "Thea's greatest contribution to our cause is to make Gaian art."

The group of Gaians raise their voices in cheery approval. The idiocy of the evil protesters' lingering odor is mitigated a bit by all this positive energy.

Thea looks around at her friends and a smile cracks her face. She loves being here. Even though she's in pain from the attack, she feels home is wherever she can be with others like these special people here, who love the planet as much as life itself.

"That be right," Junkyard breaks the hushed mood. "Let's be celebrating that, with our Green Glow Thea here. That civilization be getting what it needs. Thea's full-on heart art to the rescue! Sometimes we be altering plans and procedures to be right, and good."

With good humor as balm, Thea limps with her friends to where taxis await them.

The work coming out of Thea's studio has changed dramatically from before her landing on Planet Sober. The stop-and-stare images Junkyard used to call "fantasy with a purpose" have become more intense, more honest, more intriguing, more real. Provocative spiritual fodder given birth through enormous energy and curiosity. Thea's creative drive is now unbridled, fortified by Fast having let her into the secret of the Great Mystery. She'll never forget the distinctly weird feeling when his life's source, his energy—surged right into her. Fast's life force—what remained of his at his passing—became part of Thea's life energy. Her life force became augmented by her friend's willing his energy into hers. Just as at Big Sue's passing, her leftover life force transferred into Thea—but Thea doesn't know this yet.

Junkyard Trinnie and Maly are invited over to her studio to see the latest work.

"Whoooa, this be some intense stuff here, Green Glow," he says, making exclamation points sparkle in the air. Walking around her reclaimed studio—from a lower East Side punk band's rehearsal space with aluminum foil blacked-out windows, to a light-infused sanctuary for a heart artist with a purpose—the work space hums with energy. "Where you be getting these Irie ideas from, Honeypot? Whew! We got to be getting St. Pierre over here and I mean *fast*. Oops!" Junkyard bends over, hitting his thigh in high jubilation.

"Your Dreamtimes remind me," Maly says, ignoring her man's caprice, "of maps in our search for things sacred. Thea, you 'ave managed to capture the essence about the simple things we humans do, how everything is connected. It is wonderful work, mon amie!"

"Yes, that be it," Junkyard says. "Fern Eyes, here your Dreamtimes be catching the feeling me be having after waking up, when me be *knowing* what me be dreaming be something really important, but me can't be remembering, and it only be after trying to be piecing all them images of dreaming together when things be starting to jog my memory that it be coming to me, like that—" Junkyard snaps his fingers, "—like a puzzle be putting back together quick quick. The dream be the pieces, all mixed up. But in your Dreamtimes," Junkyard breaks off and shows his piano-keys grin, "the answers all be there, already being assembled. Easy to be making the connections for we then."

For a few moments Thea catches her breath. She feels her heart racing.

"That's exactly what these pieces are meant to do," Thea says, greatly relieved. She shows her friends what she's working on.

"See these slices of recognizable things, surrounded by incongruent images—such as messages dreams contain? The kind that are life-altering, if we can just straighten up their jumbled meaning. That's the way we deal with dreams, right? Figuring them out, searching for connections. Finding inspiration in disparate messages from our subconscious, which I believe is connected to the All of Everything."

"Most people live for simpler things, like pure pleasure," Maly says in an agreeable tone.

"To be eating and drinking, some to be making war, making more money than God be needing," Junkyard flatly adds.

"Well, these Gaia works are not for them," Thea simply declares.

"Thea, you've really got something here," Maly laughs, regarding the work, not able to keep her eyes from roaming over every inch of the many canvases. "I am going to introduce you to my friend …"

"No wait, my love," Junkyard kindly interrupts, "she be going with St. Pierre. Me already arranged it, months ago."

Thea shakes her head, chuckling. Her friends helping to get her art exposed. Things are changing. At head-spinning speed.

Upon Junkyard's insistence, she begins exhibiting at Jules St. Pierre's gallery, where Thea Bowman's Dreamtimes are received by a wildly receptive audience. It takes courage to believe these portraits of humanity's awakening will pay off as a new art form. Other styles are selling better in major art capitals than the budding Heart Art genre, but soon Thea's work is almost as sought after as Junkyard's. It will take another couple orbits around the sun for the hopelessness of the current popular dystopic art to let go its tenacious grip.

One day, after her first painting sold for a four-figure amount, Thea says to her friend, "I just don't get it, Junkyard. Between bulging human flesh and homoerotic shit and heart-hurting bestiality stuff that people get talked into hanging over their dining room tables—is it supposed to be cool? What's that all about? What's going on with the crap the art world's into, anyway? The emperor's new clothes are just a butt-naked fool parading in public—this ugly feeling art—isn't it, Junkyard? Some of it may be painted well, but—holy shit! What it's about is so incredibly pessimistic!"

"Irie, White Gurl," Junkyard says, throwing his head back, howling from deep in his throat. "You be calling it for true. Maly and me be believing that spreading fear, like down-vibe art be doing, has gone too far, m'sohn. We ought publicly be proclaiming a manifesto, we Hearts!"

"Honestly, Junkyard, if my work doesn't make the human heart soar, I'm not bothering making it anymore."

"You be right, Honeypot. People who be stepping on toes of what be sacred, there always be a price to be paying for that," he softly ends.

Both sit in silence, wondering what that unknown price could be. Wondering if the whole world will have to keep paying for what just a minority of irreverents in power insist on, from cruel world leaders to so-called freedom of expression types, like the skinheads who tried busting up the Gaia Group rally in Central Park.

"The negatives cannot be lasting in the shining light of our work, Fern Eyes," Junkyard then says. "That be why we must keep putting out the hope and the wake-up message by shocking people into feeling deeper. People need to be looking really good, and up close, at what this life be all about."

"Junkyard, you're right," Thea says. "But we Hearts know that nasty, down and dirty con jobs perpetuate Earth's problems, instead of visualizing solutions that help raise up the collective understanding. Bad art feeds off of fear and greed—and worships materialism. It's about making enormous chunks of money by promoting no-hope with degrading images. People must get off on putting themselves down, is that it, Junkyard?"

"Who can be saying, Go Green? Why waste time thinking about low vibrations. They not be helping we rise up, we Hearts know. The future be resting in our hands, with we Hearts. The fad of a dead future be over soon, you watch! Scientists and artists be getting more spiritual every day. They be joining up too, in their understanding. Life and art, they be sisters, and we them brothers. We Hearts just got to be going ahead, steady like. Focus on solutions that always be combatting negative forces. Let Irie be the artist, not the I of we. And never mind thinking about cults of dread. They be gone soon enough."

* * *

Thea becomes the most ardent and blatantly honest of the *shock-and-wake-up* Heart Artists. She's also the first woman to exhibit at Jules St. Pierre, finally ending an all-male trend in this innovative new school. In the show's *Art Quorum* review, Thea's work is described as "galvanizing, alluring, a captivating combination of embarrassment and thrill; shocking and inexplicably right. Seduce us, Ms. Bowman, please! Make our teeth sing with your Dreamtimes."

St. Pierre's Heart Artists are a substrata of visionary artists, interchangeably called *Outside-outsiders, Art Brut, Nature-ists,* or tongue-in-cheek—the *Changemakers.* Thea, Junkyard, and Maly uncomfortably react over the absurd names people are compelled to give new ideas. "It be like they have to stamp a brand name on even honesty," Junkyard sucks his teeth as he speaks.

Jules St. Pierre agrees when the subject comes up. "The more foolish, the more outlandishly pretentious a genre's nomenclature is—in the rarified world of gallery art—the better for business."

"Any press be good press," Junkyard agrees.

The Outside-outsiders begin to reshape the very fabric of elitism, the art world's drug of choice. Art aficionados start using the term *Cosmic* more often for St. Pierre's outlandish *Outrés,* after a leading critic wrote: "There really is no one genre these Outside-outsiders fit into. They're pretty cosmic."

When Thea is asked by a slick-talking reporter to explain what her work is about, she thinks a moment, then answers, "I try to not contribute to the downfall of humanity."

In *The International Eye,* the Cosmics are asked to publish their manifesto, just to set the record straight: "Through art," Junkyard is quoted in the article, "we intend to be lifting up our fellow humans from the muddy waters they be swimming in too long."

"We figure," Thea comments to the same reporter, "people are evolving collectively, as a crazy mixed-up family does. Our art honors that. We won't be known for promoting fear, separateness, or degradation of life. Maybe our Heart Art can be called sacred, as in honoring the natural, as opposed to glorifying the unnatural."

Junkyard perhaps has the best explanation of all, when he is quoted as saying: "If our art be living just halfway up to its promise of helping make the world a better, safer place to live in, then we be ought to have Heart Art available for everyone to own, not just the rich, the privileged. Art needs be a part of everyday life. It belongs in the space of everyone, not just museums or the homes of rich folks and snotty galleries."

Junkyard Trinnie's peculiarly hypnotic motifs begin to be seen on the sides of cosmopolitan buses, featured as ads paid for by unknown sources. People stop and stare at these celebratory images as they whiz down the boulevards and avenues throughout the five boroughs of New York City.

As the Hearts continue to work hard, people look around and see that many are awakening to a new dawn. A new consciousness is arising from the influence on mainstream culture. Ram Das has been spreading his joyful news of *Be Here Now* since the seventies; Esalen Institute is helping to ignite the spirit of transformation, along with many meditators inspired by Yogananda's bringing the uplifting Eastern mystical thoughts to America. Transcendental Meditation continues setting hearts afire by expanding the consciousness of ordinary folks from Anchorage to Key West, satisfying hunger pangs from previous generations' spiritually bereft bones. Heart Art is the vanguard now, helping to fill empty spaces with some of the most satisfying soul food, for those who notice or care what's happening in the outward display of human ethos.

"The trouble be," Junkyard says one day to his Hearts at a St. Pierre gathering, "that until some bigshot celeb, like *the most famous* of all, a big *Big* star, starts talking about being mindful, people then be getting into spirit things, not just fame-money-sex-playtime stuff. Until then, people just not gonna be interested in alternatives to brain-numbing trash they be used to. The entertainment industry be hell-bent on inflicting us with bull caca to keep making their stacks of bucks." Taking a breath, Junkyard adds in disgust, "The public be victims of the media world that uses creativity for anything *but* the bettering, the uplifting of we. Bucky said it right, 'the media is the massage.'"

"The truth is," Maly adds, brightening to the Buckminster Fuller reference, "art has become corrupted."

"Fast and faster, bad and badder, violent and sexy," Junkyard says and gives his teeth the sucking of their life. "Speed. Cash. Thrills. They be buzzwords that be appealing to the common folk, thanks to media moguls and the cheating hearts of them get-rich-quick types. Training folk to not be thinking for themselves."

"Oh well," Thea says, sighing. "I can't do anything about that. I just keep working. I try to not pay attention to negative forces all around. If you think about all the bullshit out there in the world, it's enough to paralyze you. If we consider degrading art as competition, instead of just a choice some people make—none of us Hearts could ever believe that the weirdly inspiring stuff we do makes any difference."

"You be right, Green Glow," Junkyard nods his head.

"See? Our Thea is now reminding *us*," Maly says, doing her Mona Lisa look. "Time changes everything!"

Thea blows air through her lips. "If I've discovered anything, it's that the language of my art has to be honesty, humor, and irony executed in an arresting manner, not necessarily beautiful or decorative. New and better ideas, that's what it must convey for me to get excited about making art. If we Hearts can't explore these things, art becomes a commercial product, not an expression of current needs—and I mean *Earth's needs* more than a society sir's or madame's. To tell the truth—I'd rather go and lie in the sun somewhere, watching the clouds pass above all day—and stop making art altogether if mine is anything less than helpful to our world. What the world doesn't need is more worthless junk."

She blinks and shrugs. "No offense, man," she nods to her friend from Trinidad.

Demand for traveling shows of Thea's work come in from museums and other venues. Commissions arrive from major cities around the world for her works in public spaces. People everywhere are clamoring for Thea Bowman's Dreamtimes.

By the mid-nineties—just as Junkyard and Maly start traveling to Trinidad, constructing their first building for the One Blood Center—in Manhattan, Thea remains in dizzy-awe about her good fortune. She meets Sophia occasionally for a catch-up dinner a couple times a season. And, no matter how much her work is in demand, Thea remains grateful, remembering how life was so rough for her, before landing back on Planet Sober.

Her exhibitions are sold out before they open. "Her renditions are nuances of magic in ordinary life," one esteemed critic wrote. "She interprets our deep inner lives as conveniently as one takes a shuttle from Washington to New York. Bowman's work allows us to leap across the raging river of our own limitations. She's built for us a safe causeway that arches from the land of pained humanism—the blood and guts of our survival—up and over to the shores of safe and practical ecstasy. Thea Bowman's work strikes a collective human nerve. A chord that sounds to most not only reasonable, but remarkably true."

Thea works, hangs with other Hearts, and visits Sophia and a few others like Jerry and Frieda from her Exchange Views beginnings. She gives up smoking, takes yoga and jazz dance classes, and practices thought-action every day by herself or with other Gaians.

One day Thea arrives back at her studio home. As soon as she opens the front door to the place she'd inherited from Fast, she knows something is wrong. It's too quiet. The sprightly pup that Big Sue had once called "my main man" doesn't saunter over to greet her, as he always does even in his rickety old age, no matter how long or short a time she's been gone. She walks into the living area of the high-ceilinged loft and discovers that Dr. Bob has lain down under the tickly leaves of his very own live ficus tree, looking peaceful as he does after a session of altering his doggie reality. As she pats his stiff face, Thea imagines him grunting happily, seeing his old gray whiskers so familiarly placed on his front paws, the way he does after a leaf's tender touch on his fur transports him from his here-and-now. He looks as if he's dozed off, in the same sunny place he always does. Dr. Bob has been the one constant in Thea's life, far longer than anyone else. It will take months for Thea not to call him for his regular evening walks after finishing work each day.

Her shadow, Dr. Bob, is gone. Yet she can't help feeling as if he too, has shared his remaining life energy with her. Why else, she thinks, does she feel *different*, right after her companion left his doggy body?

She still sees him though, under the ficus tree, lying there stoned out of his gourd, happy to be waiting patiently for her to get her act together.

Heart Art by Gaians helps revive our toxic world

33

Maly and Junkyard happen to be in New York, having officially opened the One Blood Culture Center in Trinidad the year before. They divide their time between the island and their Soho lofts, where assistants help fulfill their prolific output.

"Our plan be working great," Junkyard said to Thea the night before. "Next year we be able to live full time in Port of Spain. Then we be ready to sell the lofts here."

The three of them have planned to see a friend's performance piece together. Thea arrives early at their loft and is sitting with Maly. Junkyard called from his studio to say he's running late and will meet them at the gallery.

"So why did you stop seeing that man we met last time, ma chérie? He seemed nice, intelligent, handsome. Didn't he make you happy?"

"Yeah, he did. But we had different goals for the relationship, that's all."

"And yours were—?"

"That's the point," Thea says. "Mine are nonexistent. He had very specific ones. We finally agreed that we had no future together. And that's that."

"But you two cared about each other a good deal, oui?"

"We did. That's exactly why we decided not to waste each other's time. I heard he's recently fallen in love with a yoga teacher, or healer, I can't remember which. Our mutual friend told me he's quitting the firm and moving west to raise a family. I'm happy for him. He always wanted kids."

"And you, Thea? You never want kids? The biological clock is still ticking?"

"Making art is my offspring, Maly. That's more than enough work for me. I don't have time for a family, so it's just as well. Don't you know I'm a non-breeder, my friend? What about you?"

"Junkyard and I pray for the time we will be blessed to make a baby."

"You've been trying?"

"Oh yes, for years."

Thea isn't surprised, noting that she and Maly have never talked about having kids before. But Thea doesn't mention this.

"You'll make excellent parents," she adds. "Junkyard will have a devoted audience all the time." Both women nod their laughing heads.

"Me?" Thea says, "I'm afraid I'd damage the poor little critter."

"Why do you say that ma chérie?"

"I guess because my own folks didn't make it so easy for me."

"Oh, Thea, you're not blaming your parents, are you, for your shortcomings? That seems like a—how you say?—a cop out."

"No, I'm not, but life might have been easier if I'd had a little moral support early on. It wouldn't have hurt, y'know. I'm not complaining, mind you; it's just a fact of my life."

Thea never has been able to commit to her cascade of men friends. She loves loving them, loves the sexual release they provide, but she's always relieved to be alone when the night, or the weekend, or with Giles, the marriage, is over and she has her freedom. Sometimes she ponders how, in all her relationships, there has never been anyone who satisfied her. Not enough to take her away from needing to make art. Thea sometimes wonders if she is trying to attain something like the idea of *becoming* love itself, rather than being restrained to loving another, a single human being.

In many respects Thea is married to her art. Nothing, she'll tell admirers, will take her away from her commitment to making and disseminating Heart Art. Some men, like her latest, Wyatt, put up with her laser-like dedication—for a while. But in the end—they always want more of her than Thea is able, or willing, to give.

"My work takes as much effort from me as I've got to give," she explains to Maly as they leave to join Junkyard for that night's performance.

The next day Thea receives a call from her dealer.

"You're the one," Jules St. Pierre gushes, barely able to contain himself. Thea flushes when she hears the official news. She can't help the girlish *Yikes!* that escapes, her heart racing like a hummingbird at high noon. Her dream has come true! of being picked for what to her is the most honored role a contemporary artist can have—to represent her country at the Venice Biennale.

Life has come full circle for Thea now. From complete failure to total success. Lady Luck could not have been more kind to her. Only sharing this moment with Dr. Bob and Big Sue could have made such great good fortune taste even sweeter.

Preparations take over a year for Thea to design, execute, and ship the exhibit she calls *Varieties of Permutations*. The installation takes up an entire wing of the Palazzo dell'Arte on via Garibaldi, in the heart of old Venice. Three monstrous, freestanding sculptures made from organic materials are held together on their welded armatures with papier-mâché fabricated from copies of the Wall Street Journal and mineral-tinted sand she harvested from Painted Desert dunes in Arizona. Hung upon these three stable structures by hooks made from colorful, sawed-off high heels are many removable items that Thea designed to be lifted, purposefully, by lusty viewers wanting to steal, or simply to touch, to play with, to feel the earth-encrusted, energy-infused works. The sand used for making the pieces' outer layer is from Navajo tribal territory, given for the project with the Native Americans' blessings. She includes no instructions or details when she sets up the pieces. Thea knows human nature will do its thing. She's made it easy for the small totem-like charms and baubles to be freely lifted. Upon installation, Thea instructs the guards to turn the other way when thievery or mischief takes place at her installation. She pays them a bribe for their blind eyes.

The three gargantuan, creature-like sculptures are a hit, and more so when the crowds of people discover they can steal bits of them without any consequences. Strands of beads, shards of ceramic, glass, stone, tiny mirrors, bones, feathers, freaky dried seed capsules, and irregularly shaped bits of shell and driftwood—all loose components on display go missing from hooks that were designed for them to easily disappear, part of the exhibit's transformation process.

Thea hides her delight when Biennale officials claim outrage about the theft and vandalism. Low-wage guards are questioned and found not culpable as Thea keeps bribing them to look the other way. Thea's complicity, now public, is to prove that people are naturally compelled to own, to possess things. And if not legitimately, then to take, to steal what is considered desirable; or conversely in the case of some vandals, to destroy what appears to be abhorrent, or deemed to be sacrilegious. Extremely loved or extremely hated things catch people's attention the most. Earlier, in the designing process, she'd explained this theory to Junkyard as she was setting out to prove this commonality she suspected of human nature, in general.

"To me, it's the true reward for making art."

"To be having your work stolen?" Junkyard's face twisted in a grimace.

"Yes! That means people react to it. They'll want a piece of it! They won't be able to leave it alone. They'll either love it or hate it. No middle ground is worth the risk of getting caught for vandalism and facing the shame of being labeled a thief."

"Cheez an'bread, Honeypot, you be having strange ways of demonstrating art appreciation."

"Junkyard, to me the anticipated thievery will validate the success of the work—from the public's point of view, not from any fancy-pants critics'. People always want to own a piece of something great if they can't have the whole thing. Look at the catacombs in Rome. How folks try to grab some of that hallowed dirt when they visit down there. And how many both chunks and tiny bits of the Berlin Wall are treasured throughout the world today."

Each morning during the Biennale's opening week in June of 1997, Thea gladly replaces the stolen art pieces of the day before with extras she's brought in her luggage. Then, gleefully hiding, she practices voyeurism with gusto, watching to see which parts of the sculptures will be ripped off next from the otherworldly, insect-like, over twenty-foot anthropo-triplets. Naturally, easy-to-reach tokens are the most popular, and disappear the fastest.

Representing America at the 47th is a huge milestone in Thea's late-starting but marathon career. Her personal life has for the last decade taken a back seat to making Dreamtimes. But after the Biennale, each time she returns to her empty Grand Street loft, without Dr. Bob, she feels restless and curiously dissatisfied. *Maybe the loft is too empty, too big,* she thinks. *Something isn't right.*

Thea's Itch returns.

Even though she's overjoyed by the critical acclaim her controversial, popularly vandalized exhibit garners, shortly after returning to New York she makes up her mind. She's had enough of urban life. Enough of cold weather, enough of working endlessly with no play time. Thea decides it's time to live close to Nature again.

Junkyard and Maly fulfilled their dream and have opened the first building of their Culture Center. Gradually, Trinidad has become their permanent home, from where they keep up with their exhibition schedule and private commissions. One other major reason for their successful return to island living is the now ubiquitous internet, cellphones—and the international airport in Port of Spain.

"I need to feel the earth between my toes," Thea tells her dealer St. Pierre. "There's more to life than having a successful career. I want to feel sun on my face, to grow some vegetables, to breathe warm sea air again. I need to get out of this fucking overcrowded city!"

Before leaving for Venice, she'd gone to Miami to examine an exhibition space for a site-specific, one-person show to be held there in two years. Thea remembered then how much she loved the heat, the humidity, the wafts of tropical fruity blends dripping from leaf-riot trees. And oh, that extravagantly exotic, multiethnic blend of humanity in Miami's diverse cultural atmosphere. Within hours of arriving in America's Latin-flavored city, Thea heard her soul crying out to live somewhere nearby.

It didn't take long to discover the perfect scene to satisfy that Itch of hers. Thea wrote a hefty down payment check for her new place in Delray. Close to the sea, healthy restaurants, a yoga studio, but far enough away from Miami's air, land, and sea traffic, Delray Beach is perfect.

She packs up the loft. Excited to get out of the city and back to a more laid-back, low-speed life, Thea bids farewell to friends, extending invitations to them all to visit her, and drives south with a fully loaded U-Haul truck big enough to hold everything she owns.

The secluded estate she names *Isla à Isla* includes an elegant Spanish hacienda capped by a red ceramic tile roof, with a venerable decades-old, buttress-rooted banyan tree spreading its generous shade at its side. A formal courtyard is the link between the main house and a guest cottage within a tightly-fenced inner compound. Nearby and separate, a high-roofed building that had been the previous owner's boatbuilding business proves to be an excellent studio, with three rows of paned windows providing the northern light all artists crave. The grounds are exuberantly planted with enough foliage—the product of twenty years of skillful, selective gardening—to make Isla à Isla an idyllic retreat for making art besides a horticultural distraction one could lose themselves in.

Quickly realizing upkeeping Isla à Isla is too much for her, Thea hires a Latino couple to help. She finds their barely legible note posted on the bulletin board at Garden of the Heart, Delray's one and only health food store. Each morning in their bright yellow, old Ford pickup, Yolanda and Juan roll through the estate's gate. Yolanda does the cleaning and cooking while Juan becomes Thea's handyman, chief gardener, and extra strong arm for art moving.

When she isn't in the studio, Thea works in the gardens with Juan, something she's never done. Juan teaches her, beginning by breaking ground and enriching the humus-fragrant soil with organic material and compost. The sensation of touching bare earth begins to work its spell on Thea.

Through Thea's basic Spanish and their broken English, Juan and Yolanda show her more about living close to the earth than she bargained for. After a short while, she secretly acquiesces that they are much more than employees. This fun-loving husband and wife from El Salvador, immigrants from poverty and violence, are securely rooted in the richness of growing and nurturing natural things.

Juan is a short, sturdy man with thick peasant hands and twinkling eyes that sets Thea's heart jumping for joy every time she speaks to him in her childlike Span-glish. Yolanda's caring, maternal ways adds a touch of emotional calm to Thea's recovering urbanism. Juan works all day in the hot sun, trimming dried fronds from tall Queen and Royal palms, weeding, mulching, and clipping overgrown vines that are choking each other. He cuts back gnarled roots with a sharp machete, clears escapee bamboo stands to make way for laying new brick paths and patios wherever Thea envisions them. Within a short while, team Juan and Thea make Isla à Isla into a sculpted wonderland of tropical greenery. Thea's desired connection to sensing, touching, smelling and feeling earth becomes integral to her daily life.

She's curious to see how this new environment affects her work. The impact of Juan and Yolanda becoming Thea's new family is a surprising reward she hadn't anticipated when deciding to create a secluded home.

For the first time since Dr. Bob shed his formalwear for a suit more ethereal, Thea begins to think about getting another dog. But for now, she puts the idea out of her mind. *What dog could ever replace my space-hound anyway,* she reasons. Yet occasionally she'll drop by the Animal Shelter just for curiosity's sake.

Her friends are spread all over the globe now. Thea's life evolves into a satisfying one, just as Junkyard had predicted it would so many years earlier.

"You won't be missing your belly-button family at'tall," he'd foretold, "when you be dedicating your art to be helping the human soul to soar."

Isla à Isla becomes the beachside nest in paradise where her far-flung friends, her *heart family* as she calls them, congregate to have fun in the sun.

The comfortable and airy, tile and stucco house, a retreat from the increasing insanity of the outside world, is filled with interesting friends who love to create new ideas, as Thea does. While outside those vined walls, disturbing news of ethnic cleansing and genocide vie for importance with climate change and the deforestation of the Amazon, and the tension between extremists such as radical Islamists warring against the non-Muslim world increases; behind her tall, impenetrable privacy walls, Thea measures the tranquility of her newly transplanted life by the everyday changing growth and riotous colors of the beautiful gardens she and Juan created. She focuses on knowing that the best use of her energies is to continue creating art meant to change people's minds, expand the confusion and understanding held by too many in this increasingly urgent time of crisis for Earth, for Gaia.

Never does she regret leaving the nonstop frenzy and the mania of the Big Apple that she'd once ignored, after having first blended in with it. Since moving close to the warm sea again, Thea herself blossoms, barraged by nothing more serious than show-off-leaves of begonias, gingers, and palms as she concentrates on creating changemaking art.

She keeps busy imbibing peacefulness … and with old and new friends … releasing the abundance of creativity that comes from experiencing inner contentment. Even surrounded by crises and turmoil, enough to drive others insane who have been weakened by fear.

One day when Thea drives back from shopping for organic vegetables at Garden of the Heart, she sees Juan and Yolanda's yellow pickup is at the gate of Isla à Isla, along with another unrecognizable beat-up car with several visitors standing around. They all wave to her. Still things look peculiar to

Thea as she passes, so she slows down. Waving to the group, she glimpses an odd assortment of things on the strange car's hood. She sees a tall glass of water with what looks like a broken eggshell next to it.

When Yolanda enters the cobalt and peach tiled kitchen later Thea asks, "What was going on at the gate?"

"It nothing, Señorita Thea."

"But it looks like something, Yolanda. You're not in trouble. I'm just curious, with that glass and the egg. What's going on?"

Yolanda goes to the louvered window and checks to make sure Juan is busy outside, in the garden. Satisfied he is, she turns to Thea.

"Those people, they ask me favor. I am *curandera*."

"What's curandera? I don't know that word."

"I help people heal."

"With an egg?"

"Si, Señorita. Since girl, the magic it pass to me from my grandmother. I see the future, good and bad. I read how egg float in water. It my gift to other people. No money."

"Okay, so do my future, will you?"

"Yours, Señorita? But—you no worry. Your life good. You rich."

"There's more to life than money, isn't there, Yolanda? I never asked for it. It just happened."

"What you want to know?"

"Something important."

"Okay. Me get egg."

Yolanda comes to the kitchen table with her divination tools: a glass of water and a raw egg.

"*Digame*, Señorita Thea, what your question?"

"I want to know if my work will make a difference. If it's ... let me see how to say this better ... is it worth doing?"

"No husband. No baby?"

"No, Yolanda. That's my question."

"No amor?"

"Just what I asked, Yolanda."

"Okay, pues." Yolanda closes her eyes and mumbles a few phrases in rapid Spanish. Opening her eyes, Yolanda takes the raw egg and cracks it on the rim of the glass.

Both women sit quietly, staring at the blobby thing. Thea watches the egg spread, like a yellow one-eyed albino octopus. Yolanda intently follows the movement as the egg spreads its see-through albumen skirts, moving about by itself. As if an invisible current pulls and pushes it. At first, she has a look of surprise. Then joy fills the woman's face. The expression on her face changes again, going in an opposite mood. Thea remains silent, noticing the egg slowly moving in squid-like undulations, as if self-propelled, sinking first downward, then upward, then downward again, until it slowly comes to rest at the top of the water, glistening, rising above the surface, and its yoke's buttery color changes to a duller shade when air touches it.

Thea's impatience has worn thin. "What is it? What do you see, Yolanda?"

The woman turns to face Thea. "I no lie never," she says, glancing from Thea's eyes to her nervous fingers, playing with an invisible thread.

"No, I don't expect you ought to, ever. Do you see something?"

"Oh yes, I see, Señorita. Many times, I prove. What I see, soon be real."

"So, what is it then? Tell me."

Yolanda fidgets, looking uncomfortable, then takes a deep breath.

"You promise no tell my Juan I do egg para ti? He be very angry with me."

"I promise I won't. Tell me, Yolanda."

Thea is growing anxious. Despite her disbelief in superstitions, she respects Yolanda.

"I see sign that yes, what you ask. But a terrible price you pay for it. Lo siento, Señorita."

"What kind of price?"

"It will be bad. And big."

"You're sure?"

"Si, si. Egg never say how, or what. Your answer be yes. But things not so good, somehow. No se como. Perdoname, Señorita."

34

Thea plants the vegetable garden by herself because Juan is busy, and she likes knowing tiny things she places in dirt will soon become such big things like tomatoes, lettuce, parsley, and kale. Looming in her mind also are her childhood friends, the bugs, the birds, the nodding heads of flowers. From seed to giant stalks she watches the sunflowers dizzily towering over all others like green giants with big yellow masks on. She imagines she's a jolly insect, buzzing around each of the thousands of separate flowers within a sunflower's conglomerate inflorescence. In Delray, the sunny patch of herbs, zucchini, and beans helps Thea herself grow, helps her regain what she'd once known, back in childhood, when Nature was the only source of peace she could count on.

Digging in the earth, Thea rejoices, remembering she belongs to Nature.

She begins the next series of Dreamtimes. Awakening in the early morning sun, she breathes in fulfillment as she walks the path that leads from the house to her studio. Thea feels more alive, more comfortable in her skin than she's been since touching down on Planet Sober. Even the ominous cloud bearing the quixotic warning Yolanda had unwillingly shared isn't enough to stop Thea's excitement over life's possibilities ahead of her.

Whatever it is that's coming, she thinks, *it's not enough to stop my efforts of offering the world my visions, my reality.*

Humming the old familiar Kali chant, the one she sings to herself whenever her mind is occupied with doing something else, Thea makes art. At breaks, she walks outdoors and weeds, shaking tangled vines and weeds free from the pungent sandy dark soil that clings to its roots. Fertility bangs at Thea's senses no matter if she's in the studio or tending one of the estate's many garden plots. The scent-memory of humus bowls her over. She kneels and puts her nose one inch from the ground. Closes her eyes and takes in great lungfuls of the beloved smell of dirt.

"Returning to Nature is the best damn thing I've ever done," Thea declares, standing to return to work in the studio.

Occasionally, Thea calls Sophia to keep in touch. She also calls the only friends from Exchange Views she's stayed in contact with, those two old freaks, Jerry and Frieda, whom she and Sophia agree are the most fun of the basement crowd.

Junkyard and Maly stay closely connected to Thea from Trinidad, where One Blood quickly becomes an arts resource for the entire Caribbean basin. Thea visits when Junkyard and Maly break ground for the second building of their ten-acre complex, just outside Port of Spain. Junkyard and a pregnant Maly are in Delray for the first harvest of Thea's garden-grown juicy tomatoes, and her first vase of knockout sunflowers. Thea flies to Trinidad for their child's christening, welcoming a boisterous baby boy, Thor, the same year they are living in Trinidad full-time. While others all around her are busy reproducing, Thea hasn't the slightest stirrings of wanting a family. Long ago Sophia, herself childless, discussed this with Thea, just as Maly had.

"Making art is my mothering act," Thea answered when Sophia asked. "The raising a family thing is not my bag."

Coinciding with Thor's arrival, Junkyard and Maly form a local chapter of Gaia Group in Trinidad, with Thea, Ray, and Julia flying there for opening ceremonies. By then, people everywhere are practicing thought-action, also called mindfulness. What started off as small scattered groups evolved into a fashionable trend, just as Maly, ever the futurist designer, spoke about wishing its popularity would be, years before.

Two years previously, Ray had published *Gaia Group*, an instant nonfiction bestseller after Sarah Kempton's endorsement, herself the best example of how change starts with an outspoken celebrity promoting a worthy cause. Chatting with Ray that day on her afternoon show, Sarah's honest assessment of the importance of every individual practicing thought-action—she singlehandedly guaranteed the book's success. Ray's book sold out almost overnight, with the publisher happily printing hundreds of thousands more to keep up with worldwide demand. Best of all, Sarah exuded her praise, ending her interview with Ray by turning to the camera and softly saying:

"The entire world gets to benefit from what each one of us can do—right at home—by getting still and opening our minds to visualize a better, healthier world."

When the main building at the One Blood Center is dedicated as the official West Indian and South American headquarters of Gaia International, Sarah unexpectedly shows up as special guest for that honorable event. At Ray's invitation, Sarah leads its first televised thought-action session herself, which is beamed via satellite to everyone tuned in around the world from *The Kempton Show*, an afternoon entertainment *must* for every housewife from Boston to Bangkok.

Julia has obligations at home when Ray arrives at Isla à Isla one bright spring day. The weather is perfectly cool in the morning, becoming pleasantly sensuous with a light sea breeze that starts around noon. Thea is excited when she picks him up at the airport, this man who has personally touched her heart so deeply, and whose selfless work has affected the world in such positive ways.

"You're like the new Ghandi," Thea says, giving him an avuncular hug. Thea has come to think of Ray as not only her mentor but her surrogate father. Ray loves her for who she is, nothing more, nothing less.

"How special for you to come and help us open a new Gaia Group here," Thea says.

"Wouldn't miss it for the world, Thea."

"How's Zurich?"

"Saner than the States, but I miss the openness of our culture. Julia prefers the neutrality of their politics, that's important for her. Me, I don't really care where I am. I don't do politics, as you know."

"I love Florida, Ray. It feels like I'm home, even though there's so much to explore here: the many springs, the Everglades."

"Life has been good to you, Thea. Let's hope the future of Gaia shines as promising as your life has become in these years since I've known you."

Ray smiles at his protégé. In previous weeks, Thea had done the groundwork for starting a new group here. By the time she picks up Ray at the airport, everything is in place. Fliers have been handed out at the health food store, neighborhood gym, the yoga studio, coffee shop, library, and any public spot she can put up her poster titled:

What We Can Do NOW to Help Our World's Future.

People of all descriptions are making their way to Isla à Isla, where the driveway's gate has been thrown wide open. The sound of the front door's funky cowbell ringer on a ripcord constantly jingles as folks make their way inside. Fragrant vines cascade over the cement walls embedded with shells and topped with colored glass. Brisk ocean air mingles salt with heady scents of perfumed frangipani, ginger, and gardenia. Lavish blooms nod at people arriving at the address printed on Thea's colorful fliers. A frisky puppy who can't contain his exuberance greets everyone, wagging his tail so ferociously he keeps tripping himself.

Thea happily oversees the smooth progression of the evening. A conch shell is blown by Juan and, after introducing Ray, she turns over the gathering's rapt attention to him, who in his understated, inimitable fashion, presents thought-action to everyone. Together then, the seated crowd of forty practice how to plant positive thought-seeds. For many quiet minutes, everyone is guided to experience for themselves the satisfaction of having a viable solution for Earth's woes. "No longer do we need to passively settle for a world growing weak with evils that separate us," Ray intones. Many in the crowd claim, when Ray asks, that they're ready to join the Gaian way of life right then.

"Good," Ray says. "All it takes is the intention to practice daily and offer your thoughts as a gift. That way you're consciously supporting the upliftment of humankind and assisting the healthy future of our planet. Really, what more can any of us do?"

Throughout the evening Thea finds herself repeatedly glancing from every angle at an extraordinary person. Tall and thin, strangely seeming familiar, around her age, the striking man had been introduced to her by one of her Delray friends upon his arrival earlier in the evening as "the trailblazing architect," Michael-something-or-other. "His airports are brilliant concepts for handling the hordes of today's traveling masses, sometimes irate and always in a rush," the friend offered. Athletic and intelligent looking, Michael immediately captured her interest. The attraction feels primal and alchemical, and curiously déjà vu-ish.

Uncannily, Thea keeps noticing a weird throbbing where her Viking tattoo wraps around her left forearm. It pulsates in a most peculiar way as she observes this fascinating man from across the courtyard. Such an odd sensation, she notes, not able to remember having felt anything like it, not since she first got the Nordic knot painfully needled onto her epidermis. Inexplicably, the design begins to ache, needing to be caressed by her fingertips.

Thea touches her throbbing arm and sneaks another look at Michael. His lithe body appears fit, from his silver-tinged hair to the merry creases around entrancing eyes that keep catching hers, bewildering her. From across the spacious brick patio she keeps watching him.

Then she realizes she's walking right toward him. But quickly she stops and faces another person and begins to chat. Out of the corner of her eye, Thea sees Michael's chiseled face has a special glow; his hair and clothes are like a distracted outdoorsman, not like any office-bound architect she's ever met. As she mingles with others she keeps her antennae tuned to Michael, recognizing an instant kinship of some kind. Wondering what this elegant man's story could be.

She feels a bump on her leg. Thea leans over and gives a pat to the pup she calls Popeye, who's frolicking upside-down at her feet. Just days before, she'd chosen the energetic dog with splotchy tan and white fur because it was time, and—he felt right.

A strange sensation stirs within her. Although she's talking to someone else, she's already figured that the man standing over there, Michael, would look mighty good naked, in her bed. Thea shakes the silly thought out of her head.

*   *   *

But she can't. Something oddly familiar about him slaps Thea's memory awake. Like taking a fast, deep cold plunge on a hot summer day, she *knows* him. His face lights a muted, tiny flicker of recognition inside her. Still, Thea can't figure from where, when, or how she might know him.

She feels a rising tide. Her blood pounds. Eerily, her other tats, the coiled snake, and next her third-eye indigo dot begin pulsating. Then … this man is walking toward her. Thea looks at him and wonders who the hell he is.

"Thought-action is exactly what I've been searching for," he says with an extended hand. With a leading man's jaw of iron, terraced cheek bones, athletic airstrip shoulders, and positively the most gut-stirring voice she's ever heard, Thea is dizzy, struck speechless. "And, Thea Bowman," he says, seeming not to notice Thea's predicament, "I can't believe you don't remember me!" catching her completely off guard. "Michael Olafson," he speaks his name once more as his sable eyes lock on hers.

He reaches down and gives Popeye his hand to sniff. He touches the pup's head, triggering another wild and naughty chase off into the odiferous night by the hyper-happy dog. *Up close, Michael is even better to look at,* Thea thinks. Graceful, bursting with strength and a vitality that shoots out in waves like an electric energy field around him, he exudes good nature like some men do too-strong a cologne. His casual confidence, which echoes in that comfortable, dancey gait of his. Thea watches herself meet this man, as if a long-forgotten dream is welcoming her back.

She stands stiffly with a blank mind. Has no memory of ever having met this unforgettable man. Thea knows she looks idiotic standing, staring, not remembering a thing about the encounter he alludes to. Michael smiles broadly. He comes closer, leaning into their twosome-ness.

"It was so very long ago," he whispers an incantation of his own. His rugged features beam as he pulls his head back, obviously delighted he's caught his hostess completely unawares. Thea feels giddy and light-headed. She flushes at Michael's words, his proximity.

"I'm sorry," she haltingly whispers. "I don't remember."

His gutsy laugh startles Thea. She leans back in wariness, regarding this man whom she instantly knows, somehow, that she would love to love. Something rumbles in the pit of her stomach, that old Itch scratching itself.

Thea speaks with urgency, eager to know. "I'm so embarrassed. Where did we meet?"

"I'm the one who should be embarrassed, Thea. Meeting you is something I've never been able to forget, and the idea that you can't even *remember* me, well, it's too shattering. My poor ego." He laughs out loud again, shaking his head in feigned dismay. "Unbelievable!"

She flinches, wondering if this man is playing a really bad joke on her.

For just a moment, Thea's gaze singes the grass along the illuminated patio's edge. Across the lawn Popeye rolls on his back in the grass, kicking his paws up toward millions of stars in the frothy Milky Way. Thea and Michael stand close to a pergola that overflows with intertwined night-blooming jasmine and flaming fuchsia bougainvillea, dramatized by spotlights. She grapples with a lost scene he knows about … but she clearly doesn't.

"It was back in the Haight," Michael says, "way back in ancient history."

"Oh my God, that *was* a long time ago."

Thea tries to remember. San Francisco, late sixties: tripping and crazed, using psychedelics heavily. Rebellion, Revolution, Free Love. Shamanic Sue defending defenseless bunnies. Strenuous training in sex, drugs, Southern Comfort, and rock n' roll.

"I'm sorry, Michael, I just don't remember." Anything could have happened, back then, she knows. She was a blackout drinker. But she's feeling relaxed. And Michael's showing signs that good humor is part of his M.O.

He says, "You were hanging out in that art closet on the top floor—"

"In my attic room, you mean!" Thea feebly attempts to be amused, listening attentively, trying her best not to worry about those past mistakes.

"—with that mighty weird girlfriend of yours—"

Could it have been Sue who dragged this guy in from the cold, Thea wonders.

"—but Osgood warned me about you two," Michael says, pausing.

Big Sue *never* got sexy with *anyone*, Thea quickly assures herself.

"Osgood? Wait—you weren't one of *those*—?"

Again, Michael laughs. "When I saw you tonight, Thea, I couldn't believe you were the same person either. But I'd never forget you, not in a million years." Michael's face breaks into a kaleidoscope of a past remembered, relished, and wondrous things to come.

Ouch! Thea feels the stab of a flashback. It is not unreasonable for her to think that what this guy is saying is true. *Given my past*, she admits silently, *anything's possible. Could this be* the guy *I've never been able to remember, but knew I ought to?*

Michael breaks into her flashing thoughts. "You were on the top floor of this old gingerbread Victorian Lady somewhere in the Haight, with that outrageous friend of yours who was so notorious back then. What's her name?"

"Big Sue," Thea murmurs, noting Michael's tone lacks judgment. He's speaking calmly, openly. She's reassured instantly that he is not a threat.

"Right. That was her. Both of you were wild, beyond wild! Everyone in the Haight knew Big Sue could outdrink, out-drug every hombre north of the Rio Grande. Man, she was one messed up chick. We got so blitzed that night I met you, I couldn't find my way back home. Hey, were you there at three-fingered Louie's the night she beat the crap out of him?"

"No, but I heard about it," Thea weakly says, relieved this guy's memory of her isn't as bad as she first feared. "Big Sue fought anyone who crossed her. We must have been really hammered the night Osgood brought you up to my aerie; I can't recall a thing about you. Ha! That's what you get for trespassing into the Haight, Mr. Architect. What were you doing, a little slumming?"

Michael's manner is easy, as flexible as his buoyant personality.

"My friends told me how out-there you were, getting naked everywhere you could. I heard about that time over in Sausalito when the cops hauled you off for dancing in the buff in that wharf front bar. Hey, every guy back then wanted to know you, Thea. And those that didn't, wanted to meet Big Sue, because she was a living legend, like a two-headed rattlesnake everyone wants to party with. You two were infamous, *the wildest* chicks around. I can assure you I was not disappointed one bit that day when I insisted Osgood take me up to meet you."

"I'm afraid to burst your bubble, Michael," Thea quickly adds, "but I was only wild and crazy when I had enough booze or drugs in me to kill a moose."

He laughs. "Well, that's what everyone did back then. You were no different than the rest of us, just a little more enthusiastic. Do you remember how everyone called you the *Free Spirit of Noname?*"

"Noname?" Thea's skin bristles, a flood of forgotten remembrance washing over her.

"You remember the Noname Bar, don't you? Along the waterfront in Sausalito? Where you got your *nom de guerre*, that night you danced naked on the bar."

"What! Were you there too?" A red stain creeps over Thea's face, an instant mark of unfamiliar remorse. She doesn't know whether to run and hide or go berserk laughing over the irony of this hunk of a stranger from her past showing up. A mixed bag of emotions wells up within Thea, flooding her senses.

"No I wasn't, damn it." Michael beams, "but everyone in the fucking city heard about it, believe me. 'Specially the way you escaped." The man smiles and shakes his head in exaggerated nonsense. Altogether, his body language, his fun-loving and come-hither features spell nothing but *comfortable* to her. She's curious about being okay with this man knowing that *other side of her*, the old, scared, and horribly druggy Thea.

He's a good guy, she thinks, relaxing. *Just enjoying himself, sharing a wicked sense of humor, I can tell.*

"Osgood," Thea says, remembering vividly now, "that good-for-nothing acid-freak of a landlord of mine. He must have thought the side show of Big Sue and me was part of the rent."

"Hmmm. Sounds like cheapskate Osgood. We lost touch. I only knew him briefly."

"So you were one of his annoying freak-parade boys? He was always bringing guys up to spy on us without our permission."

"Guilty as charged."

Michael's soothing vibe erases any concerns she might have.

"It was all innocent good fun, Thea," he says, as if reading her mind. Then his voice raises. "But look at us now. Two reformed flower children of the Haight meeting like this. Ain't life great?"

Thea's cheeks flush. Her eyes dart downward, upward, anywhere but at the terribly appealing man standing before her.

"I tried to get my courage up to see you again, but I couldn't. I was engaged at the time."

A hush falls. A surge of regret presses in, of what might have been. She notices the excitement that first rushed through her, like the first waves of a strong drug, immediately die with that word, *Engaged*.

"The rest is history, as they say," Michael says. "I'm here, you're here, and in between many things have happened to us both."

"So, you're married?"

"Just long enough to have two kids. They're all grown up and on their own now. Betsy and I divorced years ago. She's a lawyer in San Francisco. Her career always came before our relationship, even before our kids. I moved to West Palm in eighty-seven. How 'bout you, Thea? Ever marry?"

"Once, down in the Bahamas. We didn't have anything in common though, no kids. I've not been lucky in the romance department," Thea adds with a barely audible, "*yet*."

Michael's eyebrows rise. "I've been too busy for relationships, the way my life is, off all over the bloody world to see clients."

Thea smiles, liking this man more than she wants to admit. She looks at his shoes and smiles at the huaraches he's wearing without socks.

"So you're free now, Thea, romance-wise?"

"Free?" She says a little too loudly. Her face bursts into sunset colors. "Well no, actually, I'm not." She whistles and Popeye bounds to her feet from where he's been sniffing nearby bushes. She bends to pat the floppy thing. "Just got this guy here to look after." She straightens up and looks directly at Michael and says, "Yes, I am free."

Michael throws his head back and roars like the king of jungle beasts, the best, most joyous sound Thea has heard her entire life.

Later that balmy night, when everyone else has left, Michael takes Thea's hands and brings her close to him in an unspoken embrace. Thea feels her heart collide with his. Michael and Thea's first tender kiss sends sparks into her deepest, darkest place, that has lain waiting to be discovered for eons. Their lips gently open and meld like a night-bloom of their own making. She reels, her mind instantly aflame, as her heart melts in the heat of recognition. She feels instantly whole. Like a huge gap has just been filled up within her. Her Itch dissipates in a puff of gentle wind from the sea.

35

After two weeks of not wanting to be apart, their decision is mutual. "Why not," Thea says to Michael, "Life is too short when you find a gift like ours."

With energy bursting like fireworks between them, creativity overflows everything they touch. Soon, an addition of a spiraling two-story building of Michael's unique sacred-geometry design is added on to Isla à Isla, to accommodate his home workspace. Thea's retreat is ample enough for both of them, a shelter from the hustle of the outside world. Michael continues to attend meetings with his architectural firm in nearby West Palm Beach, and visits clients and sites worldwide, while Thea keeps up her exhibition commitments. When they are home, they cultivate and both appreciate domestic serenity, which Thea figures must be what people mean when they say "… how you use your time on Earth makes your life either a heaven, or …."

Thea and Michael's idea of a great time together is to make a big fire with driftwood logs in the outdoor pit, get muddy together in the gardens, or practice thought-action, with or without others in their Delray Gaia Group. They keep Michael's ketch, the *Freedom*, on a dock on the Intercoastal Waterway for quick day sails out on the Atlantic, and take longer sails whenever they can, heading due east then to the south, offshore, stopping at Turtle Island or Man o' War Cay in the Abacos to eat conch fritters and dance to steel drum music when they have more than a weekend free.

In their second year together, Thea and Michael are bedazzled by their great good fortune of how lucky they were to even find each other.

"How much easier life is with a life partner," Thea remarks at this turn of the calendar.

"Maybe we already have died and gone to heaven." Michael's voice sounds incongruously in awe as he stands upright, his clothes and hands muddy from weeding in the garden.

"Darling, take off your clothes," she whispers, peering at him from under her sun visor, gauging his reaction, glad it's Juan and Yolanda's day off.

Sometimes Thea notices a glint of sequin-bouncing light as she passes the shelf in her studio where she keeps objects of inspiration. It's where she keeps rocks, shells, seeds, and bones she picks up from places she visits, to remember her experiences there, and perhaps to add them to one of her Dreamtimes. The flash of light is there again, one day while she's working nearby on a new piece: a bright flash coming from this certain shelf.

Thea walks over to check out the steady gleam of light, now that she's noticed it, originating from the shelf. To her surprise, she sees a flashing prism of vibrating white light coming from *within* the Kali rock that has lain virtually forgotten by Thea, lying there on this shelf since she unpacked it from her Manhattan studio years before.

Thea picks up the Kali rock and looks at it intently. Suddenly, it starts to heat up and she instantly remembers its power.

Midnight of the new millennium finds Thea and Michael anchored on *Freedom* out in the Keys, where fireworks can be seen deliriously exploding from a dozen different Florida islands along the broad horizon of the Atlantic that clear starry night. They are happy to greet the new era together, both swimming in the ocean of pleasure after a lifetime of wondering.

36

"You never be giving up on those dreams of yours either," Junkyard praises Thea when he calls to wish her a happy birthday in June the following year. "You see, that be one of the perks of being a Big Daddy-O. Jules be telling me about that big commission you just got for a sculpture Dreamtime for the United Nations Plaza. Attaway, White Gurl!"

Thea says, "People responding to my art reminds me of being swept away on a gigantic wave I don't have any control over."

"Right on, soul sis-tah," Junkyard cheers on the other end of the phone call. "That be the wave of power! The power of love. You got it, you live it, now others be wanting it too. So you be sharing it with your Heart Art, womb-an."

"Makes you wonder, though, doesn't it, Junkyard? How we can change so much in a lifetime. I used to feel like such a loser. Now look—you naming your new baby girl after me! The old Thea feels like a million years ago, even though it was only seventeen."

"You always be the same Honeypot, to me. You just forgot who you were for a little while, that be all."

"You and Maly and Michael are my rocks. Without you guys, and Sophia, I wouldn't have made it."

"And Miss Sophia, how she be doing?"

"I'm worried about her, honestly, Junkyard. She hasn't been answering any of my calls lately. I try to long-distance visit with her at least once a year, on her sobriety anniversary. This is the longest we've been incommunicado. It feels strange."

"She still be living in the Apple?"

"Yeah, same old apartment too. I called Jerry last week, one of our mutual friends. He told me he's worried about her too. He said something really odd about her that freaked me out. About how she'd told somebody she was taking over-the counter diet drugs, y'know, appetite suppressants. Sophia's always thought she was overweight when no one else ever did."

"That be strange," Junkyard muses. "She be the one always telling *you* to stay away from that kind of stuff—pills, even drugstore stuff for colds, right?"

"Right. Whatever's going on, this is definitely not the Sophia I know. Jerry thinks she's gone screwy. Some weird reaction to the diet pills. Maybe a breakdown, who knows? I keep trying her but she won't return my calls."

"You canna be doing nothin'?"

"I could go up to New York and see what's up."

"Well …?"

"Man, that's so hard right this moment. Two big shows coming up in the next six months, plus Michael flying everywhere from Moscow to Tokyo. You know how it is, Junkyard."

"No. You be telling me. Don't you be having Yolanda and Juan to be holding down the fort so you can be vacating for a few days, Fern Eyes?"

"Now you're making me feel guilty."

"'Tis good to feel guilty if you're supposed to be doing something else 'bout somethin', Green Glow. You always be saying how Sophia be the angel that saved you, right? Me be remembering you saying that. Remember needing Sophia like you be needing air? Was that you who be saying that way back when, White Gurl? Huh?"

"Okay, okay, I get your point, Junkyard. My friend needs me. Thanks for reminding me. I mean it."

Thea gets off the phone and promises herself to help her old friend out. If she can.

Flying up just to surprise Sophia with a visit will have to take a back seat, at least for a week, Thea realizes the next day. Her schedule is nuts. Pieces half done and chemically needing additional layers this minute, none of it can be postponed. Responsibilities consume every bit of her energy. Any spare time she has, she wants to hang out with Michael because he's in between trips this week. Next week she has time. She'll help Sophia as soon as Michael leaves. Thea grumbles as she dials her friend's phone once again, wishing she'd pick up the goddamn phone.

Two days later the couple flies for a quick overnight trip to San Juan for Michael's business. The next morning Thea checks her cellphone messages. She hears Jerry from Exchange Views, speaking low and very slowly, his voice cracked and strained, barely recognizable. The message is for her to call ASAP.

"I'm afraid I have some bad news." Jerry's hollow faraway voice breaks when she reaches him.

Shutting her eyes to brace herself, Thea holds her breath. She figures it's not going to be a rumor, like the last time, when Jerry spoke of his concerns about Sophia.

He says the words softly and quickly. "Sophia did herself in."

Neither of them breathes. "Our beautiful friend is gone," he moans.

Thea's lovely life deflates as quickly as if she's never known a happy day, ever.

A single word, No!, escapes her like a punctured balloon shooting into the air, its horrible echo floating further and further away as she stands frozen, watching her idyllic life disappear.

Thea is standing in the kitchen, hearing but not believing as Jerry continues speaking. The moments are now hours long.

What could I have done?

I should have gone to her.

Why didn't I?

Within moments Thea remembers.

Big Sue's death could have been avoidable but she didn't let anyone in, to talk to her, to save her. She wanted to die.

Sophia would have let me in if I'd gone and banged on her door, she thinks. *Her decision to do this is too cruel. As bad, or worse, as Big Sue's leaving me. This can't be! Sophia was the one who taught me how to live sober. Why couldn't she listen to her own wisdom?*

Thea's thoughts race: *Fast Forward's leaving, at least I was there to help. He let me help him. But Sophia, leaving me without a word. Without me being there to help her, hold her, save her.*

I am powerless over anyone else but myself, this proves it more than ever.

Thea's heart goes numb. She feels helpless. Left out. So very far away from love.

She asks Jerry, "Was she alone, when …?"

"'Fraid so. Somebody saw her last week and said she looked just awful. Sophia admitted to me when I asked why she was getting so skinny that she was taking that Thin-Thin stuff. It must have made her snap. You know how she was, always complaining about her weight. Christ, Thea, you wouldn't have recognized our Sophia if you'd seen her these past couple months. She didn't just get slim, she was a cadaver—before she died."

Pain chokes Thea's voice. She can't speak.

Jerry's sigh is enormous. "I ran into her on the street. That's when I called you last time. She hadn't been to Exchange Views for a long time. She looked like a living skeleton, a hungry ghost, Thea. I asked her what was going on and she just hustled away as soon as she could."

"Fucking pills," Thea whispers in disbelief.

"We figure," Jerry says, "they must have triggered a psychotic break or something. Her previous slips were opiates she hoarded from her nursing jobs."

Thea says weakly, "I can't believe she'd be so stupid."

"Whatever happened," Jerry says, "she sure wasn't the light-hearted chick we used to know. She got hooked on those things and became a miserable paranoid, like she had some kind of mental breakdown. Nobody could help her because she wouldn't let any of us close anymore. Everyone at Exchange Views knew something terrible was happening, but she wouldn't let any of us near her."

"I should have come up there when you called a week ago."

"Hey, Thea, you can't help anyone unless they want it. Quit beating yourself up. All of us tried, believe me. You can't force someone to get well."

"Of course, Jerry, I know it hurts you and Frieda as much as it hurts me. I'm sorry."

"The Sophia we all knew checked out months ago. The person's body at the morgue, that's not her. Come on up, and help us celebrate Sophia's life if you want; the real Sophia we all love. We'll all feel better after that."

In that second hot week of September, the humidity can't compare with the amount of tears Thea sheds after hanging up with Jerry. Even Michael can't console her. How can a person have that many tears in them? Thea wails her heart out. It's as if she's never cried before. Not for Big Sue, not for Fast, not for Dr. Bob or anyone she ever loved who left her. Michael puts a cold wet cloth on her temples in an effort to calm her down. Thea picks up the phone, makes travel arrangements, and brings out her carry-on, weighted by the truth of losing her personal angel.

The next morning she calls Jerry before going to the airport, to discuss the memorial and what plans Sophia's old friends from Exchange Views are making to honor her. There will be a gathering in the East Village.

"Her parents are coming to claim the body," Jerry moans. "The coroner says Sophia must have hoarded all the meds she had access to on her hospice cases. There was enough morphine and Demerol in her system to kill a football team. It wasn't just Thin-Thin that took her out."

"Shit." Thea is beyond distraught. All hope she'd had it might have been an accident, not suicide, gone. "How could she do that to herself, Jerry? She was the most spiritual of any of us."

"Guess she wanted skinny more than she wanted sane," he offers. "It's sad. She knew better than anyone how dangerous those OTC diet meds are. Somewhere along the line, wanting to be glamorous took over from her accepting who and what she was. Sophia's mind must have snapped. Either way you look at it, she did it to herself. Sophia's gone, and we have to let her go, Thea."

Junkyard answers when Thea calls Trinidad.

"How awful it be for you, my Honeypot. Let me be hugging you tight, right through this phone here. Our hearts be one. Maly and I be brokenhearted with you."

Thea wet the phone and the front of her shirt with unstoppable tears.

"Even if I didn't get to see her much these last couple years, I always felt connected to her. Sophia was my spiritual strength, my guide on how to live as a sober person. I figured she'd always be there for me. I never thought she'd ever—need me."

Junkyard switched into a firm, no-nonsense tone. "Y'got to be stopping that kind of talk now and be strong! It won't be doing you or Sophia any good at'tall to be wallowin' in self-pity."

"But I could have—"

"Wastin' yohself on regrets, that what you be doing, Fern Eyes. Sophia did what she had to be doing, period. She be the one who chose to check out, not you. Take all that powerful understanding she gave you and be using it. Don't ever lose it. That's how you be honoring her life the best, the highest way. Just be *willing* her goodness right into you, like she be doing when she be giving it to you. Use her life as a force to be making more Light in this world of darkness! Keep her memory alive in your heart and in your whole life. Be imbibing her energy, her spirit. Prove that even though her body be gone, Sophia's energy never be gone from us."

"It's true," Thea says, "Sophia helped show me who I really am."

"There it be, then. Honor that gift. And keep be giving it away to others, like she always be doing to you." Junkyard's audible breath is the embrace Thea needs right then. "It be Sophia who be teaching you way long past that you best be healing yourself first, so you can be helping others, yes? Get it together, White Gurl! If she hadn't be doing herself in, Sophia be the one telling you this, not I."

In the midst of her tears Thea has to catch her breath for a moment. Junkyard is all zip-and-zap wisdom wizard, a soundtrack of sagacity.

"Michael's driving me to the airport. I'm on my way to New York now," she says. "Some old friends from Exchange Views are getting together for a memorial."

"That be good for you and all them Views. And Sophia."

"There'll be a service somewhere. Her family's already there, to fly her body back home."

Junkyard stays silent.

Thea quietly says, "I remember meeting Sophia at Exchange Views like it was yesterday. Remember Fast giving me that black eye? I was a mess. I could barely drag myself around, Junkyard, in that raunchy, smelly old coat. And there she was, wearing an amethyst that sparkled from across the room. I always thought she looked too damn good to have ever been an addict, like I was. I never believed she really was one. How could someone that together-looking ever be like me, I thought. Sophia would tell me whatever I needed to know, like she was a mind reader. She saved me. I'll never forget how she showed me everything I know today, about living in the Light."

Thea takes deep gulps of air as rivulets etch themselves down her cheeks. The tears meet together under her chin and form one salty stream that pools in the crevice of where her collarbones meet, and slowly trickle down between her breasts.

Michael hugs Thea at the Palm Beach airport, comforting her.

"Stay as long as you need, Thee. Come home when you're at peace. Yolanda and Juan will take care of everything that I can't, so don't worry."

Flying far above Earth, all she wants to do is keep her eyes closed—forever.

Thea squeezes her eyes tightly in pain. Pushing the recline button, she tries to put some space between herself and a world that feels like it's careening toward a breakdown itself. She keeps her eyes closed as the plane ascends higher. She clearly can hear something Sophia once said to her:

"Anyone who looks inside can't be surprised at the hatred and violence they'll find in there, within themselves. The seed of evil lays dormant inside each one of us. It's our challenge to never, ever give up the inner battle, and to fight the darkness—to choose instead to walk in the Light of awareness, of heightened consciousness. But you have to know what the Dark is, in order to walk away from it. That's the trick, kiddo."

Thea quietly weeps. No one notices.

Even though she's committed as a Gaian and a Heart Artist—at that moment Thea feels the entire world spin out of control. She thinks, *How could I ever have been so audacious to believe making art can make a difference? Sophia believed in the Light, and look how she ends up, gobbled by her own darkness. That's what she chose, even though she taught me otherwise.* Thea shudders with the sinkhole thinking she can't stop. Her pain drags her further into sadness. Forgetting everything about the Light, which right now she isn't sure ever even existed.

Thea is not sure about anything anymore.

37

She feels the plane level off above the clouds. Dreamt images sweep her away. Visions—of Valala, sensations of crystals inserted under her skin, she sees herself compelled to walk over a bridge that is a gem-encrusted, enormous snake body that stretches, arching, from shore to shore, while the alarming black figure of Kali dances, all twelve of her arms waving at Thea in mixed delight and despair—until she wakes up.

Thea blinks.

There's a teenager across the aisle. Her earphone-enfolded head bobbing to silent music; her insouciance hinted at by the gum-snapping and immodest flesh folds overlapping too-tight shorts. Thea closes her eyes again and drifts. Phantoms haunt her; technicolor cartoons hallucinate a wasted life as the rumble of jet engines vibrate through her seat. Thea tries to relax. How can she? Every time she closes her eyes she's forced to watch bad reruns on her interior movie screen.

She remembers how Sophia held her hand for every new and scary thing that went *boo!* in the night, those first months of her touchdown on Planet Sober. Sophia showed her how to focus on trusting her HP, letting everything else melt away like bad, stained ice. Thea's next thought: *Why couldn't Sophia trust her own Higher Power, in the long run?*

Shifting in her seat she unconsciously moans, thinking of Sophia lying somewhere terribly cold, on an antiseptic stainless slab, her life spark extinguished. It is entirely too much, her personal angel's passing in such a degrading way. She, who helped so many to leave their earthly bodies with dignity. The truth twists Thea's guts into a ball that feels like sharp, shredded metal.

* * *

Thea's head nods. As opaque curtains of half-sleep draw close around her, her inner vision imagines what it must have been like for Sophia at the end. Marauding ghosts and other familiars watch Sophia getting hooked on Thin-Thin. The ghosts are jealous, telling her to cut all love right out of her life. Sophia forgets the demon-obedience trick she'd taught Thea. The only thing real to Sophia now is the promise of that fake-glamorous woman who tells her she's still too fat, lying to her from a badly lit hall mirror.

Nothing motivates Sophia except shrinking more and more each obsessive hourly inspection, until finally—there's nothing left for her to see in the mirror because—Sophia is no longer there.

When Thea reaches New York she checks into the Soho Crest at Broadway and Prince, in Junkyard and Maly's old neighborhood. Hardly anything has changed in the three years since she's moved to Florida. The gallery crowds are the same—in sacrosanct black. Fashion is on the streets now, standards loosened, and hairdos, shorter and flatter. Cellphones have become part of everyone's ensemble. More skin art, piercings, and a sleek asexuality set the downtown standard now. Thea's tiny tattooed indigo dot sparks between her eyebrows, pulsating as she sees the majority of people on the street are mixes of ethnic heritage. The Viking knot circling the bicep of her left arm and the snake of infinity start to strangely pulsate, just as they did that first night in the garden with Michael.

She notices glances on the street seem more tunneled, more self-involved. Thea sees solo faces that are guarded, have vacuous looks, and recognizes those people as desperately seeking success types. The general absence of camaraderie she recognizes with certain individuals is a reminder of why she'd gladly left this hostile, unfriendly place that only the career-obsessed—or those who become resigned to vie for survival in such a crowded city—claim as home.

Thea thinks of Michael, the distant and idiotically happy life she thought they had. It surges up in her as so distant now, and as amazed befuddlement.

How quickly happiness has been replaced by profound pain. So much emotion arises in her that Thea shudders uncontrollably as if she were freezing. No one pays attention as they obliviously pass her on the sidewalk.

Thea looks around the crowd as she turns onto West Broadway. Hardly any displays of joy in the streets of this new millennium, Thea notices. New Yorkers taking themselves so fucking seriously.

Lower Manhattan, still the same crazy carnival. Yet the feeling of its being home has never left her. This is where her previous existence crash landed; this is where Sophia helped to pick up her pieces. This is where Sue, Fast, and Dr. Bob left her. This is where the life force of those three entered and completed her. And now, Sophia's life energy, that Thea feels becoming part of her, fortifying her despite her sadness.

She walks down West Broadway and over to Bond Street to check if the little eatery where she and Max used to grab a midnight snack is still there; it is. She hooks a right onto Canal and walks to Hudson, leading her instinctively to Tribeca, until she arrives at Reade Street. For a while she stands looking at the front entry to Max's old loft building, the spot where Fast nearly popped her eye out of its socket. Then she walks a block over to Chambers, where she and Dr. Bob moved to the rented room after staying on the sofa at Sophia's Chelsea apartment for months. Things have drastically changed in her old neighborhood. Already an atmosphere of tightly guarded affluence rules Tribeca, she sees. Before, there'd only been a bunch of unruly brawling bohemians, like her trio of she, Sue, and Fast, scurrying between Duffy's and their other favorite after-hours bars; while in the daytime, trucks and commerce hawkers clamored on the Tribeca streets.

She tries but Thea can't picture any struggling poets, starving artists, or hard up musicians living amongst these high-end renovated loft buildings, with a BMW and a Jaguar squeezed in on the narrow streets instead of the illegal rust buckets between trucks of yesteryear.

Maudlin puppet memories invade Thea's grieving heart. The reality of why she's walking her old hunting grounds hits full force:

Life without ever hearing or seeing Sophia again is now a fact. The world is a less-filled-with-light place, Thea knows. She'll never be able to hear her friend's bell-like peals of delight again.

* * *

Thea walks further. Down Church Street, out of Tribeca, toward the two endlessly high steel-and-glass World Trade towers. They've always been her personal Siamese lighthouses—sky-high, sturdy, constantly brilliant twin beacons of hope in her personal struggle toward living in the Light. Every morning of her early days on Planet Sober she focused on the taller than tall spires as she leisurely walked down West Broadway to Exchange Views, where she learned "to live in the Light," as Sophia put it. Thea promises herself that tomorrow she'll go to a meeting there, for old times' sake.

When the gleaming towers loom into full view, a sumptuous sense of *being home* comes over Thea. She stands still and erect, mimicking them. They touch the sky, reaching high above all else, stretching to the clouds. They remind her of the many surprising discoveries she's made, about life, about love—while sitting in that basement room below the North Tower, listening to the penguins share each morning at 7 a.m. Exchange Views had been her homeport, her safety harbor; where she learned to interact with others as a spiritual being having a human-animal experience; where she'd met her Sophia, her angel, that very first day.

Thea visits favorite old spots in the Bowery and the lower East Side the rest of the afternoon.

As planned, she meets Jerry and Frieda for dinner. She hears how they have transferred their ardent devotion of marijuana and other plant-highs to become professional herbalists. Now they have a successful import-export business of medicinals made from rare botanical extracts. After eating, they end up at Tompkins Square Park and watch a group of costumed mimes on rollerblades doing daredevil routines, full speed, until two in the morning. The three old Exchange Views friends talk and laugh and weep, reminiscing all night about Sophia.

New York, the bustling, never sleeping anthill. Its familiar and ever-thrilling sights and sounds tantalize and titillate her. Thea's energy level is off the charts. It's all she can do, to sleeplessly walk to Fourteenth Street after leaving Jerry and Frieda's aromatic smelling Tribeca loft on Chambers Street at three that morning.

It's close to dawn when she pushes open the heavy glass door to the Soho Crest. As she dives between fragrant hotel sheets, she assures herself there's plenty of time to get to Exchange Views tomorrow as she drifts off. Wait. Tomorrow is today, isn't it? She smiles, the first time since hearing of Sophia's overdose.

The last thing Thea thinks about as she falls into the abyss of sleep is that Sophia hasn't abandoned her by dying. As her consciousness drifts away from the crippling sadness she's been wallowing in, Thea knows that Sophia, as she departed this Earth, willed her remaining life energy into Thea. Empowering her. Strengthening her mission here beyond anything either of them could have foretold.

Thea is asleep as the pewter dawn of first-light starts to glow brighter on this new day. This day that will be remembered forever as the day the world was forced to change. And in the same way that Thea has been empowered by Sophia's passing her own life force to her protégé, giving Thea what she needs in order to do the work ahead of her: helping the world to awaken.

Because today is the day when the entire world will hear the Great Mother's call.

Life on this planet, sober or not, will never be the same again.

38

She jolts from a few hours of deep sleep to sounds of lower Manhattan going insane. Faraway screams and loudness. Thea hears commotion through the thick door to the hallway. She runs to the window and looks out. Something unimaginable is happening—what could it be? Out the window, on Prince Street, she sees people running in all directions in total panic. She looks up. Horror! She sees the clear southern sky of morning is turning heart-clenching black. Enormous quantities of bilious smoke arising above tall buildings like rotten mushroom-shaped screams. Outside her hermetically sealed window, people frantically wave their arms, mouths wide open, silently shouting to one another. Rushing to her hotel door, hysterical muffled voices before she hears the words they're saying.

Thea opens her door. People are standing in the halls, loudly bewildered, some blank-eyed stone still. Shouts of horrendous, unthinkable things. Bombs. Downtown. Airplane. She returns to her room and throws clothes on and rushes out onto the streets that are filled with people madly running and screaming, "The city's under attack! The towers have been hit by a plane!" Everyone flies in different directions. Thea thinks she must have died while sleeping and has awoken in hell.

She whimpers, *Oh Michael, why did I leave you?* Catching her staggering breath, her very next thought is—terrorists! There'd been too many bombings in the world news lately.

She's running south, straight for her old neighborhood. She doesn't know why—she just has to. By now everyone knows it's the World Trade Center that's been hit. She doesn't notice she's running toward where everyone is scrambling away from. She gets to West Broadway and sees fiery blackness coming from precisely where she knows the towers are. She knows Exchange Views ended an hour ago; it's after nine. People's faces are frozen in fear, and hers is too. But Thea keeps going south.

She's crossing Canal Street when she sees it. A second plane. She stops. Unbelieving. Sees it flying low, slow, and—seconds later she hears it—a bomb slamming into the other tower. Screams along with everyone. Cringing, her mind blown, she keeps running. She has to. Has to be there—to help? Thea doesn't know why. She isn't thinking. Operating on automatic, she runs as fast as she can.

Maneuvering around, pushing south against the mob that is rushing north, something drives her right toward the horror. Deafening explosions. Black smoke fills the streets and rises high in the sky, blotting out the sun. While flames shoot from the towers, screams and sirens jam her ears.

She's at Reade and West Broadway, where she'd stood the night before. Everything in turmoil. Chaos and foul odors of panic sicken the most stout-hearted. No one visibly is in charge. No one knows what to do or how to handle it. Thea hears someone yell *There's more coming!* and the furor worsens. A couple of times she's nearly knocked down. She has to push against rushing people, no whys or hows. All she knows is she *has to be there*.

Police and fire trucks screech, the retreating crowd panics.

Run for your lives! The towers are going to fall! She hears but keeps going, driven by unseen forces. Worse than a nightmare because everyone knows they're awake. People in shock, injured, running, weeping, helping others, rushing, rushing away—everyone helpless. Scared witless.

Overwhelmed, she forces herself south.

The air, so dense it stings her nostrils. Everyone crying out in different languages, another tower of Babel, beseeching their own God, some cursing, everyone wailing—why—why this? Why now—why us, oh Jesus save us! Mon Dieu! Dios Mio!—don't forsake us!—everyone screaming, begging help from their Almighty.

People push past her but she keeps going, past Chambers and Warren, past Murray. Up in the sky she sees and hears the impossible black- and red-ness of massive explosions. Thea turns onto Barclay Street and stops in front of the hardware store where she used to buy lumber, hinges, screws.

The locked doors are bolted. Something tells her to hurry up and get further into the store's deep stone entryway. Then the same-something commands her to hold firmly onto the iron grating of the hardware store's sturdy door, and *stay there*.

An urgency directs her. She obeys. Thea huddles deeply in the protection of the stone archway, breathing through the bottom of her cotton shirt. She crouches low, absolutely still in the store's shadow.

She hears something awful. She looks up—up there!—where she sees between monoliths of cement, the entire height of the tower starting to collapse. Worse than slow motion. Thea believes her heart has stopped. She grabs the steel bars till her fingers hurt. All those people! she agonizes, knowing many are dying at this exact moment. She thinks not of the crowd at Exchange Views, which ended already. so she hopes they've escaped danger—but the others, she knows, who are dying right now. Trapped. Their lives snuffed out in the anguishing impact of planes and demonically collapsing tower. Powerless. *I must be dead too,* she thinks, *otherwise this wouldn't be happening.*

In homes around the world, televised deaths of faceless thousands stun the collective human heart.

She dies more with each new blast. She must bear it. She can't move. Hidden deep inside the stone portico, protected, Thea remains still as a statue—in the midst of hell on Earth. Another deafening roar. More screams, sirens, scattered people yelling, rushing by, nobody seeing Thea. Thea not seeing Thea.

At that moment she looks up, peers through the thick air and sees it.

A colossal wall—a huge tidal wave of debris and smoke—charging up West Broadway! A hundred stories of pulverized-cement skyscraper rushing right at her! The horror of the crumbling tower eating itself up paralyzes her. She turns, tightening head to knees, firms her grip around iron grating. *This is it. This insane world is ending. Goodbye, Michael.* She holds her breath, squeezes her eyes.

Goodbye, world.

"Everything's gone, and now me," she whispers.

* * *

Thea braces and holds on for dear life. The force of the debris wave hits her like a bomb. Windows blow out all around, but the stone entryway she's balled up in miraculously protects Thea from any harm.

All is Noise. Then silence (eardrums blown?).

Nothingness.

Emptiness.

Minutes pass like eons.

Senses banged to smithereens.

The wave passes.

She wonders, *Will there be another?*

Yes, there will be another.

Hiding for all eternity, Thea hears from her secret place what can only be the second tower's chest-stabbing collapse.

She does not move …

… until … all is still where she crouches in her cement cave, unscathed.

From afar she hears shouting—from others in safe hiding places, she guesses. She clings to the grating, otherwise she'll fall over. Is she breathing?

She thinks of Michael. His strength. She pretends he's with her. Keeps whispering, "Michael's here," her badge of courage.

Ash everywhere. Her hair, plastered in a sand-cast of her head. Gluey dust cements her eyes against her will. With stiff fingers she peels ash off her lashes. Cracks one eye then another. Sees people on the ground. None moving. Running footsteps muffled by ash that keeps falling. Grayness thick as chowder on the sidewalk.

People are dragging themselves, slowly, away from here. Everyone but Thea retreating. She can't move. Even if she wants to, she's incapable.

She thinks she sees something black and red moving in the thick gray fog.

Thea's heart pumps fast now, so she figures she has to be alive. Yet the air is so thick she can't breathe. Holding the doubled-up fabric against her nose and mouth she takes tiny gulps of air. She rubs more ash off her eyelashes with the inside of her clean bra.

Then she sees it! She blinks hard. Looks again.

Am I crazy instead of dead?

She can't move. Because there before her, Thea doesn't want to believe it's happening—how can it be!—there she stands—in living black flesh with red blood dripping from her mouth—Kali Durga, the destroying goddess Herself—alive! Right There! She who is called the Great Mother. She, the one who destroys demons so goodness can replace evil's empty space.

Can it be?

Thea recognizes Kali Durga instantly.

She, it is, whom Thea stares at—alive! Thea can't believe what she's seeing. But it's here, before her. Kali, the destroying goddess with a necklace of bleeding beheaded demons. Uncomfortably close. She, the Mother of the Universe, who's been Thea's personal guardian, protecting her from harm whenever asked, ever since meeting this incomparable deity in her dreams, so long ago. Thea flashes a quick thought to the hot Kali rock, like a fossil of hope, safely ensconced on a studio shelf back at Isla à Isla.

No matter how much she wishes it weren't so, before her very eyes, Kali Durga is here—moving her limbs, looking right at her! As real as flesh and blood. The naked goddess, whose skin glistens like crude oil, is coming closer to where Thea remains huddled, curled up in the hardware store's entryway. Kali stands in an impossibly angular, animate pose, staring puny Thea right in the eye. Thea feels the anvil of her sanity, and knows this is happening; it can't be whisked away or denied.

In stark contrast to the thick gray atmosphere, the shiny-skinned goddess, a mere fifteen feet away now, is as tall as Thea, and has not a stitch on but patterned lit-up designs on her black skin, and a clanking skull necklace and anklets of a thousand tiny bells. Her ebony torso ripples with sparks of kinetic blue lines and dots of energy. Her skin, taunt and slick, is blacker than black against the ashen abyss that surrounds her. Kali's red tongue flashes from a mouth that is a broken slice of blood. There is no doubt: this creature is central to the action. Whether she is flesh or not, who knows? Kali's look penetrates Thea's eyes. Thea doesn't hide. She looks right into the goddess' whirling eyes, more like glowing orbs, and gasps. Immediately Kali begins to dance, right there on Barclay Street amid this devastating human-made catastrophe. Thea is gone, transported to another place, another time, another planet for all she knows, seeing an apparition, an impossibility—she knows she's insane!

She looks up and watches. The unhuman goddess begins to twirl in an out of place, out of time manner, moving her agile limbs in a way that completely thunder-strikes Thea.

Around her, shattering cataclysms roar, discordant jumbles of hellish sounds erupt with despair, more death. Thea watches the fearsome goddess sway in ritualistic asymmetry, her many articulated hands positioned like a dark sunburst around her head. Thea doesn't want to watch this terrible, phantasmagoric sight any longer. She fights the urge to close her eyes and wait for death, wishing with all her might to be not here. Yet she's forced by something beyond her will to remain still, and watch. With eyes forced wide, she follows the impossible sight of Kali's dancing—in awe and paralyzing fear.

Crouched in the alcove, Thea's tightly wrapped arms grip her knees for strength. As she watches, she reaches out to clench a fistful of the thick settling debris. She disperses the ash and holds it in each of her clenched hands, not believing this is happening, trying to ground herself. She's compelled to touch the ash of death with shaking hands.

The ash anchors Thea's fright. Her thoughts turn to dust. She uncurls her fists and looks at the ash, the remains of so many cherished lives, proof of countless crushed dreams.

Thea's nails make half-moon marks, clutching the powdery ash in her fists. She feels scratchy particles of the *once-was* and repetitions of *will-be* in her grip: still viable seeds of lives and dreams not entirely gone, but—she senses momentous things yet to happen. Because of so many souls' abrupt departure, Thea feels their energies all around her, looking for a home. She invites the wandering energies in. Thea fights the urge to put the ash in her mouth. The desire to eat it overcomes her. She does not. Thea restrains herself, knowing she has a better way to never let go of this soul-filled ash.

She vows silently: *I'll make a glass vial necklace to put this dust in. It will be the sacred amulet I'll wear for the rest of my life, to forever remember how the destruction of evil allows new creation to come forth.*

"We witness the impossible today," she whispers aloud.

With this oath, Thea's awareness, like a bad case of tunnel vision, comes fully focused onto what the formidable goddess is unfolding before her.

Time becomes infinity.

Thea has no strength to move, yet allows the unnamable power to lift her, up and away from her stone archway. She has no will left it seems, so she remains still, sure of only one thing: she has to be here, to witness this. She has to obey the command she keeps hearing within her: *Stay Here. Watch. And absorb. To witness both the horror of human insanity and the reality of the Great Mother's cosmic dance of re-creation.*

Thea is the witness of Divine renewal unfolding before her.

Thea gathers herself at last and realizes she has stepped out from the protection of her stone alcove. Cyclonic winds lash her face. She quickly presses it into the crook of her arm. Her long, unbound hair whirls about the top of her head like blades of a chopper. Her ears roar; her eyes take in everything, every evil that's happened here—but her mind is now, oddly, calm. Her mind has been swept of chaos.

No more than a stone's throw in front of Thea, the goddess is dancing her ass off to music no one hears. The universal icon begins the dance of transformation, amidst the ashen ruins.

Thea drops her face covering and foolishly takes a gulp of the acrid tasting air. Coughing, she swears she can hear whispering. A sound like many entwined voices. A far-off drum, unified in one tremendous, recognizable voice. The sound increases slowly from a faint whisper of a distant tom-tom beat to that of a majestic Grand Chord. A primal heartbeat in unison.

A timpani-sound playing a sublimely resonating, looping beat. Thea then hears a distinct drumming-voice. She knows the sound—as well as the sight of the Great Mother's most auspicious form—is meant for her to witness.

Kali steps knees high, hopping on one bare foot, then the other in a demented Balinese dance, keeping within range of Thea's limited sight in the debris fog.

She then sees a vivid eruption between Kali's eyebrows. From the goddess' dark mid-brow, a laser-blue beam springs out, sparking like a cutting sword as it travels over the grayness surrounding everything. Thea touches between her own eyes to see if, what? To see if she's still here? "Maybe I have a head injury?" she wonders aloud. She looks at her chest. There is no blood on her except from slight cuts from flying glass splinters. Thea then feels a strange sensation as if electric shocks are rippling through her. Sizzling energy is coming from the blue beam emitted by the dancing spectacle of Kali, right *from her, into Thea*—visibly, electrically arcing—coming from Kali's third eye right into Thea's indigo dot.

Thea feels a shock as powerful as the debris wave that's just gone by.

Kali starts to spin. She changes size, getting bigger, glowing with enormous energy, emitting blue, white, purple sparks as she spins faster. Thea is even more terrified. The divine goddess is deliriously creating a spiral of supernatural force.

Right before Thea's astonished eyes, twirling Kali pumps up in size like a helium-filled Michelin man. As she grows, her twirling slows. Her spin of boney elbows, knees, and shoulders are arranged in obstreperous angularity, her cosmic form juts out everywhere. In just moments she has grown taller than a traffic signal—taller than the third floor of the surrounding gray buildings left standing—and still Kali grows and spins—growing ever upward.

Scared senseless, yet incapable of not feeling immersed with what she's witnessing, Thea can't escape being the witness. The whirling dervish-spinning goddess changes into an incalculable gigantic size. Somehow Thea, as if she were standing on the far-off Jersey shore looking over at Manhattan, can see Kali's unthinkable stature, her fearful visage, her cosmic spinning-away of demons—as if her vision were a drone's camera lens.

It's impossible, but this is what Thea sees on this Black Tuesday.

Kali Durga's spasmatic dance intensifies a thousand-fold, becoming unbearable. But still, Thea watches.

In torpedo fashion, Thea sees the goddess grow as tall as the once standing towers, their phantom shapes she straddles and spins high above, in an indisputable cosmic display of the all-powerful balance of destruction-and-creation. All the while, Thea hears a whispering cacophony of voices in her ear, as if she has earphones on, through which she hears the Great Chord. The whispers grow louder, like distant drums increasing in volume amid wind-roars of Kali's infinitely expanding, spinning form—until Thea can make out that the mingling of voices is actually One Voice, saying words she's beginning to decipher.

She clearly sees Kali has grown a mile high! still spinning ferociously.

Thea's attention turns to the increasingly loud drum beat, the One Voice she can hear are countless humans. She puts her engulfed mind to sorting out these strange, nightmarish sounds. And ... they coalesce ... becoming ... words. She hears them now, clearly:

"... TRULY ... NOW ... IN ... SPIRIT ... TRULY NOW ... IN SPIRIT ..."

Thea knows nothing, understands nothing. She just witnesses. The vision of Kali's dance. The drumbeat chorus. The annihilation surrounding her.

As the One Voice repeats these words over and over in a repetitive drone, Thea touches her cheek. It feels gritty and warm. She guesses she's still alive. The ferociously spinning Kali—the Voice that speaks above all else—is as real as the fiery horror that explodes continuously all around her, dizzying Thea's mind, piercing her sanity, overwhelming her.

teZa LORD

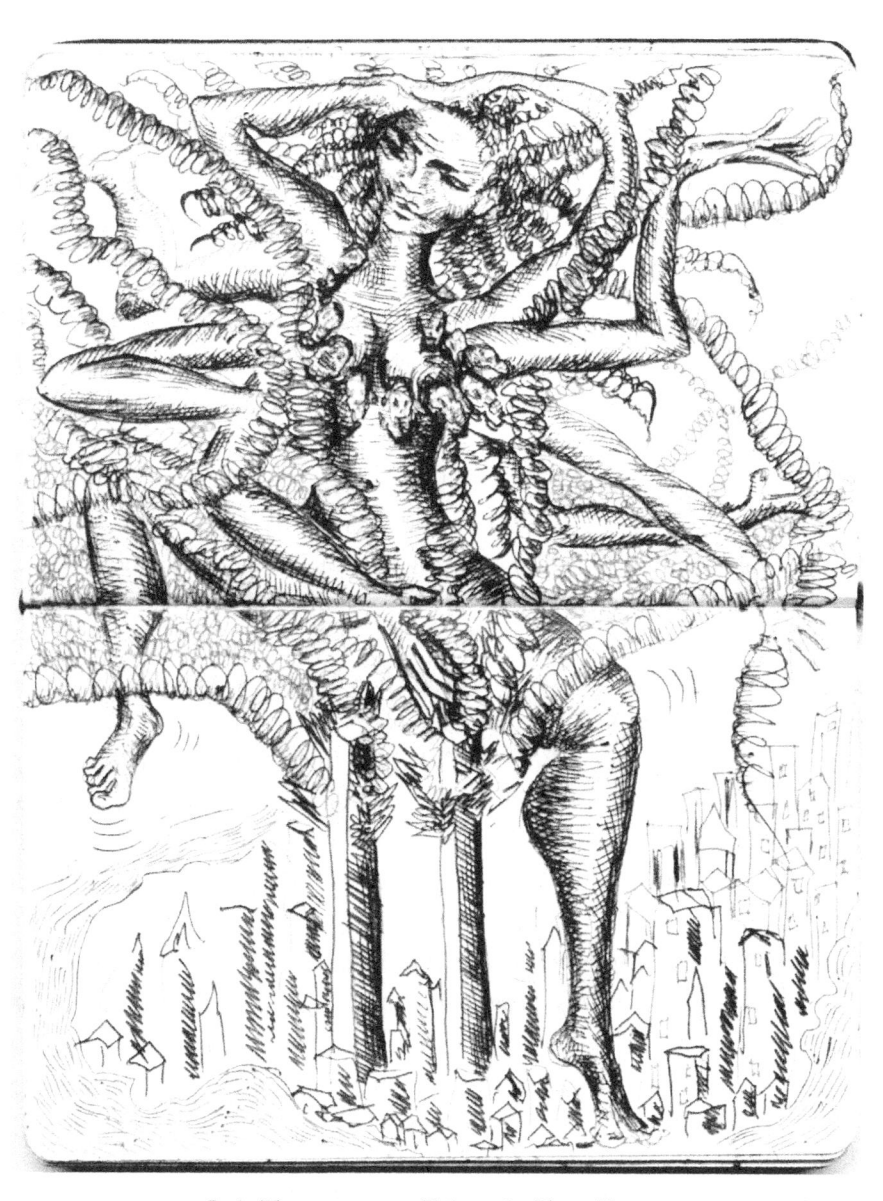

Only Thea witnesses Kali at the Twin Towers

39

The next moment, Kali instantly shrinks back to human size and stands right in front of Thea, not spinning but hopping, lifting high one foot at a time, her many arms swaying up and down and side to side—looking intently, directly into Thea's eyes.

Kali's skin appears wet. The goddess' huge firm boobs flop, keeping a metronome accompaniment to her wild dance beat. Thea sees around her neck the bloody demon skulls rattling against each other. She winces, seeing these awful tortured faces! They loom sickeningly in her vision as Kali approaches, closer. For a second Thea turns her eyes askance, she can't bear to look any longer at the severed heads, too ghastly to behold. The skulls' morbid clanking sound horrifies her.

Thea's gaze is riveted on Kali's bright fuchsia tongue as it rolls in and out of her wide crimson lips with their slash of rude red, a carnival of colors in the middle of so much ashen death and destruction. Around Kali's head are her weapon-wielding arms surrounding her like flames, increasing in number with every second of this human tragedy. And still—Kali keeps staring directly at Thea as she stomps a clumsy step. The Great Mother's neon third eye glows radioactively on her magnificent brow.

As soon as Thea recognizes the words coming from the haunting One Voice, *Truly now ... in Spirit*, she is struck with the knowledge of why Kali is making herself impossibly visible to her. The overpowering sense of knowing what's really happening comes into Thea like an uplifting, powerful wave of wordless understanding. She recognizes, seeing the horror up close, what the severed heads on Kali's necklace are.

"You're calling me to help kill the demons," Thea declares to the inconceivable vision standing before her. "You need me as an accomplice, don't you, Kali?"

Truth sweeps over Thea as she watches Kali's steps begin to slow down. Thea knows she's been led here to see, to feel, to perceive the goddess' cosmic wonder, her frightening power. It is She, the Great Mother, who has commanded Thea to be here, to witness up close what cannot be conveyed any other way. Thea knows this now, like she knows she loves Michael, whom she thinks of simultaneously at this moment of such mind-blowing realization.

As if love's epiphanies are the links to Truth.

Yes, there it is—Thea in the middle of a global catastrophe in *real time*, people all around her dead or dying, traumatized, suffering inconsolably from now to forever. But yet, Thea clearly understands. Love is the sole survivor, even when evil has destroyed all else. Love, the only salvation.

This creature before me—Thea thinks, as Kali slowly transforms into a memory—she who destroys ever-present evil thereby allowing goodness, again and again, to be re-created—here before me in living color, could she be what's real, and this so-called Earthly life—with its senseless violence, deadly insanity, and cultural embrace of materialism superseding Spirit—*could our humanness itself be the dream of madness* that suspects that the power of love is only for the weak? Is this why Kali dances her colossal manifestation, rising above such destruction, *as if this tragedy is the beginning, not the end?*

Of this, Thea's heart is now absolutely certain. Her mind, remember, has been blown to smithereens and is no longer functioning.

The goddess' thick dreadlocks, long and greasy, coil down her muscular back like sinuous snakes. As she becomes less than human-sized, slowly her high-steps become similar to those of every man and woman and in-between on a dancefloor. Kali tosses her divine head, as if finished with her task at hand. Sparks fly from her in all directions from her slowing, smaller form. The goddess and the drumbeat Voice of All that accompanied her delirium—disappearing.

Thea understands. All the horror, all the hatred—Kali consumes it all, transforms the negatives to neutralized energy within her. That is Great Mother's job, plainly, clearly.

Instantaneously, Thea realizes this is the beginning of our journey to the Light, as a global family of humankind. This singular event is the birthing of the spiritualization of the entire human race. Thea knows it. She feels it in her bones.

"Kali," she whispers as she watches the Great Mother slowly disappear into the shadows of grayness from whence she came, "you have balanced the evil of these unbelievable atrocities of humans against humans. This is why someone has to witness your dance. To help others believe. And I guess that someone is me."

Just then a young man walks by in the maelstrom on Barclay Street and notices Thea. She must look shell-shocked because he asks if she needs help. She is now combined with Kali irretrievably, beyond reason.

"I'm good. Can I help you?" Thea asks the dust-veiled guy, whose eyes are the only sparks of human color in the homogenous gray that shrouds both of them. Under a half-inch layer of ash, he wears what once was a trim business suit. He hugs a gray-iced briefcase to his chest, as if its contents contain the Secret of Life. Thea stands steady and sure as in a redwood forest, amidst the rubble raining down.

"Did you see anything, odd?" Thea asks hesitantly.

"Everything is odd, lady," the man barks.

"I mean, a huge naked dancing woman?"

The man abruptly shakes off Thea's hand that holds onto his sleeve. He loudly yells at her.

"There's nothing left! We're all finished! No one can help!" he screams. "Damn you!"

The man stumbles over himself running away.

Thea guesses she is alone in having seen the unthinkable, un-seeable Kali. Could it possibly be? That only she saw the inconceivable, world-saving One whirl madly where the phantom towers once stood? Where their foundations collapsed, where she rose up *up up*—right after they crashed down *down down*. And transmitted the clear message that filled Thea's heart with hope, replacing her shattered mind and gone-hearing, blown out from the annihilation of so much humanity.

40

Kali Durga's transformative energy crashes like a meteor of Truth, alongside the evil extremists' fuselage-bombs. Thea knows Kali's iridescent, intergalactic body was the only shade of hope in the middle of fiery human and material pulverization—the interminable sorrow of 9/11's forever changing *what is*.

From the moment Kali looked deeply into Thea's eyes during her heart-stopping, mind-bending display—Thea embraced being Kali's apprentice as her destiny.

A purpose immediately fills her. Thea knows—just as it was at Big Sue's, Fast's, Dr. Bob's, and Sophia's leaving their bodies—she is filled by a portion of each mortal life, becoming a repository of their combined lives' energy at these thousands of souls' departure, there at the towers. She is a living receptacle, a human soul-sponge. A part of the life force, the creative part of each of the innocent persons who were slain this morning leaps into her. Their creative energy does not leave planet Earth. As Thea recovers from this shock of seeing Kali, she feels the transfer of these combined energies directly into her—viscerally—as her body shakes and convulses with the invisible infusion!

She stands rooted to the ash-covered earth, feeling from above—into her emptied-by-Kali mind and then, deep within Thea's heart cave—the transfer of thousands of souls' life energy pouring into her.

The One Voice is now hers. What she's seen and heard! These are her true experiences. Her life energy is now multiplied infinitely with the unfulfilled wants and desires of the thousands of souls who perished that day.

In the middle of the ongoing nightmare surrounding the attack, images start transmitting into Thea's mind. The Great Mother opened a passage from this world—blasted free by exploding concrete and the sacrificed lives of so many—a portal into the other, unmanifested world: Durga's realm of a new world's creation.

The spiritualization of humankind has begun.

In a flash, Thea knows the kind of art she must make now.

Kali, physically invisible to Thea now, continues to transmit into her fully awakened bridge tender. Thea resolves that evil's function is to effectively ignite the inevitable destruction of *the unsustainable*, which, throughout history, has been painfully necessary for the re-creation of positive manifestation. This is the way—however gruesome it is—for the Light to outweigh the Dark, Thea realizes now.

She had to do it with her own life—just as each of ours is a miniscule microcosm of creation—over and over until she surrendered to living in the Light. And now the world's evolutionary spiral upward has been challenged, similarly, to rise up anew, having been momentarily challenged by the forces of a few radically violent, religious terrorists.

Thea recalls her childhood Genesis—*The void begat the Light. From the Dark grows illumination*—before creating images of what just transpired here and now in her sketchbook.

The membrane between the two worlds, the seen and the unseen, is punctured. The opening is permeable enough between the two dimensions so Thea can easily pass through at will, upon merely intending to do so. Thea is no fool. She realizes she's been given a mission.

Images of future Dreamtimes begin flooding her imagination, loosening the permeable portal for Thea. Now she can see, hear, feel the One Voice that has awakened within her. Thea goes sacred crazy! This she knows as surely as the gritty ash of both towers' souls she still holds securely in her hand.

41

As soon as she finds a working phone Thea calls home to tell Michael that she's safe. Best she can in a few words, she tells him what happened to her, never thinking for an instant Michael would have trouble processing such unbelievable news.

Thea senses his chilliness, his disbelief in her nightmarish report when he says, "We'll talk about these things later, when you're home. Give it time. You're in shock."

She's disappointed, of course. Shrugging her shoulders she says, "It's okay, Michael. I have to get used to not being believed. You must think I'm completely delusional."

"No, not that. I love you, Thee. Of course, I want to believe you, I'm sorry." He adds, "*It is* quite unbelievable. But I know you're not prone to hallucinations or flights of fantasy. You save all that for your work."

"I know why it happened, Michael. She took me away from all *that*. Somehow, when she danced she opened up for me a glimpse of the other side, another perspective for me to witness. I was right there, covered in ash like everyone else, but somehow I could see from another vantage point. Kali allowed me to see into her world. The unseen one is as real as our realm, the so-called real world."

"I don't know what to say, Thee."

"Don't say anything then. Just listen, please. As she spun, she showed me how we are spinning out of control. Then she let me see our world of tomorrow. We're already in the middle of a spiritual showdown culminating with today, Michael. We have to fight until evil is eradicated, like we do with deadly viruses. And then we will unite as one race, one voice, on this glorious garden planet. We'll overpower the deadly fungus of bigotry and terrorism, and instead grow Love on the skin of our living, breathing world. All those deaths will then have meant something much greater than anyone could ever have predicted.

"Michael, Kali's dance showed me that fighting evil is a holy necessity. We're supposed to face the evil and eradicate it within ourselves first—like I had to fight my destructive addictions. So now we're forced to eradicate evil that threatens humanity's spiritual evolution. Confronting all kinds of control-freak fanatics' terrorism will be the toughest battle ever fought on Earth.

"We're being forced to fight for what's right, Michael. Oh, do please understand! Kali revealed to me that our world *is now coming together* for a higher purpose. The attack on our soil is the tipping point. We've already begun the battle. She's spun the shift, like a moth making a cocoon, a butterfly its chrysalis. We humans are transforming ourselves already. Today, Kali's dance initiated all of us into the age of awakening. If we know it or not."

"You saw all that, Thee?"

"Yes, my love, I did. I saw it as clearly as detailed photos in National Geographic. Our world is at the precipice of changing, big time. But first we have to fight and slay the remaining demons, just as Kali allowed me to witness her doing. Each of us, just as the world does on a global scale, have our own demons we must slay first. After today, we choose—enlightenment or extermination. And we humans—history proves this since our cavemen ancestors—have always chosen life."

The line goes quiet.

Tired, weak, utterly drained, Thea needs Michael to believe her.

Finally, with a strained voice she says, "Our world will never be the same after today."

"I'm afraid you're right there," Michael whispers.

"My job is to make art that depicts her call to arms. I'll be sounding the roll call for others to join our Army of Light. Kali took me to inner space and back, to show me how. How unfeasible is that?"

"It's pretty hard to believe, Thee."

"It is. But I saw our little blue-seed world from space. Saw how it'll be in the future, Michael. The future of our world is without borders. Without what today cripples us: toxic minds and separation. In the future we'll be free to use our combined strength of humanity—that used to go to energy-wasters. Like arguing, and controlling, whether with things political, cultural, ethnic, sexist, religious, you-name-it: all kinds of conflicts. From now on I'll be reporting how to break our prisons of limited perspectives. I believe Kali's message. Our physical, gross world is just slower at catching up to what begins with the unseen, unlimited powers available to all of us."

42

Miraculously, Thea discovers an Acura to rent and sets off for home. Forty-some hours later, she drives through the gate of Isla à Isla. She melts into Michael's anxiously awaiting embrace. No one has figured out yet who, what, or how many are involved in the attacks. Many travelers are stranded, with all planes grounded and rental cars unavailable.

Thea slept the entire next day, recuperating from two days on the road and her life-or-death ordeal. As soon as she awakens she goes right into the studio. The images in her head beckon like church bells tolling. The work becomes a seductive drug Thea plunges into, bathing in the bittersweet oblivion of keeping Kali's conduit open, allowing the images, creating art of them.

For hours at a stretch she's single-mindedly focused: she fabricates mix media pieces like an alien-grown grove of art spices, channeling raw, ravenous creativity into an orgy of passion. "I know I'm not making these pieces," she reassures herself, "I couldn't." Masterfully, she's mixing a wide assortment of materials like a demented alchemist. Ideas pour from her as if she is a waterfall of creation, as if a maniacal, multi-talented generator is pushing her to full throttle, engaging her consciousness in an overdrive thrust she's never been capable of before. This is why she knows it's not her who is the artist here.

Divinely inspired three-dimensional Dreamtimes come to fill Thea's studio. Funnels catching the enormous outpouring of energy. In their strong armatures and bedazzling outer skins, the Dreamtimes depict trauma mixed with unabashed hope. With figures in the throes of anguish, deadly thunderbolts sent by militant demons intertwine with Truth's Light. Of creativity indescribable, whether of the good, bad, ugly, or beautiful variety.

The smell of death is close in these living memorials to Thea's passage through the membrane of our parallel realities—the real and the unreal. Coming together as solid objects, enchanting, spell-binding. Shrieking with stark, grab-you emotions.

When she needs a break, Thea walks with Popeye through Isla à Isla's gardens, smelling the earth's abundance, enjoying simply being amongst profuse beauty. Spellbound, she observes the daily unfolding of new growth, Nature's handiwork, in both her garden and studio. She watches the subtle autumnal shift of the coming dormancy that a tropical winter is. The gardens quietly accept their transformation.

Thea picks basil that has gone to seed, holding the rich odor to her nose. She drifts into a meadow of carefree glory with each breath. Every moment holds one more discovery, another detail for her to spy and wonder at in the ever-changing garden. Then Thea abruptly turns and walks briskly back into her studio for another round of focused work. The ever-exuberant Popeye keeping watch with one eye open over the commotion she makes in the studio, lying on a crocheted rug while Thea works.

Months go by before Thea can speak of what happened that day to anyone other than Michael and her close circle: Ray and Julia, and Junkyard and Maly. The day arrives, however, when she can't put off any longer talking to her dealer, St. Pierre. She picks up the phone when she sees the caller ID.

"I'm right in the middle of getting this new series ready to ship up to you," Thea assures him when he asks how things are going for her solo show in June. It was she who insisted not to cancel her show, as many Manhattan galleries were in the wake of the city's grief.

"Why haven't you answered any of my calls, Thea? Are you all right?"

She takes a deep breath. "You have to give me space, Jules. I know you were in the city then too. We all have our ways of processing the horror. You'll just have to wait and see the work to understand. Believe me, these

Dreamtimes are more important than anything I can say. Talking about what happened just dilutes it for me."

"Thea, if it weren't for Michael telling me, I would never have even known you were there, whether you were alive or dead, injured or what. How can you be like this? We've all been through a lot, every one of us in this city. The least you can do is communicate, can't you?"

"Jules, I'm sorry," she insists. "I just can't talk about what happened. It's too much. When you see the work you'll understand why. You can decide for yourself then, and see why I can't talk about it. Really, there's nothing I can say. I'm not trying to be a jerk about this, honestly. I just can't talk about it. Otherwise, the art suffers, becomes … distorted by words."

"Something like *this* happening in my studio," she tells Junkyard Trinnie and Maly on the phone, bursting with excitement. "I know whatever source that's making the art, it's not me. I only hold the tools for *IT*."

Her friends on the long-distance call invisibly nod their heads in agreement. "All true art be creating itself from outside the small of us, Honeypot," Junkyard says. Maly adds, "We feel your strength right through the phone, ma chérie! We love your energy! And now we cherish you more—surprise!—by naming our darling daughter after you, my dear friend."

Since their second baby's arrival, she's been calling Junkyard and Maly to check in on them, not to talk about what happened to her at the World Trade Center. She limits her describing to them on how the new series is going, sharing about the astounding eruption happening in her studio.

"I've never felt such energy before," Thea says. "Ideas have been gushing out of me like blood from a cut jugular. I'm bleeding art!"

"We're sorry you had to be there that day," Junkyard says, "but the work be taking you where it needs you to be going. There must be a reason why Sophia had to be dying right then, bringing you up there. There must be," his voice drifts off.

"Harness the passion, mon amie," Maly offers. "Just like how you told us you felt the energy of your friends Sue and Fast when your loved ones left. This must be what we humans do, recycle our life energy to each other. We're not glad you went through it, losing Sophia or your other dear ones, ma cherie. But maybe it's so their leftover strength comes inside yours and allows you to interpret this great world tragedy. Your Dreamtimes will make this Earth a better place for our Thor and little Thea."

"Maly be right," Junkyard perks up. "Just remember, if you do too much abstraction, nobody be catching the drift. Be specific. Dare to be the boldest you be, ever! Don't be afraid to tell the truth, as wild as it be, even if everybody be calling you nutty weirdo. Come on, wow us, Fern Eyes! Mess our heads up, wake us up—that be yours and my job! Your Dreamtimes, they always be making people pissed off, horny or happy, somehow erupting strong! Force the people to be looking deeper inside their shit, and then what? It be up to them! Transform the smelly caca to diamond brights, that be what you be slapping people awake for, White Gurl—with your art. You be head honcho Heart Artist, Honeypot! Me be christening you that, by the right of I and Ja, you be now the Irie Cosmic womb-an!"

Junkyard's and her lighthearted updrafts of joy drown out any doubts. It's like this whenever their chats turn to message art. A subject so dear for the Hearts.

"You make it seem like I'm some kind of art terrorist, Junkyard," she razzes him.

"That be it! When Heart Art be the next mainstream fad, supreme, then we be relaxing! Not till then." Junkyard laughs along with Maly who's on the extension phone.

"Me be just reminding you, that be we job, Green Glow. We Hearts be stronger now. Times be forever different. We all got to be like eggs now, hatching hope. Planting little seeds of hope for everyone, for the future.

"It be like what my Spirit Mohn prophesied, the Walrus." Junkyard starts singing in his raconteur's gravelly voice: "'*Corporation tee-shirt, stupid bloody Tuesday,*' he be right about the day, '*I am he as you are he as you are me and we are all together.*'" He finishes lines made famous from John Lennon's nonsense song.

"Oh man, Junkyard, you're too fucking much." Thea basks in her friends' radiance, his ability to find joy and humor in even life's worst things.

"Art got to be strong as real ammo, bombs, or war we be raging out in the world," Junkyard says. "Art be the only t'ing that be making t'ings change, Honeypot. Per-iod. Art changes cultures, not wars. So be keeping it light, and be keeping it real so nobody be misinterpreting nada! Light and laughter be what changes us from the inside out. Art be pointing where we be needing to make big changes. Where we be heading. The songs, the moving to rhythms; the hard-to-see, shake-up dramas, the films, stories, and tunes people loves to be pretending they be in instead of their own shitty lives. The trickery of verse 'n' visions, that be what we Hearts be doing for the people. Forget politics! It be old, way too slow and, oh you be knowing—too separating! What bull crappy politicians be!"

"Oui, d'accord," Maly exudes. "If we want our civilization to grow up like our children will, we Hearts have to take ever stronger spiritual action, to counteract the forces of the debased. Besides thought-action, Heart Art is the best tool we have to heal this terrible world-wound, mon amie. Without art, our different cultures and beliefs clash without mercy. We are like small children squabbling over our toys. It is so silly, really. And what a stupid shame we humans cannot grow up before we blow it! God is the energy of love, not hatred, no matter what different name people call the spiritual force."

"And who better," Junkyard jumps in, "than you, White Gurl, to be helping with your loud and clear art? You were *there*. Besides, it be you among we Hearts that be having the most experience with demons of your own sort—y'know, your addiction demons me be meaning. That be giving those Dreamtimes of yours *an edge* no one else be coming close to. You know that be true. It be on you, babykins. So blast that Light at us, Go Green!"

With her friends' encouragement, Thea battles privately about whether her work can ever adequately interpret what she's seen. *Is it as honest as I can make it?* She tries to stop thinking about such things, knowing she needs to save her energy to pour everything she has into her Dreamtimes. She can't afford to be insecure about sharing her visions. The time for Truth is upon the world now, she knows. She has to try, even though she knows damn well there's no possible way she could ever duplicate the enormity, the profundity of what she witnessed into mere *objects of art*. If she were a moviemaker, maybe. The expanded possibilities of animation and computer-generated images would certainly embellish her attempts, producing grander, supersized, apocalyptic impact that could stay in the public's one-second-lasting subconscious longer than tactile objects do. Film could better hint at the surreal, supernatural things she'd witnessed. *Or an Earth-shaking novel,* she thinks. That would make a better, longer lasting impression on the attention-deficit, generally art-ignorant public.

Thea's medium, however, isn't film or literature. She believes in the lasting permanence of pure, well executed, honest and true art. Something a person can see and hold, touch and feel hundreds, if not thousands of years from now. Her Dreamtimes are Thea's open-to-all memories, written in her own blood, letter by letter, word by word, blow by blow.

St. Pierre calls again wondering if Thea might be wearing herself out, working too much.

"Maybe I am," she admits.

"Don't burn out. We can postpone your show. The whole city's in a state of flux right now. No one's in the mood for buying art. You have lots of time to get those ideas out. Relax. There's no rush."

"I can't seem to stop myself, Jules."

St. Pierre's voice softens. "You've been through a lot, Thea. From what Junkyard says you've made three years' worth of work in the past months. You don't want to get sick, right? Take it easy."

But Thea doesn't want to *take it easy*. She's been feeling that Itch of hers rippling through her, pleasingly this time. Sending messages of urgency that get relieved only when she's in her studio. Another two months goes by. Her output is enormous. Michael stands proudly alongside her, watching the new work speak what Thea's words can't.

The Great Mother, Kali Durga, nurtures All of creation

43

Juan has built the wood crates to ship Thea's new Dreamtimes up to St. Pierre's gallery. She's completed twenty-two sculptures, thirteen wall-length sculptural paintings, numerous drawings, and objects of all sizes. Now Thea's exhaustion is so complete she can't think straight.

She helps Juan settle the pieces into their shipping crates, silently absorbing what she's seeing, grateful that someone besides herself is this bizarre work's creator. Michael joins to wrap the fragile ones in protective layers, before securing them in their boxes.

The most literally evocative of Thea's works is a huge mixed media on sturdy plywood, with its attached, sculpted outer edges measuring fifteen-by-seven feet. Protruding from its sturdy frame are individually applied shapes of wood, plaster, terrazzo, fragments of natural and man-made materials. On the surface is a display of Kali's gruesome figure dancing over the remaining tower as it crashes to the street below. Shocking. Vulgar, sensual in a raw, bruising slap. Repugnant, yet beautiful, a tug of war because of its moral outspokenness to the recent trauma of so many human victims. Kali is so surreal, hovering over the towers; no one could view this without gasping in disbelief. And the cosmic event itself, described pictorially so matter of fact that everyone who knows this image is antithetical to documented footage of the base, cruel, strictly human horror that day.

Can the public take Thea's depicting such brutality as a sacred ritual? As she packs Thea asks herself silently, *Will anyone understand that the attack had to be in order for humanity to continue its ever-upward evolutionary spiral?*

She won't know the answers until the works are shown.

"Definitely paganistic," Michael commented when she asked his opinion before.

Now she asks him again, "How do they strike you today, love?"

"Well, you've definitely succeeded in creating a painful initiation rite," Michael offers, and only because he was asked. "They're as powerful as petroglyphs and the deep and dark cave paintings of early indigenous, my dear. Your strongest work by far, Thee. Of course, you're taking a huge chance with your career," he adds. "But you know this already. We've discussed this *ad infinitum.*"

To her mind, depicting anything other than the cosmic dance of the Great Mother she'd witnessed, Thea would have to call herself a hypocrite. The largest sculpture-painting, a work of outrageously vibrating colors and energized strokes, in which the goddess' ponderous, nurturing breasts have been sucked dry by eons of needy, badly behaving humans, shows the deity's pain and suffering through the perspective of an omnipotent viewpoint.

Kali's empty black sacks hanging flat against her hideously deflated bony chest send chills up and down Thea's spine. When she appeared before her, the goddess' breasts were voluptuous, young and firm, the opposite of this crone's sad desiccation. But to Thea's mind, youthful breasts are too sensational, too salacious for the shockingly drastic warning, the carnage of human-bloodshed the goddess' message conveys: the call for all on Earth to awaken to Spirit.

One of Thea's renditions of Kali's grotesque dance creates the illusion of sound—a thunderous clanking of bloody demon skulls strung around her strained, sequoia neck, her numerous ankle bells are the alarming sirens of fire trucks far below on the ground—as her movements swing fiercely to the treacherous winds of fate.

Her size in relation to the tragedy is more than unbelievable. Dancing Kali surrounds plumes of smoke and human carnage, hovering over every angle of the collapsing towers. Filling the atmosphere is wildly-dancing, seen-by-all Kali, spinning her unseen work of sowing future creativity that will solve all of humankind's woes.

In scrutinizing the many works that were birthed in her studio these last months, Thea determines this one shouts the arrival of—right here and now—access for everyone, grown adult, young person, every progeny of Earth—to commune with other Unseens. Yes, Thea thinks approvingly, these temple pieces to She who is called all names yet needs no name. She who is incapable of being defined by a lexicon, because in using words to describe any aspect of cosmic consciousness, whether referred to as a Her, a Him, or an It—the Great Mother's absolute power becomes diminished because of words' innate inadequacies.

The painting she and Michael are packing now, however, which she calls "The End of Fear," is anything but inadequate. It is a call to unite in one purpose, for the sake of Earth's survival.

The sculpture-painting has the effect on Thea of a gone-berserk mandala. She feels dizzy and sits for a minute, takes a sip of water.

As final inspections are made of the crates before sealing up the entire collection, Thea is relieved. She knows her attempt to depict the alarming *Wake-Up!* that the Mother instructed her to make by her insane twirling, looming above the nightmare site, would never have happened had Kali not allowed her to observe that most sacred and terrifying dance of hers. With these works, the sound of humanity's endless possibilities for hope and redemption are empowered by the awakening of Light in the hearts of all—Earth's true form of healing—rings vibrantly loud.

"I think these works say it's okay, Michael," she says with sincerity. "Because, really, there's no accountability, right? No one else saw what I witnessed that day."

Michael leans into Thea. "You've done more than okay, Thee. You've validated Kali's unimaginable presence, duplicating for all of us to see—to witness with you!—her powerful magic, spinning faster than evil. You've shown how destroying hope within the human heart is futile. You've done it because you saw it. Who else understands? Now, hopefully, many will."

Thea smiles in satisfaction.

"The work is nothing less," Michael continues, as they observe tireless Juan moving the crates, "than what we have received from every one of those innocent souls who were killed that day."

"You're right," Thea says, searching her thoughts as if allowing herself to rationally think for the first time since Kali gave to her silent instructions.

"They're the message, the directing energy the entire world received, as a gift of transference from the martyrs killed in New York, Washington, and that cornfield out in Pennsylvania."

Michael turns to her, a look of pride on his face.

Thea is kneeling on the studio floor, nailing a cover on as she says without looking up:

"Michael, you know what? Seeing these works that came through me, but are not my creation—I know now Great Mother guides me as well as she guides all of us. It's taken this long for me to admit that if I have to, I'm willing to lay down my life to help humanity realize that what appears at first as awful, and evil, actually serves us as agents of change. Fear propels us to embrace Love more deeply. Our fears—once we realize this, are mere stepping stones, catalysts—show us what needs work, where, when, and how, as we glide toward our truly unfathomable role here on Earth, and beyond."

From its studio shelf, the Kali rock shines and heats from within.

The Kali rock

ABOUT THE AUTHOR

Artist and author teZa Lord began her art career as a scientific illustrator of plant medicines for Harvard botanists, then exhibiting visionary work while adventuring to both primitive and cultured places including working in and traversing Caribbean islands on cargo- and sailboats for a decade.

By the 90s, Lord was also committed to writing as she and her husband raised a blended family. Her nonfiction narratives: In the 'I', Zen Love, Hybrid Vigor—and the artbook manifesto, We Are One—paved the way for The Bridge Tender.

teZa was Art Director and acted in her husband Carter Lord's feature-length eco-fable Lithium Springs. Lord's current creative work is dedicated to lightening the burden of our toxic world by focusing on the individual's inner quest.

Her books, various art galleries, hundreds of ZLORD podcast episodes, MindStiller meditations, and yogic chakra explorations on YouTube are available. All Lord's literary works are also audiobooks, narrated by herself. Visit tezalord.com.

Also by teZa Lord

In the I: Easing Through Life-Storms

Hybrid Vigor: A True Reveal of Love

Zen Love: The True Journey of a Blended Family

Made in United States
Orlando, FL
14 March 2024